Alison McKenzie

⇒ THE ⇐
SAPPHIRE
HEART

Acorn Independent Press

Acknowledgement

For the other McKenzie sister, whose ongoing constructive suggestions and comments are a blessing and a curse. Also, to everyone who has read my first book. Thank you

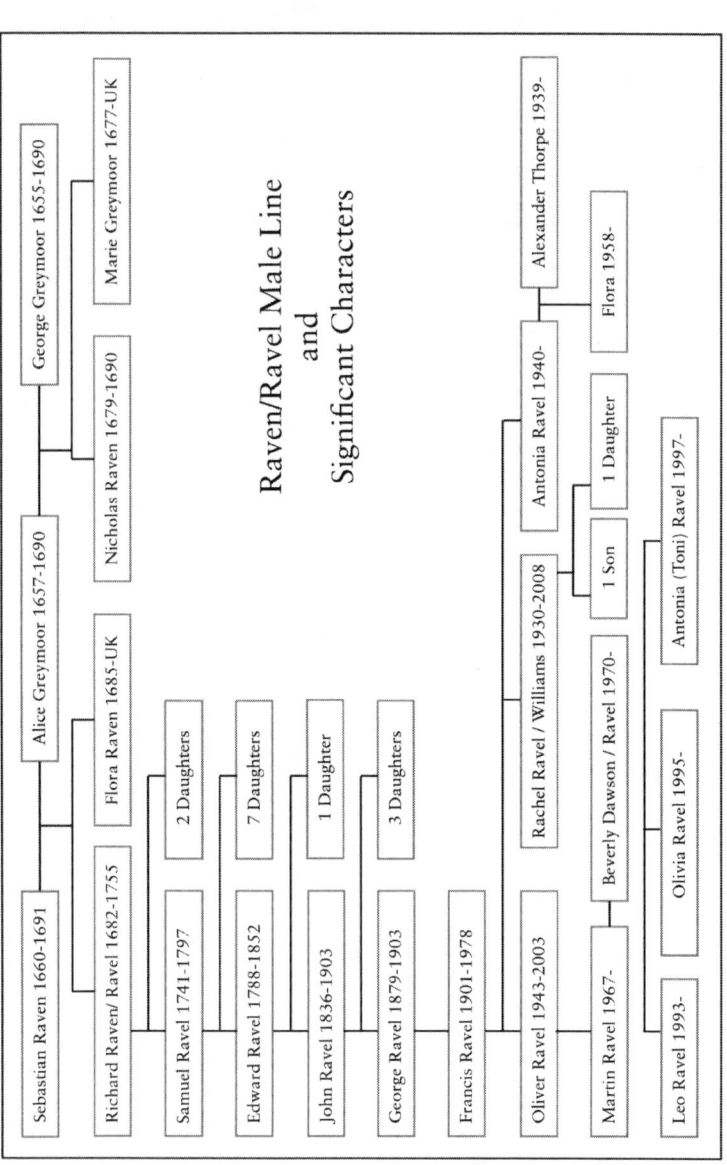

Raven/Ravel Male Line
and
Significant Characters

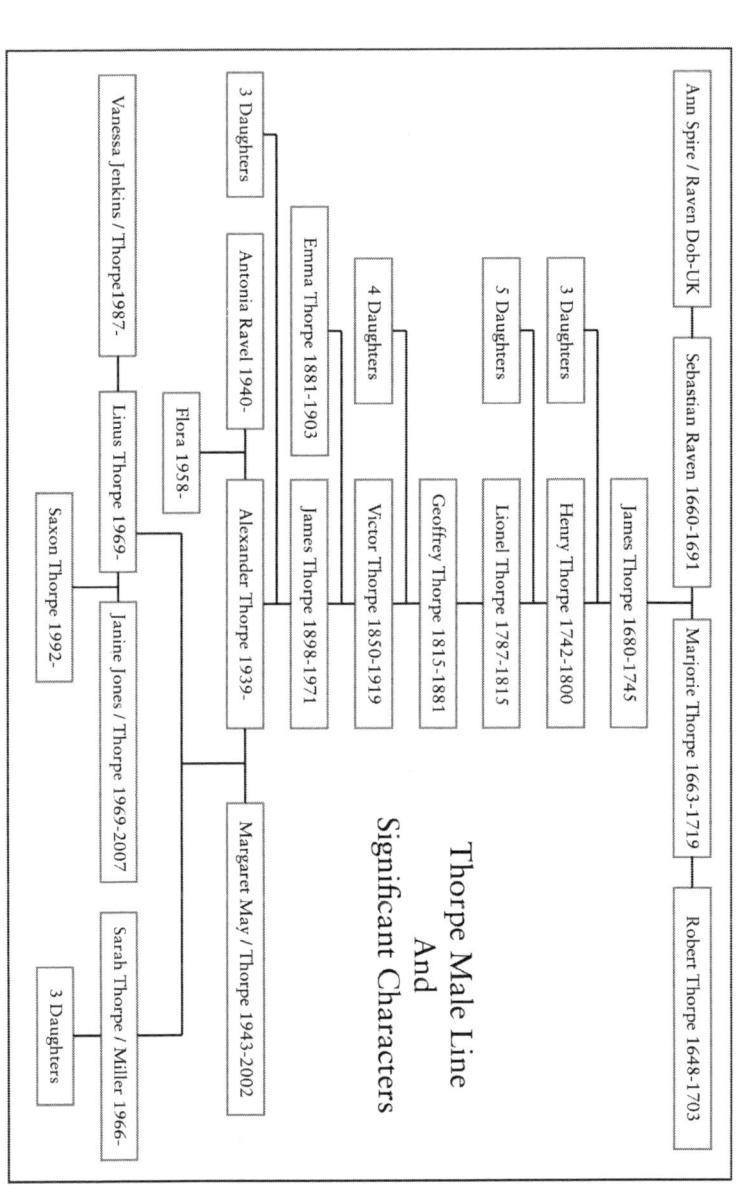

Thorpe Male Line
And
Significant Characters

Ann Spire / Raven Dob-UK

Sebastian Raven 1660-1691 — Marjorie Thorpe 1663-1719 — Robert Thorpe 1648-1703

James Thorpe 1680-1745

3 Daughters — Henry Thorpe 1742-1800

5 Daughters — Lionel Thorpe 1787-1815

Geoffrey Thorpe 1815-1881

4 Daughters — Victor Thorpe 1850-1919

Emma Thorpe 1881-1903 — James Thorpe 1898-1971

3 Daughters

Antonia Ravel 1940- — Alexander Thorpe 1939-

Flora 1958-

Vanessa Jenkins / Thorpe 1987- — Linus Thorpe 1969-

Janine Jones / Thorpe 1969-2007

Saxon Thorpe 1992-

Margaret May / Thorpe 1943-2002

Sarah Thorpe / Miller 1966-

3 Daughters

Chapter One

'You actually spoke to Saxon Thorpe?'

The discussion over the style of Olivia's neckline, on her much talked about wedding dress, came to an abrupt halt, as Martin Ravel sank into a chair and threw the local farming paper heavily onto the table next to his plate. He bit into a sandwich and mumbled 'That's that then, Littlejohn has sold.'

Toni carefully slid the paper across, began to read and failed to stifle a groan. 'The fields that look down on Shingle beach.'

'Thorpe, *bloody,* Developments,' Martin said between mouthfuls. 'If Frank Carter's right, there's going to be a holiday village built there. Why Leo still associates himself with the Thorpe lad, I don't know.' He stood up, snatched the paper from Toni and marched outside, banging two doors, very loudly, on the way.

'Frank's information isn't always sound.' Beverly tentatively commented to her two daughters.

'It'll be something equally as bad now the Thorpes have it,' Olivia added unhelpfully. She was sympathetic to the age-old problem between farmers and developers but right now, she wanted to get back to the question of how much décolletage could be seen, as she glided up the aisle of St. Mark's church, in seven weeks, two days and three minutes exactly.

Beverly sighed. 'I suppose I'd better go and pick up the bridesmaid dresses.'

'I'll do it.' Toni offered quickly. After the discouraging news her father had imparted, wedding planning was just the thing for her mother and sister to get immersed

7

in. Without wanting to appear rude, she'd heard more than enough about Olivia's cleavage to last a lifetime.

'Is the back of the van clean?' Olivia asked, looking slightly horrified at the thought of her wonderful dresses travelling in anything other than pristine conditions. Her sister's old Astra van definitely didn't make the grade.

'I was going to walk, *actually*.' Toni said irritably, thinking it could become a very *long* walk through the woods. That would fill most of the afternoon and save her from hours of more wedding talk. 'I'll try not to drag them through any hedges on the way back.' She grinned when Olivia stuck her tongue out.

Stopping to play with one of the farm cats, the only one that wasn't feral, and check the litter of kittens in the barn, Toni pondered the comment her father had just made about Saxon Thorpe. It was a good thing her brother was away, he'd have defended his friend and no doubt started a heated discussion.

Leo was finishing his year at university, studying hard for his Masters. This summer he'd come home and decide if his future and Ravel Farm, were one and the same. It would break their father's heart if he chose a different path.

The Ravel children were close in age, Leo had been born first, Olivia two years after and Toni, another fourteen months after that. They'd spent their childhoods playing and squabbling together and enjoying a freedom, of which only small village communities could boast. Saxon had been a big part of their adolescent years and for Toni, the barn always conjured up memories of him sitting on a hay bale and reading Jacqueline Wilson stories to her, whilst waiting for Leo to finish his chores. Those wistful scenes were replaced by the harsher reminders of his unkind jokes when she'd reached thirteen and overnight seemed to spring up like a beanpole and develop a face full of spots. She'd accepted a certain amount of teasing from Leo and Olly, mostly because she'd had no choice. But when Sax had added his own mean and uncalled-for comments about Dalmatians, join the dots and eventually telling her to phone the emergency services, there was an outbreak of measles, it was more than she could bear.

Over the years, she'd given the Thorpe family the benefit of the doubt because that's what she'd always done and still did, tried to see both sides of every argument. Wanting to appear open-minded, it gave her some satisfaction to listen to debates, nodding understandingly at both parties involved, almost willing one of them to convert her with irrefutable evidence. They never quite managed it. Perhaps there was a God, perhaps not. Maybe aliens exist, or they don't. As for all the conspiracy theories, Roswell, the JFK assassination and were the royal family lizards? That last one was just beyond ridiculous... or was it? The jury was still out as far as she was concerned.

One evening, after celebrating her fifteenth birthday, in the woods, Olivia had come home swearing the place was haunted. Leo had pronounced her ravings as total shite and asked Toni if she believed in ghosts.

As with politics and philosophical theories, she had no firm opinion on the supernatural. Not one to be easily spooked or hear imaginary noises, she left such thoughts and ideas to others. So, she'd shrugged and given the usual answer, 'It could be true, but then again, I doubt it, who knows?'

Her brother had rolled his eyes in frustration and accused her of sitting on the fence *yet* again. At nearly fourteen she should have the courage of her own convictions, he'd told her, irritably.

The event had coincided a day later with Saxon Thorpe handing her a tube of ointment and mumbling something about having spots on his own chest, and this stuff, he'd promised her, would help clear up even the worst acne.

It didn't matter about his hurt expression when she'd told him to go to hell. It didn't matter that she'd retrieved the tube of cream from the bin, where she'd flung it the moment he'd handed it over. It also didn't matter that the cream had started to work and the angry rash of pimples began to disappear. What *did* matter, was that she'd made a decision and picked a side, her father's side against the Thorpes, most of all, Saxon.

She didn't speak to him again after that day and as she grew into her height, her willowy figure found some curves and the last pimple departed. Boys, in and out of school began finding excuses to talk to her. Not so, her nemesis, he would walk past in the street without a second glance.

* * *

As the Second World War drew to a close, Saxon's great-grandfather, James Thorpe, earmarked two-thirds of his agricultural land and began to look into property and land development. He included his young son, Alexander, in the new family business and turning his back on decades of ancestral farming, looked to the more lucrative rebuilding that was arguably, just as important as food production.

According to Martin Ravel, over the years, Alexander had become as ruthless as James had once been. He was still a formidable character and tall for a man of his seventy-nine years. He had a head of thick grey hair and eyebrows so bushy a dormouse could make a comfortable nest and have room to raise its young. Toni had avoided him at all costs when she was younger. Even when she went with Leo to play in Saxon's swimming pool, she'd hide if Alexander came out to say hello.

As recently as a few months back, she'd taken refuge behind a hedge in Blackberry Lane, rather than have to walk past him and his awful dogs. *Satan*, and his hounds from hell!

* * *

Toni glanced at the bit of hedge now as she walked by, choosing not to dwell on the ordeal. The surrounding landscape took on the look of a randomly stitched patchwork quilt. Mostly shades of green and brown, but some yellows and white broke the haphazard design with grazing cattle adding tiny squares of polka dots.

The coastline was to the south, just beyond what had been, until now, Littlejohn's western-most fields. She walked on and reached a circular grouping of old oaks, marking the start of Raven Wood which cut a swathe through four large areas of land. Three farms and the other, a ruined manor with grounds of over two hundred acres. This belonged to the Thorpes and sported the large family home, constantly changing with modern trends and various extensions. The actual ruins had been left untouched.

Further on, and thankfully well out of sight, the remaining land that had once belonged to the large estate had been turned into post-war housing. Primrose Ridge, had over the last half century grown into a small self-contained town that didn't encroach on the local village much. It had left the Thorpes sitting on pots of money and appear to the local community as metaphorical lords of the *ruined* Manor.

Raven Wood was so dense in parts and branches so close, that the leaves formed a twilight canopy, which, at this time of year allowed the merest shaft of daylight through. It had been a favourite spot to play when they were all younger and Toni could almost picture Olly and Leo racing through the trees, with her trailing behind, whining at them to slow down. An unbidden memory of tripping over a root, blood trickling down her legs, from badly scraped knees and a white hanky wiping gently at her tearful face, came to mind. Saxon Thorpe had been the owner of that hanky and she'd been eight years old. He'd only been thirteen then, a year older than Leo, too young still to be influenced by greed.

Obviously, things had changed, Toni thought scornfully because she knew he was now well and truly embroiled in the family business, Thorpe Developments.

Her mood took another dive as she cleared the woods and reached the bottom of the gently sloping hill that marked the border of the Littlejohn's farm. From the rise, there was the most wonderful view of the sea. It was all going to be ruined, spoilt forever by what... a thousand caravans?

She stomped along the narrow grassy lane before turning into the woods to take a shortcut, her mood worsening with every step. Alexander Thorpe, his slimy toad of a son, Linus and *Saxon*. Grandfather, Father and Son, just what the community needed, a united trio of money-grabbers.

A large mound of moss-covered boulders marked a favourite meeting place for the young people of the village. Smugglers' Knoll, as locally known. Today it was empty and silent. Toni imagined she could feel a hauntingly desperate plea from the woods and surrounding fields to save them from all modern-day progress. Such a deep wave of emotion caused her to shudder and for a brief moment, she became quite teary. The sun was directly overhead and as it peeped through the high trees caused freckles of light to turn some patches of dark lichen an emerald green. Maybe once upon a time, it had been a meeting place for Druids, there was certainly an aura around the rocks. This was where Olivia had claimed to have seen her ghost. Not that any of her other friends, and it had been a large group, reported seeing or hearing anything.

Toni was talking herself into feeling spooked and suddenly, felt really cold as if an icy draft had blown through her. Time to leave the darkest part of the woods and head back to Blackberry Lane.

'Return anon, little Raven.'

She quickly spun around, her eyes darting back to the rocks. It took a moment before her legs started to follow the commands of her brain. Then she ran and didn't stop even when the overhead canopy thinned and sunlight won the battle of the shadows.

The lane ran parallel with the woods but she couldn't bring herself to glance in the direction of the trees. The sound of barking started in the distance and in no time got louder, reaching a crescendo as a canine stampede rounded the bend. Three large Dobermans bounded towards her, followed by the sharp command 'Oxeye, Brutus, Damocles, DOWN!' They dropped to the ground, a jumble of lolling tongues and wagging tails. Toni burst into tears.

'Toni, what's wrong? The dogs won't hurt you.'

Aware he was moving closer, she shook her head and tried to speak but the words wouldn't come. 'Someone w-was in the woods, a m-man I think, at the Knoll.'

Saxon's face darkened, these were the home woods, nothing ever happened here, no main roads nearby, nothing to attract outsiders not even from Primrose

Rise, apart from the die-hard walkers. 'What do you mean a *man*? Was it someone you know? Did he touch you? *Talk* to me, I'm imagining all sorts of stuff.'

Toni eyed the dogs and shifted slightly. 'H-he didn't touch me. I just got a bit scared and ran.'

'If there's some pervert up to no good, I want to know, are you *sure* you're not hurt?' As he closed in again, Toni took a step back and he stopped where he was. 'What did he look like and what *exactly* did he say?'

'I um didn't actually see anyone. I mean I kinda heard something, but I don't know, that is to say, I think, err it might have been...'

'Look, don't take this the wrong way, but are you sure you *really* heard anything at all?' He was on dangerous ground now, he could see it in her changing expression. Upset to red-faced anger in all of two seconds. 'Maybe you imagined it?' Past the point of no return. 'Or are you just embarrassed about getting frightened by the dogs?' That had done it, he braced himself.

'Sod off, Sax, go and buy up some more land, put another farmer or cottage industry out of business. You and the rest of your family can sit back and watch as they tow in the caravans and build a classless modern pub on the Littlejohn's fields. I'm sure we'll all enjoy the noise pounding across the valley and the red-jacketed plastic-smiling, wanking entertainers trying to get us all in line to dance the conga through Market Street.'

If his temper wasn't now equal to hers he'd have burst out laughing. Getting himself in check, the only way forward was to make a quick exit before one of them killed the other. 'I'm not going to waste time arguing with *you*, my girl. I'll take the dogs through the woods and make sure no one's hanging around who shouldn't be.' He turned his back on her, feeling hurt as well as angry, not unusual emotions when he had dealings with Toni Ravel. 'Tell Bolly I'll see him tonight,' he shouted back over his shoulder, not wanting to look at her again and not waiting to hear anything else she might say.

Toni watched him disappear into the trees, the three dogs running ahead. She wasn't sure which was worse, firstly, the fact that he'd all but disbelieved what she'd told him. Secondly, that he'd known her brother, Bolly, Leo's nickname from school, something to do with Ravel's Bolero, was coming home for the weekend and she hadn't. Or, thirdly, the fact that he'd called her *my girl* but had used a scathingly dismissive tone, when years ago, the way he had said it made her feel like a princess.

Return anon, little Raven, she'd heard it as plain as day. Four words, which although had scared her, had also, wrapped themselves around her like part of a kiss. No wonder she hadn't wanted to share them with Saxon Thorpe.

A family had taken over the granite boulders, the children swarmed to the top shrieking and arguing. Saxon would have liked to question the parents, it was possible they'd seen someone leaving. Mindful he had three large Dobermans, not one of which would hurt a kitten unless commanded to do so, he veered away from the noisy family scene knowing how intimidating his grandfather's dogs appeared. The sounds of shouting and arguing faded as he walked further from the Knoll.

It must have sounded just like that when Leo, Olly, Toni and himself were all much younger and playing together. He'd watched as Olivia and then Leo started teasing their little sister. Saxon had held his breath waiting for tantrums but none came. Toni had risen to the challenge with such comebacks as 'Elephant thighs,' at Olivia and 'Nice curls, did you take a photo of Nan's pubes to the hairdressers with you?' aimed at her brother. Not bad for a thirteen-year-old, Saxon had thought at the time. He'd also thought it was okay to join in but had found out to his cost that what was acceptable banter between brothers and sisters didn't extend to him. Bolly should have put him in his place, he'd have said sorry straight away and that would have been the end of the matter. Instead, Toni looked instantly betrayed and had never forgiven him.

He'd tried on more than one occasion since, to apologise, even buying some expensive dermal cream that the pharmacist had recommended, but when he'd given it to her, it had been thrown in the bin with a few choice words. By then she was fourteen, enough was enough, he was leaving for university anyway, so avoidance became the easy option.

After today he realised that's where they still stood and most likely, always would. Three years away studying for a business degree, hadn't made anyone's heart grow fonder and, in the years since he'd been home, things had probably got worse.

Bolly was still his best mate, although, their time together these days was curtailed. After an extended gap year or two, his friend had moved away to study Agricultural Science, and was now finishing his Masters in the same subject. It looked like Leo Ravel would take over from his father after all and Saxon fervently hoped that their relationship would never suffer as their parents had.

* * *

'Olly, I need to talk to you.' Toni toyed with the idea of entering her sister's hallowed space without waiting for an invitation. She could hear her talking on her mobile, which meant no one would get a look in for ages. Just as she lifted her hand to knock one last time the door opened. Olivia beckoned her in and pointed to the stool in front of the dressing table, her conversation didn't falter for a second.

Toni glanced at her reflection in the three-way mirror, she looked tired, having had strange dreams for the past two nights, which kept waking her. The green flecks in her hazel eyes didn't seem to be shining so brightly and her blonde hair lacked its usual lustre. Absentmindedly she began to fiddle with the large array of cosmetics and small jars festooning the surface of the table.

'Leave my stuff *alone*.' Olivia glared and gave a long dramatic sigh. 'Sorry, I have to go. Come over and try the dress and accessories as soon as possible, bye for now.'

'Sophie?' Toni asked, as her sister hung up.

'Yeah, I want to see the two of you together. Toni, you look *dreadful* are you feeling okay?' She walked over, grabbed a hairbrush and started to brush her sister's hair. They didn't share many close moments, but on rare occasions when they did, the tender times were silently treasured. 'The answer's yes, by the way.'

'Yes, to what, Olls?'

'My room, of course, that's what you came about, isn't it? Once I move out you can have it.'

Toni hid a smirk, she'd always coveted this room and had already planned her takeover. She certainly didn't need permission. 'Err, thanks, that's really sweet of you.' She was rewarded with a radiant smile. Olivia was the beauty of the family, masses of red chestnut hair and no sign ever, of any skin problems. A spot would shrivel up and die long before it became a blemish on her sister's lovely face. She was tall, curvaceous and sported the larger bust of the two sisters, something she never let Toni forget.

The growth spurt, Toni began at thirteen, had stopped abruptly a year later. At 5' 5" she would easily be the shorter bridesmaid, not even chief bridesmaid, that dubious privilege was going to Sophie, Olivia's best friend. The thick blonde hair ended in a shaggy bob just below her shoulders, she watched as Olivia put the brush down and scooped up the ends trying to somehow imagine what it would look like up. 'Give up now, Olly, it's not going to work.'

'It will. Sophie's sister is the best stylist for miles, she'll work her magic, don't worry. Anyhow with the coronet of flowers, it won't matter that much.'

Toni pulled a face. 'I'm going to look like Kermit the frog with something growing out of my head.'

Olivia burst out laughing, 'You won't at all, don't be bloody daft. The dresses are *moss* green and I'm going with large daisies for the coronets. I wish I was blonde like you, you're so pretty and petite, I'm going to look like a bloody great walrus following you up the aisle. At least Sophie's a size eighteen. That's an awful thing to say isn't it?'

Was she hearing right, a *compliment* from Olivia? She knew she attracted her fair share of male attention but had always assumed it was more to do with living in a small village and the lack of choice available. 'Josh is a lucky guy, I bet you can't wait to get to Cyprus and start your new life. Mr and Mrs Luscombe, Olivia Luscombe, sounds good.'

Olivia grinned. 'To tell you the truth I'm *sooo* nervous about everything, but it's a good nervous, know what I mean?'

Toni nodded. 'Can I ask you something, Olly, about your fifteenth birthday?'

'My fifteenth?' She screwed her face slightly and looked puzzled.

'Do you remember telling us something spooky happened in the woods?'

Olivia's expression changed instantly, 'I'm not talking to you anymore, I might have known you'd try to find something to make a joke about.'

'Please, Olls, I'm not joking, I *really* want to know what you saw?'

'I didn't *see* anything, and we *were* drinking, a lot. I was a kid for God's sake and the boys were messing about, that's all. Why are you asking about this now?'

'Because, I was at Smugglers' Knoll two days ago, and I thought I heard something, it freaked me out a bit. Saxon took the dogs up there to check it out.'

Olivia's mouth fell open. 'You actually spoke to Saxon Thorpe? You *must* have been scared.'

'I just happened to see him in the lane after.' She ignored her sister's teasing, pleased that she didn't appear to be annoyed anymore. 'Well did you, or *didn't* you?'

'I did, and if you ever repeat it I'll deny this conversation. Like I said I'm sure it was the booze, but I could swear someone said something and it was quite loud. All the others were on the rocks at that time, they thought I was messing around because they didn't hear it. I went really cold, it was weird.'

'What exactly did he say?'

Olivia hesitated and whispered four words. 'And now clear off, Toni. I'm busy and I don't want to talk about this ever again, thank you.'

Chapter Two

'Where did that monstrosity come from?'

Alexander Thorpe sank back into the comfortable Queen Anne chair and waited for Henry to lay his hands on the correct file.

His friend and family solicitor scratched his head and looked puzzled. 'I had the blessed thing ready for you Alex, it was *right* here.' Henry's shoulders slumped, he pressed a button on his phone and they heard a buzz in the next room. Almost immediately the door opened and a keen looking, smiling girl breezed in.

'What can I do for you, Mr Davidson?'

'Amy, can we have some tea please and have you by any chance tidied my desk this morning?' he asked hopefully.

'It's Annie, Mr Davidson, and no, I would never touch your desk.' She turned to leave but then paused. 'Is it the Thorpe/Littlejohn file you want?'

Henry shook his head, 'No, never mind, just the tea please, Amy.'

She rolled her eyes and Alexander wondered, not for the first time if he should start seeing Robert, the son, in *Davidson and Son Solicitors*. Unfortunately, he gave the impression of being a bit too smooth, at least, in Alexander's opinion. Annie was still talking about the Littlejohn folder he realised.

'I only asked because you had it on your desk yesterday before you went home.'

Henry visibly relaxed and broke into a relieved smile. 'I did, yes, you're quite correct I had it here and the will was next to it.' He got up and opened a large filing cabinet, extracting a thick folder. A noise similar to a schoolboy's whoop was heard as he pulled out a slim file and waved it at his client. 'Ha I knew it had to be somewhere around, damn thing must have slipped in there by mistake.'

Annie beamed, 'I'll go and get the tea.'

'She seems switched on.' Alexander commented when the door was closed. 'Is she holding the fort until Mrs Dale returns?' Mrs Dale was Henry's personal assistant and had undergone a hysterectomy some weeks back.

Henry nodded distractedly whilst checking something on the last page before sliding the whole thing across the desk. 'Yes, she's off for at least another month, that's the problem with older women, they all have bits that need surgically removing. Shall I get us some tea Alex, while you have a read through?'

'Annie's sorting it.' He gave an irritated sigh, it really was time to find a different law firm. It would never happen though, not only was he very particular, he was *very* loyal when it came to old friends like Henry. The door opened again and a large tray holding a bright red chunky teapot was placed carefully on the oak desk. It looked ridiculous stood amongst the delicate Royal Windsor cups and saucers, not that the last flowery teapot had matched the sugar bowl or milk jug, but it had at least been the same make.

The tea dribbled into the saucers, Annie was obviously struggling. 'Why don't you leave that, we'll see to it.' Alexander offered kindly, afraid of splashes on his newly revised Last Will and Testament.

'Thank you, Mr Thorpe, can I bring you anything else, some biscuits perhaps?'

He was about to say no, when, 'Hobnobs, please Amy' came from the floor, on the other side of the desk. 'What are you *doing* down there, Henry?'

'Dropped my blessed glasses. Oh, good Lord!' Henry spied the large red teapot as his head appeared level with the desk. 'Where did that monstrosity come from?'

'Market Street Hardware Store.' Annie looked at it doubtfully, she'd thought it would cheer up the other horrible old-fashioned china, but now she wasn't so sure.

'The Windsor met its maker two days ago,' Henry quirked his eyebrow and smiled ruefully at his friend. 'That wasn't quite the replacement I had in mind, no matter.'

'Allow me to get you a new set.' Alexander offered. *A matching one.* 'Services rendered and all that. You've done a good job with this, Henry. He may contest it of course.'

Henry waited for Annie to leave the room before he spoke. 'I'm sure he will, but it's watertight and it's not as if you're leaving him penniless. Does Saxon know?'

Alexander shook his head and read the last few lines again. 'I'll tell him, tonight. Now everything's finalised I owe it to Linus to come clean as well, it might rein him in a bit.' He blew out a breath. 'It's not a conversation I'm looking forward to.'

'You and Margaret spoilt that boy, neither of you were like it with Sarah.' Henry was one of the few people that could get away with speaking so plainly to his friend, on a personal level. 'It's made things a lot less complicated that she wants no part of the family business.'

Alexander nodded, his daughter was happily living in Boston, with his American son-in-law and three granddaughters, not that he got to see them in person very often. Once a week Saxon would dutifully set things up so he could talk to them on Skype. Lots of large round faces with huge white teeth, quite awful actually *and* they called him *Grandpops*!

That side of the family was well taken care of financially. His daughter had had more than her fair share when she first moved away and wanted to set up a publishing business. There would be more in his will, it just wouldn't be from any part of Thorpe Developments, Raven Manor, or the surrounding land. That was going to the one person he knew would protect it and try not to overturn any preservation orders, his grandson, Saxon.

Linus would be disappointed, possibly angry as well when he found out he was being overlooked in the running of the family business. His shares in the company would keep him sitting pretty and fund his expensive tastes until the day he died, but would that be enough to sweeten the blow? Thank heaven for Saxon, he was ambitious, with just the right amount of compassion and fairness. He cared about the local community and more importantly, the future.

Before coming on board, with the latest venture, Saxon had demanded that together, they went over every last detail of the proposed holiday park. When it was explained that the number of luxury lodges would be limited, and the clubhouse would be a restaurant, gym and spa, all built to the highest specifications and blending sympathetically with the surroundings, he'd agreed. Alexander was going to turn the whole project over to him shortly. Linus, on the other hand, couldn't believe they were limiting the number of holiday homes and was already trying to work out where more could be built.

It would never happen, he just had to convey that message home a bit more strongly, because from what he'd heard, Linus was looking at possibilities, which included part of Martin Ravel's land. The last thing he needed or wanted was more conflict with *that* family. 'Do you fancy some lunch, Henry? I'm meeting Saxon in the pub, he's offered to drive me home.'

* * *

'Lunchtime, Toni. Do you want first, or second break?'

'First please, Karen, I'm meeting Annie in the Swingers.'

Karen smiled, the shortened name of the local pub, The Swinging Smugglers, always amused her. 'That's fine, don't rush, it's dead in here today. In fact, take the rest of the afternoon off. I owe you time back for stocktaking last week.'

Toni wondered not for the first time, how long the small shoe shop, Pretty Feet, and her job, would survive.

'According to Vanessa Thorpe, we need to start stocking designer wellies, more upmarket trainers and high-end walking shoes. It's no good scowling Toni, I need business to pick up, or we're all in serious trouble.'

'I know, but Vanessa Thorpe, *really?*'

'Can't afford to be choosy about my customers, she spends a lot of money in here, even if I do have to hear how much more choice there is in town, *every* single time.'

Toni giggled, 'I suppose if Linus' latest wife wants to spend his ill-gotten gains who are we to refuse.' She had good memories of the first Mrs Thorpe, Saxon's mother. She'd been so kind when they'd been invited to play in the pool. Always a biscuit or homemade bun on offer. Still on friendly terms with him, eleven years ago, she along with Olivia and Leo had done their best to try and help Saxon through the emotional loss. Not easy when the fifteen-year-old had watched her waste away from cancer. Toni had been too young to understand how exactly she'd died but was old enough to know it was pretty bad. The memory of putting her arms around his neck and planting big kisses on his tear stained cheeks now stuck in her head.

Four years later Linus had brought his new bride home, all twenty-four years of her, almost half his age. By then Toni had to rely on gossip and hearsay, but understood from Leo, that it was the deciding factor for Saxon to go away to university. Until then he'd debated the local college and Open University courses, preferring to get stuck into the business, with his grandfather's guidance.

* * *

Alexander and Henry were on to their dessert by the time Saxon slid into the comfortable booth, armed with drinks. A whisky for his grandfather and a pint each for himself and Henry. He would have to make it the first and last, he thought regretfully. The Swingers sold an impressive array of different ales, but as designated driver, he would only enjoy one of them this lunchtime.

'Have you eaten, Son?' Alexander asked.

Henry watched Saxon give a quick nod, the term *son* hadn't escaped him and although broadly used, he knew it had a much more literal meaning for Alex. Saxon really was the son he'd hoped for in Linus. The codicil to the Will, now signed and witnessed, had on the surface appeared an easy decision for his old friend. Henry was most likely the only person to know the heartache and great disappointment behind firstly, the decision and secondly, putting it into action.

'I say, Henry, is that your employee chatting away to the Ravel girl?' All three men looked toward the bar, where Annie and Toni were drinking fruit ciders and laughing over a shared joke. 'Hope she can keep her mouth shut.'

'She's a good worker and they all have to sign confidentiality clauses.'

Alexander heard a note of doubt in his voice, he'd have to hope for the best, or at the very least she didn't know the contents of his will or other business dealings. 'Isn't Martin's other daughter getting married soon?' he directed the question to Saxon.

'Err yeah, Olivia. I think she intends to move away for a couple of years, from what Leo was saying. Her fiancé is in the air-force, a long-term posting in Cyprus.'

'That'll be a big change,' Henry smiled. 'Very nice too.'

Alexander nodded in Toni's direction. 'Damn pretty, that one.'

'Stop that *right* now. You know everything that's happened, so don't pretend that you don't.' Saxon narrowed his grey eyes to show his displeasure but he had a twinkle in them. When he wasn't being watched, his gaze kept creeping towards the bar, Toni Ravel certainly *was* pretty and a lot more.

While he'd been away studying, he'd pushed all thoughts of home aside. But since returning, three years ago, he'd been aware of letting his mind drift on occasions and Toni often came unbidden into his head. It was because she was Leo's sister, he'd told himself. When he'd watched her leave the pub one time with Lawrence Carter, obviously, he felt protective. The same justification excused the fact that his brain nearly scrambled when she'd climbed on the back of Ian Littlejohn's Honda Fireblade and they'd roared down the high street. How he'd stopped himself from driving after them, he didn't know. Ian was a complete jerk *and* he'd been drinking. Saxon had got no sleep that night and found an excuse to call in at the local shoe shop the next morning, just to make sure she was in one piece. Two pairs of socks and an unfriendly scowl later, he could at least breathe easier, until her next escapade.

Toni played with a beer mat, doodling a beard, moustache and glasses on the three sorry-looking men dangling from the end of the Hangman's ropes. The mats matched the large sign outside of the Swinging Smugglers Inn. A popular B&B for walkers and renowned for a good Sunday Carvery.

'Don't ask,' Annie smiled apologetically. 'I can't say anything, it's more than my job's worth and I really like working at Davidsons.'

'Fair enough I don't want to get you in trouble, I just wish you hadn't mentioned the folder.' Toni heard deep male laughter and followed the sound to the far booths. 'The bloody Thorpes are here.'

'Bothered much?' Annie grinned.

'No, why should I be?'

'I think the farmer's daughter doth protest too much.'

'Shut up, not funny.' *Not where he's concerned.*

Annie changed the subject to her favourite topic. 'I hear Leo was home.'

'Yeah, not that I got to see him much.' Another nail in Saxon's coffin, for hogging her brother nearly the entire weekend. 'Sunday lunch was a real hoot. I'm sure Olly thinks Leo doesn't know the definition of the word *Usher*, she must have said it at least thirty times, while we were eating. Leo was being a *complete* knob, asking stupid questions just to wind her up.'

Annie sat straighter as Henry Davidson walked past, looking pointedly at his watch. 'Bloody cheek, I've only been here forty minutes. I suppose I better go. Laters.'

Toni smiled, her friend's lunch break was forty-five minutes and it was at least a five-minute walk back up the hill. Out of the corner of her eye, she saw movement, Saxon and the Antichrist were getting ready to leave as well, she didn't want them walking past and be forced into a polite acknowledgement.

'I'll give you a lift,' she offered quickly.

'In the van?' Annie asked warily.

'Of course, don't diss the van, it's one of the only trustworthy and honest things around here.'

'*Thanks*, I love you too!'

'Best friends not included.' Toni began a mammoth search for the keys, in a handbag that Vanessa Thorpe would give to the coal-man as a spare sack. By the time half the contents were on the counter and the Barman watched fascinated, the Thorpes had gone, leaving an echo of soft laughter in their wake.

* * *

'I want to talk about something when we get home, privately.' Alexander tried to sound casual but obviously failed.

'That sounds ominous, something wrong with the planning?' Saxon asked.

He was thrown for a moment wondering which planning Saxon meant. An extension of Primrose Rise was also underway. That at least was safe to leave in Linus' hands, as long as he stuck to the proposals already agreed. His son had a bad habit of making changes without consultation and presenting them as a fait accompli. 'No, Saxon, this is something very different, a personal matter.'

He didn't say anymore and Saxon tried to work out what personal issues they might have, whilst watching the shapely backside of the girl in front as she got into the driver's seat of the twenty-year-old Astra Van.

'Are you going to help her out or are we to be stuck here for another ten minutes?' Alexander asked, as he also watched with a wistful *if only I was fifty years younger*, appreciation.

'Give it a minute,' Saxon grinned.

'You have a wicked streak. Heaven's above!' Alexander strained to see through the rear windscreen of the van. 'That *bloody* bag is getting emptied out onto the front seat by the look of it.'

Saxon unclicked his seatbelt and opened the car door. They'd pulled up behind Toni whilst she'd been filling the tank with diesel. Using the pump behind, he'd felt a little irritated, when she'd blanked him and proceeded to continue as if he wasn't there. Finishing first he'd sat back in the driver's seat resisting the urge to switch on the ignition. His grandfather began to chuckle and nudged his arm, she'd only left a huge bunch of keys hanging out of the petrol cap. They could see her looking around, reaching into pockets of a discarded jacket, and now it was the bag's turn for an intimate search.

Toni was getting more and more pissed off, mindful she was muttering to herself and fully aware who was waiting for her to pull away. When the sound of jangling keys filtered through the window, she didn't need to look, knowing exactly who'd be holding them and no doubt enjoying every second.

'Are these what you're looking for?' Saxon crouched slightly and dangled the keys in her face.

'Blast.' She grabbed them and thrust the ignition key into place. After three attempts the engine reluctantly gave a splutter and after pumping the accelerator it pathetically roared into life reminiscent of a geriatric lion's death rattle.

'My *pleasure*,' he murmured, starting to walk away and not expecting any thanks.

'Err, Sax, wait up. Did you find anything, in the woods the other day?'

He was tempted to ignore her but of course, he didn't. 'Kids were playing on the rocks, I couldn't really talk to the parents, not with the dogs. Are you sure whatever you heard wasn't from a way off, the wind can distort things?' He daren't mention her imagination again, she was already starting to bristle.

'It was pretty clear, I'll take a look one evening this week.'

'*Don't.*' He surprised himself with the force behind the word. 'I mean… don't go alone, you never know, someone *could* have been hanging around the other day.'

'Well, clearly you don't think that's a possibility and I'm not one of your demolition squad, you don't get to tell me what to do.'

With that she rammed the gear stick into first, the grating noise causing Saxon to wince. Not having time to formulate an answer, the van screeched away and he had to take a quick step backwards, nearly tripping over a flagstone.

Alexander shook his head, unable to hear what they'd said but seeing the outcome. 'That's girl's trouble, stay well away,' he half-heartedly advised.

'Don't worry, I intend to.' He also knew he couldn't let her search the woods on her own. Now all he had to do was figure out how that could be prevented.

* * *

Vanessa sat at her dressing table digesting what she'd overheard a day ago by hovering outside of Alexander's study. Linus was out again, maybe he had a bit on the side? she laughed and dismissed the thought as an impossibility. Why would he go looking for second best and who would want him anyway?

Being a golf widow had become a tad tedious and for that reason, she had to decide what to do with this new information. From what she'd understood, it could affect her long-term future. That was of course if she chose to stay in this backwater. She hated the green fields, muddy lanes and awful smells that descended every time the wind blew in any direction, their home being bordered by farms. The topic of muck spreading was something that guaranteed a full-on debate. Certainly, it was talked about at every given opportunity in the local pub. No wonder she avoided the place at all costs.

Six years ago, the future had looked so wonderfully and affluently rosy. The head of the family, an old man of seventy-three, was bound to step down any day and hand the reins over to his only son. As for her nineteen-year-old stepson, he was an entirely different matter. Saxon, only five years her junior, could get her juices flowing with a single look. She was convinced he was totally begging for the guidance of his, only too happy to oblige, stepmother.

Her nightly dealings with Linus, which quite often left her more than a little unsatisfied were sweetened a great deal with the thought of Saxon taking his father's place between the sheets. It didn't help when the object of her desire took himself away to university instead. At least the long holidays offered her a teasing glance of his maturing and athletic body, especially in summer around the pool. For the bored young housewife, it was a promise of things to come. Whether he was there alone or with friends she would find an opportunity to drape herself across a sun lounger and breathe in the testosterone-charged air. When they made excuses to leave earlier than originally planned she would never have assumed it had anything to do with her presence.

Living away from a big city, bored with Linus and missing Saxon, she'd started to look for a more permanent diversion and found one in the form of Robert Davidson, son, in the law firm that the Thorpes chose to use. Two years younger than her husband, but far more attractive and with a full head of hair, it didn't matter to her that he had his own fat *countryfied* wife, no doubt happily chained to the kitchen sink. If her own husband thought she was content sitting at home reading magazines, while he played golf, he was very much mistaken. Weekly Saturday shopping trips to the nearest town included a clandestine meeting and a bit of afternoon delight, in a small country hotel on route, and as time went on, a midweek assignation was also added.

Three years ago, Saxon had returned and once more taken up permanent residence in the family home. Less desperate now, because of Robert, Vanessa still wanted what she thought would be an easy conquest. Now, totally frustrated that he was taking *playing it cool* and *hard to get*, too far, she wondered what other approaches may win him around.

A critical look in the mirror showed her blonde hair could use a few highlights and giving her forehead a prod, perhaps another Botox session, soon. Not that Linus would notice. When she shared her little secret, *if* she did, he'd take notice then. Lips pursed, the anger began to grow and fester, eventually, it would settle and common sense would dictate the course of action. Should she make an effort to pursue Saxon and not give a damn that his father was going to be overlooked in Alexander's will, or, should she advise Linus to start making plans now?

She hadn't heard *everything*, because Saxon had burst out looking at his watch with the old man right behind. The conversation had ceased abruptly, looks of accusation had crossed their faces when they saw her pretending to straighten a picture. Aware it was the lamest thing ever, but being caught blatantly listening, what else could she do? Saxon *had* given her a small smile of acknowledgement, at least, before tearing out through the front door. She couldn't help wishing he was rushing up the stairs to her bedroom with such a determined look on his face.

* * *

Nine o'clock, surely, she wouldn't come now? Saxon decided to call it a night. This was the second evening he'd waited to see if Toni would appear. He couldn't do this all week. It was only the thought of hearing a remark over the breakfast table, 'Do you know what happened to Toni Ravel at Smugglers' Knoll? That *poor* family, right before the sister's wedding as well.' He could almost see Vanessa pretending heartfelt sympathy when actually, she'd be greedily scanning the next few lines of the morning paper hoping for another juicy morsel. Perhaps how many times she'd been attacked or the fact that the murder weapon was found discarded on the large boulders like some kind of trophy. *Get a grip.* He nearly shouted the words out loud, forever grateful he hadn't when he heard approaching footsteps.

'*Sax,* what the bloody hell are you doing here?'

Chapter Three

'Sebastian Raven at thy service.'

Saxon frowned. 'I told you *not* to come here alone.'

'And I told you, I don't take orders and anyway, I'm clearly *not* on my own. I seem to have acquired a guard-dog, which actually I don't need or want. Perhaps I should call you Oxeye or Damocles, or the other stupid name.'

Saxon raised his hands in a gesture of submission. 'You know what, just do what you have to do. This is the second night I've sat here, so ignore me and when you're ready to go home give me some sort of sign. *Not* that,' he snarled as she stuck her middle finger up at him.

He was still talking, she knew because his mouth was opening and closing, but a cold chill had wrapped around her body and held her almost immobile. 'Sax.' He hadn't heard her, he was still babbling some nonsense. 'SAX.'

'Thou returned, little Raven, as I desired, but who is with ye?'

'Who's there?'

'Thou hath brought a boy, a champion perchance?'

The voice seemed distant and caused a ringing in her ears, she had felt something similar when she'd fainted, many years ago. Voices and sounds nearby but distorted so they sounded a long way off.

'Sooth, another Raven, I hoped it wouldst be so.'

'I don't feel too good.' A wave of intense nausea forced Toni to move from her petrified state. Bending double, she began to retch violently.

'I beg thy pardon; our connection is stout.'

'Toni, are you okay?' Saxon helped her to stand. 'You're *freezing*!' He took his sweater off and forced it over her head, feeding her arms into the sleeves.

'Didn't you *hear* him?'

'Hear who?' He was still sceptical but began to circle the trees. If someone was hiding nearby he'd find them. 'Stay by the Knoll and shout if you see anything.'

Toni hugged herself in the large sweater, it smelt of freshly cut grass, gorse and something else, rosemary and bergamot soap, that was it, a smell she always identified with her childhood, probably because Saxon had been such a big part of it. He was talking to her while he searched, even when he walked around to the back of the large boulders he kept asking if she was okay. She was about to answer that she felt a little better when the chill surrounded her again.

'Dost ye believe I am here?'

She still felt sick and cold, but oddly, not at all frightened. There was something about the voice that put her at ease. 'I don't *think* I'm going mad, so yes, I guess so. Was it you that spoke to Olivia?'

'Olivia?'

'My sister, it would have been about seven years ago. She said someone called her a raven.'

'There wast one buxom beauty, I recall. Time means very little, verily it couldst be thirty years past, or a matter of weeks.'

'*Who* are you talking too?' Saxon asked anxiously. 'There's no one here. Come on, I'll walk you home.'

'Can't you hear him, Sax, not even a little bit?'

He shook his head and looked puzzled, 'I don't know what this is about, I thought it was some stupid joke, but you were in a really bad way just now and you're still *so* cold.' He started to rub her arms. 'We're leaving, *now*, I'll carry you if I have to.'

35

She took a few steps, too bemused with the whole situation to argue. They'd hardly gone any distance before she heard faint laughter and saw Saxon turn to look suspiciously back at the Knoll. 'You heard *that*, didn't you?'

'Wait here.' He started to walk back and knew instinctively she was following. 'Can't you ever do what you're told?'

'You don't get to…'

'Yeah, I know,' he sighed, 'tell you what to do.'

'Back so soon?'

'I thought you couldn't tell the passing of time, maybe I've been away for a week!'

'Saucy wench, too much to say and too clever, a true Raven.'

'Raven?'

'Toni, *please* stop this?' Saxon was beginning to get really worried about her state of mind. '*Jesus*, it's cold.'

'Just try, Sax, I have to know I'm not insane.'

'Come, knave, try harder.'

Saxon's mouth dropped open, 'There *is* someone here.'

'I desire ye both to see me properly and methinks 'twill help. Come hence to the cave anon.'

'The cave on Shingle beach?'

'Aye, wench, if tis the bay south of here you speak of.'

'I'm working tomorrow.' Toni said automatically. 'When should I come.' It didn't occur to her that perhaps she shouldn't be answering, let alone agreeing to a meeting.

'*Working*? That knave doth not provide sufficiently? Art ye in service then?'

'I work in Pretty Feet, the shoe shop on Abbey Road, in the village.' *I'm babbling, but I'm actually having a conversation with… whatever this is.*

'A cobbler's store, so that is thy craft. A strange trade for a mistress. I wouldst crave a fine pair of boots if I couldst wear them.'

'Who are you calling a *mistress*?'

'Not the correct word? Over time the way I speak hast altered mightily, I shalt try harder not to revert to the speech of mine own time.'

Saxon was still too stupefied to say anything even though he wasn't happy that Toni seemed to be accepting all this so easily.

'Is this knave a simpleton? He speaks not.'

Toni couldn't help grinning, she was acclimatising to the cold feeling that seemed to accompany the mysterious voice, and all traces of nausea had faded. It left her buzzing with a feeling of heightened energy, adrenalin she guessed.

'What is all this? Who are you?' Saxon finally pulled himself together enough to ask.

'Sebastian Raven at thy service.' The tone sounded mocking.

'I'll come on Saturday morning. Will you know when it's Saturday?' Toni asked excitedly.

Saxon stared at her, he was furious. 'Absolutely not.' He spluttered.

'Absolutely *yes*,' she replied calmly.

'I'll warrant ye wouldst not desire to leave the wench alone with me, young Thorpe?'

'Of course, I wouldn't and how do you know my name? I'm not sure what all this is, but if you think you can harm...'

'*Harm... HARM* one of mine own blood?'

The roar echoed around the Knoll. Toni grabbed Saxon's hand and she felt him grip it tightly.

'Forgive me,' Sebastian's voice quietened, 'I beg thy pardons, the invitation is for both of ye, in fact, tis imperative ye come together. There is much to say and much to do.'

'Please let me take you home, this is enough now.' Saxon was overcome with the same sickness Toni had felt earlier.

Sebastian smiled to himself as he watched them leave. A Thorpe and a Ravel, both of his bloodline. This was the closest he'd come in over three hundred years to make some recompense and put an end, once and for all, to the family curse.

Saxon and Toni walked in silence until the farmhouse was in sight. 'I won't come to the door, but I'll watch until you're inside.'

'I know my way.' She gave a small smile; the reality was creeping back fast. This was Saxon Thorpe who'd walked her home. She'd dropped his hand pretty quickly when they'd left the Knoll, now she wasn't sure what to think or feel about the evening's events. 'Nothing's changed, you know.'

'I'm well aware of that. I'll meet you at the top of the cliff path on Saturday morning, shall we say, ten o'clock?'

'I'm grateful for your help, but like I said, I don't need it.'

'That's too bad, cos it seems our resident ghost does.'

'*Ghost?* Yeah, I suppose that's what he is, shit, it makes you think doesn't it?'

'Goodnight, Toni.'

When she got to the door she turned to give a quick wave, but Saxon was already walking away. *I can't like him again, I'm not a kid anymore and anyway, he's the enemy.*

* * *

A pregnant runner bean sprang to mind when Vanessa looked at Linus' naked lanky frame and pot belly in the bedroom that night. Saxon was the real heir to the family fortune and he was by far the more superior specimen of male *Thorpeness*. Vanessa rather liked the made-up word. So far, she'd only flirted a bit, now she would make it count. He'd be unable to resist what was so attractively and generously offered. She'd have to keep Linus sweet as well, just in case things went tits up. What a pity he hadn't inherited Alexander's physique and thick hair, if anyone had missed out on all the good-looking genes when they skipped a generation it was her husband.

The front door clicked shut. 'Saxon's home,' Linus said from his spread-eagled position on the super-king divan.

Oh God, he thinks he looks sexy. Vanessa managed to paint on a smile. From her very first day in this house, she'd hated sharing it. Her and Linus, Alexander and his continuous supply of mutts and Saxon, all living together like the cast of *Dallas* in the Southfork-Ranch. Actually, having Saxon so close had changed her mind somewhat, he was a different matter entirely, it was the old man she couldn't abide. Always peering above his spectacles, trying to catch Saxon's eye when she made a comment or looking down his long nose because she was wearing a new piece of jewellery. What did the old fool think all the money was for? New church roofs and providing the means to keep the local primary school open? That's why charities and local councils gave grants and bursaries. The Thorpes shouldn't have to dip into their pockets to keep poor relations and decrepit old buildings afloat. If the kids had to catch a bus to the nearest town, so what? They'd all benefit from growing up more streetwise!

This backwater and the people in it were like the land time forgot. Linus was just as bad, he loved the thought of being a big fish in a small pond. She looked at him sprawled on the bed and her gaze slid between his legs, big fish? she gave a snort, more like a limp sardine. Just another thing that had skipped a generation. From the surreptitious attention she paid to Saxon's crotch, she'd bet *his* jeans held a mighty monster from the deep. Now, all she had to do was unleash the beast. In the meantime, Robert would have to suffice.

Despite what Vanessa thought, people didn't bother to compare the Thorpe men, not in looks anyway. Yes, it was obvious the grandson took after the grandfather, but Linus' mother, Margaret, had been popular among her peers, so to inherit her looks was almost a way of paying tribute and help keep her memory alive. It was the other comparisons that left Linus wanting.

No-one liked to do business with him, he wouldn't exactly renege on a deal, but neither was his word his bond. Written contracts often had subtle differences to the hours of verbal discussion that preceded them. Alexander had learnt early on, to watch his son carefully. Nearly all the bad feeling towards his family could be traced back to projects he'd left in Linus' hands. It broke his heart, or so he'd thought until his beloved Margaret passed, only then did he truly discover what a broken heart really was. It was around that time he began to coach Saxon in the family business and was delighted that values such as honesty and fairness appeared to be abundant in his ten-year-old grandson.

Linus had insisted on sending Saxon to private school when he reached thirteen, Alexander couldn't argue the point having done the same with him from an even earlier age, a decision he'd come to regret. Fortunately, the chosen school was not too far and weekly boarding was finally agreed between the three of them. If Saxon had got his way, he'd have stayed at the local secondary school with Leo and his other friends.

The bad habits and superior attitude that Linus developed, buying friendship with money, and learning how to cheat in exams thankfully, didn't repeat themselves in Saxon's education. Even today Linus believed himself popular and well thought of. He couldn't see that the hangers-on considered him a meal ticket. As fast as he made it, Linus enjoyed spending money and he could be magnanimously generous to the *right sort* of people.

The one genuine and devastating loss was the premature death of his wife, Janine, five years after the mother he'd also adored and who had spent a lifetime spoiling him. He deeply regretted having so many affairs and the vasectomy he'd had and not mentioned. Janine had so dearly wanted another child, a brother or sister for Saxon and asked for tests to be done on them both. Linus had guiltily told her not to bother, they loved their son, what would be would be.

Alexander had known his daughter-in-law had wanted another baby. It seemed to be par for the course that Thorpe men only ever had one son, plenty of daughters to make up for it, apparently, but only ever one male child. He could trace the family tree back as far as 1815, courtesy of a family Bible which recorded the death of Lionel Thorpe at the battle of Waterloo. His widow gave birth the same year to Geoffrey Charles Thorpe. There were two more entries before that one, but the aged ink was now illegible. One son, all the way down through those two hundred years, over seven generations. If the Thorpe men had gone away to fight, be it the Crimean, Boer or First world war and no son had been born they seemed to make it home in one piece to ensure the begetting of one. Strangely, the same trait was shared by the Ravel family, although, he wasn't sure how far back that went. Certainly, in the last hundred years, only one boy was born to the father before him. Daughters, it seemed weren't affected, they could marry and produce a large brood of healthy boys, enough to form a football team if they so wished. It seemed almost abnormal and Alexander had pondered on more than one occasion over the rather bizarre coincidence.

* * *

'It fits like a *glove*,' Beverly enthused as Sophie slipped the bridesmaid dress over her head. 'Such a beautiful colour,' she skimmed her fingers across the green silk. Across the room, her younger daughter appeared to be imitating Houdini.

Toni was still struggling to get into her own dress and now she was afraid she'd got the zipper snagged. 'I'm stuck,' she finally admitted, readying herself as the stampede of three charged over with instructions to 'Stand still.' 'Don't tear the material.' 'Get it off, GET IT *OFF*.' The last, being Olivia's frenzied contribution.

In the end, it was Sophie who deftly released the zip and started to laugh. Toni knew if *she'd* so much as smiled first, Olivia would be mad. Thankfully they all saw the funny side. The dress, was of course too long, even in the strappy high heels. Beverly pinned it up and told them she could manage the hemming, it wouldn't need to go back for any further alterations. Olivia breathed a sigh of relief, now they were here, she wanted the dresses where she could keep an eye on them.

Toni wandered downstairs, blaming Sebastian Raven for the entanglement, in fact, she'd blamed him for everything that went wrong over the last three days. Talk about a distraction, it was all she could think about, and why wasn't she scared? He filled her thoughts entirely and the need to see what he looked like was becoming an obsession. Please don't let him be some headless horseman or look like Beetlejuice. She'd spent hours on Google looking up ghosts, hauntings, Smugglers' Knoll and paranormal sightings on the south coast.

She didn't find out much she hadn't known already. Raven was a popular name, if she combined it with a search in this area, Raven Manor came up. A large manor house belonging to the Raven family during the reign of Henry VIII. Raven Wood and much of the surrounding land had been owned by the same family. Although the house had kept its name, the history was patchy. The Ravens must have flown, she smiled at her joke and typed in Sebastian Raven DOB, nothing. He did seem to be some kind of Japanese cartoon drawing and also a character in a vampire novel, that was quite cool, maybe she ought to try and download it. She hadn't read a book for ages.

* * *

A light drizzle was falling, and every so often Saxon switched the windscreen wipers on so he could see when Toni arrived. He'd had second thoughts about even coming this morning, but yet again it was the thought of her going into the cave alone. In the harsh light of day, he'd been trying to think of any reasonable possibilities for what had happened. It annoyed him that he couldn't and as Toni had done, wasted a great deal of time on the internet.

Vanessa had started to really piss him off as well over the last two days. Whenever he entered a room she appeared a few seconds after. If he went to the kitchen to make a quick coffee she'd be there, pulling out the expensive percolator and making smutty innuendos about sweet, dark and strong. He wasn't interested in anything she had to say, the woman was a complete waste of space. What *had* his father been thinking? It wasn't the mother replacement issue, his father deserved to be happy and was too young to spend the rest of his life a widower, it was *Vanessa,* she was awful. Every cliché could be applied, gold digger, being the most pertinent. If she jiggled her silicone tits in his direction one more time he'd leave home and move into a portacabin on the new site.

The Astra van pulled into the car park and rattled into position next to his Cherokee. Because of the weather, theirs' were the only two vehicles. Toni jumped out and threw him a scowl. If he'd been trying to imagine the complete opposite of Vanessa, it was Toni Ravel.

'Are you just going to sit there or what?' she shouted.

He exhaled loudly and got out of the car, 'And a good morning to you too.'

'Sorry, Sax, I'm kinda pissed off with everything this morning. Karen phoned, the Saturday girl's sick and I had to let her down. I hate saying no, she hardly ever asks me to work on a weekend, the extra money would have been handy as well.'

'You should have done it, we could do this another time, according to the... err ghost, he doesn't know what day it is anyway.'

'Yeah but this is ideal, no one will be here in this weather.' She started to walk down the path towards Shingle beach. 'Do you think he meant the main cave?'

'Must have, it's the only one head height. I've got a torch; did you bring one?'

'I didn't think, but then I knew you'd be useful for something.'

'How're the wedding preparations going?' he asked, trying to keep up the momentum of small talk.

'None of your business.' She ran ahead and reaching the bottom first, slipped on the wet stones.

'Break your neck, why don't you?' he muttered. A giggle filtered back and he savoured the sound. When had she last laughed at something he'd said?

They both remained silent upon entering the cave. It was narrow and went back a fair way, which meant they were in semi-darkness well before coming to the dead end.

'WHO GOES!' The booming voice echoed loudly.

'Oh, crap.' Toni grabbed hold of the sleeve of Saxon's hoodie. 'Bloody hell, Sebastian, is that you?'

'Mine pardon, Ravens, I couldst not resist I knew 'twas ye of course. Missy, thine use of coarse language is most unbecoming. I hast known old, bawdy tavern slatterns with more refinement. Come hither and let me see ye.'

From the fistful of material Toni was twisting more and more tightly, Saxon wondered if his sleeve would still be attached to the rest of the top.

'Ah quaint, I bethought it wouldst be so. I can see ye both better when I am in solid form.'

Her fingers relaxed a little, '*Quaint*, is that a compliment?' she whispered to Saxon.

'And thou, Master Thorpe, quite splendid, a real credit to thy ancestors.' Sebastian stepped forward as Saxon switched the torch on.

'Holy Saints in heaven,' A pair of emerald green eyes reflected in the torchlight. 'What is yond shining weapon? Dost not point it at me.'

Toni's mouth dropped open at the sight in front of her. She let go of Saxon's sleeve and cupped her cheeks unable to tear her eyes away. '*Wow!*'

45

Chapter Four

'He's my ghost, I saw him first.'

Totally drop-dead *gorgeous*, which seemed a little ironic, as he really was dead. Toni could hear him a lot more clearly, no more penetrating half-whispers. Instead, a rich, warm voice that reminded her of a strong baritone, the kind that should sing Christmas carols in a church choir. And the way he spoke, a mixture of comical and charming, old English mixed with more modern words, she loved it.

'Why are you acting so weird?'

Damn Saxon Thorpe, intruding on this extraordinary and spellbinding moment. She ignored his question and opened her eyes wider, fighting the poor light. Sebastian Raven was tall, maybe half an inch taller than Saxon, that pleased her, with a *he's bigger than you* childish reasoning. It was difficult to make out the exact colour of his hair with only the torchlight, but she could definitely see some hints of red, not unlike Leo and Olivia's, and her father's come to that. Also, she wasn't very good at ages. Saxon would be twenty-six at the end of the year, she though Sebastian looked a few years older.

Saxon moved closer and she gave him a reassuring nod in a bid to stop him muscling in even more. Something strange happened then, for a second it was as if the two faces merged together and she started to notice uncomfortable similarities. Saxon's hair was much darker, there was a word for it but she couldn't quite remember, an animal name when brown was almost black... sable, that was it.

The noses were the same, straight, not big but well defined, as were the lips. She tried to concentrate on

Sebastian only, but it was impossible not to compare them. Thick eyebrows, one day Saxon's would grow bushy like Alexander's, two polar bear armpits. She would make sure he trimmed them of course. What the *hell*? she wouldn't even know him then, certainly not by choice anyway. She forced her attention back to Sebastian and focused on his clothes, that did the trick, much more interesting than a navy sweat top and jeans.

A long grey coat with a deep collar fell to his knees, it was open and a light green, heavily embossed tunic reached the same length, the material didn't look in the least aged. Long boots met the green hem and Toni couldn't help wondering what might be underneath.

Sebastian puffed out his chest and took a step forward. 'Tis been a long while ere I hadst a reaction like this. Art thou faring well, Knave, ye art quiet again?'

'I'm not a *knave*.' Saxon forced out between gritted teeth.

Sebastian winked at Toni.

'Can I touch you?' she asked still feeling rather overcome.

Both men turned quickly, one looking positively ecstatic and the other, frowning so hard, he might be in acute pain.

'Be mine *guest*.' Sebastian pulled his coat wide open, eagerly awaiting her touch.

Toni put her hand cautiously on his chest, the tunic was a thick velvet. Beneath, he felt firm, as she would have expected, but then something seemed to give way and her hand began to sink a tiny bit into the material. Sebastian's smile started to fade.

'Toni, I think you should stop.' Saxon gave her shoulder a gentle shove and moved her back.

'It was like... I don't actually know how to describe it, a thick cake-mix? No, tougher than that, bread dough. Can I try again?' She didn't wait for an answer but reached forward about to place her hand on the same spot.

Sebastian braced himself, 'Try a little lower wench, dost not be afeard, I am made of sturdier stuff down below.'

Toni started to lower her hand and then realised where he'd directed her. Her hand flew back as if it had been burnt. 'I don't *think* so.'

'Shame.' He chuckled and didn't miss how quickly Saxon had grabbed Toni's hand and was still gripping tightly even as she tried to wriggle it free.

'Art thou still out of sorts, boy? She doth not wear a ring, so ye art not wed. Lovers then, mayhap?'

'No, certainly not, we're just...' *What are we?*

'Betrothed?' Sebastian asked hopefully.

Saxon shook his head and tried again. 'We're...'

'He's my brother's friend.' Toni said managing to retrieve her hand.

'Yes, Bolly's mate,' Saxon said with a look of relief.

'*Bolleee's* mate?' Sebastian shook his head, 'Strange words. I wast hopeful thy connection to each other wast stout, still, there is time.'

'Not happening, there'll never be enough time for that,' Toni muttered.

'Right back at you.' Saxon replied.

'So, I cannot interest the two of ye in a little adventure?'

'An *adventure*?' Toni responded much too quickly for Saxon's liking.

Sebastian smiled, the girl would be willing, he'd bet his last gold coin if he still had one. The boy... a different matter, he wouldn't allow her to go gallivanting into the unknown, that was for sure. He had feelings for her, he'd bet his last gold... *Damnation.*

'What *kind* of adventure,' Saxon asked cautiously.

'If ye concur, ye shalt need to work together.'

Together, Toni's heart sank, but an *adventure,* with a ghost and a *really hot* ghost. She glanced at Saxon, he was tempted. Oh, he'd spoken in his usual head up his arse way, but Toni recognised the suppressed excitement.

'Maybe *I* could help you out, with whatever it is.' Saxon offered. 'It would be easier if it was just one of us.' He was feeling a bit wicked and wanted to rile her, especially after the way she'd drooled and almost copped a feel of phantom playdough man.

'You *bastard,* Saxon Thorpe, how bloody *dare* you? I'm in, I'll do it, whatever it is.'

Sebastian nodded trying not to show his glee. He didn't approve of the word *bastard* at all, it was too near to home. Another time he'd take her to task, but not today, not when he had them right where he wanted.

'I cannot hold this form for long and I sense much animosity. Avaunt and bethink how ye can improve thy situation. Come hither anon, or to the Hunters' Stones, I shalt hear if ye dost call.'

'The *Hunters' Stones*? Do you mean Smugglers' Knoll?' Saxon asked.

'I dare say,' He gave a terse laugh, 'Sooth, Smugglers' Knoll.'

'Sooth,' Toni giggled, 'and avaunt, what do they mean?'

'Avaunt means away, and sooth... well, tis *sooth*. I shalt try harder to maintain thy manner of speech, some words hast adapted through the years, others I fear shalt never change. Ye must comprehend mine family wast country folk and lived away from the big city. Speech wast changing mightily in those places, but for us, 'twas slower.' He grinned at them both. 'It shalt be a most higgledy-piggledy discourse methinks.'

They had acclimatised to the chilly atmosphere, but as soon as Sebastian left them, it became noticeably warmer. 'He's definitely gone.' Toni said.

Saxon may have been five years older than Toni and about twenty years wiser but the word adventure had him bubbling with as much excitement as it did her. He'd tried to play it cool to draw Sebastian out a bit, but he'd stubbornly refused any more details today. On the way back up the cliff path, he muttered quietly 'I'm sure *boy* is no better than being called *knave*. I may have to threaten to have a bloody exorcism performed here.'

Toni was working out a hundred and one ways to persuade Sebastian to let her do this thing alone. 'Getting in a tizzy, Sax?'

'Hardly, and speaking of *tizzies*, watch your temper. He didn't appreciate your swearing.'

Damn him, she couldn't argue the point, she was well aware she swore too much at times and hadn't failed to notice the fleeting look of displeasure on Sebastian's face a few minutes ago.

The Littlejohn brothers had been a bad influence and could be blamed for her choice of less than polite language. At a time when she was unconsciously grieving the loss of Saxon in her life, she'd turned to his complete opposites. Leo made his feelings very clear, they were wastrels the pair of them, just waiting for their parents' land to fall into their laps, so it could be sold off the next day. No wonder the family was going under.

Annie, Toni's friend, had had a thing for the younger brother, the double dating, which was mostly just hanging together, went on for a year or so until thankfully, both girls saw the light. Of course, it hadn't stopped Toni getting on the back of Ian's new motorbike two years ago. He'd been keen to show off and she knew Saxon was in the Swingers that night. When he came into Pretty Feet the next day to buy socks, she couldn't help the feeling of satisfaction as he handed his money over. She could still get a reaction from him.

'How do you want to do this?' Saxon asked, bringing her back to the present and their looming problem.

'On my own,' she responded immediately.

'Yeah well, I'd rather do it with Bolly, he's home for good in two weeks, at least we should bring him on board.'

'No way am I going to let you push me out. I know your family likes to intimidate people, well it *won't* work with me, he's *my* ghost, I saw him first.'

Saxon burst out laughing, he couldn't help himself. 'Christ, Toni, are you twenty-one or eleven still?'

'Twenty *actually*.' She was a bit hurt that he hadn't known she'd not had her twenty-first yet. Not that he'd be getting an invite.

Of course, her birthday is at the end of August. 'Yeah, I knew that. Look if we *are* going to do this thing together and we don't know what it is yet, how are we going to explain it to everyone?'

'Do we have to actually be seen with each other? Perhaps we can do different bits and just message each other, *I* don't know.'

'That might work, but I get the idea it's not what Sebastian has in mind, he seems pretty clear we should be getting on better.'

'While you're buying up every bit of land and building high rises all over the place we'll never get on.'

'Stop exaggerating, the blocks of flats in Primrose Rise are only three stories high, we haven't built anymore since then.' He pushed his hand through his thick hair and leaned back against the door of his jeep. 'This is about the fields, isn't it? Meet me up there tomorrow and I'll show you the plans.'

Toni gave a nonchalant shrug, but her interest was definitely piqued. 'Trust a *Thorpe*? You could show me anything, how do I know you'll be telling the truth...'

'Right that's it then, this isn't going to happen, we can't do it. When have I *ever* lied to you? Ask your narrow-minded little self that question.' He opened the car door and got in, slamming it noisily behind him.

She'd pushed him too far and if the situation wasn't rectified all this would be over before it began. Saxon was right, it sounded like they would have to work together and he wasn't a liar. The engine started, she banged on the window. At first, she thought he was going to ignore her and drive off, but then, the glass moved a fraction.

'I'm not apologising through a one-inch gap!' The window came down half-way, the engine was still running. 'I'm sorry okay.' The engine revved, she could see his foot pumping the pedal. 'I'm *really* sorry and yes, I would like to see the plans.' The engine settled to a purr and the window came all the way down.

'What time's best for you?'

'I help Mum on Sunday mornings, we still do lunch for everyone, so, after that... about half three?'

A memory of sitting around a massive pine table with all of the Ravels, the farm workers and usually an apprentice or two, came into his head. He gave a terse nod, put the car into gear and roared away.

Man, that was hard. She got into her van and looked at the waterlogged windscreen. The wiper blade on the passenger side didn't work, grabbing a cloth she went back out and dried it off as best she could, thankfully the drizzle was quite light now. Saxon's car was a way off, but she could still see it in the distance. *Narrow-minded*, what a bloody cheek. She considered herself very broad-minded, always trying to see the other person's point of view, except when it came to the Thorpes and *that* was going to be a problem, unless of course, Saxon could change her opinion.

* * *

It had taken Linus a couple of days to make sense of and reconcile with, his father's news about the will. At first, he was outraged and if Alexander came into the same room, Linus would mumble some incoherent excuse to leave.

Since then he'd began to see things with a bit more clarity. Most importantly while the old man still lived, nothing would change. It had been abundantly clear for some years that Saxon was being groomed in Alexander's image, and actually, it didn't matter to Linus. If he had inherited as he'd assumed, he would, it would all go to Saxon one day anyway. With the recently added codicil, which had been thoroughly explained the other evening, the money he was being left, plus the shares in the company would see him through nicely. It wasn't so bad really, Saxon could do the work and they'd all reap the benefits.

He also knew his father was feeling guilty, that was rare indeed and might be used to his advantage. What his father couldn't stomach was sulking, two days was enough. In the morning he would appear agreeable, which having had a chance to think things through, wasn't far from the truth. Some of his own deals going through on the back of the Thorpe name were near completion, kicking up a fuss now would only draw attention to them. The profit he made would be secreted away into his Jersey account. Vanessa was only allowed to find his monthly, high-street bank statements and if she believed those, hopefully, it would curb her spending a little.

He would have a home here for life, Alexander, had said. Unless he and Saxon found a reason, they couldn't live under the same roof, then he would have to move out. That wouldn't happen, he had no wish to fall out or become a burden to his son. Vanessa was a different matter, he almost relished the thought of watching her face when the will was read. He had no doubt she intended to pack her bags and leave as soon as Alexander took his last dying breath, well, if she thought she was getting half of everything she'd be sorely disappointed.

How he wished he could turn the clock back six years, he'd have never married the bitch. At the time she'd made him feel good and occasionally, still did when she could be bothered to accompany him to meals at the golf club or ladies' night at the Freemasons' lodge. In the early days of their marriage, they'd always been out socialising, clubs, the theatre, dinners and the Casino. Now if she went out she preferred to go alone. No doubt she was screwing someone, and when or if he could be bothered to discover who it was, she'd be out on her ear.

Vanessa had never wanted children and asked him if he would consider having a vasectomy. He didn't let on that he'd had it done already and made a big thing about doing it to please her. It had become difficult afterwards not to agree with everything she'd wanted. Dear God, he'd offered his balls on a plate and she'd proceeded to break them, grind them and finally, sweep the dust away.

If he'd done one percent of the things she regularly accused him of he'd be a happy man. There was *Rita* of course, she worked behind the bar at the golf club and went a long way to soothing his damaged ego.

Linus had decided years ago he was probably going straight to hell when he departed this mortal world. He was guilty of at least five of the seven deadly sins and with the exception of *Thou shalt not kill,* he'd easily broken the other nine commandments, many times over. He glanced at his sleeping wife, there was still time to crack the last one.

The smell of bacon wafted up the stairs, Saxon was cooking breakfast, he always made plenty on a Sunday morning. Slipping on his dressing gown, he made his way to the kitchen. The parasite that was his second wife would most likely sleep until late morning and then demand to be taken out for lunch. Why not? Perhaps he'd suggest the Swinging Smugglers, that would really upset her.

Vanessa felt when the bed was empty and stretched out her body revelling in his absence. She was feeling quite pleased with herself. She thought she knew something Linus didn't, that he had no idea he was being cut out of his father's will. Considering how well things were going with her stepson, she'd decided to keep it that way. Saxon was definitely interested, he could hardly take his eyes off her the other day when she'd worn her new extra tight t-shirt. Swinging her legs over the side of the bed, she looked in the mirror. Were her breasts starting to sag just a little? She was thirty-one now, maybe she should consider a lift and another small implant. This was the time to spend Linus' money, while they still had it, although his balance hadn't looked too healthy the last time his bank statement had been left lying around.

* * *

Sunday breakfast at Ravel Farm consisted of Toni and her mother, sharing a plate of hot buttered toast. Olivia was away for the weekend with her fiancé, and it was the one morning of the week Martin accepted a cup of tea in bed and enjoyed an hour alone with the Sunday Paper.

'Are you okay, sunshine?' Beverly asked. 'You seem quiet lately, I know I haven't had much time to spare, what with fussing over Olivia.'

Toni laughed, 'You love having one of us chicks to fuss over.' She saw her mother smile. 'I'm fine, just a bit worried about my job and this holiday village is on my mind.' She didn't say she was meeting Saxon later to talk about the plans.

'About the fields, I wouldn't say this if your father was in the room it would only start a huge debate, which would turn into an argument. I went to see Norma yesterday afternoon.'

'*Mum*, you walked all the way to the Littlejohn Farm? I'd have taken you in the van.' She ignored the shudder her mother tried to hide. 'Were the boys there?'

'Where else would they be? That lazy pair, *don't* get me started. I'm so glad you finally came to your senses over Ian. If they'd only help out a bit the farm could be saved, but all they want to do is play those horrible noisy video games, drink beer and expect handouts. Did you know Gus has dropped out of college? That's the second course he's given up on. Norma looked so upset when she told me.'

Toni had known Gus was jacking in his course. She also knew that Ian had bought his brand spanking new Fireblade from a loan his father had given him two years ago and still hadn't made any attempt to pay him back. 'It'll all go to me and Gus one day, may as well get some benefit now,' he'd boasted. Leo had been right when he'd warned her four years ago, they were wastrels. 'Are things really that bad?' she asked.

'Pretty grim. If Norma had her way, they'd sell completely, and you know how much she loves the place. Anyway, as I was saying, I don't like the fact those fields were sold any more than you or your dad, but I at least understand why. Alexander Thorpe gave them a very fair, actually, *more* than fair price and apparently, some shares in the new development. *And*, it was Pete that approached Alexander about the sale.'

'Satan, couldn't believe his luck.' Toni was still cross about it but even as she snapped her reply, felt a little foolish. 'I've heard it's not going to be quite the holiday park we first thought.'

Beverly looked at her daughter with surprise. 'Have you now? well you'd be right about that, according to Norma, it's going to be high-quality lodges or something. Anyway, I can hear your father moving around upstairs and this won't get the veg prepared.' She brought a large basket of seasonable vegetables to the table and gave Toni a peeler. 'Only six of us eating today, you do that lot please, while I start making the crumble. And by the way, don't call him Satan!' she chuckled.

'I'm going out later Mum, can I do the dishes when I get back?' For some reason, the Sunday crockery didn't make it into the dishwasher, something to do with the gold leaf design decorating the rims. Because of that, all the roasting tins were done by hand as well, it was a traditional weekly nightmare which had been hers and Olivia's job as far back as she could remember.

Olivia being older and bossier usually donned the marigolds, washing as quickly as possible and leaving Toni with a huge pile of drying to do alone. She only stayed to help with the putting away if they were being supervised. Leo didn't have to do any *women's work*, as Beverly called it. On more than one occasion, Toni had moaned to Annie or anyone else who would listen, that she had been born into the most archaic and sexist family in the whole of the county.

'I'll do the dishes today love. You go out and enjoy yourself.'

'Thanks, Mum.' Toni beamed, wondering what her mother would think if she knew Saxon Thorpe was the main part of her afternoon plan. 'Are you sure?'

'Yes dear, perhaps you could fit in a visit to Great-Aunty Antonia after work tomorrow, instead?'

Toni groaned. *The care home, full of crazies. I knew there'd be a catch.*

Chapter Five

'No one will believe you're my new BFF.'

Sharing bacon sandwiches and maintaining the safe boundaries of small talk effectively achieved a pleasant breakfast for father and son. Saxon knew his father had been told about the will and surprisingly, no reference had been made to it at all. Either he was calculating his next move, or just possibly, had accepted things? Saxon had even got an invite to lunch, and feeling a bit guilty for declining, suggested one evening in the week perhaps? Linus looked pleased and the amiable atmosphere continued until Vanessa joined them.

When she finally graced them with her presence, Saxon was her obvious target. She pulled her chair close and whispered in a suggestive conspiratorial manner about being seen out with an older man. When he'd reminded her, that *older man* was his father and *her* husband she'd retreated slightly and shot him a venomous look, quickly replaced with an awkward smile and high squeaky giggle.

'Silly.' Vanessa said, taking the opportunity to put her hand on his arm, 'You know that's not what I meant,' and began to stroke him.

With an inward sigh, Saxon extricated her well-manicured hand and edged towards the door, using the excuse that his room needed tidying. He didn't care that it made him sound like he was fourteen years old, escape was more important.

Alexander was also out for lunch, and when they'd all gone Saxon revelled in the solitude. With the whole house to himself, music was soon blasting through the empty rooms filtering through the built-in sound system all the way to the outdoor pool where he swam furiously until beaten by exhaustion.

The swim had cleared his head and Saxon found himself looking forward to the meeting with Toni. The few hours alone in the house had brought a bit of clarity and strengthened his resolve to try and make things better between them. She was the sister of his best friend, it was time this nonsense came to an end. He would offer an olive branch or even the whole tree if necessary, it would be interesting to see if she took it. Was it possible to rekindle a friendship lost, justify his family's latest business scheme and discuss adventures and ghosts? The whole thing seemed surreal, and he couldn't work out which part was going to be the most challenging.

If Sebastian's presence gave him a chill, Toni's had the opposite effect. He heard her approach and felt when she sat on the grass next to him, not too near, of course, she was keeping a reserved distance. A warm flush started to spread as he wondered if she'd speak first hoping her tone would be at least a little friendlier today?

* * *

Toni had been in a good mood until a visit to Great-Aunt Antonia had been suggested. Her father's Aunt, who she'd been named after. Although, no one ever called her by her full name, not even her parents. The actual sitting with and talking to the delusional old lady was no hardship, Toni was very fond of her. It was being surrounded by the other peculiar inmates. During the last visit with Olivia, two months previously, they'd been subjected to a *flasher*, who insisted on standing right in front of them and raising her skirt every two minutes. Having to watch Olivia's fit of giggles, Aunt

Antonia's outrage at the *skirt lifter* and the poor care assistant trying to diffuse the situation had strengthened Toni's resolve to never grow old.

It had made her think about her family and on the walk over to meet Saxon, Toni had tried to recall her family history. Her mother's family was impossible to trace, the grandparents were hale and hearty and presently residing in Spain. There were a lot of brothers and sisters on that side, but because her mother and one of the brothers had been adopted, the bloodline ended with them.

Her father had been an only child, but *his* father had had two sisters, one was Antonia and the other, Rachel. She was dead now but had married a naval officer, William Williams, that always brought a smile when the family-tree was being recounted. She'd had a son and daughter, who in turn had seven children between them. So, there were a lot of second and third generation cousins.

Because Martin was the only one to share the same surname as Antonia, the home tended to call him first if there were any problems. Thankfully, that didn't happen too often.

She would have tried to go further back, but the hill was quite a climb and needed her full concentration if she didn't want to arrive puffing and panting for breath. Also, her mood had lifted again, and she was prepared to give Saxon a chance to redeem himself. She really wanted to do this ghost thing and after listening to what her mother had had to say, she had a proposal to put. Whether it was a good idea or if he'd go along with it, she wasn't too sure and if he did, how on *earth* would she tell her father?

Saxon saw her eyeing the brown folder and decided not to waste any more time. 'Shall we do this? You'll either hate me even more or hopefully, begin to realise that the Thorpes aren't *quite* so bad as you thought?'

'I expect it'll be somewhere in the middle,' she gave him a grin.

'Progress indeed.' Saxon grinned back. A large folded sheet detailing planned lodges, footpaths, newly planted garden areas, water features and most importantly the clubhouse and spa were laid on the grass. The two of them pored over it and then spent the next hour walking the area. Saxon pointed out where everything on the plans related to on the ground. He answered all her questions honestly and if he didn't know something, he came clean, rather than try to wing it.

It was obvious he wasn't trying to dig himself out of any part of her sometimes-difficult interrogation and in truth, Toni was impressed. Nothing would beat leaving the countryside untouched, but these plans weren't anything like the picture she'd conjured up from prejudice and hearsay.

'I have to say, this has *almost* been a pleasure.' Saxon smiled when he heard Toni give a snort. 'This proposed site really is designed to attract nature lovers, bird watchers, walkers, those sorts of people. Or simply couples that want to relax, hole up together and get away from the rat-race. It's not adults only, but there are no kids' play areas and the local stony beach is hardly conducive to toddlers with buckets and spades.

'Yeah, I get that, this coastline is too savage, hence our ghostly smuggler. Talking of which, I tried to find him the other day.'

'What?' Saxon stopped smiling and his eyes darkened.

'Calm down, you didn't miss out, I walked down to the cave and back through the woods, he didn't appear. I didn't even feel a shiver.'

'You were going to ask him to cut me out, weren't you?'

'Funny how you jump to that conclusion so easily, perhaps you were thinking the same thing?' She raised an eyebrow at his guilty look. 'Anyway, from what he said to us, it's all or nothing, which is why I've been thinking.'

'That sounds ominous.' Saxon was a bit pissed off that she'd considered the same thing he had, but not wanting to ruin the first pleasant conversation they'd shared for years, he quickly changed the subject. 'Let me show you the car park and most importantly the clubhouse and spa.' They walked to the far end of the fields and down a more gradual slope until the land levelled out. 'This will be the only point of access from the road, but we have to be able to get delivery vehicles here, and of course the building equipment.' He showed her on the plans where a lane would cut in from the main road to the village. It was really only an extension of an existing lane that cars could use to access the next cove. Even stonier than Shingle Beach.

'What were you going to say just now?' Saxon asked.

'About what?' Toni answered absently, too busy thinking about the situation of the large building that would house the main reception, a restaurant, pool and therapy rooms. She was looking at the plans and shaking her head.

'You said he wants us *both* and you'd been thinking?'

'Ah yes,' she folded the sheet, not very well.

Saxon had a flashback to the times he'd stayed overnight with Bolly on a Saturday. The next morning over breakfast, Toni tried to look so important opening the pages of the large Sunday broadsheet, which was nearly as big as she was. After scanning the few pictures and pronouncing them *boring*, it had to be put back together before taken upstairs with Martin's cup of tea. The result was a misaligned jumble, causing Beverly to tut noisily. He took the plans and folded them carefully watching as she crossed her arms and gave him an irritated look.

'I haven't finished with those yet, but yeah the other thing, it was about us actually.'

Saxon couldn't have been more surprised. 'What do you mean, *us*?'

'Well, *obviously*, we can't make any decisions until we actually know what Sebastian wants. We may never see him again, of course, but I think he needs us to find some personal item. An old trinket, or weapon, or his *skull*.' She pulled a face at the thought.

'His *skull*! What the Hell?' Saxon roared with laughter. 'You've been watching too many films.'

'*Whatever*, the point *is*, all this could be over in less than a day and if so, well then, that's the end of it.'

'You're right, and if that's the case, at least we've proved we can have a civilised conversation, so it's not all bad. I've quite enjoyed this afternoon.' He hadn't meant to say that out loud, but it was done now.

'Hmm, that brings me to my idea. No one will believe you're my new BFF. If we're seen together once, that could be explained away, we could even tell the truth and say you were showing me the plans. If we're caught again, *then* what? All my friends know I wouldn't give you the time of day.'

'Gee thanks, we'll just have to be careful I guess.'

Toni nodded. 'Yes, but Leo's home in just over a week, I think we should pretend we're... *together*.' She looked down and held her breath.

Saxon stopped dead in his tracks and stared. 'Did you actually say that?'

'Yeah, I did, only for this of course, while it lasts. When it's all over we can flip a coin and see who gets to dump who.'

'*Harsh*, and that won't work, not if Bolly's around. Can you imagine what he'd say if we were actually a *couple*? Bloody hell, Toni, and then I *dump* you? He's going to love that.'

'Well... we'll mutually break up, all friendly like. I don't know, can you suggest anything better?'

He ran his fingers through his hair and shook his head. 'Are you absolutely sure it's worth all the aggro?'

I'm not sure about anything. 'We'll only be pretending. When in your *whole* life did you ever think you'd see a ghost? We've found one that talks to us, a real *live* ghost that wants *us* to share an adventure. It's the sort of thing only written about in kids' storybooks.'

'Real *live* ghost. That's a warped oxymoron, trust you to come out with it.'

'You're the bloody moron,' she muttered. 'I'm not going to let this go, I have a really weird feeling that he's got something important to tell and it's connected to what we find *and* us doing it together?'

'If we do go for your idea, it'll need some planning, I mean our families, what are we going to tell them?'

'Don't stress about it yet, Sax. When we know for sure what we're dealing with, we'll make a decision.' She grabbed the plans back and began to unfold them again. 'This isn't going to work at all, whoever designed the clubhouse is obviously not a spa user?'

Saxon hurried after her, she was pacing the perimeter of what would be the spa. Staying quiet, he left her to it and thought about all she'd said. Realistically it was the only way, but at what cost?

'Look where this is situated, right next to a car park and the reception? Lovely, relaxing on the massage couch and listening to car engines revving up, doors banging, people checking into the lodges, you get the picture?'

'We need to move the spa to the back of the building.' He agreed, pleased with this distraction.

'Also, if I was staying here, I'm not sure I'd want to walk down, have a nice facial or mud-wrap or whatever and then have to trudge back up the hill. Even worse, what if my place was at the far end?'

'You're absolutely right and we're definitely not having cars at the top. Damn, this could change the clubhouse plans completely. The idea was to keep it down here, so locals could use it as well.' It was his turn to pace while Toni stood and watched.

'How about a pool of half a dozen golf-type buggies for transport, sort of on request, or, if you have enough staff they can ferry them around? I'm sure it wouldn't apply all the time. The sort of people that would stay here will be quite active and think nothing of walking back after a meal in the evening, unless the weather was bad. That may put them off using the restaurant. What's going to happen on arrival with their luggage and stuff?'

'That *has* been thought of.' He grinned, enjoying this discussion immensely. 'A chauffeured car will take them to their lodge, the only one that would have access to the top, apart from laundry and maintenance, of course. Fancy a job here?'

'Now you really are pushing your luck, I'm not cut out to be a taxi driver or a beauty therapist, bimbo.' *Nor work for the enemy*, she reminded herself.

'Ravel, you snob, isn't one of your cousins into this sort of thing?'

'Ella does a mean set of Shellacs and I was only joking about the bimbo bit.'

'*Shellacs*? You've lost me now. Seriously though, you'd be fantastic with the lodge bookings, and things like that.' What was he thinking? This, *pretend couple,* business was getting him carried away.

Just for a moment, Toni almost forgot who they both were and wanted to ask more about the potential job. It sounded a whole lot more gratifying than finding box after box of shoes for customers that were sometimes less than grateful. 'At least Pretty Feet is still Thorpe-free.' She turned her comment into a joke, by laughing, also aware of breaking the fragile truce they'd gained during the afternoon.

'Well, the offer's open if you change your mind.'

'How soon is this happening?'

'Soon, it's all signed, the planning's been approved, give or take moving the spa.' Saxon thought about his father's suggestion, three times as many lodges and a push to buy the bottom field from Martin Ravel. Thank God, his grandfather had put his foot down before anything had been said, not that Martin would ever sell to them, but even a whisper on the breeze would have seen the two families at daggers drawn.

'You swear this is the final plan and there's nothing else you're not telling me?'

Could she read his mind? Toni had moved up close and was standing right in front of him, he should be angry at her question, but he wasn't. 'I swear, okay?'

'Okay, I believe you,' She said brightly. 'So, when are we going *ghost-busting* again? Not tomorrow, I have to visit the crazy home.'

'Your Aunt Antonia?' he saw her nod. 'How about Tuesday evening?'

Toni grinned, he was every bit as keen as she was. 'The Knoll will probably be busy, and we'll be seen together, but the tide is no good for the cave.'

'We'll have to chance the Knoll, leave it till nine o'clock, the young kids will have gone by then and hopefully, being a school night, the older ones won't be around.'

'I wonder why he just doesn't pop up in a bedroom somewhere?'

'Would you really want that?' She waggled her eyebrows and he remembered how enamoured she'd been the other day. 'Don't answer.'

They walked together along the lane until it split, Saxon took the north fork and Toni carried on straight ahead.

Deep in Raven Wood, Sebastian felt a warm glow of satisfaction.

* * *

Glen-Croft, Nursing Home, was every bit as manic as Toni had come to expect. Every nurse and care-worker had her utmost admiration, this certainly wasn't a job she could do with such patience and understanding.

Antonia was presently indisposed. Lizzie, her named carer for the day confided that she hadn't *been* for two days. Finally, things were looking hopeful and they didn't want to interrupt the long-awaited toilet result. Too much information! The staff here were great but why the hell were they *so* obsessed with bowel actions?

'Have a seat lovey, I'll get you a nice cuppa. I'm sure she won't be long.'

Toni was unable to prevent a *resistance is futile* grimace. Giving the chair in the residents' lounge the once over, she sat herself down in anticipation of a long wait and a cup of insipid milky tea.

Dolly and Joan were sitting opposite on a two-seater settee. The first few times Toni and Olivia had noticed them, they'd thought that they could be sisters as they were usually holding hands. Then Olivia suggested, partners, together at a time when they would have found a relationship in the outside world difficult to deal with. Neither was true, apparently, they just seemed to gravitate towards one another. Toni had rather wished Olivia's romantic notion was correct, it would have been cool for them to end their days in an environment where they didn't feel they had anything to hide.

Today a small teddy bear was the focus of their attention. Toni was forced to listen to such comments as, 'Look at his little nose.' 'Would you like to stroke his ears?' 'He must be getting tired now.' Curling her feet beneath her in the large armchair, she wished she could magically disappear.

Five minutes later all hell broke loose. An elderly gentleman shuffled in, snatched a cushion from behind a thin birdlike woman sitting in the chair next to Dolly, placed it on his Zimmer frame and discovering a burst of speed he hadn't demonstrated for some years, took off to the far side of the lounge. Finding a seat to his liking, near the television, he proceeded to make himself comfortable.

Toni watched in horror as the small lady jumped up and started shouting at the top of her lungs.

'THIEF, THIEF, PILLOW THIEF.'

'Now then Mary, what's the matter?' A calm-voiced nurse asked. The shouts of pillow thief, continued until Mary was led away, for a *quiet rest.*

The culprit poked out his tongue at the retreating women. Toni got the impression he'd known he'd get that reaction, especially when she saw him throw the cushion onto the floor, proving he hadn't wanted it in the first place.

To top it all, the commotion had upset Dolly and Joan, the teddy bear was now being pulled as if it was the prize in a tug-of-war competition.

'Don't touch him,' Joan shrieked

'Horrible *bitch,*' Dolly screamed back.

Toni moved to the other side of the room, this brought her near to the old chap that had started the trouble. He caught her eye and gave her a wink. She began to laugh, but whether or not it was in desperation, she wasn't sure.

'Your Aunt is ready now, lovie, but she doesn't want to come in here.'

Toni couldn't move quickly enough and followed Lizzie along the corridor to Aunt Antonia's room. A small oasis of sanity in a desert of absurdity, depending of course, on the old lady's mood.

'Antonia, my dear girl, come and sit down and tell me the news.' The only family member to *always* use her full name looked exceedingly pleased with herself. The waft of air freshener coming from the ensuite gave a clue as to the reason why.

'Hello, Aunty.' They exchanged a kiss on the cheek and Toni perched on the bed next to the substantial reclining chair. She ran through a quick report on everyone's health and then the plans for Olivia's wedding, being interrupted three times and having to hear the indignant retorts that no one had told her Olivia was getting married.

Aunt Antonia waited until the talking stopped and then craned her head forward peering most intensely. 'How are the girls, Beverly?'

Toni groaned, she shared her mother's small build and colouring, both having honey blonde hair, but the resemblance stopped there. The hazel green eyes, in particular, were very much from the Ravel side. 'I'm *Antonia*, Aunty.'

'I know *that*,' the old lady snapped. 'Well dear, what's the news?' Toni was saved from answering when the door was flung open and Mr Corbet, a short, bald-headed gentleman, barged in.

'Have you got my teeth?' he snarled.

'Toni poised her finger on the call-bell. It was unusual to have any residents on this floor with violent tendencies, but she knew all forms of dementia led to unpredictable behaviour and this particular client was renowned for his unpleasantness.

'Clear off shorty.' Aunt Antonia shouted. 'This is the ladies powder room.' She turned to Toni, 'I find bald-heads most unappealing.'

'Have you stolen my *teeth*, woman?'

Toni pushed the button, this wasn't going to end well, he was starting to remove his trousers.

Two members of staff arrived promptly and escorted Mr Corbet back to his room. The shouts about his teeth soon changed to shouts about another part of his anatomy. In her enthusiasm to hold his trousers up, the younger carer was giving the poor old boy a wedgie.

'Be careful of my bloody balls girl, I'd like to be a father someday.'

'I'm so sorry,' The nurse poked her head around the door and looked very apologetic. 'He's not been sleeping well lately, keeps saying there's a ghost in his room.' She grinned and shook her head. 'It's just his new blind, it isn't fixed properly and keeps flapping.'

'What's that about a ghost?'

'Nothing Aunty, the old man reckons he saw one.'

Antonia closed her eyes and sank back against the soft cushions. 'I wish I could see him one more time. Tell Sebastian to visit.'

Toni's mouth fell open, she hadn't mistaken what had been said. 'Aunty, wake up, tell me about him.'

'Hello Beverly dear, how's the family?'

'*Sebastian*?' Toni prompted.

'Ah, but you know all about him I can tell. He's a rascal, don't let him near Olivia and Antonia, he likes Ravel girls.' With that, her head dropped to her chin and soft snoring started almost instantly.

Toni gave her Aunt a goodbye kiss, the old lady made a snuffling noise but didn't stir. The door to Mr Corbet's room was firmly shut but raised conversation, mostly concerning dentures and testicles, could still be heard. Walking past the main lounge, Toni looked in to let a member of staff know she was leaving. Dolly and Joan were once again reconciled, holding hands and walking around the room desperately looking for something they thought they'd lost. The *pillow thief* waved the teddy bear in the air grinning at a quiz show host on the television.

'A typical afternoon,' Lizzie said, waving her off with a cheery smile.

Not quite so typical Toni thought as she got into her van. It seemed Sebastian had left a lasting impression on Great-Aunt Antonia and she wanted to know how... and why?

Chapter Six

'What's with the raven stuff all the time?'

Biting back an oath of frustration that Saxon had come alone, Sebastian resigned himself to the inevitable confrontation. Really, he should ignore the boy as he'd done with the wench only a few days past. He certainly wouldn't materialise, why waste precious energy? Young Thorpe could shiver and feel uncomfortable, it would serve him right. 'Good Morrow, Knave?'

Saxon felt a chill go through him, it didn't help that the sun was low and was unlikely to find its way through the dense trees. 'Can we discuss what it is you want Toni and me to help you with? Is it dangerous? That's what I really want to know.'

Sebastian softened a little, *Doth the boy care, or is he seeking knowledge for his own benefit?* He studied Saxon before answering. 'Tis no risk to thine life.'

'To be honest, I'm probably in more danger from Toni if she knew I was talking to you without her.' Saxon was beginning to feel a little light headed. 'I don't care what you or she says, we're not going to break into a museum to retrieve some lost artefact that you may wish to have returned. And I certainly won't have her scaling down a cliff face to a hidden cave. If that's what it takes, I'll go alone. You're not putting her in danger, get it?'

Sebastian's first impressions had been correct, this member of the Thorpe Dynasty was worthy. 'A *little* climbing mayhap.' He hurriedly put Saxon's mind at rest. 'Nay cliffs, nor museums, well I bethink not. Is a museum a house of curiosities?'

'I... guess so.' Saxon was having difficulty thinking straight, why wouldn't Sebastian show himself? He could be heard better and this awful cold and nausea didn't seem to occur.

'Thou art thinking of our girl's safety that is good. I would'st never put either of ye in harm's way.'

Saxon snorted. 'Forgive me, but I'm not exactly reassured.'

'God's saints, what a big milkmaid,' Sebastian's laugh echoed around the Knoll. 'Dost not waste mine time coming alone again, not unless I request it of ye.'

'I haven't finished yet...' Saxon had instantly warmed up and all signs of queasiness had vanished. Sebastian had gone. *No cliffs and no stealing, and we're not at risk of death. That's the best I'm going to get*. He was far from happy, but it was better than nothing.

* * *

Toni and Annie were in the snug at the Swingers, trying to avoid the unwanted attentions of the Littlejohn brothers, Ian and Gus. Annie was desperate to find out Leo's plans and was most put out that her friend didn't seem to know much.

'Last Christmas he was still keen on going abroad,' Annie said miserably. 'I heard him talking to Sax about it. They were sat in this very booth and he was trying to persuade Sax to do something similar.'

Toni knew her brother had mentioned the possibility of another trip away. Six months working on a farm in Australia, some kind of exchange scheme. When he'd first dropped it into the conversation, at Christmas, she'd hoped a nice tanned Aussie boy was going to arrive on the Ravel Farm doorstep in his place, but apparently, it didn't work like that. He hadn't mentioned it again since, so the family wondered if it was still happening. Leo had always been full of big ideas and plans, only a handful ever came to fruition though. If he could focus himself on one project long enough and, if it was the farm, he'd turn the place around. Her father had done wonders, but he was struggling now, set in his ways, he didn't like change, even though he wasn't short-sighted enough to know it was inevitable. He and Leo would work well together because he'd let his son take the reins when it came to new schemes. They'd already sat for hours making plans, Martin listening carefully to Leo's proposals and wishing he'd had that sort of opportunity and relationship with his own father.

'According to Dad, he's going to stay for the foreseeable and anyway, Sax is far too busy with...' Damn, Toni realised she shouldn't even be mentioning his name, let alone have knowledge of what he was or wasn't doing.

'Too busy with what?' Annie didn't miss a thing. Her friend had been acting a bit weird lately and according to Lawrence Carter, he'd seen the pair together yesterday afternoon walking near Raven Wood. 'Is there something going on that you're not telling me?'

'I asked him to show me the plans for the new holiday development, don't make anything of it.' Her friend looked as if she had a hundred questions to ask, but was forestalled by the rude interruption of Ian, his brother not far behind.

'Wassup?' he asked, squeezing himself in next to Toni.

'Piss off, we were having a private conversation.' Annie left him in no doubt he wasn't wanted.

'Gus, get the drinks,' he yelled back, ignoring her protest. 'I didn't see your shit-heap of a van in the carpark, so I'm guessing you're not driving tonight.'

'No, but we're both working tomorrow, something *you* wouldn't know about.' Toni looked resignedly at Annie and mouthed, '*One drink only.*'

Gus arrived with four pints of strong ale and four shots. Toni groaned. That would take her ages to drink, she'd been nursing a half of cider for the last forty minutes.

'Wassup?' he parroted Ian and slid along the bench, ending up far too close to Annie.

'We were talking about work, so you won't be able to join in.' Annie quipped.

'*Funny*.' He pulled a face and drank his shot, urging the others to do the same.

It was then, that Saxon, Linus and a scowling, overdressed Vanessa walked in and were shown to a reserved table not a million miles away. Linus had chickened out on Sunday and taken Vanessa to her favourite restaurant for lunch. After a few hurtful remarks in the bedroom last night, he'd wished he hadn't bothered and decided to get his own back by bringing her here this evening. By the time he ordered a curry, something he was not allowed to indulge in at home, her wrath would be well and truly incurred.

Saxon's eyes locked with Toni's for a brief moment before noticing the company she was sharing and the number of drinks on the table. He recognised a quiet look of desperation and a smile of understanding passed between them. His own predicament wasn't much better, but his father had invited him and he would at least try and make the best of it.

After her husband had spent over a hundred pounds on their meal yesterday, Vanessa had been surprised at the suggestion to eat out again. About to decline, the Monday night's soap offerings, a much more appealing thought, her mind was changed when Linus mentioned he was asking Saxon to join them. That, of course, made all the difference. Imagining an expensively tasteful restaurant in the city centre, she dressed appropriately. When the Rolls pulled up in the carpark of the local village pub, she could have screamed. Now looking and feeling ridiculously out of place she moodily pushed her portion of grilled salmon around the plate.

The food in the Swinging Smugglers was excellent. Using local and seasonal fare as much as possible meant the menus were changed frequently. Midday deals were also popular and with the recent addition of Den-Zone, a play area for toddlers, saw many young parents lunching together. It also gave part-time employment to two of the village girls. Thankfully it wasn't open in the evening, the volume of children's noise often creeping into the pub's lounge.

Vanessa may as well have been eating ashes, she was so angry that she could hardly taste the food. Saxon was discussing cricket of all things, with Linus, whilst constantly looking across at his friends. She casually glanced over to see what had caught his interest. Two girls who looked familiar and the Littlejohn boys, nothing to get excited about. Had it been a girl on her own, that would have been different. She cheered up a bit, there were no women here that could hold a candle to herself, surely her stepson could see that?

By the second course, she'd managed to steer the conversation to decorating the sitting room and was pleased to see Saxon paying attention.

Purples, blues, or shades of pink? Saxon couldn't give a shit. When would Vanessa shut her mouth and eat her bloody crème-brulee? The raucous laughter and smutty innuendos coming from Ian and Gus were not going down well with the other punters. Poor Annie and Toni looked like they wanted to die. The pints had been finished and he'd heard the girls' refusals, but another round of drinks had miraculously appeared on the table, accompanied again with more shots. He knew Toni was a lightweight where alcohol was concerned. Leo had mentioned it and he'd witnessed it himself more than once.

The brothers got up, Gus was swaying and Ian didn't look too healthy. 'We're off to the Ass Cracks,' Gus chortled. 'You two coming?'

'How old are you?' Annie said disgustedly, 'we used to call it that in school, no one does now.' The Brass Tacks was a pub on the Primrose estate, bought up recently and modernised by a large chain, it now had a fancy name, which hardly anyone used, preferring the old one.

'C'mon don't be boring, we'll drive you home after.'

'You have got to be kidding me,' Toni looked at them both in horror. 'Ian, you can't let him drive?'

Ian looked questioningly at his brother, but Gus just laughed. 'I'm not over the limit, *much*, it's only three miles away. Who'll be driving along the country lanes on a Monday night?'

'It'ssss fine.' Ian slurred, trying to convince himself as much as them. 'If you don't want to go we'll drop you home on the way. It's pisssshing down in case you hadn't noticed.'

Much to Vanessa's dismay, just as she thought Saxon was on board with the Ralph Lauren luxury drapes, he jumped up and marched off. Linus who had lost the will to live after the cricket conversation had dried up, smiled over his bourbon and told his wife to buy whatever she thought best. Somewhat appeased she pushed her uneaten dessert away and poured another glass of wine instead.

'A word, Ian,' Saxon pulled him to one side, not apologising for nearly unbalancing him in the process.

'Gus is way too drunk to drive anyone anywhere, and you're well over the limit as well.'

'Bloody hell, Thorpe, since when did you start monitoring what we can and can't do? Shhhove off and mind your own busy... businessssh.'

'I would say, go ahead and kill yourselves if you want to, but not with the girls in the car. Toni, is Leo's sister, or had you forgotten?'

'Course not, he's a mate.'

Hardly, dickhead. 'Not for much longer if he finds out what's going on here, and he *will* because I'll tell him. Did you know he's back next week?'

Something finally sunk in, and Ian seemed to sober up quickly. He'd been on the receiving end of Leo's fist once before, that had been to do with Olivia, a few kegs of cider and a party on Shingle Beach. 'Okay, okay, I get it.' He picked up his brother's car keys and started to guide him toward the exit. Everyone was relieved when he got his phone out and called a taxi. 'We can still drop you two off,' he said remembering the girls just as they got to the door.

'No thanks we'll take our chances in the rain.' Even in the comparative safety of a taxi, Toni didn't want to be squashed in the back seat between the Littlejohn brothers, because she knew with complete certainty, Annie would call shotgun. 'I guess we better phone a cab as well.' She said to her friend.

Saxon was still hovering and overheard. 'We'll drop you both home.'

She had no idea how to respond and not sure how she felt about him talking to Ian on their behalf but the point became moot as Annie happily accepted the offer for them both.

'We'll have another... err coffee, while you finish your meal.' Toni said, feeling awkward with Saxon so close. She watched him walk back to the table, his father was casting glances that hinted of more than a little interest in her and Annie's direction.

Vanessa sat with lips as pinched as a cat's backside. Linus smiled to himself as he pulled out of the carpark well aware of the ructions that were brewing and would meet him full-force behind closed doors. He'd told her to dress casually when she'd asked, but her fashion faux-pas would no doubt be his fault. The earlier attempt to play footsie with Saxon had seen his son scoot across the bench and engage in a debate over the county cricket scores. They'd used to go together at one time and watch the game, why had they stopped?

Rear mirror spying, was proving very enlightening. Annie sat quietly in the middle, but it was the odd looks between his son and the Ravel girl that were telling the real story. Not flirting exactly, something more, a shared secret perhaps? Linus had his eye on some of Martin Ravel's land but wasn't foolish enough to think it would fall into his lap. It would take a lot of persuasive negotiation and pretty little Toni Ravel may be the key.

Annie was the first out, she thanked them all and scurried up the short drive of a pleasant country cottage. Linus knew this gateway well, he often made a drop off here. The father was a maths teacher, at the school that accommodated the majority of the children from Primrose Ridge, he had left home some years ago, a messy divorce had ensued. The mother worked behind the bar at the Golf club. She was called Rita.

Saxon and Toni shuffled slightly, giving themselves a bit more room. Vanessa glanced around reassuring herself the girl in the back was no threat. Blonde hair hung at an odd length in a tousled mess. Nice eyes, she begrudgingly conceded, a greenish hazel, were they green or gold? It was hard to tell in this light, like the hair, was it long or short? It seemed nothing about Toni Ravel wanted to be seen as clear-cut. If she'd voiced her observations, Saxon would have replied, 'That's Toni all over, never wants to commit to either side.'

'You can drop me just here please.' Toni said as the farmhouse came into sight.

'Nonsense,' Linus replied, 'We'll drop you at the door, you'll get soaked otherwise.'

'Sorry,' Saxon whispered quietly. He knew the last thing Toni would want was her father seeing *his* father's Rolls-Royce Phantom pulling up outside.

'I guess if we are going ahead with our plan, this will pave the way a little, and if not, well, it's just a lift home.' Toni said quietly.

Saxon gave a nod. 'Do you still want to do tomorrow if it is raining?'

'Yeah, the forecast is good. I'll meet you in the lane at nine o'clock.' As Annie had done, she politely said thank you to all of them and disappeared inside so quickly Saxon and Linus began to laugh.

'I don't know what's so funny,' Vanessa said sniffing, 'The car stinks of cheap perfume, some dreadful flowery smell from that animal-friendly shop no doubt. The one between the vegetarian cafe and the organic greengrocers on Market Street.'

'You seem very familiar with the local shops, darling.' Linus commented.

'I buy your aftershave there.' She gave him a condescending smile. 'After this evening, it's just as well, it seems we're on a *budget* for some undisclosed reason.'

Saxon tuned out of the strained conversation and watching the first flash of lightning streak across the sky to illuminate the Ravel lands, hoped the Met Office had their facts right.

* * *

Thankfully, the farming weather had been correct. Toni watched a few kids leave the woods as she approached the place in the lane she was going to wait for Saxon. Explaining the lift home last night hadn't been nearly so bad as she'd anticipated. The rain had got even heavier and as she'd put her key in the lock, the door had been thrust open by her father, scowling at the reversing Rolls. Just as he opened his mouth a huge clap of thunder echoed overhead causing Toni to shriek and nearly bowl him over in a bid to get past. Beverley, hearing who had dropped her off, was immediately grateful and told her husband to stop overreacting, it had been an act of common courtesy. Martin, in the end, had to agree, he couldn't quite bring himself to be gracious about it though.

'I love the day after a storm, don't you?'

Toni jumped, she'd been so busy watching the woods she hadn't heard his approach. Can't fault a white shirt and dark jeans, she thought. A bit dated on some perhaps, but not Saxon Thorpe. Marching ahead and disappearing into the trees she left him with no option other than to follow behind.

'Good evening, Ravens, how dost ye fare? I pondered at which hour ye wouldst come. This place seems to be plagued with blasted youngsters. Oft I try to gallow those folks hence, but mostly they dost not notice me.'

'Pardon?' Toni asked. 'I didn't catch that last bit.'

'I sometimes try to scare them away.'

'Ah right! Sebastian, can we see you, cos this is really difficult, it's not easy to hear properly and it's bloody cold?' Toni turned to Saxon who was now standing next to her. 'What's with the raven stuff all the time?'

'I haven't got a clue. Were things okay last night after we dropped you off?'

'Yes thanks, the storm helped. Mum was pleased and Dad just had to go with it in the end.'

'Perchance ye hast come to speak with *me*, thy private discourse can be conducted anon.'

Toni once again was in awe of the figure that materialised in front of their eyes. Were ghosts supposed to be so damn good looking? 'Jealous Sebastian?'

'I wish I hadst reason to be.' He appraised them both but his dark green eyes lingered on Toni's tight t-shirt and moved slowly towards her figure-hugging leggings. 'Thou art a sight to behold in such apparel. I cannot believe ye wouldst grant me such a feast for mine eyes as to appear in undergarments.' With his gaze not leaving her for a moment, he addressed Saxon. 'How can ye bear it so stoically without some form of dalliance?'

'This isn't *underwear*.' Toni began to feel self-conscious, especially when Saxon began to smirk. 'Perhaps I should have thought more about what I wore tonight but both pairs of jeans are in the wash. For God's, this is the twenty-first century.'

'Forgive me, Saxon, 'twill be hard to endure tonight if the wench flaunts her body so openly. Allow me to explain a little about the name, then we shalt converse about the treasure and the... nay, I shalt leave the curse for another day.'

'The *curse?*' Both Toni and Saxon said together.

'*Another* day I hath said.' He winked at Toni.

She couldn't help giggling and wondered if the women of his time would have been enamoured by his cheesy and sexist seduction. No doubt Sebastian Raven had been quite a player. And yes, her leggings would appear as some sort of undergarment, or men's hose, wasn't that what they called their tights?

'When you two have finished flirting perhaps you'll tell us about the treasure.' Saxon said irritably.

Ah, tis not I that is jealous. Sebastian kept those thoughts to himself. The atmosphere between these two was already different from when he'd seen them in the cave. 'So, Master Thorpe, thou fancy thyself a treasure hunter? In which case I hast a story to tell. Tis a great shame the seating here is rough.'

'Can't you just come to one of our houses?' Toni asked. 'When the rest of the family are out.' She added hastily.

'I am limited wherefore I can travel, the woods, of course, the Manor, of which we shalt speak anon, a few odd buildings, hither and thither and the caves hence, but not the tunnels. Tis all methinks.' He heard the word '*tunnels*' repeated excitedly by Toni.

'And the treasure, is it in one of those places?' Saxon asked.

'Tis not far hence, unless some blackguard hath hadst away with it.' Sebastian shook his head. 'Nay, methinks I would know if the Sapphire-Heart wast gone.'

'The Sapphire-Heart! Wow, that really *does* sound like treasure.' Toni said. 'Is it a ring, or a brooch, or a necklace?'

'I shouldst not hast made mention of that stone yet. The real *treasure* as ye calls it, is not the precious gems, but worth just as much to its rightful owners.'

'Who *does* the rest of it belong to and what exactly *is* it?' Saxon, wanted to know how they were going to retrieve whatever it was and where from. It was very frustrating not getting a straight answer.

'*Patience*, young Raven, listen well. Church Relics lie below the Abbey, or I shouldst say, Manor, they art one and the same.'

'The *ruins* do you mean, on Sax's land?' Toni asked eagerly.

Sebastian took a stick and started to make a rough drawing in the dirt. He soon threw it down in disgust.

'Tis hard to hold something for any length of time. Dost ye recognise this?'

'Err, not really.' Toni tried to make out something familiar on the roughly drawn map. 'What do you reckon, Sax, do you think that could be Blackberry Lane?'

Saxon nodded. 'I think so, but there are no defining lines to any of the individual properties. I'm not even sure where your farm starts.'

'Properties?' Sebastian looked puzzled. 'Tis all Raven land, and hence,' he pointed to some earth he'd scratched a bit deeper, 'wast the Thorpe Estate.'

'Hmm it's not like that now,' Toni picked up a stone, 'Would the Manor be here Sebastian?' She placed it on the drawing and watched as he studied what she'd done.

'Aye, methinks, tis correct, about two miles due north of the coast.'

'That *is* the the ruins then, there's buried treasure on your land. Shit, how *bloody* typical.' She said frowning.

'Wench, I cannot abide any more of thy cursing.' He disappeared and the cold chill was more than uncomfortable. Like the first time he'd spoken to them, it caused Toni to feel light headed and nauseous.

'Well, you really pissed him off, well done Ravel.' Saxon said angrily.

'Sebastian, you bastard, show yourself.'

The air settled around them and he appeared once again. Toni unconsciously took a step toward Saxon. Their ghost had a face like thunder.

'I may be a bastard, missy, but I dost not desire ye to cast aspersions on the fact I wast born the wrong side of the bed sheets.'

'I'm sorry, I didn't mean to be such a dumbass.'

Saxon came to the rescue before Sebastian combusted with fury. 'The word doesn't really mean that, well it does, but not in the way you've taken it. Words and

85

phrases have different connotations now. Anyway, no one cares if your parents are married or not these days.'

'Humph.'

'Lots of people use words like that now.' He didn't say that, in his opinion, Toni swore more than was necessary.

'Damn it all, tis unacceptable. Hast ye ever bethought of teaching the wench some manners? Ye hast a stout belt I see, that shalt work well enough. I shalt even disappear for a few minutes while ye gives her a beating, or, I'd be joyous to gaze.' He added hopefully, his anger beginning to abate.

Saxon wasn't quite quick enough to disguise the fleeting grin. The look of complete outrage and horror on Toni's face had seen to that. It was only when he noticed something else, fear, that she was trying so desperately to hide, that he stopped smiling and turned back to Sebastian. 'For all our sakes, I'll assume that was a joke. But just to be clear, I'd *never* hit a woman.'

'*Nay*? Sebastian asked, with genuine puzzlement.

'Nay... I mean *no*, absolutely not.'

'Pity, it doth sort a gross amount of problems. Watch thy tongue in future wench and we shalt leave it at that.' He looked again at the thick leather belt Saxon had looped through the waist of his jeans and gave a wistful sigh.

Saxon put a hand on Toni's arm. 'It's alright, he didn't really mean it.'

'Jesus and all his Saints,' Sebastian roared. 'Return on the morrow. I cannot bear the sight of the two of ye any longer. Wench, wear something less revealing, and ye Knave, grow a pair of stones.'

Saxon and Toni weren't sure whether to laugh or feel insulted. Saxon took a photo of Sebastian's rough drawing on his phone and seeing Toni looked a bit pale threw his arm across her shoulder in an act of camaraderie.

'Do you think he's dangerous.' Toni squeaked, not shrugging his arm off.

'Well I doubt he could physically hurt us, and I'm pretty sure that's not his intention.' *He has a nasty temper that's for sure.*

His arm was still around her when they bumped into Frank and Lawrence Carter in Blackberry Lane. Two sets of raised eyebrows greeted them.

'That's how it is,' Lawrence said quietly to Toni. 'I did wonder after seeing you with him last week, and what Ian said yesterday, kinda confirmed things.'

'And they say it's women that gossip!'

'You and Sax, that's more than mere gossip.' Lawrence, although disappointed, was dying to get to the Swingers and spread this little gem around.

'What are we going to do now?' Saxon asked when they'd gone.

'Plan A, I suppose, you're my new boyfriend. Won't Leo have something to say about that? Come to think of it I don't even have your number, maybe that's the first thing we should exchange to seal the deal.'

Saxon nodded and got his phone out. 'The Manor, I can't believe it, I mean it's been no more than ruins since the fire, nearly two hundred years ago. There *can't* be anything hidden there? He called it the Abbey first, did you notice? I'm sure I've heard that before. I'll have to look up the history, I can't remember it well enough.'

'Yeah but Sax, he mentioned tunnels, and sapphires, the Sapphire-Heart. That sounds well expensive.'

'When are you free next?' he asked, desperate to find out more.

'I've got Thursday off, the tide turns really early, I know that cos Gus wanted to arrange a beach barbecue.'

He scowled at the mention of Gus' name. 'I know it's early, but if we can get to the cave at six in the morning, the water will only be ankle deep, no one would be around.'

His enthusiasm was infectious and Toni hadn't noticed that they'd walked as far as the fork in the lane still with his arm around her. 'Thursday then, and let me know what you find out about the Manor once being an Abbey.' His friendly wave reminded her of a time long ago. She smiled and waved back.

Chapter Seven

*'You're not exactly asking for my
hand in marriage.'*

Still being met by total silence on the third attempt to gain entry into her sister's bedroom, Olivia opened the door and barged in.

'Olly, what the hell!' Toni pulled the headphones out of her ears and frowned. 'You'd go mad if I did that to you.'

'You *do,* do it to me and I'm not standing out on the landing forever.' She pushed Toni's feet out of the way and sat on the end of the bed. 'I want to know what's going on with you and Sax.'

'Who told you?'

'Lawrence act... hang on, what do you mean who told me? You're not denying it. OMG, Toni, is it true then, the two of you?'

Toni stopped herself from frowning again. It had got around even quicker than she'd expected, twenty-four hours to be precise. It was only yesterday evening that Lawrence Carter had seen them. 'Look, it's early days, I don't want Dad upset, in case things don't work out. Stop grinning like a cretin.' This charade of a relationship with Sax was going to be the talk of the village. She'd been naive to think it could be kept low key. Now she'd have to have the conversation with her parents after all. And what the hell would her brother say when he came home on Saturday?

Olivia couldn't stop smiling, as she voiced those very thoughts. 'Whatever will Leo make of it? He won't be happy if his best mate is all loved up and not available for a lad's night out.'

Had Saxon thought that side of it through? Toni wondered. He'd begrudgingly agreed, that the pretend romance was the easiest way forward, especially since gaining the knowledge that they would be potentially treasure hunting at the ruins together. What other excuses could there possibly be for her to be on Thorpe land with him? Not only that, she'd made him promise he wouldn't start looking without her. He'd given such a resigned smile and not even attempted to argue. It had been kind of cute.

'I guess you'll be needing a plus one for the wedding after all?' Olivia continued an air of smugness in her voice. 'Or a plus two as you're already bringing Annie. All that crap about me following the man I love and moving away. You'll soon see what it's like when you have someone else to think about.'

'I don't know about that.' Toni said anxiously. 'The wedding's five weeks away, we may not even be together then.'

'Who are you kidding, this won't be some minor dalliance, Sax isn't like that, I bet with him it'll be really serious. All joking apart, if it wasn't for his family, he'd be the perfect boyfriend. I'm going to readjust the seating plan, you were never on the top table anyway, so it's not too much of an issue.' She realised what she'd said, her best friend was maid of honour, not her sister. Although Toni hadn't seemed to mind, she did feel a little guilty. 'Err sorry I didn't mean it like that.'

'It's fine, just don't get carried away, Olly, pleeeease.'

'Yeah, yeah whatever, Saxon Thorpe, *who'd* have thought.'

Toni dramatically threw herself back onto the duvet and rolled over to face the wall. Now Olivia knew her secret the urgency to speak with her father had just increased by a hundred percent.

The following morning, Toni's alarm woke her at half past five. She scrambled out of bed and dressed quickly having decided the night before, a summer dress, denim jacket and ankle boots may be more appropriate, in Sebastian's eyes.

Relieved that there was no sign of Saxon's car, she rushed down the cliff path. If she was going to apologise it certainly didn't have to be done in front of him as well. By climbing across a few low rocks, she managed to keep her boots dry, the cave floor was generally above the tide line unless it was a particularly high one.

'Sebastian,' she called softly, 'Are you here?' she called a little louder, and finally, after the third attempt, he appeared. 'I owe you an apology.' Toni put a hand on his arm trying to ignore the peculiar feeling, which reminded her of the green oasis her mother stuck dried flowers in. 'I'll try to watch what I say and, err be a bit more ladylike when I'm around you.'

'Tis all right really, things hast changed over the years, not for the better methinks. I gaze the passing of time as a spectator. Sometimes I hear youngsters using far foul language than ye hast, they speak of female body parts, those rogues need a valorous whipping.'

'You sound a bit sad.' Toni went so far as giving him a hug, aware his torso firmed slightly as he pulled her roughly towards him. Untangling herself she stepped back, 'I appreciate it's difficult, and I agree that young children swearing is totally unacceptable. But Sebastian, you *have* to get over these sadistic tendencies you have for punishment, it just doesn't fit in with today's politically correct form of child discipline. The majority of parents don't even give their kids a smack.' She touched his arm again, the spongy feeling definitely gone. 'How come you feel firmer today?'

'Tis the effect thou hast on me.' He laughed loudly as he saw her face redden. 'A most becoming blush, it goes a long way to win me over. I am melancholy no longer.'

Toni grinned, pleased that he'd apparently forgiven her for calling him a bastard, and also a little flattered. 'I wanted to ask you something last time, but you disappeared and I didn't get a chance.'

Sebastian looked a bit wary. 'I told young Thorpe, ye art in this together or not at all, I bethought 'twas clear.'

'Oh, err no it's nothing like that.' *That bloody Saxon tried to talk to Sebastian alone, just wait till I get my hands on him.* 'This is actually about my aunt or great-aunt to be precise. I think she may have met you. I'm not sure when exactly but I guess fifty or sixty years ago? Antonia Ravel, I was named after her.'

'Ah yes… Antonia, I recall, I so nearly hadst the young Thorpe as well.'

'Toni racked her brains, Linus wouldn't have been old enough, he probably wouldn't have even been born. Did he mean, Saxon's grandfather? 'Was he called Alexander?'

'I hast nay notion. Didst thou say ye wast named Antonia also?'

'Yes, it just got shortened over time and I prefer Toni.'

'Well, I sooth dost not. Praise the Saints ye hast a suitable and quaint name, after all. From this day, I shalt use it. Frown not, Antonia, tis not becoming.'

'I asked you about Alexander Thorpe.' She reminded him irritably.

'And I already hath said thy meaning escapes me, Antonia, thy aunt, came to me oft, and told me she hadst fallen in love.'

Toni looked at him in shock, her *aunt* in *love*? This was a revelation. Before she'd begun to lose her mind, Aunt Antonia had sat Olivia and Toni down and all the bad points and every negative scenario of being a wife or letting a man break their hearts was drummed into them. It had coincided with Toni's falling out with Saxon, over the *pimple* incident, more ammunition that persuaded her that Aunt Antonia knew what she was talking about. Boys would only let you down.

'I hadst desired they wouldst be the ones, but he hurt her and wed another. I saw her a few times thereafter, but then, she ceased coming.' He sighed. 'That is how it hath always been, I find one of ye, but rarely a pair. It hast to be a pair, dost ye comprehend?'

'Not really.' *Antonia and Alexander, did they have a thing?* 'Umm, Sebastian, you do know Sax and I aren't together, as in, being a couple?'

'Aye, Antonia, ye hast made it abundantly clear but fate cannot be fought. Tis one thing I hast learned, love and misprise art two sides of the same coin.'

'*Misprise?*'

'Hate, love and hate. Ah, Antonia thou shalt learn as thy ancestors didst, our families always deal with passion in some form. Oft a love affair, or a plot so deadly, wouldst be worthy of great writings.'

Toni wasn't sure whether to laugh or not, but he looked so serious, she was afraid of offending him again. The decision was taken away as she heard someone approaching and braced herself for a telling off from Saxon 'Hi, Sax,' she said a little too cheerfully as he entered the cave.

'Good *Morrow*, Saxon.' Sebastian smiled.

'Morning, Sebastian. You should have waited for me in the car park, Toni,' he said accusingly.

'We didn't arrange a specific meeting point, I knew you'd see the van and guess I'd already gone on ahead. Afraid I wanted a *private* conversation?'

'*Cease*,' Sebastian said firmly. 'I hast made a decision, ere I speak of the treasure, it hast come to mine notice ye shouldst learn more of thy ancestry. Mayhap 'twill aid in determining why thy relationship is not as it shouldst be.'

'There *is* no relationship.' Toni said at the same time Saxon asked why he kept referring to them as ravens.

'Dost not rail at me with thy questions, remain silent and hark mine words. The Raven part of the family shalt become apparent. Antonia, come hither and sit.' Sebastian motioned to a flat rock near the back of the cave, Saxon followed and found his own rock to sit on.

'Um, one quick thing.' Toni said, trying to ignore the ghost's darkening glare at being interrupted before he'd even begun. 'The last thing I want is to annoy you again, but if this is going to be a long explanation do you think you could try not to put in those old-fashioned words… err possibly, pretty please? I can't always follow what you're saying.'

'Tis not a matter of choice, mine spoken word is nothing as 'twas. No doubt if mine kinsmen heard me speak today, they wouldst bethink me possessed by an evil spirit.' He gave a small smile. 'Tis important though, so for ye, I shalt try.' He was rewarded with another quick hug and the satisfaction of seeing some bewilderment in Saxon's eyes. The boy had his chance to stamp his authority. Now he could watch and learn what rewards the threat of a firm hand reaped.

It was a good thing Toni had no way of knowing Sebastian's thoughts. Her apology had been necessary. The hug although instinctive, was also calculated. He'd enjoyed the bodily contact earlier, if a few cuddles could keep him sweet it had to be better for all of them, plus she had quite enjoyed it as well.

Saxon wondered why Sebastian had suddenly started calling Toni, Antonia. He assumed she'd apologised but didn't think it likely the two things were related. He stopped bothering to work it out as Sebastian started to fill in a few blanks in the Ravel/Thorpe/Raven family tree.

'Now whither to begin? With the Thorpes methinks, as they came first.' Sebastian looked thoughtfully at Saxon. 'Of course, truth be told, ye art not of pure blood.'

'What? Are you saying I'm not really a Thorpe?'

'Wend back um...' Sebastian started to count on his fingers and gave up. 'Err many generations and ye sprang from a mix of Thorpe and Raven. A cuckoo in the nest, there wast many, but on this occasion, 'twas a Raven that planted it.' *Mineself, but I cannot admit to that yet.*

Toni's face broke into a wide grin.

'Dost not look so smug, Missy, ye art only here today due to a goodly share of incest, rape and adultery.' Saxon and Toni stared at each other both trying to digest what they'd just heard. Sebastian continued, oblivious to their feelings, 'Somewhere amongst all those shenanigans came mine humble self. Thou art both from mine bloodline, both Ravens.'

'Are we?' Toni whispered.

'I guess, that's why he calls us *Ravens*. It's a family name, nothing to do with the birds, but I don't get it?' Saxon wasn't buying any of this. 'He still hasn't told us who the *Raven*s are?'

'Does this mean our families are related...' Toni let the words fade away, not sure she wanted to explore that particular avenue of thought.

'Well, of course, thou art,' Sebastian sneered. 'So is half the blessed countryside if ye behold the thought that way. We art all God's creatures, after all, brothers and sisters every one of us poor sinners.'

'Please don't start quoting the Bible, Sebastian.' Toni managed a small chuckle. She wasn't really in the mood for humour after the afternoon's disclosures. 'Do you know more about our families, things that happened before you were born?'

'Aye, the Ravels arrived with William the Conqueror, and the Thorpes, as I hath said, wast here first. Originally of Danish descent, I believe, and took English land in the ninth century.'

'You're a Viking.' Toni said to Saxon, slightly in awe.

'And your ancestors were French.' Saxon smiled. 'That makes sense, Maurice Ravel, the guy that wrote Ravel's Bolero was French. Makes Bolly's nickname even more fitting.'

Sebastian tutted with impatience. 'Mine comprehension, tis King William granted his men packages of land, oft with the dwelling included. The Ravels wast of Nobel French Blood. Three brothers came to square... err fight at the side of the Conqueror, two wast killed. The last, Henry, wast knighted and gifted most of the land in this area, which belonged then to the Thorpes.'

Toni and Saxon were spellbound, these discoveries came from a time before any written records could confirm or deny the story, and whether or not it was true, it was certainly fascinating.

'I say *belonged* to the Thorpes, sooth, those gents raided and pillaged their way across England two hundred years afore. As with most Royal bequests, the aim wast to place a loyal retainer in lodging, but also maintain peace, so, if a daughter of the house wast of marriageable age, the King preferred they shouldst be taken with the land.'

'So, a Ravel married a Thorpe?' Saxon asked, seeing where this story was leading.

'He didst and the marriage wast a valorous one and produced many children. Some years anon, more family crossed the channel, one being a sister of Henry. Things didst not wend so well for that lady. Betrothed to another

French Nobel, she wast compromised and left with issue by a member of the ousted Thorpes.'

'Issue?' Toni queried.

'Child... babe, she wast raped, and left pregnant.' Sebastian clarified.

'Wow, this is like some television epic. Are you sure it's all true Sebastian?' Toni asked. 'I mean when did you come into the picture?'

'A picture of what?' Sebastian looked puzzled.

'Were *you* there, at the time? The Raven family, were they Saxons or Danes or something else?'

'Dost not complicate matters, Antonia.' He looked a bit annoyed to be put off his stroke for the second time. Some names and dates he'd made up, but in general what he was telling them were the facts as had been passed down, through the generations. Some bearing written witness, mostly though, by word of mouth. 'Now whither wast I?'

'Henry's sister,' Saxon prompted. 'She'd been attacked.'

'Aye, the lady wast left with child. Of course, the marriage didst not wend ahead, she birthed a son and promptly hanged herself.'

The atmosphere in the cave changed instantly. These may only be stories, but if a tiny bit was true, that baby was possibly an ancestor of both Toni and Saxon.

'Through the years, the two families seemed to oft find themselves entangled. Marriages, affairs, revenge killings. One thing wast consistent, every generation wouldst see some kind of pairing be it a good or evil one. Tis hard to recall so much and try to bethink how to deliver it to ye. Mine words got so muddled through the years. A Thorpe wench visited me here oft during the years the big flyers were overhead, she used much strange diction.'

'Big flyers, *aeroplanes* do you mean?' Toni asked, but Sebastian was lost in thought.

'That must have been during the second world war, which means it may have been an aunt or grandmother of ours?' Saxon sat up straighter. 'What was her name?'

'Doodlebug.' Sebastian suddenly said looking pleased with himself. 'I wouldst speak that word in discourse, but I know not its meaning.' He looked at their bemused faces. 'Hast I said it incorrectly?'

'Err no, but you probably won't get the chance to drop it into a conversation any time soon. It was the name given to a flying bomb.' Toni could see he was now looking totally baffled and wished she'd not said anything. 'Umm, never mind let's not get into that now, just think of it as something truly awful.'

'Truly awful,' he repeated. 'Verily I hast not remembered it in vain then. Victoria wast the wench's name, in answer to thy question, Saxon. She spoke oft of Dunkerque, I hath heard of that coastal fortress, it belonged to the Spanish, until Cromwell's men took it and sold it to the French, HA! it became a Pirate's harbour thereafter.'

'That's so cool.' Toni said trying to picture it.

'I doubt my great-aunt was referring to that particular invasion.' Saxon laughed. 'She was the eldest, born ten years before Grandad, he was the youngest of four, three older sisters,' he grinned. 'Sometimes I think it's not so bad to be an only child! When exactly do you fit into this history lesson, Sebastian?'

'Yeah, and who are the bloody... sorry, who are the *Ravens*? you still haven't told us.'

'And we're no nearer to learning about the treasure.' Saxon grumbled.

'Sebastian grinned. 'I shalt tell ye next time, and anon I shalt tell ye properly about mine life.' He looked at them both, so far so good, they were thirsty for knowledge, it would make their bond stronger. The family history would certainly hold their interests. '*We* art the Ravens.' He made a huge sweeping gesture which included himself. 'The Ravels took the name for a period of years which included mine own birth, I wast the last ere it reverted back to Ravel.' He saw Saxon was about to speak and shushed him. 'I know what ye art going to say, ye art a Thorpe, but recall what I spoke earlier, ye art both from mine direct bloodline, and although, there art many Ravels and Thorpes living within the whole of England, mine direct descendants art the only ones to be concerned with. Let us meet at the Abbey anon.

'He's gone again,' Toni said getting up. 'Completely gone, I'm not cold, so he isn't even lurking. Christ what a control freak. We're at his beck and call.'

Saxon nodded, letting her rant for a few minutes. When he stood up as well, his legs were stiff. 'We've been sat here for three hours!'

'It didn't feel like it. That was *so* good, do you think it's all true?'

'I guess like all stories that pass down through families, an element of it must be. And there's more to come by the sound of it.'

'Why would the Ravels change their name? Something bad must have happened, I want to know.'

'Me too, but right now I want some breakfast and I'm dying for a coffee. Fancy coming with me, my treat?'

'Yeah, go on then, we're meant to be a couple, after all.' They'd reached the car park and she noticed his car wasn't there. 'You walked,' she began to grin, 'in which case, you'll have to get in the *van*, and I'll drive us.'

Saxon hadn't taken that into consideration when he'd made the spur of the moment breakfast offer, he could hardly retract it now. 'Okay then, you choose where,' *and I'll just hope this heap of junk makes it.*

Saxon drank his second coffee while Toni tucked into her second bacon butty. She was looking at something on her phone and eventually, between mouthfuls, spluttered out 'Valorous, to be valorous is to show valour: to be valiant and courageous. Hmm, that definition doesn't quite fit in with how Sebastian used the word.'

'I think it can mean good or great,' Saxon said, looking over her shoulder. 'Perhaps he used it in that context, what did he say again?'

'He used it a couple of times. 'Um, a valorous whipping, and the marriage, that was valorous too.'

'Valorous whipping?' Saxon quirked an eyebrow. 'I didn't hear that bit, what was he threatening to do?'

'Nothing that *you're* thinking,' she said, feeling her face grow hot. 'He was talking about young kids using female body parts as swear words.'

'Understandable then, if he got in a such a rage with you calling him a bastard, think what he'd do if you used the 'C' word.'

'Well, I never would. Even I'm not *that* bad.' She wiped the grease from her lips and finished her mug of *strong builders'* tea.

Much to Saxon's amusement, she'd taken them to a transport café, just outside of the Primrose Ridge estate. She may have liked his offer of treating her to breakfast, but she obviously didn't want to be too beholden.

'I think we should make a move, I need to talk to Dad soon before someone else does.' Toni told him about the conversation with Olivia yesterday.

'In which case I'd better name drop you over supper tonight. Should I come to the farm with you now?'

'Err no thanks, Sax you're not exactly asking for my hand in marriage!'

She dropped him at the main gates of his family home, looking at the Manor ruins in the distance as she drove off. *This is really going to piss Dad off. I hope it's worth it.*

Chapter Eight

'Perhaps we can dig up a sense of humour for you.'

Toni looked at her father's empty chair, dreading the talk that she'd just psyched herself up for in the shower.

'If you want Dad, he's already gone with Frank Carter to an auction. I'm not expecting him home for tea.'

Frank Carter, those two words felt like nails being hammered into her coffin. By tonight her father would know every rumour and piece of gossip going. The only way to salvage a small amount of damage was to *fess up* to her mother. 'Um, can I talk to you a minute?'

Beverley sat down at the table and poured tea from the heavy silver teapot that had been passed down through at least four generations of Ravels, each subsequent owner receiving it somewhat dubiously. Olivia had said in no uncertain terms that she didn't want to inherit it, what on earth was the point of buying teabags? And Toni threatened to plant a flower in the hideous thing if it ended up in her hands.

'You know Linus gave me a lift home the other night?' she took a sip of tea. 'Well, Sax and I have sort of become friends again.'

'I did wonder dear, Norma mentioned something to me yesterday in the hairdressers.'

Ian and Gus, Oh my God this bloody place. 'What did she say exactly?'

'Apparently, he wouldn't let Gus drive you or Annie home.'

'Gus was shit-faced... sorry, I mean drunk and Ian wasn't far behind. We wouldn't have got in the car with them anyhow.' Toni said indignantly.

'Don't snap at me, and *don't* swear, I'm only telling you what I heard. You were also seen last week on the Littlejohn's... Thorpe's field with him.'

'Does Dad know?'

'I'm trying to drop a few hints, but I wanted to talk to you first. Are you *more* than just friends, love?'

This was it, the point of no return. How easy to just say no, and that would end this farce. But then, how would she explain the next time they were seen together, or the time after that, it was bound to happen, and soon. 'Yes, I think so.'

Beverly nodded. 'I always liked him, but Dad won't be happy. He'll take it extremely personally.'

'Oh God, I really wanted to tell him this morning, but I think Frank's gonna do that for me.'

'I have to say I am a little *surprised*, it was only a couple of weeks ago you sat here and said awful things about the family.'

'I know, perhaps I was a bit hasty. Sax showed me the lodge plans and they're not nearly as bad as I thought.' She didn't mention how tempted she'd been with the offer of a job. When all this ghost and treasure hunting business was over, she and Sax would revert to... to what? she actually didn't hate him now, maybe they really could be friends? When she made a big thing of them splitting up, eventually, it would be far easier for Leo if they remained civil. 'I better get to work.' Toni hugged her mother a bit longer than usual. 'Do you think you could...'

'I'll have a word,' Beverly smiled. 'Let's hope he gets some bargains today, it'll put him in a good mood.'

'If Frank Carter's opened his big gossiping blabbermouth, it'll take more than a piece of farm machinery to do that.'

Beverly watched her daughter leave and felt a tinge of sadness. This whole feud business was ridiculous, and she'd tried on more than one occasion to tell Martin just that. He never listened to reason, just spouted out the same answers that his father had always given, 'That's the way it's always been.' Or 'There's bad blood between us.' *Men*, they were all as stupid as each other at times.

Toni pulled up in the parking bay behind Pretty Feet, just as her phone rang. *Saxon*, what did he want?

'Hi, Toni, are you working today?'

'Yeah, I finish at two o'clock, why?'

'I want to have a poke around the ruins, I knew you'd go off on one if I didn't give you a head's up.'

'You bloody well wait for me, I'll come straight over when I'm done here.' She was about to hang up, 'Err, I don't have to come to the house and ring the bell, do I?' she heard laughter on the other end.

'Message me when you get here, I'll come out. But um, Toni you can't exactly camouflage the van you know.'

'I've told Mum about us.' Silence, that had shocked him.

'Right okay then, well in that case... see you later, *girlfriend*.'

So, it begins, Toni thought, unlocking the back door of the shop.

Karen spent the morning trying to give Toni jobs so the two of them weren't constantly sat around drinking coffee. It was getting increasingly difficult, the lack of customers only heightening the anxiety she was trying to keep hidden. After taking a quick lunch break, she called Toni into the office, keeping the door open so as not to miss a rare potential sale. 'I'm really sorry about this but I'm going to have to cut your hours.'

Toni gave a resigned nod, she'd expected worse but even so, she only worked twenty-seven hours a week as it was, how many more could she afford to drop?

'I'm also reducing Heather's hours, by the same amount. The Saturday girl, already only works the one shift, plus a bit extra in the school holidays. I'm so sorry,' Karen said, finding the conversation very difficult. 'Can we try twenty-two, and I promise you'll be first for overtime?'

What could she say? It had to be yes. Twenty-two hours was better than the zero-hour contracts a lot of other people her age had to deal with. 'It's okay, I know we're struggling, maybe when the Thorpe's holiday lodges are finished things will improve?'

Karen nodded miserably, surprised to hear Toni making any sort of positive comment about them, and more to the point, mention the Thorpe name without spitting it out in derision. The rumours could be true after all, about her and Saxon, although, now wasn't the time to have a natter and gossip. 'The err, salon might want a receptionist on a Saturday,' she added helpfully, watching her friend grab her bag.

Reception work in a salon that dealt mostly with her mother's age range of clientele, no *thank* you. Still, she'd have to do something and fast. No savings, no five-year plan and no wish to marry and start producing babies, well not for years at any rate.

She parked the van in the road, some distance from Saxon's home, rang him and waited. This way they could take the old footpath and walk to the ruins unseen from the main house. *Walk*! oh no, please let her trainers be in the back.

The sight which greeted Saxon was Toni's behind, sticking out from the back of the van and clad in a short, tight-fitting, black skirt. For some strange reason, he imagined Sebastian standing next to him, enjoying the same view and didn't like it. Not used to jealousy and not recognising it in this instance, it left him feeling frustrated. Before he could call a greeting, Oxeye bounded toward the van and leapt past Toni straight into the boot. She shrieked and fell backwards holding one bright red Converse. Damocles and Brutus rushed at her from both sides. Saxon shouted and the dogs immediately sat down. He mustn't grin, she'd go berserk. Thankfully, Oxeye saved the day by emerging from the back of the van with the second trainer. Toni wondered if he'd drop it if she asked. She was saved from finding out by Saxon. He helped her up and retrieved the trainer, still trying hard not to look amused as she swapped her footwear.

'I should have gone home and changed properly. I wasn't expecting the dogs.' She eyed them warily, all were sitting calmly, Oxeye watching her slightly wet trainer, with a look of desire.

'Sorry, I should have warned you. As soon as I said I was going for a walk Grandad called the dogs. Don't worry about Oxeye, he's only young and a bit exuberant.'

'*Young*, he's bloody huge.' Toni had never taken any real notice of the dogs before, too busy trying to avoid them if she heard the familiar barking nearby. Now, she could see that one was a bit smaller and not quite so thick set as the other two. He also had a mischievous look if that was possible for a *hound from hell*. Oxeye, knowing he was being talked about, thumped his tail on the ground. 'Is he related to one of the others?'

Saxon waited for her to lock up and they began the short walk along the road before cutting through an opening in the hedge. 'Damocles was used for stud, so we had the pick of the litter,' he explained.

'And yet he shares the colouring of the other err, what's his name?'

'Brutus.' He smiled. 'He's the sire of Damocles. The dogs are Grandad's remit, he's always had a thing about this breed. He says the next one will be from a different line, a breeder he's used in the past.'

'Three generations under one roof, just like the Thorpe men. No bitches allowed?'

Saxon thought of Vanessa and had to stop himself from saying, only in the dog world. 'Oxeye was a very obvious choice, the biggest and strongest, Grandad can always spot one that's going to be obedient, easy to train and a credit to its bloodline.'

Where did he go wrong with Linus then? That skinny weasel looks like the runt of the litter. 'I bet they wouldn't dare misbehave in Alexander's company. No pissing on the Silk Isfahan Rug, or chewing a Louis Vuitton ankle boot?'

Saxon raised an eyebrow, he wouldn't bite, not this afternoon, things were pleasant and he wanted to keep them that way. 'They don't live in the house, well that's not entirely true, they spend a fair time indoors, but at night they're most definitely outside, so no snooping around the ruins on your own Ravel, or you may end up as dog food.'

'*Funny!*' she mumbled, eyeing the dogs and giving a small shudder. The two older ones hadn't paid her a moment's interest after initially sussing her out. Oxeye seemed to have taken a shine to her, or perhaps it was the trainers, he spent a lot of time running in circles around both her and Saxon.

'Our rug came from Ikea and Grandad doesn't own any Louis Vuitton's, by the way.'

'It was a joke, Sax, perhaps we can dig up a sense of humour for you, while we're looking for the treasure?' She looked up to see a twinkle in his eye, he'd been teasing her and once again she was transported back to a time when his jokes would have had her squealing with laughter.

'I would say race you to the ruins, but the thought of what would happen to that little black skirt if you started to run is unthinkable... for this time of day.'

He was still teasing, and much to Toni's irritation she was enjoying it. 'I bet that was your plan all along, phoning me at work, knowing I'd want to rush over like this.'

'It worked, didn't it?' he grinned. 'Anyway, we're here.' The top of what had once been a tower loomed above them. 'I have no idea what we're actually looking for.'

'A big red cross on the ground hopefully. Failing that some kind of trapdoor, but it's certainly not going to be obvious.' Toni stood in the middle of what had once been an extremely large manor house. It was as exciting and atmospheric as she remembered it from years ago when they often used to come here to play.

Olivia, was the Lady, *naturally*. Leo and Saxon would play the good and bad knights, Sir something or other, and she was... in the *kitchen*, pretending to prepare a feast from the picnic Saxon's mother had packed for them. 'Why were you a Knight, while I had to be the sodding scullery maid?'

That was the point he lost control and burst out laughing, visualising her on the road flat on her ass and then, tentatively eyeing the dogs the whole way, whilst trying to pull her skirt down and now this ridiculous remark on top of everything. The same memories flooded back and he imagined that he heard the echoes of their childish games. When he finally looked at Toni, she was wiping tears of laughter away. They shared their first honest, warm, emotionally charged moment, which left them both reeling slightly from long-buried feelings.

* * *

Someone who did own a pair of Louis Vuitton boots was Vanessa, and as soon as she'd seen Saxon leave with the dogs, she'd pulled them on. A walk along Blackberry lane, just the two of them, would be an ideal opportunity for a little harmless seduction. Hurrying behind, she was surprised to see him go in the other direction. This way skirted around their land and met with Eastdown lane, which eventually, led to the main road. They couldn't be going that far because the dogs weren't on leads, she didn't think they even owned any, apart from the red velvet one she kept in her bedside cupboard. That had been a waste of time, the one occasion she'd tried to play *naughty puppy* with Linus, was virtually over before it began. Staying power was not his forte. She'd bet Saxon could have played all night.

That was odd, she heard voices around the next bend, one of them, definitely Saxon's. Staying out of sight she moved cautiously nearer. That trollop from the other night, parading around and taking off her shoes? What were they doing together? All thoughts of seduction gone, Vanessa followed at a distance, saw where they were heading and returned home. She'd take the jeep and drive over the grass to meet them, thinking of a convincing excuse on the way.

* * *

'Do you think Sebastian would come here if we called him.' Toni finally asked after they'd been looking for some sign of loose flooring.

'He did say he could come to the Manor. Try it,' Saxon said. 'These flagstones aren't moving. If there is a concealed entrance to a cellar, we'll never find it. Well, not without weeks of trying to lift each one by digging around it first. Let's hope he can at least point us in the right direction because I don't think this is an option, otherwise.'

'Sebastian, are you here?' Toni called a few times, the note of exasperation becoming increasingly obvious. The dogs began to growl while displaying quite bizarre behaviour. Saxon couldn't control them at all.

'Be silent hounds and know thy place.' Sebastian glared at the dogs, which were now trembling. They lay down, paws in front of their faces as if shielding their eyes from his cold stare. 'Ye Gods wench, hast thou any notion of what ye hast summoned me from?'

Toni looked at him questioningly and felt a little dazzled. This was the first time seeing him away from the half-light of the woods or in the darkness of the cave on Shingle beach. The brilliant sunlight showed him in his full glory and he certainly didn't disappoint. Yet again she couldn't help noting the similarities with Saxon.

'Raven Manor, I hast not been hither for a long while.' He looked around trying to get his bearings. 'We art standing in the great hall; the main staircase wast over yonder, come.' He marched away leaving them to follow.

'Summoned you away from what, exactly?' Saxon asked. 'What does a ghost do in his spare time?'

'I wast at the sandy bay along the coast hence, watching beauties parading around in skimpy underclothing.' He shot a warning look at Toni. 'Not something thou shouldst be dressing in, Antonia.'

'Sebastian, they were bathing suits, for swimming in the sea, or lying in the sun, to get a tan. Everyone wears them.' He was looking at her as if she was speaking a foreign language. 'Tanned you know, *sunbathing*? Getting a nice shade of golden brown?'

'Lying in the *sun*? To make their *bodies* brown? *Burn* themselves? Art, they *addle-pots*? Women's skin shouldst be fair, their complexion as whey-faced as moonlight.'

'Wow.' Toni grinned and nudged his arm. 'You have the heart of a poet.'

Poet? More like a lecherous old perv! Saxon thought. 'We were hoping you could help us find the cellar.'

'Cellar? why art ye wasting time looking for that?'

'Isn't that the way to the tunnels and the treasure?' Toni asked.

'Holy relics hidden amongst kegs and flagons of wine. In a cellar used by serving maids? Nay.' He scoffed as if they couldn't have suggested anything more ridiculous. 'Tis the outside, underground store ye seek, near the stables.' He strode straight through the building and as he came to what must have been one of the back entrances, stopped short. 'Fire and damnation, whither hast the blessed thing gone. The north-west corner of the main stable hadst concealed the entrance. Verily tis a disaster.' He walked onto the grass and scrubby bushes of gorse and began to stamp around. 'It hast been too long, I cannot get mine bearings.' He gave another few stamps in one particular spot, leaving an indentation with his boot. 'Hmm,' he murmured looking pleased.

'Have you found it?' Toni asked, excitedly.

'Nay, but I cannot usually make such a mark. I seem to firm up when thou art close, dearest girl.'

Toni threw Saxon a grin, but he didn't look too happy. 'So, what can we do now?'

'Thou shalt wend in from the other end.'

'The real smugglers' caves.' Saxon asked. 'Further along the coast?'

'Aye, well, not the main ones exactly, young Thorpe. I shalt pray ye can get all the way through still.'

'You do remember our talk, don't you Sebastian?' He didn't care that Toni was listening. If the tunnels weren't safe he wasn't going to let her go in them. 'Toni has a brother; would he be a Raven? and should he go with us?'

'Saxon, *NO*,' Toni shouted. 'How *dare* you ask that without discussing it first.'

'He wouldst be a Raven sooth, tell me dost ye have a sister? The lady must be an unwed maiden or an older spinster, or mayhap a widow of childbearing age?'

'No, I don't. Does it matter?'

''Tis *everything*, without such, another Ravel, a male one at least, is of nay use.' He watched Toni carefully. She was furious and he couldn't help but be drawn to the fire in her eyes. *A passionate wench. Young Thorpe is a fool.* 'Our girl is upset, Saxon, ye must make amends, I warrant.'

'I'll never forgive you. What an ass I was to think you'd changed. You just can't help yourself, wanting to take charge, call the shots, just like the rest of your family. Bloody hell I *really* was beginning to think you were different after all. But no, bring Leo in and push me out.'

'Toni, I-I'm sorry okay, I didn't mean that at all. The tunnels could be dangerous, or we could end up trapped, someone should know where we're going.'

'Saxon speaks true words. If danger wast to befall ye I cannot alert anyone. The tunnels are stout though, I wouldst not allow ye to wend through otherwise.'

She looked from Sebastian to Saxon. Both men were obviously concerned, but Saxon looked downright miserable. '*Fine*, you can tell him where we're going, *but*, you do *not* mention Sebastian or the treasure or *anything* else. You can make up a story about how *we* found the entrance by accident and that *we're* going to explore it and *he's* not coming with us.'

'Antonia means business, not a lady to be messed with methinks.' Before either of them could argue further, he turned sharply. 'Someone comes, tis no Raven so they shalt not see me unless I desire it so.'

Saxon heard his name being called and groaned. 'It's Vanessa, what the hell is *she* doing here?' *And she's driven my car, bloody cheek!*

'Saxon, darling, I saw someone here and thought it may be vandals.'

He forced a smile, it was disconcerting to see Sebastian walk around her, taking in every detail and then give a look of disgust.

'A doxy, if ere I saw one. I care not for this wench.'

'The sales-assistant, isn't it?' Vanessa walked towards Toni and stuck her hand out. 'I've seen you in the shoe shop. I didn't know you and Saxon were friends?'

Toni, looking puzzled, gave her hand a quick shake.

Saxon walked over and put his arm around her pulling her close, it was especially gratifying after her outburst a few moments ago. 'Vanessa, you know Toni Ravel *surely*? Leo's sister? We gave her a lift *home* the other night.'

'Oh yes,' her voice had a silky edge. 'Sorry, of *course,* I remember, I didn't make the connection. I wasn't paying much attention that evening. His *youngest* sister, isn't that right?'

Stuck up cow. 'That's right.' Toni said cheerfully, recognising an opponent straight away, but for what reason, she couldn't imagine. This was Saxon's stepmother, married to the slime-ball Linus, perhaps she was just overprotective, but it seemed unlikely.

'Toni's my girlfriend, we were keeping it quiet because as I'm sure you're aware, the families don't exactly see eye to eye. But... well, it's time it was out in the open now.'

'Girlfriend! how *nice.*' Vanessa's teeth were clamped shut but she did manage to force a smile. Sebastian was literally a few inches in front of her, and she kept waving a hand as if to brush away a few midges. 'You must come for dinner, I absolutely insist. Friday night?'

Toni wasn't sure what to say so Saxon answered for her. 'Cheers, Vanessa, that'll be great, Toni doesn't like cabbage though, or not much that's green actually.'

'How childlike.' She gave a tinkling laugh, which didn't cause one muscle of her face to move.

Botox perhaps, or not? Either way, there was something decidedly unfriendly about Vanessa. Toni, forgetting their earlier argument smiled, he'd remembered she wasn't keen on green leafy vegetables. She gripped Saxon's hand and felt a reassuring squeeze.

'Thou art courting. Didst ye both forget to tell me this?' he asked, before looking back into Vanessa's cold blue eyes. *I hast seen thine like afore. She fears ye, my little wench. I wonder why?*

Chapter Nine

'This isn't fair Verona and I'm not Juliet.'

During her lunch break, the following day, Toni met Annie in the Swingers and wondered if something good might come out of her sham relationship. Perhaps she could instigate a few opportunities where her best friend and brother were thrown together. Oh dear, this boyfriend/girlfriend situation was *really* going to rile Leo. Toni chuckled at the thought of him playing gooseberry for once.

'What's so funny?' Annie demanded. 'I've just been telling you about the case Robert Davidson's taken on, a pretty mucky divorce. Did you hear *anything* I said?'

'Err, yeah, sorry. Henry knows one of the parties involved in a divorce thing so, he can't do it and he's passed it on to Robert because he's shit-hot with divorce stuff.' Toni gave her friend an apologetic look.

'I said that like... *fifteen* minutes ago. I've told you all the ins and outs since then, you didn't listen to a bloody thing, what's so important?'

She had to tell Annie, her best friend would be really upset if she heard it all second hand. 'I'm seeing Sax and I have to tell Dad tonight, well that's if Frank Carter didn't do the job for me yesterday.' Toni didn't think Annie's mouth could drop any further but when she mentioned the dinner invite, it did.

'Oh, my God,' Annie squealed. 'I thought *something* was going on with you two, but actually going *out* together? Oh, my *God*,' she said again, even more loudly.

Toni cringed, everyone was starting to look and she was beginning to feel like an awful fraud, none of it was real. Telling the people she loved and cared about was a whole lot different to just talking about it with Sax. 'Keep your voice *down*, you'll hear all the details later, let me get Dad over with first. Then we can conveniently arrange some *foursomes* with you and Leo.' That shut her friend up, she noted with satisfaction.

Annie's mind was already beginning to calculate how this could work to her advantage. 'Are you sure there're no uni girlfriends?'

'None that he's mentioned and Mum and Olly always give him a pretty good grilling when he's home.'

'Blast, this is just getting interesting and now I'm late.' Annie grabbed her things and rushed out of the pub, leaving Toni alone with her thoughts, the inevitable talk that she really had to have with her father that evening still being the main one. She really hoped her mother had smoothed the way a little because now adding a dinner invitation into the equation wasn't going to help matters, not if Annie's reaction had been anything to go by.

* * *

Saxon, Linus and Alexander were standing together on what was going to be the carpark of their new development. Everything had been approved, and the first obstacle, access from the narrow beach road, was being addressed with one of the contractors. Saxon could see his grandfather was getting irritated with the comments Linus kept offering, which translated to every single item on the itinerary being made bigger, cheaper and suggestions at how to fit in three of something where there was only the provision for one. The last remark, about missing a trick by not turning the bottom field into a trout lake and adding some smaller lodges, or semi's perhaps, which would need even less space, was the last straw.

'Linus, you're only here as a courtesy and a distant hope you may actually have something helpful to offer. That field belongs to Martin Ravel as you very well know because we've had this conversation. And as for doubling up the number of lodges, forget it. I don't care *what* the planners will allow, *this* is how it's going to be. If you want to recreate another God-awful place like that one along the coast, what's its name? Sunny Park... something or other, sod off and do it on your own, preferably in the next county.'

Saxon waited for an explosive retort, but it didn't happen.

Linus gave a shrug. 'In which case, Father, Saxon, I shall indeed bugger off and stop wasting my precious time. See you both later.'

They watched him get in the Phantom and drive away without a backward glance or, giving a thought to the fact that he'd given them a lift there earlier, and they would now have a long walk home.

'That boy will be the death of me.' Alexander muttered. He finalised things quickly and shook hands with the contractor, agreeing on a start date of the Monday of the following week. Phase one would be the reception, restaurant and bar and the first thirty lodges. Phase two, the spa, gym and remaining forty-five lodges. There was and never would be, a phase three.

'I think perhaps I should go and bring the car back for you, Grandad.' Saxon suggested.

'When I can't walk home, just shoot me where I stand and leave me in the nearest ditch.' He saw his grandson grin. 'Anyway, I wanted an opportunity to talk to you alone. You can tell me why in God's name I have to sit opposite Toni Ravel at dinner on Friday night when only a couple of weeks ago you had no interest in her whatsoever?'

Saxon took a deep breath and stuck to the story they'd both decided to use, basically the one where she'd demanded to know more about the lodge plans and to keep on good, neighbourly terms, he'd taken the trouble to show her. The attraction had grown quite quickly from that afternoon. He went on to explain some of her ideas about the spa, and the golf buggy type transport system.

'She's a bright one, I always thought so. Those ideas are sound, are we taking them on board?'

'Already done.' Saxon smiled. 'I've had the revised plans drawn up. The actual building is no bigger, so the architect doesn't envisage any problems, we'll go through it properly tonight if you want.'

'Yes indeed. Saxon, just because she's bright doesn't mean she's the right girl for you. There's some family history you don't know about. It's personal, I don't really want to share it unless Martin brings it up. Just be careful, getting in bed with the Ravels won't be trouble free.'

Saxon flushed at the metaphor and the image it conjured up of him and Toni very definitely getting into bed. Hell, what was he thinking, it wasn't real and she was like a little sister to him. It could never be anything more than that.

'Young Thorpe I wish to speak with ye.'

Jumping slightly, Saxon hadn't realised they'd walked so near to the woods. He'd been paying attention to the conversation and couldn't think of an excuse to just abandon his granddad, so had to ignore the summons and carry on.

Sebastian had no intention of being ignored, he could sense another of his blood, one he'd seen before, but had not been open to him. 'Knave make thy way to the stones, now.'

Saxon pretended to answer a text, he was curious but also irritated at the way he was expected to dance to Sebastian's tune. Although in fairness, when Toni had called for him the other day, he *had* torn himself away from the bikini-clad girls on the beach. 'Err, Grandad something's come up, do you mind if I see you later at home?'

Alexander wondered what or who, had caused him to look so shifty. It wasn't like Saxon to be secretive. Still, if it was this girl, he couldn't expect to be party to all the ins and outs. Toni Ravel... Antonia... no, he mustn't go there, it was years ago. Margaret had forgiven him, although she had never found out the full story. There was no reason history would repeat itself, but he'd watch this relationship carefully. No Ravel girl was going to hurt his grandson, the way they'd hurt him.

'I'm here Sebastian.' There were a few dog walkers around and a woman with two small children playing on the Knoll.

'Walk hence from the sun, one hundred yards shouldst suffice.'

What does that mean, towards it or away? Saxon could see two women walking towards him, from which he deduced Sebastian meant the opposite direction. Just as he was trying to acclimatise to the familiar chill, which had been getting a lot easier lately. Sebastian stood in front of him in the flesh. He glanced around making sure no one was walking this way. 'Aren't you worried about being seen?'

'Nay, only mine bloodline can see me unless I wish it otherwise. Hast I not explained that once already?'

Had he? Saxon couldn't remember. Sebastian was looking flustered something must have happened? 'Is everything okay, why did you want me?'

'Antonia and ye art courting? Shalt a betrothal announcement follow anon?'

'Ah, it's not actually like that. Sorry, we did tell you we'd never be a real couple.'

'Then wherefore this façade to trick folk? I am heartbroken. I dost not comprehend. Our wench is lovely, high in spirit and a real beauty. I can see ye art not immune to her charms, thou art jealous when she gazes at me.'

Saxon was pretty sure Sebastian was joking but just in case he wasn't, he would at least appear to take the conversation seriously. 'I can't think of her in *that* way, it feels wrong. Let me explain how things are?' Saxon told him how he'd practically grown up with Leo and his family. He'd seen himself as a sort of older brother and protector, the same with Olivia to a degree, but something about Toni always drew him to her side. He went on to explain how he'd hurt her feelings right at a vulnerable time, age-wise. She'd never forgiven him or accepted his apology. 'This is the closest we've been in years, I value having her friendship again, I won't jeopardise that.'

Sebastian listened carefully and looked thoughtful for a few moments. 'She was once as a little sister. Hmm, tis the answer, of course, dost ye not see? If things hadst not happened so, thou wouldst still be experiencing that same relationship. Speak truly, dost ye behold that voluptuous body and see thy sister still?'

It had only been the day before she'd been wiggling about in that tight skirt, not to mention everything else that came flooding into his mind uninvited. 'No... you're absolutely right, those times have gone.' *Toni like a sister, no bloody chance. When or how had it changed?*

'Thou wouldst not wish to imagine swiving thine own sister.' He laughed loudly. 'Although sooth it hast happened more than once in our family history.' *The boy looks horrified, I hadst best cease or things shalt never progress.* 'I tell ye young Thorpe, those feelings *hadst* to change, the falling out between ye, happened for a reason. Now the relationship is like new, no sister or brotherly love to hang between ye. Dost ye grasp what lest I speak?'

'I do, but it doesn't matter, she won't have me.'

'Wouldst ye wish it so?'

'*Perhaps*, but I couldn't tell her, not yet anyway.'

'The treasure seeking shalt take a while, hence lie miles of tunnels below and I cannot wend there to get mine bearings.' *And I shalt damn well make sure it doth take long enough for her to feel the same.* 'Go now and bethink about things and dost not look at me so oddly, I am trying to speak in thy tongue.' *Another Raven lurks hither.* Sebastian disappeared quickly. *I should hast been paying more attention to what or who wast around.*

Alexander hadn't meant to spy, it had been Saxon that had veered towards him. Who on earth was he talking too? Some guy in fancy dress by the look of it. An Adam Ant tribute act, stand and deliver, he chuckled to himself. He'd have bet good money Saxon was on his way to Ravel farm, so he was surprised to see him pick up his pace and walk towards home. Whoever that odd character was, it was the person that had texted him earlier. Good Lord! what was that awful chill, he began to feel a bit light headed and hurried to Blackberry lane to find the sun.

* * *

'I'm sorry, love, I'm not sure about this, not sure at all.' Martin looked unhappily across the fields of potatoes. 'We'll need to start irrigating tomorrow.'

'Don't shut me out, I know you're upset, but is it really Sax you dislike so much?'

Martin studied his daughter, he'd heard the news from Frank and spent the whole of yesterday in a foul temper. Earlier this morning, Beverly had confirmed it but put a slightly different slant on the story. It didn't help, not really. In fairness it wasn't the boy, it was the Thorpes, in general. For some reason, their families seemed to entangle themselves, and usually not for the good.

'It's the thought of you marrying a Thorpe, you'd become one of them.'

'*Dad*, this isn't fair Verona and I'm not Juliet.' *And Sax certainly isn't Romeo and we're not star-crossed lovers. And anyway, none of this is real.* Was that the tiniest bit of regret she felt? No, it couldn't be, it was the tense situation, her emotions were all over the place.

Martin allowed a small smile. 'Ye must follow your own path, I won't disown you or throw you out of the house and tell you not to darken my door. *Joke*,' he said weakly.

'I'm glad you clarified that.' Toni linked her arm with her father's. 'It really *is* early days, and once Leo's back and they start doing boy things who knows what'll happen?'

'They're a bit old to be putting *boy* things before girls, love. I shouldn't worry about that. You always want to see two sides to everything, but sometimes there isn't an alternative, remember that.' He blew out a deep breath and kept his real feelings hidden. He had no problem with the boy that had used to come and play here but that child had grown into a man. Saxon was following in Alexander's and James' footsteps. He was a Thorpe through and through. 'I can't exactly give you my blessing, and I'm not happy about it, but I won't make your life a misery. I'll be watching him very carefully though, and you can tell him that.'

'Could have been worse, you're being watched.' Toni messaged Sax later that evening.

'I better behave then.' Came back with a smiley face. 'Do you know anything about some family history? the last 75 or so years?'

'I have a feeling there was something with our grandfathers? Gonna do a bit of digging. What's the arrangements for Friday, is it still happening?' Toni was almost hoping he'd say no.

'Of course, shall I pick you up, say 7 pm?'

'What's with all the messages?' Olivia leaned across every time she heard the ping on her sister's phone.

'None of your business, but if you must know I've been invited to dinner.' She quickly messaged Sax back. 'Cool thanks.'

'Dinner *really*? Is he taking you somewhere nice, what are you going to wear?'

'I haven't thought about that, it's at his place.'

'What do you mean you *haven't* thought, honestly, Toni, you're hopeless at times. In that case, we're going to town tomorrow and *I'll* drive. I'm not getting in that death trap of a van.'

* * *

'Nothing fancy, Olly, or too revealing, I have to sit opposite or next to Linus and Alexander.' She wasn't sure what was more shocking. The large pile of dresses, Olivia had brought into the changing room, or, the shiny price tags, displaying amounts way over what she could afford. 'Isn't there something on the sale rack?' She asked hopefully.

'Are you joking, this is your time to shine, not sit back and play the poor neighbour.'

Toni was about to protest, but then remembered Vanessa's smirks and snobby looks of contempt, the other day. She sifted through the choices quickly and pulled out a dark crimson cocktail dress, the cheapest and fortunately, in her opinion, the nicest.

'Oh, Toni, that's lovely.' Olivia looked at the tight-fitting bodice, well aware she'd never get her ample chest into a style like that. It had a faux crisscross design at the back, which gave the illusion of an old-fashioned corset top. The skirt fell to mid-thigh and had some small dark brown beading. Not enough to make it into a party dress, but enough to add just a little extra.

'Over the top?' Toni asked looking at her next choice which was much dearer.

'Not at all and you can dress it down with sandals rather than high shoes.' Olivia declared the dress a winner and didn't even glance back at the stupefied sales girl.

'I'm so sorry, Toni winced, let me put some of these back on the rack for you.'

'Nah, you're alright, I'm off on my break now, the part timer's doing an extra shift, she can tidy up.'

'I'll give you half towards it.' Olivia offered. 'I know you wouldn't have spent more than that if it had been left to you, but sometimes you just *have* to.'

Toni grinned. 'Thanks, Olly I'll buy the coffees and you can show me the pictures of the married quarters again. And I'll smile and pretend I love every single cushion cover you're going to describe in great detail.'

Olivia burst out laughing, grabbed her sister's arm and marched her to the plush new Brazilian coffee bar in the Mall, knowing Toni's first word would begin with an F and the second one would be pretentious.

* * *

Saxon knocked on the door at one minute to seven. Beverly answered and ushered him into the hall, it was the first time he'd set foot inside the farmhouse, for over eight years. Although his friendship with Leo had grown stronger, he'd felt less welcome here. Whatever the reasons, it had been easier to wait in the lane, meet in the Swingers, or get Leo to come to his house. *Regrettable* didn't seem a strong enough word for how a short span or repetitive behaviour could cause such monumental chasms.

There was a short, polite conversation with Beverly, no sign of Martin or Olivia and thankfully, before things grew too awkward, Toni came down the stairs and stood beside him.

Will they expect me to give her a kiss on the cheek? 'You look lovely,' he said leaning over and risking it.

She muffled a squeak of surprise which luckily her mother didn't notice. 'Err thanks, you too.'

He was practically pushed out of the door and all the way to his car. When Toni got into the passenger seat, he heard an exaggerated sigh of relief. 'It wasn't *that* bad! At least your dad didn't welcome me with the ancient family blunderbuss.'

Toni began to giggle. If he'd meant to alleviate her tension he'd succeeded a little, but the nearer they got the worse she began to feel. 'Damn, I had a bottle of wine to bring and I forgot it.'

'Good, you don't need to bring anything, this is meant to be a casual meal, just a friendly sit down and...' He stopped dead. Vanessa was waiting in the doorway wearing a long evening dress, her hair was immaculate, styled in an up-do, nothing out of place whatsoever.

'Right, a normal teatime in the Thorpe household then.' Toni muttered.

'What the hell's she thinking?' Saxon answered.

Trying to look like the sophisticated business man's wife, as opposed to the farmer's daughter, would be my guess. 'Maybe she's just trying to make an effort, eh Sax?'

'Maybe.' *But I doubt it.* He looked closely at Toni's hair as they walked from the garage to the house. It shone in the evening sun and bounced on her shoulders as she moved. *Natural and beautiful, just perfect.*

'*Toni*, I can call you that, can't I?' Vanessa gushed. 'You look charming, what a *sweet* dress, it's amazing what you can get in the Mall, isn't it? Let's go in and have a drink before dinner, did you bring a bottle of something you'd like us to open, no? Oh well, not to worry it's a good thing we have plenty.'

Chapter Ten

*'Wabbit? Pardon, mon frère, but this is the
rabbit you seek.'*

Saxon guided Toni through the hallway, she could see a
palatial living room to one side and three closed doors
on the other.

'Have you been here before?' Vanessa asked.

'I've been in the kitchen when Sax's mum made us
snacks. We used to come here to play in the pool. I don't
recognise very much, it seems a long time ago.'

'I like to think I've improved the place. Oh, Saxon
darling, nothing against your dear mother, but... well,
times and fashions have moved on, haven't they?'

'I taught you to swim, Toni, do you remember?'
Saxon said, concentrating on her remark about the pool
and trying to shut Vanessa out. For a moment, he lost
himself in a memory of childhood games and his mother.

'I had proper swimming lessons *actually*, with Olivia,
you did teach me backstroke, though,' she conceded.
The more she looked around and noticed things, the odd
picture, a silver vase with a yellow rose, the more she
began to feel nostalgic. 'Your mum loved roses. I can see
her now pruning the long ones that grew over the arch.'

Linus come out just in time to hear what was being
said. 'Janine's climbing roses, I still look after them for
her. Welcome, Miss Ravel, it's nice to see you again.
Come through, Mrs Howard won't be ready for another
half hour.'

'Mrs Howard?' Toni looked enquiringly at Saxon,
thinking another guest was joining them for dinner.

'The domestic.' Vanessa said irritably. She didn't want the conversation to gravitate to the past all night, or more particularly the virtues of Linus' first wife.

'She comes in three times a week and does a few bits, she's also an excellent cook, so you can thank her for tonight's meal, not us.' Saxon grinned.

'A godsend,' Linus added. 'Nice to have a woman's touch.'

It hadn't been a personal dig at Vanessa, but it was certainly received as one.

'It's not just female territory you know, the kitchen.' Toni said before she could stop herself.

'Quite right,' Alexander nodded, also joining in the conversation as they reached the conservatory. 'Saxon is somewhat of a Master Chef, did you know that, Miss Ravel?'

'Um, yes, I think I do remember he liked to err, cook... stuff.' Why was she always tongue-tied around Satan? 'Um, please call me Toni.'

'Well then, good evening, Toni, nice to have you here. What can I get you to drink?'

What should I ask for? Nobody's drinking wine, I don't want him to open a bottle on my account.

Alexander hid a smile, he could have a lot of fun baiting this lovely young woman if he had a mind to. He wouldn't of course, not for the time being, at any rate, he needed to find out if she had any hidden agenda first. 'Would you like a beer? Or something lighter?'

'A beer would be good, thanks.' The lights strung across the pool looked magical and she started walking out onto the patio, an exclamation of delight on her lips. The dogs stirred and Oxeye made his way over. She managed a pat on his head, which seemed to suffice. 'Oh, this is lovely.'

'Saxon did it especially.' Alexander said quietly, handing her a glass of cold larger.

'Something to nibble on?' Linus smiled, offering a tray of canapes.

'Oh, olives, not really my thing, err sorry, Mr Thorpe, they look very nice though.'

'No problem,' He knocked the offending green olive from the top of the salmon and cream cheese blini, using a cocktail stick. 'That's got rid of the oily little bastard,' he said with a twinkle in his eye. 'Call me, Linus.'

Saxon looked at his father in shock. Toni burst out laughing and accepted the (olive free) offering. Alexander wondered, not for the first time, how his son could have been attracted to a pair of false eyelashes and big breasts. An older version of Toni Ravel would have done wonders for him. It was rare to see Linus make a joke or laugh. If he did, his wife always seemed to be on hand to put him down.

Vanessa hung back and glowered as she watched the three men crowd around their guest. *A novelty I suppose.* 'I'll check what time Mrs Howard will be serving the starters.' She said, trying to claw back some attention. Saxon threw her a smile which she accepted as if he'd bestowed some kind of exclusive invitation, analysing its meaning all the way to the kitchen.

'I'm sorry,' Saxon said at the first opportunity to get Toni on her own for five minutes. 'I did say I wanted just a casual meal.'

'You mean you *don't* do this every night?' She walked with him to the far side of the pool. 'My illusions are shattered.'

'*Funny.*' He grinned. 'Actually, egg and chips are a resident favourite here.'

'I don't believe that for one minute, not with your dad and grandad praising your culinary skills.'

'I do like cooking a proper meal when we're all here to eat together. You and Leo cook, don't you?'

'Yeah, a bit. I prefer one pot things, shepherd's pie, stew, spag-bol. Less washing up. We don't all have a Mrs Howard tucked away ready to spring into action when required.'

Saxon couldn't detect any sarcasm in her tone, and she was still smiling. 'Perhaps one night I'll cook a meal, just for us? Not a Mrs Howard in sight.'

'I'll look forward to it.' Everything was so light-hearted and the fairy lights were so pretty, even though it wasn't dark yet. When they started walking back to the others and Saxon held her hand it felt like the most natural thing in the world.

The starters were cleared and the main course about to be served. Mrs Howard explained to Vanessa, she was leaving at that point. They all knew because they could overhear the entire conversation from the dining room. Vanessa screeching in a frenzy and Mrs Howard's calm and frank argument that it had been arranged earlier and no, sorry, it couldn't be changed. Her son needed picking up from football practice. The dessert was in the pantry, and the clotted cream, in the fridge.

Get that silly bitch under control. Alexander's good manners and feelings for his son's embarrassment wouldn't allow him to speak the words aloud. But the dark glare he sent in Linus' direction left them all under no illusion as to what he was thinking.

For the first time, since his mother died, Toni felt huge waves of sympathy toward Saxon. She'd thought he lived some sort of charmed existence here. A beautiful luxurious home, thriving family business, an estate with its own ruined Manor... everything she could only dream of, and yet, not one of the three men sat at the table looked happy. Was Vanessa the reason for it? She wasn't qualified to answer that, but the woman was either well on her way to inebriation, slightly insane or just plain awful, and it was pretty obvious she fancied the pants off Sax. Her sympathy also extended a little to Linus and Alexander. She'd been here less than an hour and so far, these family dynamics were a real eye-opener.

Linus disappeared muttering something about needing the bathroom, Saxon gritted his teeth, got up and went into the kitchen. Whatever he said was delivered quietly and within a few minutes Vanessa was once again seated, a large smile painted on her face and an even larger glass of red wine in her hand. An extra bottle had also been placed on the table and she covertly topped up Saxon's glass. Linus scuttled back to his seat avoiding eye contact with everyone especially his father.

'This all looks delicious.' Toni said breaking the silence and eyeing the huge joint of roast beef, fluffy Yorkshires and golden crispy potatoes. There were three covered dishes of what she suspected were vegetables, hopefully, carrots and something else that wasn't green would be in at least two of them.

'Yes, indeed. Thank you so much, Mrs Howard, you've done us all an enormous favour.' Alexander smiled kindly at her. 'You hurry along now, I know you have prior commitments. We're extremely grateful.'

Saxon and Linus concurred and Toni nodded, grateful this woman wasn't from the village and she didn't know her. Even Vanessa managed a grudging mumble of thanks. The next five minutes was taken up with noisy and polite enquiries as to who wanted what. 'Can I pass you the French beans, Alexander?' 'Gravy, Linus?' 'Horseradish, Toni?' 'A glass of Malbec, with the beef, Toni?' 'Carrots, you eat them, don't you?' 'Another potato or roast parsnip, Vanessa, before I put some of these dishes on the side out of the way?' 'Let me top up your glass, Saxon, darling?'

And then finally... peace and quiet whilst everyone savoured the slightly rare and succulent meat and everything that went with it, all cooked to perfection. When Toni did allow a furtive glance around the table all three men gave her a friendly wink, totally unaware the other two had done the same.

Everyone helped clear all signs of the main course away. Everyone except Toni, she wasn't allowed to do anything. She waited patiently to see what would arrive next, hoping it wasn't going to be something soaked in heavy liqueur and presented in a cloud of blue flames.

'Strawberries.' Saxon smiled, putting the dish of red juicy fruits in front of her. As she made a small '*oooh*' noise he was tempted to pick one up and feed it to her.

'Cream and sugar.' Vanessa offered, placing a bowl of each nearby. Toni helped herself to both and passed them on to Alexander.

'Thank you, I believe these are yours actually, the strawberries.' He smiled when she looked puzzled. 'We bought them from the greengrocers in Market Street. I think Ravel farm supply them, am I correct?'

'Oh, yes we do, these are the first, another two weeks and the fields will be full of students.'

He nodded. 'Saxon told me your suggestions for the clubhouse, I have to say you spotted things we hadn't. It'll be much easier to alter a few drawings than change rooms around later on.'

'And the buggies,' Linus said, ignoring Vanessa's warning look. 'A bloody good idea, well done.'

'Any more *ideas*?' Vanessa asked snidely.

'Well yes, I have, but it's not really my place...'

'Come on, tell us.' Saxon said encouragingly. He looked at his grandfather who was nodding and looked genuinely eager to hear what she was going to say.

'Well... the strawberries, for instance, everything could be sourced locally, and menus changed to fit in with availability. It's what they do in the Swingers all the time.'

'We've already thought of something along those lines,' Alexander smiled.

Vanessa snorted, 'Oh well.'

'Umm, also I was thinking, you know in hotel foyers they have glass displays with things for sale? I thought...'

'We could make a killing.' Linus interrupted.

'No,' she threw him a disgusted look, 'I meant use things from the local shops. Where I work, for example, Karen, the manager, is struggling to keep afloat. She has some really nice accessories, handbags, scarves, purses.' She looked at Vanessa, trying to get her on board, 'She took your advice and ordered some designer wellies and walking shoes. If you displayed some of those, well, then you could take a percentage, or however, you do that side of things. Also, Castle's jewellery and watches, do you know he does most of his trade online now? Jimmy Castle and his daughter design the most wonderful pieces, to order.'

'I didn't know that.' Vanessa said, planning to look in on some of the smaller shops she'd never bothered with before. With Saxon's attention fixated on what was being said, Vanessa manoeuvred the bottle of wine and sloshed another top up into his glass. If he drank all of that without realising, there'd be no lift home for the little slut. She could phone for a taxi and good riddance.

Toni had hardly stopped to take a breath for the last half hour. 'This could be a really a good idea as well. A small hairdressing salon but run in conjunction with the one on Abbey Road. Perhaps one of their staff up there permanently or on a rota basis or something. That would be up to them to arrange, of course. Fine details.' She shrugged. 'Should I go on?'

'Please do.' Alexander coaxed, hiding a smile.

'Okay, err, well, they could pay a small rental for the room, or again you take a percentage. The younger girls who go there to work get fed up. The salon can never employ a fully qualified apprentice, as soon as they finish training, they're off. There's not enough variety in this village. All the local clientele want are shampoo and sets and the odd trim, most of them are so... old.' She stopped for a moment and looked at Alexander. 'Um present company excepted?' she grinned. 'Take my sister, for instance, she wouldn't be seen dead going into the village for a trim, which is so stupid cos, they're like really cheap. I bet she'd go up to your place though, and probably have a treatment or something at the same time in the spa.' *This isn't for the Thorpes' benefit, it's for the good of the community.* Who was she kidding? Toni had let her herself get completely swept away by the excitement of it all.

'Tell me, Toni do you go to the local hairdressers to have your hair styled?' Vanessa asked, looking thoroughly bored.

'I don't exactly have it styled, but I go for a trim every couple of months.'

'Thought as much.' She murmured into her wine glass.

'Bless my soul.' Alexander sat back, scratched his chin and remembered what he'd thought only a few days ago about having to sit opposite Martin Ravel's daughter over dinner. 'These ideas of yours, are not as easy as you think to implement.' He caught Saxon's eye, his grandson looked as if he was about to burst with pride. 'But, they're all do-able. I'm extremely impressed, young lady.'

'You are? Good, I have more suggestions.'

'I think that's enough for one evening,' he laughed. 'It's certainly given us something to think about. Don't say anything yet, to your boss, I mean. I'm not in a position to make offers or promises at the moment, I have to give all of this some careful thought.'

'I understand, hopefully, something will happen before Pretty feet closes completely.'

'Is that likely?' Saxon asked.

'My hours have been cut, again, along with Heather's, the other part-timer, so who knows?'

Saxon took a long drink trying to recollect if she'd mentioned that before. 'Damn, how much have I had to drink? Did anyone top this up?'

'I gave you a refill, darling,' Vanessa said looking concerned. 'Is that a problem?'

'I was going to give Toni a lift home, I *can't,* now can I?'

'I'm *so* sorry, I totally forgot, I just love to see my men relaxing. You don't mind getting a taxi *do* you, Toni?'

'No of course not. I wasn't expecting a lift anyway but thanks for thinking about it Sax. Now you're over the limit, you don't have to be careful anymore. Have a few more drinks, enjoy yourself.' *God knows I would if I lived here.*

'It's a warm evening, you can always walk the girl back, eh son.' Linus leered slightly. 'A *romantic* walk through the woods.' Vanessa looked daggers at him, that was not the plan at all.

Saxon and Toni both knew a walk through the woods would be anything but romantic. Not with the scrutiny, they'd be under from Sebastian. It was just as well they weren't looking for romance in their *make-believe* relationship.

'Let's move back to the conservatory.' Alexander suggested. 'Would you like another drink or a coffee, Toni?'

'This is fine,' she gestured to her wine, which Linus immediately topped up for her, and hovered behind her chair.

'Tell me.' He helped her from her seat, offering his arm. 'Your father's fields, the ones that run parallel to…'

'To the land your family have just acquired from the Littlejohns?' she finished for him.

'*Dad*!' Saxon rushed across and took Toni's other arm forcing Linus to retreat.

'It's fine, let him have his say.' She said in a deceptive honeyed tone, 'I'd love to know what you were all planning.'

'Nothing Toni, I swear it.' He forced her to look at him. 'On Mum's grave.' He whispered, aware his father was going to undo all the goodwill that had been forged between them over the last few weeks. 'I promise you this is nothing to do with me *or* Grandad.'

Toni nodded. 'Okay, but I still want to hear him out.' She turned her attention back to Linus who was beginning to shrink slightly under Alexander's piercing stare. 'What exactly is it you want to know, Mr Thorpe?'

'Oh well, err only wondering why your father doesn't farm them, and err… please call me Linus.'

'Those fields don't belong to my father, Mr Thorpe, although that's not the reason we don't use them.' She had everyone's attention now, it was almost laughable. 'The soil isn't great, although we could sort that if it was the only issue. They flood at the bottom sometimes in a high tide and the winds race down the slope from the Littlejo… err, your land. It's only the very low fields that are a problem, my grandfather used to rent them out for grazing.'

'Not your *father's* land?' Alexander said still surprised by her earlier statement. 'I'm intrigued and *not* for any ulterior motive.' He glared again at Linus. 'If not Martin's land then who does it belong too?'

'Oh, it is *Ravel* land, it's mine actually,' she grinned, enjoying the looks on all of their faces. She let Saxon guide her to a comfortable wicker seat with large plump cushions.

He sat down beside her. 'Toni, that's great, I didn't know you were a landowner,' he said looking pleased. 'It's your business, you don't have to tell us anything else.'

'What and disappoint your dad?' She whispered. 'He's nearly pissing himself with a need to know.' *I've been waiting all night for an opportunity to drop Antonia's name into the conversation.* She waited until everyone was seated. Saxon and Alexander seemed relaxed but were obviously keen to hear her news. Linus was hanging on her every word and Vanessa... well, she looked positively enraged. *Oops, I seem to be the centre of attention again.*

'I have to go back to my grandfather's time, Oliver, he had two sisters, Rachel and Antonia.' She looked straight at Alexander, had he flinched a tiny bit? 'The farm was passed down to him, Rachel married well, money was never going to be an issue for her. Things were different for Antonia. Something happened, I'm not sure what, but she fell out with the family or rather, her father, Francis. When Oliver was granted power of attorney, because Francis went a bit odd, probably dementia. He gifted her the bottom fields. Dad said once, he remembered him saying that she'd asked for them, but I don't know if that's true.' She waited for the few exclamations to die down. 'Did you not hear the story?' She directed the question at Alexander.

'I didn't, but I assume because you've asked me, you're aware Antonia and I were friends at one time?'

It was Saxon and Linus' turn to looked shocked. 'Just *friends*?' Linus asked his father.

'Please, Toni, continue.' Alexander said ignoring the question.

'Antonia rented a cottage about twenty miles away which she eventually bought. She missed the village though, and according to Dad, talked about Raven Wood a lot.' She glanced at Saxon, wondering if he would draw the same conclusion, she had.

'My aunt never did anything with the fields and when she recognised she was getting a bit *forgetful*, wanted to make sure nothing could be used as funding if she did end up in a home. She wanted to give it to me and Olivia, knowing that Leo would have the farm, and it would be no benefit to Rachel's children, they lived too far away.' She stopped and looked thoughtful. 'Apparently, there's also some kind of trust set up, but I guess we'll find out about that when she dies.'

'So, it's yours *and* Olivia's.' Saxon said. 'Bolly's never mentioned that.'

'Dad made him promise. Aunt Antonia gifted Olly the cottage, and me, the land. Twenty-eight acres to be exact. She needn't have worried about selling up to fund her care, she's so barking mad now, every time she has a review, social services agree her needs require full state funding. The family top it up though, that's why she's in one of the better homes.'

'How exciting.' Vanessa said, her voice dripping with sarcasm. 'Such a *long* story as to how you came to own some not very fertile fields.' She gave a tinkling laugh. 'And what will you do with them?'

Toni gave her a scathing look. Linus was sitting on the edge of his seat, she noticed. 'Well, a lot of it is still being farmed, by Dad. I suspect the ones adjacent to your lands will probably always remain fallow. I quite like the idea of turning some of it into a nature reserve one day.'

Linus groaned. All that land ripe for development was going to become infested with wildlife.

'Partridges, pheasants, grouses, all safe from the hunting season.'

'Grouse.' Saxon, corrected with a grin.

'*Grouse*? are you sure?'

'Yes, Toni, don't you remember the story of The Three Little Grouse and the Albatross?'

'Oh yes, of course, he wanted to blow their nest down. Hang on, grouses... *grouse* don't nest in trees, are you sure that was a real story?'

'As real as you wanted it to be, it was *your* story. I started you off and you wanted an albatross that would huff and puff and...'

'Blow their nest down.' Her eyes held unshed tears she was so completely lost in the moment, everything and everyone else was forgotten.

Alexander gave a small cough. 'Err as much I don't wish to break up this literary moment from your youth, I have to say, your idea of a wildlife reserve is admirable. Perhaps a nature trail wouldn't be out of the question?'

'Hmm leading down from the lodges no doubt. In which case I'll be after some Thorpe investment. As long as you have no guests by the name of Elmer Fudd. No muskets allowed on my land.' She grinned.

She was joking, but in Alexander's head, he was already on the case.

'Wabbit? Pardon, mon frère, but this is the rabbit you seek. I'm no rabbit.' Saxon quoted. The two of them burst out laughing.

Vanessa gave a convincing titter and suggested in a loud voice she'd phone a taxi for Toni. Totally ignored by everyone she did it anyway, so when the doorbell rang, ten minutes later and she announced the cab was waiting, they all looked at her accusingly. 'I did ask,' she said pathetically.

Toni looked at her watch. 'Probably late enough,' she said to Saxon, regretfully.

He knew she was talking about her father. 'Small steps,' he smiled. 'It's a pity we'll have them all on side eventually and then have to mutually break up.'

'Yeah, well that's a way off. I think you're getting an invite to the wedding, so whatever happens, it won't be until after that.'

'I had a text from Bolly earlier, I've just read it.' He walked with her to the waiting taxi. 'He's arriving on Sunday. There's a leaving party on Saturday night he wants to go to.'

'The last hooray,' Toni snorted. 'He's finally going to put his student life behind him.' She turned to the door and gave a wave. 'Your family are watching!'

He gave her a quick kiss on the lips. 'Sorry, it would look a bit odd if I didn't do that. And it's the last hoorah by the way.'

She unconsciously ran her tongue over her bottom lip. 'Seems I'll have you around to put me right for a while longer.'

Alexander sat alone in his study long after the others had retired to bed. He sifted through everything Toni had told them, scribbling himself a reminder to 'phone Henry, ref Pretty Feet'. That was something he could help with if the current owner of the building was open to a sale or small investment.

What a revelation that girl had been, he wasn't in the least surprised Saxon had fallen for her. They were well suited, but then, he'd thought he and Antonia had been the same, once upon a time. Should he pay a visit to Glen-Croft? No, best not, sleeping dogs and all that.

140

Chapter Eleven

'Thou hath slain him with the magic telephone.'

After watching Leo unpack his first bag, which loosely translated to tipping a mound of washing in the laundry basket, Toni got up from her perched position on the side of his desk. 'Are we cool?' she asked.

He had his back to her so she didn't see the broad grin that nearly split his face apart. 'It's a bloody shock if you must know. I'm not sure about him sacrificing himself like this. It'll probably end in tears, and knowing that poor bugger's luck, his tears.' Catching a glimpse of her angry face in the mirror he burst out laughing. 'I'm a bit pissed off my best mate's going to be all loved up, but apart from that, it's brilliant. Treat him gently, Toni.'

'You really suck sometimes; do you know that?' she said, stretching over to give him a whack.

'Hello, losers.' Olivia pushed her way past the suitcases, gave her brother a big hug and flopped down on the bed. 'What have I missed?'

'Toni's, in *lurve.*'

'No, I'm bloody not, don't be such an asshat, Leo, and for God's sake don't make jokes like that in front of Dad.'

'Right, that's my next question answered then, the old man's not pleased?'

'To be honest, he's taking it better than I thought, but no, definitely not behaving like someone who's been on a happiness course. We're just kind of silently agreeing not to mention it.'

'Not the same at Thorpe *Manor* is it, Toni?' Olivia sat back, loving an opportunity to stir the pot.

'Oh, *do* tell?' Leo grinned again. 'Have you charmed all three generations with your beguiling wit, beautiful face and colourful language?'

'Piss off both of you, I'm going.' She pushed past him, a ghost of a smile playing around her mouth.

'Do you have a planned assignation with lover boy, or can I have him this evening?' Leo shouted across the landing.

'He's all yours.' She began furiously texting Saxon as soon as she got to her room. '**Leo's turn 2nite. DO NOT tell him anything X**'. She deleted the kiss, put it back in, started to delete it a second time and finally decided to leave it, but changed it to lower-case, '**x**'. *Christ, I'm getting stressed about a sodding friendly kiss on a text!*

Her phone buzzed. '**Yeah no probs. Need to see Seb about tunnel entrance. Tomoz afty, you still free? XX**'

Two kisses, and both in uppercase! Why had she noticed that before even reading the short message? She texted back with a time to meet at the Knoll. One or two kisses? upper or lower? Oh, God!

Toni needed to arrive a bit earlier than the time she'd texted to Saxon because she wanted to ask Sebastian a few more questions about her great-aunt. He'd dismissed the mention of Antonia a little too quickly the other day and the fact that even in a confused state, her aunt remembered his name and their encounter, that had to mean something. Also, if Alexander *was* implicated, as Toni suspected, it could be awkward to talk about it in front of Saxon.

* * *

All plans changed the next day when the manager of Glen-Croft phoned mid-morning and asked to speak to Martin. She was sorry to say his aunt may have had a stroke and had been taken to the hospital. It was of her opinion they should go quickly. Toni was summoned home from work. Olivia put the little boxes she was making for wedding favours away with only a small murmur of protest. Then the whole family piled into Martin's estate with Toni squashed between her older siblings in the back seat. It had been like that when they'd gone out for day trips. The only difference today, no one was singing Disney songs.

Arriving at the county's main hospital, at midday, did not bode well for the likelihood of finding a parking space. In the end, Leo suggested they all get out at the main entrance and he would find the elusive empty bay. If the lit-up sign still showing parking available, was to be believed, there should be one somewhere.

The family hurried to the medical assessment unit, and once there, faced the second battle of finding a nurse that was free long enough to point them in the right direction. It wasn't too long before someone in a light green uniform looking for all the world like she was in charge of not only this particular ward, but the whole hospital and bearing the title 'Health Care Assistant' came to their aid.

Escorted to a side cubicle where his aunt was, Martin asked if a Doctor could explain what had happened. With a great sucking in of breath and shaking of her head, the Health Care Assistant, obviously not pleased at being asked a second request, took out a small notebook and scribbled 'DOC FOR CUBICLE 5' then rushed away, terrified she may be asked to make cups of tea for the visitors.

'They were called auxiliaries in my day.' Beverly muttered.

Olivia and Toni hung back to let their father sit in the only chair, so he could hold Antonia's hand. Beverly stood behind him whispering words of encouragement.

'Why are you whispering, Mum?' Olivia asked. 'Isn't the whole point to let her know we're here?'

'It's a hospital love, you're supposed to be quiet.' She said this just as a clanking, metal, dinner trolley was wheeled past the open door.

'Is she awake do you think?' Toni asked, edging a little closer to the bed.

Martin shrugged. 'I think so, she gave my hand a squeeze.'

'Hello, Aunty, it's Antonia,' Toni said loudly in the patient's ear.

Whether it was the recognition of hearing her own name, they weren't sure, but her eyes opened and focussed briefly on all of them. She looked at Toni and tried to speak, but even though she was only mouthing what appeared to be one word, it was virtually impossible to decipher.

'That sounded a lot like *Daddy*,' Martin said, 'Which is odd because she never called him that in her life. Are. You. Asking. For. Father?' He enunciated every word.

'I highly doubt that they never spoke again, after...' Beverly fell silent aware she may have said too much.

'After what?' Olivia demanded.

'Family business,' Beverly said, still whispering. 'There was a row and she left home.'

All sorts of scenarios flashed through Toni's mind, but the one that stuck was an illicit love affair between Antonia and Alexander. The fact that she never reconciled with her father smacked on something pretty serious. She leaned even closer and tried again, saying her name clearly and then putting her ear right next to her Aunt's lips.

'Diary.'

'What did she say?' Martin and Beverly asked together.

Diary, Toni heard it plainly that time, she looked at her family's expectant faces. 'I'm not sure, sorry.'

'She was the last of that generation, you know, my father and Aunt Rachel have both gone.' Martin muttered quietly.

'For goodness sake, Martin, don't say *was*.' Beverly chided. She lowered her voice to even less than a whisper. 'She's not dead yet.'

Leo arrived at the same time as a young male doctor, who introduced himself as the House Officer. He went on to explain which consultant was on take, meaning the one taking all the medical admissions for that day. He had the case notes and next of kin details but was pleased to be able to confirm them with Martin.

'It's far too early for a diagnosis.' He said apologetically. 'It certainly appears that she's had a small stroke, but we need to run a few more tests.'

'And then what happens?' Beverly asked.

'Well usually in a case like this she would transfer back to the original nursing home, assuming they can meet her needs. As I said it's really too early to say.'

'But she's not going to die?' Toni asked the question they all wanted to ask.

'I can't answer that, she's elderly, and...' he noticed the tears threatening and put on his more compassionate voice. 'Whatever sort of trauma she's experienced, is bound to have a huge effect on a lady of her age. However, she looks strong, so all being well,' *if she doesn't have a second massive stroke in the next few days,* 'we'll do our best to get her back to,' a quick look at his notes, 'Glen-Croft.' He finished with a smile.

The family stayed a while longer, tea and biscuits did eventually arrive and when they were ready to leave, the nurse in charge promised to phone them if there was any change. 'I have another number here for Mrs

Ravel which I'll just double check with you, a Marilyn Helmsley?'

'That's my cousin.' Martin informed her. 'Antonia's niece, I'll phone when I get home and let her know what's happened. That side of the family live quite a bit further away, but by all means, contact her if you can't get hold of us.'

'Thank you, we wondered if it was a daughter or granddaughter?'

'My Aunt never married, even though all your staff address her as *Mrs* Ravel.'

'Duly noted.' The staff nurse smiled. 'It's bad practice I'm afraid, we don't always think. It's quite possible *Miss* Ravel will be moved to another ward within the next few hours, please don't be alarmed by that, it's normal procedure.'

'Of course, and call her Antonia, she'll prefer that anyway.' Martin smiled back wondering how they had time to call anybody anything with the pressure of work they all seemed to be under. He stood still and closed his eyes for a moment trying to work out how he was going to fit daily visits into his busy schedule, then remembering Leo had come home, relaxed.

A diary, where the hell would that be? Toni had tuned out of the chatter in the car on the journey home, too busy imagining what secrets may have been written many years ago. She picked up a few words Olivia was saying about tax. 'What's that about, Olls?'

'Christ, keep up. It's to do with how long ago we were given the land and the cottage. Eight years ago, Dad thinks, even though we didn't know about it until your eighteenth. Henry Davidson was dealing with the paperwork, it might be worth checking.'

'Why? what difference does it make?'

'Because if she dies too soon, we could have massive tax bills.'

'I'm sure it's fine,' Martin said looking in the driver's mirror. 'She's been in Glen-Croft for nearly four years, and I'm sure it all went through at least four years before that.'

'*That* long,' Leo looked surprised. 'I suppose it must be, I was just going into 6th form.'

'I was thirteen,' Toni commented.

'All tall and spotty,' Leo laughed, 'Who'd have thought you'd stop growing and end up a short-ass?'

'I'm average height *actually*, but thanks for reminding me about the spots.' She gave a hard dig to his ribs making him yelp.

Beverly swivelled in her seat. 'Stop it the pair of you, anyone would think you're still thirteen and seventeen years old.'

Leo grinned and Toni wondered why she'd ever got so worked up by Saxon's teasing. It had only been the once; Leo and Olly's had been constant the whole of her life. She remembered some of her own unkind comments towards them and ruffled her brother's buzz cut. 'Don't let the pubes grow too long.' She grinned at his warning look and wisely kept quiet for the rest of the journey.

* * *

Toni waited impatiently at Smugglers' Knoll, or the Hunters' Stones, as she was beginning to think of it. Fortunately, the woods were deserted, most likely because a light rain was falling. Saxon had answered her messages earlier, sorry to hear about her aunt and yes, he'd meet her at seven o'clock, instead. The diary was foremost in her mind, but she was still a bit upset from the hospital visit in general. Just walking through the ward on their way out had been pretty traumatic.

An emergency bell had sounded and the resuscitation trolley was yanked from its residing place. Nurses had frantically tried to usher a man away from what was most likely his wife, whilst pulling curtains around the bed. The scenario was still playing on her mind. The man had been about the same age as her father, which meant, the extremely poorly woman, could just as easily have been her mum. How did people do that job? She'd thought the staff at Glen-Croft admirable enough, but these doctors and nurses were something else.

'Antonia, thou art alone and whey-faced, what ails ye?'

'Oh good, Sebastian, you're here, Saxon's coming soon but I wanted to talk to you privately.'

He eyed her suspiciously, never completely happy when either of them approached him making demands or asking questions. 'How can I be of service?'

'My Aunt Antonia is in hospital, on death's door, she could literally die at any minute.' Toni laid it on a little thicker than necessary. 'She mentioned a diary; do you know if she kept one?'

'Antonia, mine lovely wench.' Sebastian went quiet and Toni wasn't sure if he was referring to her or her aunt. He seemed lost in a world of his own for a moment before he started talking again. 'Such a terrible burden to bear alone, cast out, but then the lady wast not the first. I couldst tell ye a story of a Thorpe father that hadst killed his own daughter for bringing such shame.'

'The *diary*?' Toni asked again. 'Did she ever mention it?'

'I hardly knew the lady, let alone, such secrets?'

She glanced at the time on her phone, Sax would be here any minute. 'Please Sebastian,' she walked over and laid a hand on his arm, 'she told me in her almost dying breaths to read it.'

He turned and studied her face. 'Didst she truly speak that?'

Toni nodded, mesmerised by the close contact and his hypnotic green-eyed stare. Surely whispering the word diary, implied she go and read it, didn't it? Reaching a hand toward his face, she stroked his cheek.

Sebastian rested his face in her palm. 'Wench, thou art very dear to me.' He moved her hand slowly to his lips and kissed it gently.

Toni forgot everything including Saxon's imminent arrival. Dogs barking somewhere in the woods didn't even begin to register. Eventually, pulling herself together she moved back a little remembering why she was there. '*Do* you know where the diary is?'

Without letting her hand go, he looked thoughtful again. 'She transcribed her innermost thoughts to paper. I know not whither 'twould be. I saw her again, some years anon...' he stopped, that was Antonia's secret. 'She told me she lived alone in a cottage, wishing not to witness certain folk, *together*.'

'*Together*? Did it have anything to do with Alexander Thorpe?' Toni felt Sebastian stiffen a little, as much as that was possible for him. '*Please* tell me?'

'Find the diary, mine love, it shalt reveal the truth. Tis all I can speak on this matter. You may stroke me some more before thy beau comes hither.'

'You're *outrageous* Sebastian, and he's not my beau.' Toni smiled and stretching up kissed his cheek, he turned quickly and just for a second their lips touched.

'Please accept mine most humble apology.' Sebastian moved away as two dogs rushed toward them. 'I shouldst refrain, but ye art so lovely.' He let the dogs bark for just a moment. 'To the floor, hounds.' Oxeye and Damocles dropped like stones.

'You two look very cosy.' Saxon said accusingly. 'What are you concocting, Toni?'

'Nothing at all, I was telling him about Antonia.'

Saxon's glare immediately softened. 'I'm sorry, was it very bad?'

'Hospitals, you know,' she gave an indifferent shrug. Inside she was feeling just the opposite. Sebastian was a ghost for Christ's sake. And now Saxon was here looking all gorgeous and protective. For some reason, what she was feeling for one was transferring to the other. 'Why only two dogs today?' she asked, trying to distance herself mentally and physically.

'Ah, well that's a bit of bad news as well. Brutus died in the night, quite unexpectedly really, he was the oldest of the three, but it was still a shock. Actually, when I got your text, it worked out better, cos it meant I could help Grandad bury him.'

'Oh, Sax, I'm sorry to hear that. Was he upset? Are *you* upset?'

'He's very much, what will be, will be. He doesn't like to show his feelings. When we, or I should say I, was digging and your message came through, I told him why you were at the hospital and he went very quiet.' It was Saxon's turn to shrug. 'I'm okay though, Oxeye's my favourite, I'd be upset if anything happened to him.'

'Not a good day for news, is it?' Toni's phoned beeped, she looked down and pulled a face.

'Problem?' Saxon asked.

'If you call *Gus* a problem, then yeah.' Toni didn't notice Saxon's eyes narrow, she was too busy debating whether or not to open the message.

'What's he *sent*?' he almost spat out.

'It's a snapchat and I just know it's going to involve genitals of some kind.'

Sebastian had no idea what a mobile phone was, let alone *snapchat* but he did understand the word genitals and moved closer.

Saxon's face had darkened, he was virtually ready to snatch her phone away. 'Is he sending dirty photos of himself?'

Toni looked up as both men hovered, one either side. 'Nothing that bad.' There had been one occasion, on her sixteenth birthday. She'd threatened to make it public if he ever sent a second. 'It'll be a cartoon or a joke, or some picture, he'll have drawn a co... well, you know. Everyone will have been sent it not just me.'

'Open it,' Saxon said icily. If that pathetic little pipsqueak was sending disgusting images he'd bloody well kill him.

She hesitated for a second but realising this was one battle not worth fighting she did as he asked. A picture of Barney Rubble, from *The Flintstones* fame, had a speech bubble saying 'Time for another Bamm-Bamm' and of course the obligatory cock and balls were drawn over the top. She had to fight very hard not to giggle because one look at Saxon's face, told her, he would definitely not find it amusing.

'Witchery! Tis a magic box of lurid pictures; wherefore wouldst ye possess such a thing?'

Saxon was fighting his own inner turmoil, trying to reconcile the fact it was indeed a harmless joke, but desperate to know what Gus had sent previously. 'It's a communication device, Sebastian. A telephone, have you heard of that?'

Sebastian nodded. 'I comprehend that word, and hast seen many folks with boxes such as this one. They prod constantly and speak to them.'

'Generally, they're a good thing. If Toni was in trouble, she could speak into hers and someone would come to help.'

'B-but somebody hast drawn this disgusting image, a rogue, I warrant.' Sebastian's eyes flashed in anger. 'Doth he not know thee art courting?'

Toni was glad that the picture had played for its ten seconds and now disappeared.

'Call that gent out,' Sebastian roared at Saxon. 'Horse-whip him.'

'Delete him, Toni.' Saxon said carefully, knowing he had no right to ask.

She took a breath, brought up her contact list and pressed a button. 'He's deleted.'

'*Deleted!* Thou hath slain him with the magic telephone?'

'Nothing that radical, but he won't be bothering her again.' Saxon fought the urge to laugh. He was still mad at Gus Littlejohn, and he'd give him a piece of his mind when he saw him next. Not so much because of this one snapchat, but he did have very serious reservations about that guy, for many reasons. 'The dogs are getting restless, I should make a move.'

'Why didst ye come tonight?' Sebastian asked, calming down now that the picture was gone, the small box put away and Gus, hopefully, had got his just rewards.

'Oh yeah, nearly forgot.' Saxon said. 'Where's the entrance to the tunnels, on this side, as we're not going to get through from the ruins.'

'Wend to the top of the Manor tower, behold towards the coast and call that twelve of the clock. Draw an imaginary line at eleven. Thither is the cove ye seek. Hmm, the path down hath long gone. Ye shalt need a small boat.'

'Or we could climb down...'

'NO!'

'NAY!'

Toni put her hands up to her ears in mock annoyance. 'Commands in *stereo* now. Okay, I get it, no climbing.'

'I can get a boat,' Saxon said quickly, before he had to explain what stereo was, 'but unless the sea is like glass forget it, those rocks are deadly.'

'Why dost ye bethink that part of the coastline wast used by smugglers?' Sebastian murmured. 'The cave is obvious if ye art stood facing the cliff. Wend to the back. At the top is a ridge and a small opening which ye hast to crawl through. I hast done it, so shouldst be a simple feat.' He glanced at Toni. 'Thou shouldst wear thine underwear again and take a sturdy lantern, tis a long and dark way to wend to the Manor.'

'Sebastian, if we find anything, what are we meant to do with it?' It was the first time either of them had actually asked that question and it had only just occurred to Toni.

'It must all be returned to the Holy Church, of course.'

'*All* of it? Even the sapphire necklace?'

'Nay, mine wench, I told ye, that hast nothing whatsoever to do with the church. The necklace hadst a different owner and shalt not be found in the same place. Tis work for another day.'

'Okay, we are talking Catholic church, right?' Toni asked for clarification.

'Tis the only one, and the reason many valorous men wast killed, hiding these riches from King Henry.'

Toni's mouth dropped open. 'Henry VIII? Is that when you lived Sebastian?' You said you'd tell us your story and how you're related to us.'

'I didst make such a promise, ye art quite correct, but I didst not live then, sometime anon, in the seventeenth century. Now I grow weary, I hath held this form for too long. Find the treasure little Raven and all shalt start to unravel.' He faced Saxon. 'There shouldst be no danger, the tunnel wast sound but, 'twas a valorous idea to alert others. I wish ye good fortune.' He gripped Saxon in a tight hug patting his back. With Toni, it was an excuse to kiss her lips again, and this time keeping her angled from prying eyes he took his time. 'I forgot the most important thing, directions, 2 rights and 1 left, the full length of the tunnel. 2 and 1, remember it well, tis easy to lose oneself or become befuddled with the dead ends.'

After he'd disappeared and the chill had left them Toni was still rooted to the spot. Saxon hadn't seen the kiss properly but was looking at her strangely, and if the truth be told she felt strange. This time it was she that reached for his hand and held it tightly, not even realising until the farmhouse was in sight, he'd walked her all the way home.

'I've been wondering how we can involve Bolly,' Saxon said before letting her go. 'He's going to want to come with us. We'll have to suss out this cave first, make sure the small tunnel hasn't collapsed, and we can get through to the bigger one, but then, I think we just tell him we discovered it and we want to explore, take it from there.'

Toni didn't argue anymore, all that talk of 2 to the right and 1 to the left, dead ends and getting lost had unnerved her a little. 'What about him seeing the treasure?' she asked.

'If it's even there. This all happened during the reign of Henry VIII, five hundred years ago. It's probably long gone.'

'Hmm, I doubt it, I think Sebastian would know. Whether or not we can actually *find* it, is a different matter. What do we actually do with it?'

'I'm sure it'll all be online, failing that, we hand it over to the police.'

'Don't let Sebastian hear that.' Toni grinned. 'I have a feeling he wouldn't approve at all. Do you think he was a smuggler?'

'Who knows,' he shrugged. 'I'm looking forward to hearing his story.'

'When can you get hold of a boat?'

'Anytime, that's not a problem. The weather isn't looking good for the next couple of days though.' He heard a car approaching and looked along the road. 'That's Bolly, don't say anything yet, not until we've taken the first step and checked the cave out.'

'Okay, um Sax, if that's my brother you can't just say goodnight and shake my hand, we'll have to at least pretend...' she never finished what she was saying because Saxon had pulled her into an embrace and his lips were covering her own. It was impossible to freeze her facial muscles like a statue especially with the taste of Sebastian's kiss still lingering. She moved her mouth a tiny bit and was lost in the most wonderful passionate kiss she'd ever experienced.

'Sorry' he pulled back a little, 'I couldn't help myself and you intimated it had to be authentic.'

'Did I?' she said almost dreamily. 'I thought I said pretend?' Even as she spoke the words she was leaning towards him.

A horn blasted making them jump. 'Get a room you two.' Leo shouted jovially, driving past them at snails' pace just to make a point.

'If he's coming with us, I'm bringing Annie.' Toni said determinedly.

'I'm not sure that's a good idea.'

'It's a bloody brilliant idea, I want that guy fixed up and Annie's been after him for ages. What better opportunity than stuck together in a tunnel, discovering treasure, if that doesn't do it, nothing will.'

'Okay, if you say so. I know he's gone now, but... can I kiss you again?'

Chapter Twelve

*'This relationship is going to be
a work in progress.'*

Toni switched off the alarm and took a moment to lie
in bed wondering where she should start to look for the
diary. The cottage seemed the most likely place, and as
luck would have it, Olivia was between tenants which
meant it was empty. She'd need an excuse, perhaps if she
offered to go and clean? Would Olly buy that, or would
she accuse her of wanting to take Sax there for some
nefarious reason? *Sax*, thoughts of their kiss just kept
popping into her head.

That had been two days ago and she was due to
meet him in the Swingers this evening, along with Leo
and Annie. After Leo had driven past the other night,
they'd stayed together for a while, but apart from a
tentative arrangement, which had been confirmed by
texts messages, they hadn't spoken. There had definitely
been something, a real thunderbolt from the blue,
cliché moment, but even more troubling was the other
kiss she'd received that day. A short but intimate kiss
that had stirred similar feelings. So now every time she
pictured Saxon's silvery grey eyes, Sebastian's dark green
eyes would be twinkling instead or vice versa.

**'I can get the boat this afty. Tides and weather good.
R u working? x'**

Toni texted back immediately. **'Finish at 1. Where
shall I meet you x?'** This was good, an opportunity to
see Sax alone, rather than feel awkward in front of her
brother and friend. If she was having misgivings it stood
to reason he may be as well.

'Short black skirt v sexy, not practical ☹ take other clothes. I'll pick u up xx'

Her breath hitched. He hadn't made jokey references like that until now. She quite liked it. If he was picking her up from outside Pretty Feet she'd better get a move on, it was pointless taking the van which meant a twenty-minute walk. She'd forgo her morning shower if she was going to be crawling around in tunnels later. A nice soak in the bath with a very expensive bath bomb she'd been saving, would be something to look forward to when she got back.

Even at twenty years of age, her mother wouldn't let her out without something to eat first thing in the morning. It was the farming blood in her, Toni mused. The days when they'd be up at first light, go and do two or three hours work and then come back for a huge breakfast before starting all over again.

Fortunately, the primary objective of this farm was producing food. They'd never had livestock to worry about, so no animal feeds or milking, she gave a small shudder and spared a thought for Lawrence Carter. She was aware he had a crush on her and had done for some time. The fact that he was two years younger was a bit off-putting, but mainly it was the thought of all those cows. Growing up on her parent's farm had been a wonderful blessing, but she wasn't cut out to be a farmer's wife, not in any shape or form.

Now she had Sax as a pretend boyfriend, or was he? If half the things Sebastian said were true, perhaps their families were always destined to either fall madly in love or murder one another.

'What's so funny?' Martin asked watching Toni grin at her slice of toast.

'Oh, nothing, I was miles away.'

Leo smirked, about to make some rude comment involving Sax and bed, but with his father there, thought better of it. 'So, what's all this in aid of tonight?' he asked instead.

'Just a night out, no hidden agenda.'

'Hmm, that's why you've asked Annie is it? Trying to fix me up the minute I come home?'

'Not at all, she's my friend and I want to see her, same as you want to see your mate.' Toni shifted uncomfortably and tried to change the subject. If she was masterminding situations in which they'd be thrown together, she'd have to be a bit subtler. Tonight, was perfect though when she and Sax talked about the tunnels, both Leo and Annie would hear about them together. It would stand to reason that they'd both want to be involved.

Martin and Beverly gave each other a conspiratorial look. A nice girlfriend would be just the thing to put the Australian visit out of his mind. Just because it hadn't been mentioned, didn't mean Leo had forgotten about it.

'Anyone driving to the village in the next half an hour?' Toni asked, hopefully.

'Something wrong with the van?' Martin asked.

'Saxon is picking me up straight from work, that's all.' She tried to keep her tone matter-of-fact. He wasn't exactly one who must not be named, but she did try and not mention him too often in her father's hearing.

'I'll drop you down love,' he offered. 'I need to have a quick word with Henry Davidson.' Hopefully this thing with Saxon Thorpe would run its course and die a most welcomed death. If not, he'd have to accept it, but it wasn't going to be easy.

Karen waved Toni into the small office and poured them both a coffee. 'Good news, or at least I think it is. I'm getting a new landlord, I didn't even know the building was up for sale.'

'Why is that good?' Toni asked. 'He or she might have all sorts of designs on the place, at the very least the rent will go up.'

'Well when I read the first few lines, that what I thought right away, but apparently not. They want a list of everything that needs repairing *and*, I'm getting one month's free rental, as a sort of 'welcome offer' I suppose.' She smiled. 'The rent is guaranteed to be fixed for two years, at the same rate I'm paying now. That's pretty damn good, I was expecting a big increase in September.'

'Blimey, Karen, that's great, who's bought it?'

'Can't you guess?'

Of course, it had to be Thorpe Developments. How on earth had Alexander managed that so quickly, or was it always on the cards? She shouldn't flatter herself thinking he'd done it because of what she'd said over dinner. Still, he had seemed quite open to her idea about selling items in his foyer. What a difference that could make to Karen's business.

* * *

Martin sat patiently while Henry Davidson found the correct file. An A4 folder was extracted and also a letter. He strained trying to make out the name on the envelope, it was definitely his aunt's handwriting, but he was the wrong side of the large desk to read it properly.

'That's strange.' Henry went to the door, opened his mouth to call a name and then hesitated. 'I want to say, Amy,' he muttered, 'but I know that's not right.'

'Annie,' Martin offered helpfully, knowing his daughter's friend well. 'Annie Page.'

'Yes indeed,' Henry smiled. 'Annie, could you come in please?' He motioned her towards the filing cabinet marked 'M to T'. 'Have you been tidying these files recently?' he asked hopefully.

'I've refiled whatever you've left out, but I haven't removed anything.'

'In that case, I have a job for you, I've mislaid an envelope, from Antonia Ravel's file. I can only think that somehow it's fallen to the bottom and then perhaps been misfiled elsewhere.' He looked apologetically at Martin, who had no idea there had even been an envelope. 'It's addressed to your daughter and was to be read with the will.'

'Really, which daughter? Have you any idea of the contents Henry?'

'Your younger daughter, Antonia... Toni, I believe she calls herself. It was sealed, I haven't read it.' He turned to Annie and smiled. 'When I'm out of the office next, please start a thorough search of the other files and check the actual cabinet itself, otherwise, that will be all for now, err Annie.'

'Of course.' She grinned at Martin on her way out, who following the remarks over the breakfast table, tried hard not to look too appraisingly at her.

She hadn't quite closed the door when she overheard, 'I do know that it was some kind of explanation why Olivia got the cottage and Toni the fields, which to all intents and purposes, don't hold much value.' It was no good, she had to shut the door at that point, but it had certainly piqued her interest and not only that, she'd seen Robert Davidson with his hands in that particular filing cabinet about a week or so, ago. Should she have mentioned it? No, surely their work overlapped, he'd have every reason to take files from his father's office, she'd just never noticed him doing it at any other time, usually, his personal assistant, Mona, would fetch anything he needed.

Martin's brow creased. 'I must admit I did wonder. I can't see it ever being given planning permission to build on, but then, of course, we all thought the same with Littlejohn's fields.'

Henry wasn't being drawn into that debate. He'd done a lot of work on behalf of Alexander Thorpe for that particular job and client confidentiality was of utmost importance, plus Alex was a good friend. He also liked Martin Ravel, even if the man did have tunnel vision as far as the Thorpes were concerned.

'On a more useful note, the cottage and lands gifted to the girls are perfectly safe, which is what you wanted to hear. It was as you thought, eight years ago.' He smiled and offered his hand to Martin. 'I'm sorry to hurry you, but I have another appointment in ten minutes.'

'No problem, thank you for seeing me at short notice, Henry.' As he stood, Martin managed to lean slightly across the desk and read the name written on the envelope. *Alexander Thorpe,* he stifled a gasp. Damn the woman, what the hell did she have to say to him?

* * *

At the end of her morning shift, Toni rolled her skirt and white blouse into a sausage and stuffed them into her large shoulder bag. Putting on her jeggings and an old purple t-shirt, she said goodbye to Karen and waited on the pavement, just outside of the shop.

Within a few minutes, she saw the red Cherokee approaching. It had belonged to Linus until three years ago but he'd hardly ever used it, preferring to be seen in the Rolls. It had been given to Saxon as a graduation/ welcome home gift. Today there was a large trailer attached and on it, an inflatable dinghy.

They sat side by side both looking at each other a bit awkwardly. Saxon about to put the car into gear, leaned over and kissed her cheek instead, it broke the ice. 'That's got that out the way then,' he laughed and they both relaxed.

Travelling further along the coast than Toni expected, she caught sight of the Marina in the distance. 'All this way, why?'

'We're here actually,' he said, pulling into a narrow lane which looked seldom used. 'It's the nearest point I can get the car to the water's edge, otherwise, it *will* be all the way to the Marina.'

'Is this your boat?' She asked as he parked and started to unload the dinghy. He seemed to know what he was doing. 'I expected a little wooden thing with oars.'

'This has got oars, but I think you'll appreciate not rowing all the way.'

'You use this for the *luxury* yacht, don't you?' It came out a bit scathingly, she hadn't meant it to.

Saxon stopped what he was doing, walked over, put his hand on her shoulders and backed her up against the car. Then he kissed her. 'Right,' he drew back slightly, 'I've been wanting to do that since I picked you up, and I don't want this to turn into an argument. First off, are we… going out properly now, or is this still pretend as far as you're concerned?'

'I-I don't know, I mean every thing's changed hasn't it? The parents know, the hard part's done, I guess we could give it a go, and revert back to plan A if things don't work out.'

'Solid commitment, that's what I like about you Ravel,' he chuckled. 'Hedge your bets as usual.'

Toni compressed her lips which was difficult, given that he'd just kissed them. 'I said yes, didn't I?'

'In which case, my girl, I need to clear the air about something. No, on second thoughts, let's get going, we can talk while we motor towards the cave.'

No escape. After her childish remark about the yacht, Toni had a feeling she knew what was coming.

It didn't take long to launch the small craft, Saxon let her throw her trainers on board and jump in early. He waded out a little further, pulling the dinghy and ignoring her laughter when a wave caught the bottom of his shorts. He climbed in, and they were off. The last thing either of them wanted to do was spoil the mood, but this needed saying, he'd tried a few times before, hopefully now, she'd be a bit more receptive. If not, things would never work between them. 'I want to tell you a bit about how the family business started.'

'I'm sorry about that remark earlier, you don't have to justify anything to me.'

'No, I *don't* but that's what's so bloody frustrating, I feel I have to... I want to.' He saw her nod and carried on, keeping a close eye on what he was doing. The sea was calm, but they didn't have life jackets so he wasn't going to show off or take any chances. 'My grandfather and his father worked hard for every penny they made. There were no lucky breaks, they didn't buy shares low and make a fortune or anything. It was slow and steady. Yes, they sold land after the war and made a killing, something the rest of the farming community has never let us forget, but it was *their* land to sell.' He waited for some smart retort if anything she looked a bit embarrassed and kept her eyes firmly on the sea, rather than him, but she *was* listening. 'Whatever people say, Grandad's done more, financially, for this village than anyone else.'

'Sax, you don't have to say all this, I do know and I don't understand why Dad feels so strongly about things. As far as I'm aware there have never been any business deals between the two families.'

'I don't get it either.'

'Did you know Alexander was going to buy Pretty Feet?'

'Yes, it was a decision he made literally in the last few days and he's in the process of doing so, even a cash purchase doesn't happen overnight.'

Toni smiled, 'And was that sound business sense?'

'In the short term, probably not. But he'll be getting rent, and pretty much all property is an investment. We're here.' He switched off the engine and took hold of the oars.

'What can I do to help?'

'Keep a close eye out for rocks below the surface, I'm hoping we can get close enough to climb up and pull the dinghy out after.'

As luck would have it, that's exactly what they were able to do. Saxon steadied the craft while Toni heaved herself onto the first flat rock they came to. She did scrape her knees a bit but kept quiet when she saw how difficult it was for Saxon to disembark.

He supposed it was his fault for not making it clear she was meant to lean over and hold it steady for him! At least she gave him a hand to pull the dinghy onto land, which, with the motor as well, was heavy. 'The tide is on the way out, so it should be perfectly safe.' He took her hand and they cautiously made their way across to the cliff face.

'Will four of us fit in that?' Toni asked looking dubiously back at the little raft.

'Yeah, it's designed for four and I've been in it with Dad, Grandad and Vanessa.'

'On your way to the mega yacht,' she laughed.

'Very funny, I wish.' This time there was no animosity, he knew she was teasing him. 'More smart remarks like that and I won't take you out on it.'

'Wow really, Sax, you can sail it on your own?'

He began to laugh. 'It's a sports cruiser, 33ft, no sails required. To be honest, I *haven't* taken it out alone, but Dad has with Vanessa, so it can't be that difficult. It actually belongs to him.'

Digesting this new information, she should have realised something flashy like that would be owned by Linus. Still, a trip away, on their own, or perhaps with Leo and Annie one day. She really needed to work on those two.

They studied the cliff face together. Saxon tried to find any remains of a path leading down from the top, but there was nothing. If it had been there in Sebastian's time, there was no evidence of it now. He did, however, find an opening, that only showed up if he stood with his nose almost touching the rock and looked sideways. 'I think this crevice is what Sebastian meant.'

'Hmm, I don't see how it's a secret, not over all these years, someone's bound to have explored this coastline, given the smuggling history. Although, it certainly wasn't obvious from the boat.' She rummaged in her bag and brandished a torch at him. 'I remembered.' She said feeling pleased because he'd obviously forgotten.

'Well done, I can't believe...'

'That you didn't bring one and you're not perfect after all?' She finished off his sentence and smirked.

'This relationship is going to be a work in progress, I can see that.' They made their way through the opening and continued inwards. 'This is more like a fracture; do you really think Smugglers would have used this?'

'I can't see it, especially if they had to climb and find a narrow opening.' She shone the torch upwards, 'I mean, they'd have their swag bags to contend with.' She heard him laugh, and they both followed the beam looking for some kind of narrow overhang.

'Could that be it?' Saxon asked, dying to grab the torch and take control. About twelve feet up, the wall curved in slightly, even with the light shining it was hard to make out what was above. 'I'll go first, all we need to establish is that there is a larger tunnel on the other side. We're not exploring alone okay?'

'Yeah okay, no need to get all bossy about it.' She watched him climb and tried to shine the light where it was needed. When he'd reached halfway, he told her to follow. The climb up was a bit tricky and he kept offering to help. She couldn't climb and hold the torch so reluctantly handed it over. They reached the ledge together and there was just enough room for one of them to pull themselves up. The opening when they did find it was well concealed. 'Perhaps we really are the first people to come this way in many years. You go through first, Sax.'

He smiled to himself, she was scared, but would never admit it. He laid flat and began to wriggle through, hearing her scrabble onto the ledge after him. It was tight, but he was slightly smaller than Sebastian and if the ghost was telling the truth, he'd been through here. 'It's not too far,' he called back. 'Only about two metres, just let me make sure it's possible to actually get out at this end and then I'll shine the torch so you can see.'

Toni started to follow as soon as his feet began to disappear, worried that she was going to be left in darkness, she preferred to keep the torch beam in view. He'd dropped out of sight and panicking a little, she moved more quickly, her bag snarling up beneath her body.

She'd stopped moving, her hips had stuck fast and she wasn't going anywhere. The light shone straight in her eyes and a torrent of abuse was followed by a desperate, 'I'm stuck.'

'Toni, calm down and keep still, you're half my size. I'm on solid ground, by the way, the tunnel is almost head height and it climbs steeply upwards. Give me your hands, I'll pull you.'

She managed to free one hand but the other was wedged under the bag strap. 'I can't go backwards either. Shit, what am I going to do?'

He now had both his hands on her shoulders and managed to push her a few inches, but that was all. 'I don't get it.' He was too puzzled to find it funny, which was just as well because Toni was working herself into a frenzy. The torch beam caught the leather strap on her shoulder and he gave an exasperated tut. 'Tell me you didn't try to come through with that bloody great bag? How could you have been so stupid?'

'You're not helping,' she shouted before bursting into tears.

'Okay, I'm sorry. Right, let's think about this.' Purposely keeping his tone upbeat, he wondered if there was a possibility of breaking the strap. Suddenly her eyes flew open and she gave a piercing scream. Saxon, seeing her look of abject terror had never felt so helpless in his whole life.

Sebastian had known right away that Toni was in trouble, his link with her was very solid. He chuckled, maybe he was more open to the younger pretty ones, the ones he'd like to swive, although he didn't recall a connection this strong, before. The holy artefacts were going to be found soon and returned to their rightful place. Would that pave his way into heaven, or were his own sins too great? How could he atone for something when he wasn't sorry, and what would his lovely girl think of him when she found out the truth?

Toni felt two hands on her thighs, she began to kick her legs from the knees down, the only part that had free movement.

'A most shapely bottom, tis hard to concentrate on what I must do.'

'Oh my *God,* Sebastian, is that you?'

'Of course, tis me. Wouldst I allow another to feast his eyes on thy predicament?'

Before she felt herself starting to move backwards, Toni felt definite stroking on her inner thigh. The hands lingered there far too long. Finally, she was manoeuvred and turned and Sebastian loomed right above, his mouth inches above her own.

'Mine dearest wench, thou art safe.' He dropped a kiss on the top of her head and disappeared, materialising almost instantly on the cave floor below, where he waited for her to join him.

Saxon scrabbled back through the tunnel and climbed down the rocks in record time, his arm now possessively around Toni's shoulders. 'I thought you said this cave was somewhere you couldn't appear, and how did you know we were here?'

'I hath said I cannot be in the tunnels, I know not why certain areas art forbidden. Heigh-ho, verily this cave is fine. In answer to thy question, I shalt always know if ye needs me.' He took Toni's hand, turned it over and, bringing it to his lips, kissed her wrist. 'That took a gross amount from me, to physically hold ye about the legs and pull.' He didn't mention the willpower it had taken not to fondle her more. 'I shalt take mine leave now.' He turned to Saxon. 'Wast the tunnel still open?'

'Yes,' he answered, a little sullenly. There something going on, certain looks, things that weren't there a few weeks ago. He was glad Toni was unhurt, she'd been genuinely frightened, he just wished he had freed her himself.

'Good, dost not forget, right, right left.'

Toni gripped Saxon's hand, 'I think we should leave too. How are we going to pretend we know the way?' she asked as they emerged into the daylight. 'Leo will want to be in the lead with you, so you're going to have to encourage him to follow somehow.'

'Yeah that's going to be tricky, he'll have his own ideas, like taking alternate rights and lefts, which normally I'd suggest as well.'

They'd reached the dinghy and because the tide had gone out further, had to walk with it. 'It is heavy, I'm glad we didn't carry it down the cliff path at Shingles,' Toni commented after a short distance. 'I'll bring a smaller bag next time as well.'

'Are you okay now? I'm sorry I snapped, I got a bit scared myself.' He admitted.

'I'm fine, thanks and it was bloody stupid, you were quite right.'

The journey back seemed much quicker, Saxon dropped her at the door rather than the lane. Beverly came out and waved when she heard the car.

'I think you'll win Mum over quite quickly.' Toni smiled. 'See you tonight, I'll walk down with Leo.'

He nodded not wanting to kiss her in front of her mother. A few minutes after he'd left, Toni had a text.

'Looking forward to it XXX'

Chapter Thirteen

'Very well, Lucifer it is'

Some months previously, Robert Davidson had started looking into, what he considered were a few rather worthless fields for his client, Linus Thorpe. He'd listened carefully to the schemes and nodded politely, knowing there wasn't a hope in hell of Martin Ravel selling one inch of his land to the Thorpes. But, if Linus wanted him to start proceedings, he'd take his money, he was screwing the poor sod's wife so a few grand between friends was nothing.

More recently, he'd decided it was time to at least take a tentative look at the job, and was surprised to find the land didn't belong to Martin Ravel, but actually his younger daughter. The previous owner being a resident of Glen-Croft Nursing Home, another Antonia Ravel, this one, in her late seventies. Following a bit of digging in his father's filing cabinet, he found copies of the transfer of land and also a cottage, to Olivia Ravel, Martin's other daughter. Why would the two girls be given gifts, where the values differed so drastically? More rummaging turned up Antonia Ravel's will and two letters, one addressed to Alexander Thorpe and one to Antonia (Toni) Ravel, her great-niece.

Curious as to what she would have to say to a Thorpe, he decided regretfully, against tampering with both envelopes and slipped Alexander's back into place. A door closed softly and he swung around to look who was there. The apprentice, Annie, was still around, that was alright, she wouldn't suspect anything, he had every right to look at files of his father's if he chose to.

He pocketed Toni's letter and read it later at home, planning to replace it the next day. The contents, if true were astounding, he had to get his hands on that land and the best way would be through Linus.

Feigning surprise during a recent phone call as Linus informed him that Toni Ravel owned the land, and as luck would have it, was going out with Saxon. Robert listened politely, his would-be business partner playing right into his hands.

'How opportune,' Robert enthused. 'Much easier than having to deal with Martin. Would Linus consider a sleeping partner, on this venture? He'd recently freed up some money and would like to reinvest.' Linus had agreed to think about it.

The following Saturday afternoon, just at a climactic moment, Robert's phone lit up. As soon as he was physically able, he rolled off Vanessa, watched her scurry away into the bathroom, wonder how satisfied he was actually feeling and listened to his voice mail. A yes, from Linus.

Vanessa must have thought his look of pure gratification was due to her performance, she couldn't have been more wrong. Neither golf partner nor current sexual dalliance would know the reason he was so ecstatic.

The only small problem was that he'd lost the damn letter, and so, couldn't return it to the folder containing the will and other papers.

* * *

As very often happened on his way out, Saxon had been waylaid by Vanessa. Passing her bedroom, he'd heard, 'Saxon darling, will you zip me up?' How bloody inappropriate was that? She'd *almost* made a grab for him, but either changed her mind at the last minute or he, sensing her intention, had taken a step back just in time.

He took great pleasure mentioning that Toni was spending the next day here, with him. Her face had been a picture, as much as was possible with her inability to show any emotion from the fillers and Botox. *Why* did she have all that stuff done, she was only thirty-one, and attractive. Not his sort, but he had to admit she looked good. Was it really for his father's benefit? The two of them hardly seemed to notice each other these days. Linus spent at least three evenings a week at the golf club, whilst Vanessa, disappeared every Wednesday, and Saturday. They certainly appeared to have a wide circle of friends that they preferred to socialize with separately.

He was still brooding on it when he entered the pub, his eyes sought Toni out immediately. She always dressed casually but looked so bloody gorgeous, even now in jeans and a short bright red top, she could run rings around Vanessa and her designer gear.

Perhaps what Sebastian had said was correct, they'd had to go through a kind of *rite of passage* to come out at the other end and see each other in a different light. Whatever it was, he was filled with an inner contentment, it felt right, him and her, and even though it was very early days, and things were a bit tentative, he knew without any doubt, it was going to work.

Toni rushed across as soon as she saw him enter the Swingers.

'Are you that pleased to see me?' he grinned.

'Don't be daft, I came to waylay you.' She saw his grin start to fade. 'Well, yeah I'm pleased as well,' she stretched up and gave him a quick kiss. 'I thought we'd get some drinks and take our time.' Rolling her eyes in Leo's direction, Saxon saw him talking animatedly to Toni's friend.

'Ah I get it, give the lovely Annie a chance to work her magic.'

'You're beginning to sound like Sebastian, that's the sort of thing he'd say.'

'I'm not sure how to take that?' he said, sounding a bit affronted.

'Just don't start saying heigh-ho, or singing, Hey Nonny-Nonny.'

'Saxon gave a laugh. 'Come hither to the bar then, wench.' His eyes twinkled, 'What are we all having?'

They put the drinks and some bags of crisps on a tray, Toni started to delve into her huge bag for her purse, which had to be there somewhere. Saxon arched a brow and paid the barman quickly.

'I wanted to pay for them.' Toni protested.

'I'm sure you did, love, but we'd be here all night.' He eyed her bag with derision and looked away before she noticed. 'Have you said anything yet?'

'No, that was something else I wanted to talk to you about. The whole point of telling Leo, was so we'd have someone on the outside who knew where we were, should anything go wrong. Now we've decided to ask them to go with us, all four of us could be trapped or worse.'

'You're right,' he said thoughtfully, 'what do you want to do?'

Toni was pleased that he was asking her opinion, she knew Sax liked to take charge of things. 'It would be *fun* to all go. I'm sure if we're really careful and marked our way properly, it'll be okay.'

'And you leave that great haversack at home.' He indicated at her shoulder bag.

Toni put up with Leo and Saxon's juvenile handshakes, greetings and silly behaviour for the time it took to finish the first round of drinks, by then she'd had enough. Annie, on the other hand, didn't really care what Leo did, as long as she was with him when he did it.

By the time Leo had returned with more drinks, Toni decided if they didn't start the tunnel discussion soon, it wouldn't happen at all tonight. 'Guess what?' she nudged her brother's arm to get his attention. 'When we were out in the boat, Sax and I found a cave, and there's a tunnel behind it, fancy coming with us to have a look?'

Leo looked at Sax feeling a little hurt that it hadn't been him in the boat discovering caves and tunnels. He quickly resolved that that was the way it was going to be from now on. Plastering on a smile, he asked, 'When are we going?'

'Well, if Annie wants to come as well it'll have to be a weekend and the tide has to be right.' Toni said quickly before the boys started arranging things and taking over.

'We can only reach it using the dinghy.' Saxon explained. He got his phone out and they all waited patiently while he checked a few things. 'Weather's okay for Sunday, it wouldn't be much fun if we got there soaking wet, and... the tide is, good at...'

'Christ, get on it with.' Toni interrupted, 'how long does it take to look that up?'

'Patience.' He turned the phone so she could see it was taking a while to load. 'The signal's crap in here.'

'Switch the sodding data on then, Scrooge.'

'Yeah, why didn't I think of that?' It had been on all along, but he gritted his teeth and didn't say anything. 'Here we go, half twelve. Is that okay for everyone?'

Toni glanced at Leo, they were both thinking of Sunday lunch. 'We'll tell Mum the four of us are going out to eat.' *If she thinks Leo and Annie are out together, she won't say no.*

'Well, that's exactly what we'll do then, we just won't be going to any restaurants.' Saxon said. 'Make sure it's just a few sandwiches or a cold pasty, something to eat, as we're walking. The first tunnel is very narrow, we won't get food hampers through it.' He raised his eyebrows, but seeing the look on Toni's face, didn't elaborate.

'Yeah most likely if we keep heading right or eastwards, it'll take us parallel along the coast to the main caves.' Leo said.

'Actually, we *think* it may run north, and Toni and I decided if there are forks we're going to have a kind of route which we'll map out as we go.'

'That's a good idea,' Annie piped up. 'If it does join up with the main tunnels, it would have been discovered years ago. Far more likely, it goes in the other direction, or inland. If it doesn't just end right away.'

Leo looked at her excited face, he knew Toni was trying to set him up with her friend. He'd resisted before because he was away and also just to make a point. She was quite cute though, and clever. Her apprenticeship at Davidson and Son was just part of her studying. With a weekly day release to the local college, plus extra coursework online, she hoped to eventually get a job in the law courts. It was refreshing to talk about something other than agriculture and with a pretty girl as well.

Annie was still in a heightened state of excitement over the thought of exploring possible undiscovered tunnels, and best of all doing it with Leo. 'I wonder if they will reach as far as the woods?'

Saxon smiled at her enthusiasm, he could see why she and Toni were such good friends, they were very alike in many ways. 'I guess we'll find out on Sunday, I'll get some kid's chalks, the giant stuff, and we'll make a map as well. Now then who's having another drink?'

It wasn't a late night, both Leo and Annie had to be up early. Toni had the next two days off, this three-day week had its advantages, but she had to admit to getting pretty bored. Now she and Sax really were going out together, she let her mind wander to his offer of a job. Maybe she'd mention it again when her dad had had some time to come to terms with things.

'Mum's picking me up on her way home from work, Annie informed them. I'm sure she'd drop you home, Sax, if you wanted a lift, it's a long walk otherwise.'

'Yeah, thanks, Annie.' He glanced at Leo, 'You are going home now, right?'

'Course I am, why?'

Toni began to laugh. 'He doesn't want me walking home on my own, I mean, bloody hell, it's half past ten, anything could be lurking out there, axe murderers, sexual deviants, ghosts!'

'Very funny,' Saxon pulled a face. 'Just bring an extremely tiny bikini tomorrow. I'll make us lunch and eat it while I'm staring at you.'

Toni felt her cheeks getting warm. 'I'll see what I can do.'

'What are you doing for the rest of week Toni?' Annie asked.

'Err,' she tried to concentrate, 'With Sax tomorrow and then Wednesday, I may nip over and clean the cottage for Olly. She's gone to stay with Joshua's mum for a couple of days. Thursday and Friday, I'm working.'

Leo made a snorting noise into his beer, and Annie looked at her oddly. 'Blimey, you must be bored, if you're actually volunteering to *clean*.'

Saxon had had a bit too much to drink, but he still took everything on board. Toni had too much time on her hands and not enough paid work. With any luck, if things carried on as they were, he'd make sure she had a job, running the spa, or working on reception, or maybe managing the restaurant. A *smart cookie,* Grandad had called her. She could also look into the nature reserve she so badly wanted. If it was possible, he'd help her achieve it, and enjoy every minute. When had he started to care quite so much? Always, he answered his own question, even during the years they weren't speaking. At university, he'd gravitated towards dark-haired, dark-eyed girls. His friends had made jokes about it, saying he definitely had a type. Now he knew why there was only one blonde he'd ever be interested in, and she was right here.

* * *

Linus recognised Rita's car as it pulled into the drive, only a minute after his own. For a moment, nothing made sense. Rita, here? he'd just said goodnight to her at the back of the golf club, a quick kiss and a promise, for a day out together soon. He'd waved her off and gone back inside to finish a conversation about Stanley Uxbridge's handicap. It couldn't have been more than ten minutes, what could have happened between then and now? When he saw Saxon getting out he went cold, had they been found out? Did his son know he was having an affair? If the worst happened he'd admit it, pay Vanessa off and marry Rita like a shot, he loved her after all.

Linus watched Annie, who he now knew was her daughter, wave goodbye and say something about Sunday. He had to admit to a huge feeling of relief. As much as he wished his desires to become reality, he had to get rid of his present wife first. She was also having an affair, he was sure of it. Just a while longer to sort some money out and then he'd hire a private detective. With any luck, he could serve up the divorce papers with the Christmas turkey.

* * *

The van was making a most unhealthy noise. Toni chose to ignore it and focussed her thoughts on Saxon instead. Only a few weeks ago she'd just about have managed a polite greeting of some kind, now she couldn't wait to see him and share another kiss or three.

Oxeye announced her arrival, by barking madly and jumping at the van. Saxon eyed the old Astra and tried not to show the contempt he held it in. He'd heard the exhaust banging and a grinding noise as she'd slowed to a halt. It hadn't needed one of the dogs to warn him she was here.

The driver's door was flung open, causing a loud clunking noise in the hinges. 'Hey.' Toni grinned, oblivious to all imperfections in her beloved vehicle. She reached down and patted Oxeye who was almost euphoric to see the red trainers again. 'Have we got the pool to ourselves?' she asked hopefully.

'Pretty much, but there is a slight change of plan, come in and I'll tell you about it while you get changed.' She started to laugh and he realised what he'd just implied. 'I meant, after,' he grinned.

Toni threw a sarong around the small red bikini and walked with a confidence, she didn't feel, towards the pool.

'Wow,' Saxon exclaimed as the sarong came off.

Her confidence soared for real. Today was going to be most enjoyable if she could bait him that easily.

'Do you want a swim, or just sunbathe?' He asked.

'Do you have any floaty things?' Those would be the first items she'd buy if she ever owned a swimming pool.

Saxon opened the lid of a large oak locker and pulled out exactly what she'd hoped for. 'We've only got one lilo at the moment, Dad broke the other and we all keep forgetting to replace it. We'll have to share.' He waggled his eyebrows suggestively.

'Go on then.' She hid her smile and slid into the water, which thankfully was heated.

They played like the two children they had once been, pushing each other off and tipping the lilo over. Unlike children, however, were the touches, gropes and strokes, which led to the inevitable kissing and cuddling on the inflatable, just as Vanessa made a grand appearance to announce she was going out. No amount of plumping makeup would compensate for the almost invisible line her lips morphed into. She refrained from banging any of the doors on her way out, glad that they hadn't seen her. The time couldn't come soon enough to leave this place. Linus had no idea she was frequently syphoning small amounts of his money into her own account. With any luck, it would all be over by Christmas.

'Grandad's asked me to go and view a puppy with him later.' Saxon finally revealed.

'Oh, that means our afternoon will be over sooner than I thought.' Toni tried to hide her disappointment.

'I could say no, but he doesn't ask me for much, and it's over forty miles, I'd rather he didn't drive, plus it's easier to put the small cage in the back of the jeep.'

'That's okay of course you must go. What time?'

'He's arranged to be there at three o'clock, but when I told him you were here, he suggested you come as well.'

Toni was about to say forty miles in a confined space with Satan was one step too far, but with Sax nuzzling her neck, she didn't want to go home early. 'I'd like that.' She spotted a large wooden shed and assumed Linus and Vanessa had installed a sauna. 'What's that?' she asked, pointing towards it.

'I'll show you.' Saxon took her hand and they walked around the side of the house. 'Do you remember I told you the dogs don't stay in the house at night?'

Toni nodded. Now they were closer, she could see a large flap on the side which opened into a small wired compound. Inside was quite roomy as well and there were dog beds, extra blankets on shelves and even a heater. 'Not a bad kennel, it looks cosier than my bedroom.'

'Don't exaggerate,' Saxon laughed, but yeah it is pretty luxurious. They don't roam the land at night like the Baskerville Hounds, but they would certainly bark enough to frighten anyone off that shouldn't be here.'

'Pity about the sauna though.'

'Sauna? Is that what you thought it was? That's over with the hot tub.' Saxon pointed to another covered area. He didn't mention he never used it if Vanessa was around. Being stuck in there once with her was one time too many. He'd actually felt quite terrified when she hinted at having nothing on under her robe. Thankfully she'd been joking, but he was quite sure she'd have stripped completely if he'd so much as looked interested. 'Wait till you come and visit in the winter. I'll stock up on the birch twigs. If you say yes, it could be valorous!'

Toni started to laugh. 'Yes, to the sauna, but *no* birch twigs.' She laughed again when he pretended to look sad. 'I'm hungry now, is it lunchtime?'

Saxon removed the hot cheese and ham pizza from the oven and placed it on a wooden board. He used a wheel to slice it and heaped salad leaves with some kind of fragrant oily dressing onto Toni's plate.

'This isn't shop bought. Bloody hell, Sax, you've made the base and everything, it tastes fuc... bloody good.'

He arched a brow but didn't comment on her *almost* swearing. 'To be honest, I usually buy the bases, it was only last night I realised there weren't any in the freezer. So, you're properly honoured, Miss Ravel.' Toni grinned and tucked into another two slices of the delicious pizza.

When lunch was finished they went back outside, lay down together on the double circular sunbed, pulled the shade over the top and promptly fell asleep. It was only Alexander surreptitiously clearing his throat a couple of hours later, that had Saxon looking at his phone. 'Oh hell, is it that time?'

'Time to see the puppies?' Toni mumbled groggily.

'Yeah, you'd better put some clothes on first though, I don't think Grandad's heart would take that skimpy red number too well.' He reached over and handed her the sarong.

With Saxon doing the driving, Toni automatically started to get in the back. She felt Alexander's hand on her arm.

'I've already cut your afternoon short. Please sit in the front, next to Saxon.'

Toni smiled gratefully. Alexander Thorpe kept surprising her.

* * *

Six robust and bright-eyed Doberman pups leapt up, wagging their tails. Toni was amazed to see the change in Alexander, he looked like a young boy in a sweetshop.

'This is going to take a while.' Saxon warned her.

There was more dog noise coming from another room, Mrs Gently, the breeder, smiled. 'Come and have a quick look,' she beckoned to Toni. 'Our little collie cross came into season at the same time, it's entirely my own fault, I just didn't think.'

The pups were smaller and to Toni's mind, a lot cuter. 'Wow look at these, Sax, aren't they adorable, perhaps your grandad would take something different for a change?' She picked up what was obviously the runt of the litter. 'I could easily take you home,' she kissed the squirming mass on its head and looked wistfully at the others.

Saxon smiled. Watching Toni play with the puppies tugged on his heartstrings. He disappeared outside and searched the contacts on his phone. 'Bolly, can you do me a favour? I need you to speak to one of your parents...'

A great deal of conferring was taking place in the other room. Toni re-joined them just as a decision had finally been made.

'This is the one.' Alexander announced, looking pleased. 'Not too withdrawn or skittish and just as importantly, not overly energetic.'

'Very sweet.' Toni said her mind on the other little puppy.

'*Sweet!* Good Lord, intelligent, healthy, confident, those were the words I was hoping for. Tell me, Toni, what would you name him?' He obviously expected something utterly ridiculous or girly, whichever the case, it wouldn't be an option.

'Lucifer,' she said without even thinking.

'That was quick.'

'I was um, inspired.' She hid a smile.

'Very well, Lucifer it is. Now then, Mrs Gently, let's have a look at the mongrels.'

'You're a good customer, Mr Thorpe, this is the fourth pup we've sold you over the years and been grateful for your stud dog from time to time. If you want one of the little Doberman/Collie crosses, you're welcome, no charge.'

'That's very generous,' he homed in immediately on the largest, and Toni sat back, a bit surprised but resigned at being here for another hour.

'She wants the *little* one, Grandad.' Saxon whispered.

'She would, that pipsqueak is half the size of his brother. Hell, he's smaller than the bitches.' He turned his attention to the runt and was pleased to see it might be on the small side, but otherwise looked healthy and seemed to have a good temperament. 'Are you sure about this, Saxon? If she refuses it'll be your responsibility.'

Saxon grinned. 'I know but she won't refuse, she's been playing with him for ages. Leo's sounded Martin out, he said yes, so no problem.'

'Does he know it's a gift from you?' He asked dubiously.

'Yeah, I guess so, but at the end of the day he's a buy one get one free, Toni can always play that card.'

Toni leapt up when she saw Alexander inspecting the little tricolour pup. She tugged Saxon's sleeve. 'Is he really interested in that one? That would be fantastic, I could come out for walks with you and see him.'

'What about a name for *this* little specimen?' Alexander directed the question to Toni, once again. 'He's certainly not a Lucifer.'

'No, he's much cuter. All your other dogs look like their names. This one really wouldn't suit being called Bloodaxe or Deathray. I'm not really sure.'

'What would you call him if he was *yours*?' Saxon asked. Ignoring a slight spluttering noise emanating from his grandfather's direction.

'Quando.' she smiled. 'I always wanted Dad to use that name when we used to have dogs, but he never would.'

One sensible decision by Martin Ravel. Alexander thought. 'I'll take the little one, Mrs Gently. Is he ready to go today?'

'You've surprised me with that choice.' She smiled, looking at Toni and wondering just how much influence she'd had with the selection. 'He's ready, all vaccinations and worming are finished. I have four viewings next week, you came just at the right time.'

'Jolly good,' *I doubt he'd have been chosen, but still.* 'Saxon, get the boot ready, we have the travel cage for Lucifer, but Toni will have to sit in the back with... Doombringer on her lap.'

'*Doombringer*!' She saw Alexander's eyes twinkle. 'Oh, you're joking, very funny. What *will* you call him?'

'Quando of course,' Saxon answered as if it was obvious. 'He's yours, Toni.'

'He's m-mine? Oh, Sax, I'd *love* to have him but I'll have to check at home first.'

'All done, love, Leo's asked your mum and dad, and they said yes.'

She didn't know what to say and just wrapped her arms around Saxon, pressing a small kiss to his lips. The puppy somewhat squashed between them gave a tiny 'yip' and stretched up to lick whoever's chin was nearest.

Chapter Fourteen

'Throw a spanner?'

The cottage was in sight, at last, it had been a longer drive than Toni remembered, and the van was making even worse noises. '*Please* don't give up on me,' she tapped the steering wheel, 'I can't afford to replace you just yet.' Not having slept particularly well, due to going downstairs three times in the night when Quando started whining, she wasn't at her best. A breakdown in these remote narrow lanes, would not be good.

Luckily, Beverly had fallen instantly in love with the friendly puppy and cancelled her hair appointment so she could stay and keep him company. Without the pressure of having to rush back, Toni could at least take her time searching and even clean a little if absolutely necessary.

The sheds and attic were the most likely places to begin. Here, on her own for the first time ever, Toni began to realise the value of the place. It had never bothered her before, now for some reason, it did.

Antonia had carried on living here after the deeds had been changed. That had been part of the agreement. Toni thought more carefully about it. Olivia may own the building, on paper, but it could have been many years before she could sell or rent. If not for dementia, their great-aunt may well have resided here, quite happily for another twenty years. She admonished herself for the earlier bout of envy.

The loft hatch was secured, previous tenants not having access. Toni remained hopeful there were things lying undisturbed and discoveries to be made. Dragging a chair from one of the bedrooms she gingerly stretched up and made a grab for the padlock. Success, the first key on the ring fitted easily, the lock sprung open and the hatch fell by the hinges, nearly knocking her out in the process. Now all she had to do was find the light switch and pull the ladder down.

* * *

'A *nature* reserve,' Robert Davidson sneered. 'Are you serious?'

Linus nodded and scanned the view of the coastline from one of Toni's fields. 'This would be a lovely place to build a house... or fifty.'

Robert wasn't really listening, he was more intent on trying to find a clue as to where something could have been concealed hundreds of years ago. Christ, it was going to be like finding a needle in a haystack. But, if this so-called Sapphire-Heart was anything like he was imagining, it could be worth millions. 'Do you still want me to look into planning, Linus?' There wasn't a hope in hell of getting it, but he had to keep him interested. 'I'm quite confident if we don't rush things, I can get it through. Buy it now, sit on it for two or three years and then we'll reap the rewards. The Ravel girl will be happy with some money in her pocket. Just persuade her it'll be enough to start her sanctuary crap a bit further down the coast, away from all the dog walkers and holiday ramblers, or whatever.'

Having got to know Toni a little, Linus doubted very much if she'd go for it. He'd have to convince Saxon they'd be doing her a great favour. 'Don't spend any money just yet, Rob. Find out what you can. The new builds at Primrose Rise are all but finished and I can commit to this properly then. If you don't need my input anymore today, I'll be off.'

'That's fine, I'll wander around a bit and see if there's anything we can use to our advantage as prospective buyers.' Robert walked in the opposite direction to Linus. There had to be some kind of marker or small hillock, *anything* which would give an indication of where a priceless treasure could be buried. Surely whoever put it there, would have wanted to retrieve it someday. How many years ago was it buried? The information in the letter was sketchy. Looking around he now realised he'd have to advise Linus to buy the full twenty-eight acres, that wouldn't be so easy, his client was only interested in the first three fields, the ones not being farmed. Of course, the whole thing *could* be nonsense, which was why he wanted to use Linus' money. If by some miracle, planning *was* granted, then he'd be quids in whether or not the necklace existed. If it all came to nothing, well, the contract would be dissolved, *wording* was everything, he'd play Linus Thorpe at his own game.

From the fields above, Saxon was watching. He'd seen the Rolls winding its way through the narrow lanes, it was pretty hard to miss. Stopping what he was doing he could just make out Robert Davidson. Damn it, Toni would go mad if she knew his dad was still interested in her land. She'd made it plain enough over dinner, a wildlife park, or nature reserve was what she wanted. He'd already started looking into things and when the time was right he planned to surprise her with a few facts and figures.

Saxon loved his father but right now, he didn't like him very much.

* * *

'How's the cleaning going? Bet u look hot in a little apron!! ☺ XX' Toni smiled at the text but wasn't in a position to answer it at that precise moment. Carefully walking across wooden beams, as the loft had never been boarded, she was making her way to the second of three large trunks. The first had been stuffed full of tablecloths and other linens, yellow with age. They were, at least dry, and spider free. She'd had to take out and replace every item, not wanting to miss a notebook which could have been placed between coronation tea towels and knitted tea-cosies.

The second trunk contained clothing, and handbags. Again, a thorough search was needed but apart from hairgrips, a hair net, safety pins and an old Victorian penny, there was nothing. Beginning to feel hot and uncomfortable and still having to balance on beams, Toni lifted the lid of the third and last trunk. It was full to bursting with books. If a diary was going to be anywhere it would be here, but this was going to take ages.

Two hours later and two-thirds of the way down, her prayers were answered with not one, but three diaries. She sat down carefully on top of the trunk and checked the dates. 1957, Antonia would have been seventeen years old. Toni struggled with the light of the one small bulb to read the first entry.

I saw him again today, Father would be very angry. Alexander and Sebastian are so much alike.

She dropped the small book in surprise. This could be her writing about Saxon and Sebastian. She picked up another one, it mentioned the Queen's coronation on the first page, that would have been 1953. Flipping to the end of the third and last diary, it was dated December 2010.

My seventieth birthday has prompted me to put pen to paper one last time. Everything that's important is either recorded on these pages, or in the hands of Davidson &

Son, Solicitors. I have loved two men but can only leave a written message for one of them. My sister Rachel's children have all been left some items of jewellery. My will states who gets what, and how it can be retrieved.

I loved my brother Oliver the best, and so, my nephew Martin and his family will get the lion's share. I don't care if it's fair, I'm doing exactly as I wish. Had I done that fifty years ago, things would be very different. Leo will inherit the farm, from his parents, as is right and proper. I have decided to gift my cottage to Olivia and all the paperwork has already been signed. I suspect she will be the one to find and read this diary.

Toni felt a bit guilty but carried on regardless when she saw her own name appear.

Antonia, my namesake, will have my land and that also has already been signed over. She is the only one in this family that always sees two sides to everything, and in this particular circumstance, an open mind will be essential. The letter I have left with my will holds the explanation of why it is more valuable than she will ever imagine. I hope the girls have found Sebastian, he will be invaluable with the recovery of the Sapphire-Heart. I only wish I'd had the motivation to find it myself. Sadly, I lost the inclination after everything that happened. There is a chance the necklace doesn't exist, then again if it does, Antonia will be rich beyond her wildest dreams.

The words on the page began to morph together in the bad light. There was still more on the last page to read, something about a trust for Flora. Not to mention the other two notebooks, full of her aunt's spidery writing. The childhood scribblings in the first diary may hold secrets about the family, things her father didn't know or didn't want to tell them. She packed everything else away carefully and climbing back down the ladder sealed the hatch and made her way downstairs.

Remembering the earlier text, she sent Saxon a quick reply. **'Not a good scrubber, my bad. Fancy a walk with Quando tomoz? How's Lucifer? xoxo'** She'd planned to ask him to meet up tonight, but Antonia's diaries were calling. Especially after a mention of Alexander, Sebastian *and* the sapphires, plus another name, Flora? She needed to re-read those pages carefully.

'Tomoz good, Lucifer pissed all over Vanessa's handbag ☹ Got a spare collar and lead you can have XX' Toni quickly replied before the drive back. **'Lol is it all chains studs and Doberman like? I was thinking a nice blue one xx'** She heard the notification a few minutes later but had to wait until she arrived home to read what he'd said. One day she'd have a car with Bluetooth!

'Ungrateful wench, tomoz then with BLUE collar. FYI I'll keep the studded one just 4 u! XX' She went red, even though it was a joke and no one could see her. Keeping the three diaries concealed in her large shoulder bag, dropped the cleaning stuff in the kitchen and found her new puppy asleep on her mother's lap, in the lounge. Thank goodness the cottage had been relatively clean because she'd run out of time and resorted to spraying air freshener into every room on her way out.

After supper, Toni took Quando and the first of the diaries into the barn. She shut the doors so that he could play safely and also learn that farm cats should not be messed with.

Reading these girlhood memories, Toni got a feeling of a dreamy fanciful child living within the bounds of a strict household. The very first entry had been made during 1950 when Antonia would have been ten years old. She wrote mostly about helping Mother and Grandma Eunice in the kitchen. There were a few paragraphs about school and occasionally a whole page about her life as a pirate or woodland fairy.

Some of the ramblings were so ridiculous or faded that Toni almost missed the mention of Alexander's name. She slowed down a bit and tried hard to imagine Sir Alexander Goodly, brave knight of King Arthur standing high at the top of Smugglers' Knoll, while the damsel in distress, Lady Antonia Fairface, watched from below as he vanquished a dragon. These games were not unlike the ones she'd once played with Leo, Olly and Sax. Toni struggled to read the date, June 13th, 1952, that would make her aunt twelve years old and Alexander, thirteen or fourteen? So, they played together? There were a few more mentions of him, usually with other children's names as well.

Something that did catch her eye near the very end of the diary, was the mention of The Hunters' Stones. Only one person, or ghost to be correct, called them that. Saxon had Googled the name after their first encounter. Smugglers' Knoll got a small mention, *A large pile of natural stones, a popular landmark within Raven Wood.* It went on to name the village and county, there was no reference to the Hunters' Stones at all.

Desperate to start reading the second diary, Toni told her parents she was having a long soak in the bath and going to bed straight after to read her novel. Quando found Beverly's lap and her father gave a dismissive goodnight wave.

Martin was still thinking about the missing letter and was undecided whether or not to mention it. Henry would most likely find it amongst his other files, and it wasn't meant to come to light until the reading of the will anyway. Beverly had taken a call from the senior nurse at Glen-Croft to inform them that Antonia appeared to have improved now she was back in familiar surroundings but was running a slight temperature and seemed very sleepy. All this was on his mind. If his aunt should die, he wanted everything in order and that included any last wishes, either in her will or in those letters.

Midnight came and went. Toni had work in the morning, but she'd reached a really interesting point and didn't want to stop reading. The year was 1956, Antonia had just celebrated her sixteenth birthday. The entries were inconsistent, sometimes three days in a row if something was happening, and then maybe nothing for a few weeks.

I thought now I'm not a schoolgirl anymore, Alex would be more interested. He still treats me like one of his sisters. Everything's about Margaret May, now!! Margaret this, Margaret that, I hate Margaret May!!! She's taking him away from me!!!!

There were a few blotches on the paper, which made it difficult to read. Toni wondered if they might be tear stains.

I haven't seen Sebastian for two weeks. I think he's angry because Alex doesn't believe me and won't come to meet him. I'll go and look for him tomorrow if I can get away from the farm. Father seems to watch me all the time. I daren't mention the name Alexander Thorpe anymore. For some reason, he's not keen on the family. Mother says it goes back to my grandfather and great-grandfather's time. She won't say what, but I found out from Grandma Eunice that it involved a drowning. I'm going to ask Sebastian, he tells me everything. I wish he was real I think I love him more than Alex!!

A drowning? Antonia's great-grandfather, that would be around the late 1800s or the turn of the century, perhaps. Toni made a few notes, something else to research. She flicked through a few pages looking for the names she was interested in, another time she would read them more thoroughly.

Alex put his arm around me today, I was so happy until he told me he's getting engaged to Margaret May. She's joining the WRENS.

There was a thin line through the next sentence, but Toni could still read it.

I hope she gets posted away and dies somewhere horrible and foreign. I didn't mean that. Maybe he'll forget her if she is sent abroad, or maybe she'll meet somebody else.

The entries jumped ahead another couple of weeks. Toni crept downstairs quietly to make a strong coffee, as long as she put her light out by two o'clock, she could get six hours sleep. That would give her another hour to read.

Toni's memory of her aunt, before she became ill, was of being very matter-of-fact. Everything black or white, no shades of grey whatsoever. Yet in these pages, she came across as a romantic whimsical young girl. What had happened to change her outlook on life? The failed romance with Alexander? It must have hurt her very badly if that was the reason.

Toni eventually saw the name she really wanted to read about, Sebastian's. Taking a large sip of coffee, she hardly noticed it was too hot and burnt her tongue. With a loud tut, she half-heartedly put the mug down and was oblivious as it overbalanced creating a large brown stain on the bedroom carpet. Fully immersed in the latest instalments of the teenage Antonia's life, Toni read until she eventually fell asleep at three thirty, the diary clutched tightly in her hand.

* * *

Pretty Feet was having a busy half hour. Mrs McKee had brought in four of her six children for holiday shoes. The equivalent would cost half the price in the supermarket by the Primrose estate, but village folk tended to support the local businesses and Toni felt that that should be applauded. The more she turned a blind eye to the mess being made on the racks by the two younger girls, the more their mother kept buying. By the time she'd finished, the children had an assortment of canvas casuals, flip-flops and trainers and Mrs McKee had two pairs of new sandals for herself. The bill was high and Toni, knowing most of this particular stock was going into the sale soon, offered a 10% discount. Karen was out for the morning, but she would be more than happy, she'd often encouraged Toni to do just that, especially with regular customers.

There was a lull, during which much tidying was required. For the fifteen items sold, there were twice as many waiting to be re-boxed, and the racks looked like Frank Carter's prize bull had been on a rampage around the shoe shop.

At least while she methodically put everything away, she could go back over what she'd been reading during the night. The necklace and the letter were still foremost in her mind, but for once, she'd forced herself to read everything in order and some of the revelations had left her reeling. If Toni hadn't known she'd be working alone this morning, she'd have been tempted to pull a *sickie*. Such was her need to find Sebastian and discover if Aunt Antonia's written account of what had happened with Alexander was actual fact, or a product of a fanciful imagination?

Flora. She'd spotted the name whilst still in the attic yesterday. Having now read more and realising exactly who she was, the possible implications for both families, were little short of astounding

The small bell on the counter dinged, not once, but half a dozen times. Pulled from her reverie Toni inwardly groaned when she heard Gus Littlejohn calling, *shop*, in an over-exaggerated fashion.

'Hi, Gus,' she put on her best professional smile. 'How can I help you?'

'I can think of any number of answers to *that* question.' He smirked. 'On your own?'

Toni groaned again, this time, loudly. 'Have you come for your dad's order or are you actually planning to spend some money of your own today?'

'Dad's boots,' he grinned. 'I'll have a pair of socks, that packet hanging up there.' He pointed to the display behind the counter and was most disappointed when Toni took a pole and hooked them down.

'You thought I was going to climb the ladder in front of you?' She rang them through the till without waiting for his answer. Gus was so predictable.

'You've got boring now you're shagging Sax Thorpe,' Gus grumbled. 'Who incidentally was your worst enemy until a few weeks ago.' He was still angry from his telling off in the Swingers, the night he'd wanted to drive her home.

'£4.99,' Toni said, pretending not to be fazed by that comment. Inside she was seething, how *dare* he say that? She produced two large carrier bags and put a box in each.

'What's he bought?'

'Hunter Balmoral Classics and Muck boots...err,' she jostled the box to read the label 'Scrub,' she finished. 'They're all paid for, tell him to bring them back if he needs a different size.'

Gus nodded and handed over a fiver for his socks. 'Keep the change,' he grinned sauntering towards the door.

'Gee thanks, asshat,' she mumbled dropping the penny into the charity box on the counter. *And by the way, you're deleted. I've slain you with my magic telephone.*

Karen was delighted with the morning's takings when she came in at lunchtime. Toni asked if she could forgo her break and leave earlier, which was fine. So, at half past three, she got in her van and drove as fast as she dared to the bottom of Raven Wood. Saxon was coming around after tea and she was looking forward to spending time with him and walking Quando. The puppy hadn't been on a lead yet, it would be quite an adventure for him. Right now, though, she had something more pressing to do.

The Hunters' Stones were far too busy with school children. A regular occurrence at this time of day. She headed east, taking the same route that Saxon had a few weeks before. When she was far enough away, she felt the air around her grow cold.

'Heigh-ho, wench, alone *again?*'

'This is personal stuff, nothing to do with Saxon,' she began. 'Well, perhaps it is indirectly.'

'I am pleased to see ye but get to the point.'

Toni tutted. 'Sorry if I'm keeping you from something, more bathing beauties to perv at perhaps?'

'Perv? I know not thy meaning Antonia, but I see ye art troubled. Mayhap a kiss shalt clear thy thoughts.'

Toni started to laugh. 'Nice try. I've found Antonia's diaries. And she *did* have a thing about Alexander, Sax's grandad. It also mentions the Sapphire-Heart necklace.'

'Verily tis important.' He moved closer.

Toni was very aware of Sebastian's body touching hers. It was becoming difficult to remain focused on why she was there. 'It *is* important yes, but who is Flora?'

'I know *not*.' He said, a little too emphatically.

'I think you do. My aunt wrote in her diary that we should ask you.'

'*We?*' She knew not that you wouldst be with Saxon. Methinks tis trickery, Antonia.'

'Me and my *sister*, I meant. It was obvious one of us would find her diaries eventually. I wouldn't trick you.' She gave him a beguiling smile and allowed herself to rub up against him a little. A soft sigh was the tell-tale sign that he'd been won around.

'In that case, Flora wast the name thine aunt gave to the babe she hadst with Alexander.'

Toni gave a small smile. *That's exactly what I thought.* 'She hinted at it, but even though she wrote her innermost feelings, I think she was afraid of someone finding it, her parents perhaps.'

'Or mayhap her sister, they didst not receive each other well.'

'Antonia and Rachel didn't get on? Is that the reason she gave me and Olly the cottage and land I wonder? What happened to the child? According to the diary, she asked for help. Alexander, that *bastard*, s-sorry Sebastian, but he was, didn't stand by her. He married Margaret.'

'Come sit, dear heart, dost not rail so.' He took her arm and guided her to a large tree trunk, which had lain there since the mighty oak had been toppled by lightning, years before. 'Alexander wast going to break his betrothal and doeth what was gallant. He travelled overseas to tell the lady in person.'

'So, he did know Antonia was pregnant and abandoned her anyway. Margaret was Saxon's grandmother, so in the end, he didn't do the right thing at all.'

'Dost not judge so harshly, mine girl, he is no doodlebug. Things art not always as they seem. Of what else doth the diary speak?'

'She went to see Alexander's father. It's hard to tell from the little bits she wrote. I do know that after seeing him, she ran away. That *poor* girl, seventeen years old, pregnant and afraid to tell her own family.'

Sebastian shook his head. 'She told her own father, also. He cast her from the house. Thou art correct that she went to seek aid from James Thorpe. That gent lacked valour, he didst not want his son mixed up with the Ravels. He told her that Alexander hadst gone to wed Margaret, and if she be wise, she wouldst wend somewhere far off and rid herself of the babe.'

'So, *both* fathers let her down. According to the diary, Alexander had told her he was going to break things off with Margaret. Obviously, when his father said differently she must have thought he'd been lying. Hang on though, why *didn't* he break it off, he'd already left England?'

'Thorpe hadst sent a… missive which arrives quicker than a gent can travel. I dost not recall the name.'

'A telegram?' she offered.

'Aye,' he shrugged, 'I bethink tis it. He told his son there wast no babe. Antonia hadst played him false to ensnare him.'

'Shit, I thought Alexander was bad, but his father takes the *bloody* biscuit.'

Sebastian let her swearing go, this time. He could see she was upset by all this new information and thought it best not to ask about the biscuit reference.

'Where did she have the baby?'

'Some miles hence. It wast given the name Flora, 'twas mine own suggestion. Hadst it been a strapping boy he wast to be named for me. Of course, hadst that been the case, Saxon wouldst not be here, as his father wouldst not exist.'

'*What*? why not?'

'Tis the curse I tell ye, one son for each generation. Alexander wouldst have had his share.'

'Sebastian, I'm sorry, but a curse is one step *too* far for me to believe. What happened to Flora?' She quickly asked before he could get angry.

'The child went to a Godfearing couple. Antonia visited here on occasion to see her brother and of course, mineself.'

'And what do the sapphires have to do with my aunt...' Sebastian's lips had found her own, she should push him away but it felt good and right now she wasn't thinking too kindly about the Thorpes.

As if reading her mind, and with the greatest willpower, he regretfully withdrew. 'I humbly beg thy pardon, I cannot control mineself, tis not Saxon's fault. And as for Alexander, ye hast to understand, Antonia wast relentless in her pursuit of him.'

'But she was so young.'

'Nay seventeen is hardly young, and the knave wast not much older. She flirted shamelessly. Oh, she loved him I warrant, but she still bethought if he swived her, he wouldst be hers.'

'So, what now, should I tell Sax he has an aunt? Linus has a sister and Dad has another cousin, bloody hell that would certainly throw a spanner in the works. They'd all be related to this one woman, who's quite possibly had children of her own.'

'Throw a *spanner*?'

'Forget it, like doodlebug, lock those words up in your head and don't use them.' She grinned, still feeling a bit embarrassed from her reaction over the kiss... *again*.

'I cannot say what thou shouldst do. Tell thy betrothed if tis the right thing. Or mayhap after ye hast found the holy treasure.'

'Hmm talking of which, about the necklace...'

'Finish reading the diaries, they speak of what I hath told ye this day. Find the church relics and we shalt speak anon. I must wend now, I find it hard not to misbehave with ye.'

* * *

199

Later that evening when Saxon had fastened a blue collar around Quando's neck and Toni realised he must have gone all the way to the pet shop in town to buy it, she kissed him. This new, exciting and still fragile relationship was too precious to put at risk. She would tell him everything about the diaries and Flora, after searching the tunnels. Then, the only secret between them would be her feelings for Sebastian, and they would stay well and truly buried from now on. There would be *no* third kiss.

Chapter Fifteen

'What is it with girls and their bladders?'

The next few days passed far too slowly for Toni's liking. She was looking forward to Sunday. Treasure hunting with Saxon, how cool did that sound?

Every so often she picked up the third diary, managing with great difficulty, to ignore the last page and methodically carry on from where she'd left off. The second one was finished and had pretty much reiterated what Sebastian had said. She kept wondering about the mention of the letters that were with the will. The one addressed to Alexander probably explained everything *he* needed to know. If it was the wish of her great-aunt to wait until she was dead before he found out, she ought to respect that. But, what *if* Alexander died first? It would be unlikely, given that Aunt Antonia, recovering from a minor stroke was now being treated for a chest infection but, it was possible. Also, there was the being honest with Sax, thing. If he kept a secret involving *her* family, she'd be really pissed off.

Friday evening was spent with the Thorpe's. Alexander had insisted she bring her puppy and she and Sax had taken all the dogs to the ruins. Lucifer and Quando wanted to keep running off, but Oxeye and Damocles seemed to keep the pups in line. Toni had to admit that Alexander certainly trained his dogs well.

Saxon, fished a folded card from his pocket. 'Olivia sent me a wedding invitation, but I'm obviously not allowed to bring my other girlfriend.' He showed her the *plus one*, it had a heavy black line through it.

'Trust Olly.' Toni laughed. 'Other *girlfriend*! Mess me around at your peril.' She gave Quando a shout, the little dog looked fleetingly in her direction before charging off with the pack. 'I was going to tell him to go for your throat, but it seems you've had a lucky escape.'

'How about you go for my throat instead?' Saxon pulled her close, kissed her and was unashamedly delighted when she gave his neck a small nip.

'Sorry couldn't resist.'

'Always follow your instincts love,' he smiled. 'Far more fun than sitting on the fence and wondering what might happen if you did or didn't.'

You wouldn't say that if you knew I'd kissed Sebastian. She pushed the thought firmly away and grabbed his hand, pulling him on towards the ruins. The weather had other ideas, a short summer shower caught them completely unprepared and they turned to hurry back to the house instead.

They were both laughing, despite being soaked. Saxon grabbed a towel from the bathroom and started to dry Toni's hair, which caused more frivolity. Vanessa's scowls made no impact, and Linus, flitting around in the background in the hope of dropping another hint about the land, slunk away, recognising now was not the best time.

The two puppies were given a quick, rough towelling by Alexander. He gave Quando the once over, snorted at the blue collar, but had to admit he was quite an engaging fellow. Lucifer, he noted with satisfaction, settled quickly with the older dogs while this little scamp jumped up, turned a few circles and found a comfortable spot cuddling into his lap. Not able to reach his mug of tea without disturbing him he sat back resignedly wondering if Toni had his grandson wrapped around her little finger as well.

'All set for Sunday?' Toni asked a little later as she ushered Quando into the passenger seat of the van.

'Chalk, torch, spare batteries, water... anything else?'

'Paper and pen I suppose, we may need to draw a proper map as well as chalk the way.'

'Yeah, good thinking, I'll get the dinghy with Bolly and we'll pick you and Annie up on Shingles.'

It seemed a lot of extra motoring for them, but aware her brother had taken a massive step back to give her time alone with Saxon, she quickly agreed and gave him a kiss goodnight.

The van had hardly moved before the usual rattle was followed by an unusual banging which ended with a very loud and definite thud. Toni was forced to get out and inspect the damage. 'I need my van. *Bloody* hell, I'll have to borrow some money from Dad to get it fixed.'

Alexander and Linus came out to see what all the commotion was. Part of the exhaust lay on the drive a few yards from where it should be.

'Can't I still drive home, no one will see at this time of night?'

'No but they'd certainly *hear*. I'll drop you back.' Saxon said firmly.

'And we'll get this sorted.' Linus offered. It wouldn't hurt to get in Toni's good books. He genuinely liked Saxon's girlfriend and any help they gave would annoy Vanessa. Win-win, he thought, a little wickedly.

She looked at each of the three men, not wanting to be beholden to the Thorpes but realising that now she was involved with Saxon it was inevitable. 'Thanks, Linus.' She was taken slightly aback by his beaming smile.

'No trouble at all, I'm sure Pete Alford will pick it up in the morning. We'll let him know you need it back asap.'

'Pete knows the van well.' She said, which caused all three men to hide a smirk. There was something reassuring in Linus choosing the garage her father used. 'Thank you very much, ask him to send the bill to the farm, please.'

It was less than a five-minute drive home. Saxon came around and opened the passenger door. She realised she took his good manners for granted most of the time. 'Thanks Sax, I really mean that.'

'Goodnight for a second time.' Saxon gave her another kiss, which was cut short due to Quando's whining for attention. 'What are you up to tomorrow?'

As much as she would have liked to see him again, the last diary needed finishing and it was Olivia's run through at the church. 'Dress rehearsal,' she said miserably. 'And I've promised Olly to help her pack up her room.'

'Ah okay, Sunday it is then.'

* * *

After waiting with Annie, on Shingle beach for what seemed like ages and then being relegated to the back of the dinghy, Toni wasn't in a very good mood by the time they were all standing in the small cave. Leo was already trying to take charge and had suggested a few strategies they should follow.

'I don't know how we're going to keep to the right, right, left that Sebastian told us.' Toni scowled. 'You're not taking this seriously.'

'Oh, my God, Ravel, did you really just say that? Come here.' Saxon ushered her to one side while Annie continued to sort out the snack lunch they'd brought with them. 'Did you miss me yesterday? Is that why you're acting all cranky, or are you just jealous of your brother?' He kissed her before she let loose a tirade of choice language. 'I can't seem to get enough of you, what's that about?'

'God knows, but it'll help keep you in your place.' She giggled and began to feel better.

Leo shone his torch towards the overhang. 'Put my sister down, Sax, you and I can go in first and lead the way.'

'Actually, Bolly, I've been thinking about this. From what I saw quickly the other day, the tunnel is fairly narrow. I think we should keep the girls in-between, just in case.'

'Do you think it *could* be dangerous? If so, Toni's not doing this.' He wanted to make a similar remark about Annie but thought better of it.

'It's far better they're with us, rather than following along afterwards on their own. You know that would happen.' He heard his friend give a resigned sigh and understood only too well. 'I'll go first and you can help the girls through the small opening up top.' He handed him the packet of thick chalks. 'We need to know our route is being marked properly, would you really trust either of them to do that?' It was a good thing Toni knew what this conversation was all about, but Annie didn't, and she was looking daggers at them and muttering something about 'sexist pigs'.

'Yeah, you're right.' Leo sounded a bit disappointed. 'Keep Toni behind you then.' He lowered his voice. 'If I've got to watch someone's ass the whole way through I'd rather it was Annie's. I can't get over how you two just happened to find this place by accident, what a stroke of luck. Even if it does only go a short way and hits a dead end, it's still a good afternoon out.'

Saxon nodded, thankful and a little surprised that it had gone quite so easily.

Without the encumbrance of any inappropriately sized hand luggage, they soon made it through the narrow tunnel. Then after a brief respite of being able to stand full height had to stoop almost double and follow the rocky passage in a steep incline for what Saxon guessed was approximately two hundred metres.

Toni's eyes were glued to his muscular backside. She was tempted to give it a quick fondle but afraid he may jump and hit his head on the low ceiling of rock, thought better of it.

When Saxon straightened to full height, he gave a murmur of appreciation at being able to stretch, they were still heading upwards but not so steeply. The first fork was also approaching, which Toni could just see, but Annie and Leo had their view blocked. 'Okay, Bolly get the chalk ready we're taking the right fork here.'

'Okay, what are we doing right, left, right, left?'

'That would make sense if we wanted to keep fairly straight.' Annie chipped in.

'We'll play it by ear, maybe go with gut instincts for a while, or see which tunnel looks easier. We can always come back and try something different.' Saxon hoped it wouldn't open up to a discussion.

Before her brother could protest, Toni agreed it was a good idea, why not be random? Leo shrugged, feeling a bit redundant at the back and marked the first turn with an arrow drawn with the pink chalk.

'Shall I plot in on the paper?' Annie asked, 'You don't want to have to do that as well.'

Leo handed the notebook and pen over. 'Are you okay with confined spaces?'

'It's a bit late if I'm not,' she smiled. 'Thanks for asking though. I hope we can walk upright the rest of the way, and it's not *all* uphill. I didn't realise how unfit I was. I suppose working in an office all day, isn't quite the same as being out and about in the great outdoors.'

Leo grinned. 'You'd be surprised how much time I spend doing paperwork. Come over one evening, I'll show you some of the new ideas if you're interested?'

She nodded enthusiastically, 'I'd love to, Mum works four evenings a week, so I get pretty bored home alone. Toni usually comes in at least once a week and we watch a film, but she's got more important things on her mind now.'

'You do go out though, right? Are you, err seeing anyone?'

'A boyfriend, you mean?' They'd started walking again, so she had to keep turning around. 'No, not for a while, what about you, anyone from uni?'

'I purposely steered away from relationships because I was planning another trip away, but... things are changing, Dad needs me here.'

'Toni mentioned something about Australia, was that it? You should go if it's what you really want to do.'

'We'll see, it was never important, just a fancy, I guess, a sort of *last stand* before settling down.'

'Leo, if you don't want this life, you should say, I had the opportunity to move away a few years back, live with my Dad, but I wouldn't leave Mum on her own. I think I love the village too much as well.' Annie hoped she wasn't sounding like some boring country maid. If Leo hadn't wanted a relationship with all those clever girls he'd been studying with, what chance did she have?

'I think I'd always come back to the farm eventually. Our ancestors have been here for hundreds of years, it must be in the blood.'

'I can't boast anything like that, I just like the village, I guess.'

Leo was so engrossed in the conversation he was having with Annie, that neither of them noticed when Saxon took another right fork. The quick left that followed was charted and marked, but by then the map was already incorrect.

After the first half an hour, the novelty of walking through the dark tunnels, trying to shine torches at their feet and ahead at the same time, was beginning to wear off. Toni listened to snatches of conversation going on behind her, she would have liked to talk to Saxon a bit more, but he was concentrating on the right, right, left thing and she daren't put him off.

The tunnel opened and thankfully there was room for all four of them to stand together. Annie handed the sandwiches around and officially declared it lunchtime. 'The air's a bit better here, we can't be too far below the surface.'

'Are we nearly there yet?' Toni refrained from putting on a childish, sing-song voice.

'We haven't come far enough, I doubt we've even cleared the woods.' Saxon felt Toni tugging at his arm. 'What is it?'

'I know exactly where we are. Look at the rock, it goes all the way to the top of the cavern.'

'The Hunters... err, Smugglers' Knoll.' Saxon exclaimed. 'We're right below it.'

'So, we're heading pretty much northeast then.' Leo said, 'Do you want to swap places for a while Sax?' he asked hopefully.

'I'll carry on a *bit* longer then you can take over.' He guiltily watched his friend grumble quietly and resume his place behind Annie.

'Don't feel bad,' Toni whispered, 'It was *our* discovery, after all, Leo can bloody well stay where he belongs, at the end.'

Saxon began to laugh and because the tunnel remained a little wider he was able to hold her hand for a while. The going remained easier for a long stretch and after another twenty minutes or so, he whispered, 'We must be over halfway now, as the crow flies.'

'Or the raven!' Toni whispered back. 'We still haven't found out about that. Sebastian said the Ravel's became Ravens. What's that got to do with *your* family, and why did they change *back* to Ravel?'

'We need to get those questions answered.' Saxon stopped as another fork approached, this one went in three directions. 'Left,' he shouted and waited until he heard the chalk scraping on the wall. If they did have to retrace their steps, it could still be easy to go wrong if they didn't pay attention. 'We'll demand Sebastian tells us exactly what happened in the past, no more secrets, agreed?'

'Agreed.' Toni confirmed, but she wished he hadn't mentioned secrets. The last diary had uncovered an astounding revelation. She was fighting with her conscience as to whether or not to share it, as well as everything else, with Saxon. The Alexander/Antonia affair was going to be hard enough to explain, but the Sapphire-Heart was the reason Aunt Antonia had given her, what everyone assumed was a piece of land worth a fraction of the cottage. At some point both families would have to be told, but when? What a dilemma for someone who didn't like to make decisions.

One thing was for sure, she was going to have to persuade her best friend to get hold of the letter in her aunt's will. That was something she really did feel guilty about. No way did she want Annie to jeopardise her position in Davidson & Son. Perhaps she could take a quick photo of the contents, message it across and the letter could be resealed. So much to think about, but how exciting. She gave Saxon's hand a squeeze and as they took another fork, she called 'Right,' to Leo and Annie, wondering just how many chalk marks they'd actually find on the return journey.

*** * ***

Vanessa, watched Linus stack the plates in the dishwasher, feeling a little less contempt for him than usual. It had been a novelty to eat Sunday lunch at home with Saxon and Alexander both out. Feeling how she did about Robert, at the moment, she had *almost* enjoyed her husband's company. By the end of the meal, however, her feelings had reverted to normal and she'd quickly remembered why she had to get away from this boring man. Her plans would have to be postponed slightly because only yesterday, things had taken an interesting turn.

Leaving the hotel, after her Saturday afternoon rendezvous with Robert, she'd agreed to pick up his dry cleaning, a job normally reserved for his fat, countryfied wife. Mrs Davidson was obviously failing in her duties both in and out of the bedroom. Robert realised he'd not seen his favourite work suit for some time and must have forgotten all about it until Vanessa happened to mention she had a few items to collect. She was particularly keen to retrieve a very expensive cashmere pashmina and generously made the offer to pick up his suit at the same time. Whilst waiting for the assistant to hand everything over, her thoughts darkened and an image of the new puppy swam before her eyes.

Lucifer, not knowing the difference between a cerise wool shawl which had been handmade in Nepal and a grey fleece blanket with a black pawprint pattern, had somehow dragged it out to the kennel and slept on it for an entire night. The next morning he'd proudly left it perilously close to the climbing roses and the newly forked manure, lovingly worked in by Linus, the evening before.

She'd eyed the Doberman puppy wondering if there was some way to dispose of him. It hadn't been difficult with the old dog a few weeks back, he was already on his way out. Brutus had weed on her bedroom carpet, for goodness sake, *twice*. The men hadn't seemed to care that he was losing control of his bodily functions. There was absolutely no point hanging on to anything old, useless or past its sell-by date. This young dog was different, unfortunately, and anyway, the old man would only go and buy another.

She paid for the laundry and was handed a small plastic pouch containing things they'd removed from the pockets of Robert's jacket. Getting into her car she looked quickly, some change, a container for his contact lenses, a photo of his two red-cheeked children and an *opened* envelope with... Antonia Ravel's name scrawled across the front.

Which was why she was feeling a little more benevolent towards Linus today, quite certain he knew nothing about any sapphires. No, her poor sap of a husband was buying land for what he thought would be an investment in a few years' time. The fact that her lover, very soon to be, ex-lover, wanted in as a silent partner, she'd only found out from listening in on telephone conversations and reading emails, over Linus' bony shoulders.

She'd wondered why Robert was so interested in those fields. Never in her wildest dreams had she thought treasure was buried there. A necklace over three hundred years old. According to Antonia Ravel, Sebastian, whoever he was, had said it was on route to the new king, William III. No doubt intended as a gift for Queen Mary. Unfortunately, the necklace would have to be broken down and the stones sold separately. Unless of course there was no record of it. A search online should reveal that. *The Sapphire-Heart*. The name alone sounded lavishly extravagant.

Who was Sebastian? A historian friend of the old woman, perhaps? It could mean of course the treasure was long gone if other people knew of it. Whatever the possibilities, she wasn't going to sit back and watch someone cheat her husband, not when that someone wasn't including her in the deal. Now all she had to work out, was whether or not it would be better to have Toni on side, or completely out of the picture. Saxon had been going on about some nature reserve, if they became even closer, he'd be investing his own money and then she'd never sell. Perhaps better if she wasn't around, as in, permanently. Vanessa could approach the family and cut her own deal, offer to do what their dear daughter had wanted, a sanctuary for wildlife, all in the Ravel name. What a fitting memorial for such a dear sweet girl, so unfortunately taken before her time. Once the necklace was in her possession, Linus, along with his finances, hidden or otherwise, could take a run and jump off a very high cliff

* * *

'I think we're getting close.' Saxon whispered. The conversation from the back had long dried up, a few moans had drifted forward about how much further? The tunnel had taken a downward route and the air had become very stagnant in parts. He'd been afraid that they'd be forced to call it a day, but then, after another steep incline the floor levelled and the air became fresher again. It must mean they weren't too deep, perhaps crossing the expanse of grassy field that led to the ruins? It was impossible, only using torchlight in the otherwise sheer darkness, to see what sort of ventilation was above. They had also noted that old wooden uprights now supported the tunnel in places. All four of them were feeling nervous. 'It's quarter past two,' he announced. 'I propose another fifteen minutes and then we go back, perhaps try a different route another day.'

Toni understood that he expected to reach their goal within that time. It would be an easier walk back, mostly flat or downhill, but still another good couple of hours. The excitement Leo and Annie had felt earlier had long dissipated. If they decided they'd had enough, Toni knew everyone would have to go back together, because those two were bound to get lost on their own.

Luckily, they all agreed with Saxon's suggested time limit, and when, five minutes later the tunnel ended in a large man-made cavern they frantically shone their torches around. The gasps of astonishment and awe filled the sacred space and appeared to bounce back from a raised oblong structure standing in the middle.

'What the hell. Wow, where are we?' Leo asked.

'That looks like an altar of some kind. I think we're beneath the Manor ruins. That's approximately the direction we've been heading in.' Saxon was disappointed it was too dark to see Toni's expression.

'Are you sure you haven't been here before today?' Leo asked suspiciously.

'Honestly Bolly, on… your sister's life.' He laughed.

'Bugger off Sax, don't you dare swear on me.' She shone her torch at the altar, there was a lot of dirt that needed to be wiped off, but underneath there were inscriptions. 'This *could* be Latin.'

'It used to be an Abbey at one time.' Saxon had remembered what he'd planned to say if they did all find it together. 'It changed during the reign of Henry VIII.'

'Then this could be a secret place of worship.' Annie concluded 'They obviously tried to save the building from destruction by the Protestant King.'

'Where are the relics?' Toni whispered.

Saxon shrugged. 'Perhaps there aren't any, or they were moved long ago. Let's look in all the corners and we'll see if the altar moves at all, something could be hidden under it.'

'Blimey you're almost clever sometimes, I'd have never thought of that.' She had an urge to kiss him, but that would have to wait because right now, she had an urge for something a lot more pressing. 'I'm desperate for a pee, guys. If I go back down the tunnel, don't follow me.'

'Oh, me too, now you've gone and said it.' Annie admitted.

'What is it with girls and their bladders?' Saxon looked at Leo and smirked.

'Err, well I've had a piss already, it's one advantage of being at the back.'

Annie swivelled around and grinned at him. 'I didn't hear you?'

'I can be a very discreet pisser when I have to be?' They all laughed.

'That's cos he's got a very discreet little... you know what.' Toni grinned at her brother and ducked quickly as he threw something at her. 'Bloody hell, Leo, don't go lobbing rocks at me.'

'Sorry I thought it was a lump of earth.'

'This isn't just *earth*.' All thoughts of needing to relieve themselves vanished as Annie rushed across and the two girls gently broke years of ingrained dirt from a small orb. 'I think this was an incense thing, look there's a bit of chain still attached.'

Leo gave a low whistle. 'This is quite a find Sax, and it's on your land, what do want to do about it?'

'We have to inform the police, and maybe the Catholic church, what else *can* we do?'

'Yeah but you're going to have journalists here, archaeologists, historians. Do you want them traipsing all over the place?'

'Of course not, but it's in the public interest. We'll have to fence the ruins off somehow, at least temporarily. There's the footpath from Eastdown lane that leads here, luckily it doesn't go anywhere after that, so it's not a right of way to walk across our land.' He dragged his fingers through his thick hair, only just realising the impact this was going to have. It left him feeling uneasy about whether or not he was doing the right thing.

'Sounds like you've got it all worked out.' Leo said, again a little suspiciously.

Toni squeezed his hand, 'It's the only thing *to* do, Sax, you can't hide it. Who knows, maybe the village will benefit and you can leave a few holiday brochures lying around here.'

Saxon chuckled. 'That's my clever girl always full of ideas.' He wrapped his arms around her, the doubts and uneasiness began to lift. She'd always had that effect on him, even when his mother died, she'd been the one to soothe his misery. 'Thanks, love I needed that.'

'You're welcome,' Toni's torch had been shining upwards while they cuddled and now she gave him a nudge. 'Look up, Sax, right above the altar, I think that could be the corner of a flagstone.' The other two heard and all aimed their torches so the light hit a small area on the ceiling.

'We could reach that,' Leo said jumping up on the altar and holding his hand out towards Saxon. His friend took a swing up and both of them began to push the stone directly above their heads. 'Shit, it's not going to budge.' Leo said, dreading the thought of the long walk back and more than aware he hadn't marked the route properly.

215

'You could poke a knife up around the sides, maybe loosen something.' Annie said.

'*Yep*, a knife would be just great, as would a stick of dynamite.' Leo answered sarcastically. 'Oh, I say; any of you happen to have one or the other?'

'Asshole.' Annie mumbled, tipping the contents of her tiny shoulder bag onto the floor. 'I thought a penknife, string, bits and pieces like that might come in handy. Which is why I suggested it.'

Leo jumped down immediately. 'I'm sorry I didn't mean that. You're right, I am an asshole.'

'Yep he's right,' Toni chipped in. 'Definitely the biggest asshole I know.'

Leo ignored his sister's remark and studied Annie's face. 'Are we okay?'

'I don't know,' she gave a tight smile. 'What do you mean exactly, do we need to be okay?'

'I mean, can I spend the rest of the day with you, not those two other assholes as well, just us.'

She giggled. 'I'd like that, my mum's working so I could cook us some tea?' She gave him a quick kiss on the cheek. 'There may be more for dessert *if* you don't piss me off again.'

Leo laughed and Toni, watching them interact together, felt immensely satisfied with the afternoon's outcome, for more than one reason.

The girls held a torch in each hand while the boys tried to cut around the square slab. Saxon had been sure they'd just hit more of the hard stone, but surprisingly the knife was moving through the earth and as bits filtered down, eventually, they were followed by wisps of grass. When they'd freed it as much as possible they began to push again and almost at the point of giving up Leo felt movement on his side.

'Rest your arms for five minutes.' Toni suggested. They did and with a second burst of strength the slab began to move and daylight flooded in like a heavenly sunbeam.

Saxon helped Leo out first and then each of the girls. Then, the three of them leaned back in, grabbed his arms and pulled. He landed face down in the warm grass just behind what used to be the old stable, flipping over on his back, he grabbed Toni and gave her the kiss she'd wanted in the dark underground chapel. 'We never did try to move the altar. I need to go home and speak to Grandad about all this, will you lot do me a favour?'

'Keep quiet about it until you've informed the authorities?' Leo guessed.

'Yeah, let's put the stone back, I don't want any idiots falling in.' Can you spare me a couple of hours tomorrow Bolly, to pick up the dinghy? It'll be fine there tonight.' Luckily with Bolly's help, the dinghy had been pulled in much further and left way above the high tide line.

'Yeah sure, Annie and I are heading off now, I'll pick you up tomorrow Sax, is your car okay parked out all night as well?'

'It's fine, everything can wait until tomorrow.' He looked at Toni, 'Do you have to go home right away? You can spend the evening at mine, I'll borrow a car to take you back later.'

'Let me give Mum a quick ring and make sure Quando's okay. I feel a bit guilty, but I've got tomorrow off so I'll make it up to him.'

Later that evening, Alexander, Linus and even Vanessa were hanging on Saxon's and Toni's every word. Toni showed them the small orb and they described the inscriptions on the altar as best as they could. The photos Toni had taken on her phone weren't great, but they got a general idea.

'It certainly sounds like a hidden chapel.' Alexander agreed. 'How astonishing, all those years right under our land.' He shared Saxon's misgivings about the oncoming intrusion, but also knew that first thing in the morning it would need reporting.

Toni glanced at Linus, he was quieter than usual and his eyes had a misty sheen. 'Are you okay?' she asked.

'Err yes, Toni, thank you for asking.' He turned to his son. 'I was just thinking about you in those tunnels. Jesus, you could have got lost and you had the *girls* with you.' *Rita's daughter for one.* 'Don't think I'm not impressed by what you've found, but if you were a few years younger I'd bloody well give you a hiding.'

Saxon knew very well without Sebastian's instructions they *would* have most likely been lost. 'Thanks, Dad, I love you too.' A sense of camaraderie that had been missing since before Saxon's mother died slowly began to creep back.

Linus decided against mentioning Toni's fields tonight, for the first time it didn't seem so important. His son was safe and happy, wasn't that what it was all about. He looked at his watch. Rita would just be starting work now, no one here would miss him if he slipped off to the golf club for a few hours.

Chapter Sixteen

'Dogs and wenches should be treated the same.'

On the drive home, Toni asked Saxon to stop somewhere as she had something to tell him. Suspecting it wasn't going to be quick, he drove to the cliff above Shingle Beach and they sat together in silence for a few moments, watching the moon's reflection on the dark ocean.

'When I went to visit my aunt in hospital, she whispered something about a diary,' Toni began. She went on to tell him about finding the three notebooks in the attic, talking to Sebastian and how Antonia and Alexander had been friends.

'He's never mentioned her,' Saxon said thoughtfully. 'I wonder if she was friends with Grandma as well?'

'I *highly* doubt it. Don't get mad that I haven't told you this before, I've only known a short time and... well, it wasn't my secret to tell.'

Saxon looked at her strangely, then sat back and listened in silence while he heard Toni's summarization of the first two diaries. 'So, you're suggesting they had an *affair*?'

Oh dear, he sounds upset. 'I only finished the last diary yesterday, it starts in 1956.' She glanced across, Saxon was staring straight ahead, she tried to hold his hand but he pulled it away. 'This isn't *my* fault, I can't help it if my great-aunt was a flirt and your grandad couldn't keep it in his pants.'

As if a veil lifted, Saxon dragged his gaze to Toni, he immediately reached for her hand and began to apologise. 'Tell me the rest, love, it's a bit of a shock.'

Toni let out a sigh. 'Most of this comes from the third diary, but Sebastian filled in the blanks, it seems she also encountered our friendly ghost. During my last visit to Glen-Croft, she had one of her spectacular *odd* moments and said she wished she could see Sebastian again. That's what first got me wondering, and when she whispered the word *diary*, I just...'

'You just had to investigate didn't you Ravel?' he gave a terse laugh. 'It's okay, I'm already imagining the worst like they had some sort of secret marriage, you may as well put me out of my misery.'

She breathed a silent sigh of relief, knowing things weren't quite that bad. 'Your grandma, Margaret, was in the WRENS and posted off to Gibraltar. Antonia must have thought it was her best chance to win Alexander around. I'm absolutely certain she truly loved him. Anyway, in November 1957, my aunt celebrated her seventeenth birthday. There was a party in the woods,' she smiled. 'Some things don't change I guess. Well, it ended with Alexander walking her home, and she wrote about them drinking cider, some local brew, more like paint stripper no doubt.'

Saxon had been holding his breath, but he allowed a small smile. This was hard to hear, all his life he'd been told how *in love* his grandparents had been. He was still hoping it was a sick joke. But he knew in his heart Toni would never do that to him. He was falling in love with her, and how could it continue if she'd stoop to something like that. No this was all true, or, she at least believed it to be true. 'Go on love, I'm getting the picture, they *did it*, on the way home, didn't they?'

'Yup, and although she didn't write details, thank God, she wrote enough to let on they both... erm enjoyed it and did it again a few more times. The upshot of it all was, by spring, she knew she was pregnant. Alexander promised to marry her, but said he needed to speak to Margaret in person, as they were engaged by then.' She glanced across, Saxon looked like he was in physical pain, but she had to get it all out, now she'd started. 'Aunt Antonia's father, my great-grandfather, threw her out of the house. Her sister Rachel gave her a pretty hard time, they didn't get on apparently. She was close to her brother, Oliver, he gets mentioned quite a lot in the diaries. I assume he wasn't allowed to offer any help if he even knew, of course, he was a few years younger, the baby of the family.'

'Christ Toni, she was *pregnant*, what happened?'

'This is where it gets really sad. Antonia went to throw herself on the mercy of *your* great-grandfather, but he was having none of it. He said his son had gone to Gibraltar to *marry* Margaret, which was untrue, he'd gone to break up. He gave her some money and told her if she was sensible, she'd go away and get rid of it. Then he sent a telegram to Alexander and said the whole thing had been a hoax, and not to break off his engagement after all.'

'An abortion! They were illegal and unsafe back then. I know my grandma would have been heartbroken, but you'd think both the fathers would have wanted their grandchild? I don't understand.'

'Well from what I can gather, and I need to talk to Sebastian again, something happened in the generation before theirs, concerning our great-greats. There's mention of a drowning, see what you can find online, Sax, you're better at it than me, I think it was your ancestor that died and mine that got the blame.'

'Just another chapter in our twisted family saga.'

'We're doomed, aren't we?' Toni gave a sad smile.

'No, we are *definitely* not, don't *ever* say that again.' It was said with such conviction that Saxon surprised himself as much as he'd surprised Toni. 'So, poor Antonia got rid of the baby and presumably, Grandad never found out.'

'Uh-uh,' Toni shook her head. 'She had it. Flora, a little girl. She was given to a couple in the country somewhere. By the time Antonia came home, Margaret had left the WRENS and Alexander had married her. I don't think they ever spoke again. They must still hate each other. He thought he'd been tricked and she thought she'd been abandoned.'

'So, I've got a second aunt somewhere, and maybe, some more cousins.' He leaned forward and put his head in his hands. 'I have to tell him.'

Toni was resigned to the decision she knew he'd make. 'Do you want me to be there with you?'

'Let me think about it. Can he read the diaries?'

'Ah, that's a bit awkward. I'd have to remove some pages. There's something else I have to tell you.'

'I don't think I can take anymore, not tonight, but I can't leave it either, go on.'

'There's nothing more with the families. This is about Antonia's love affair with Sebastian.'

'What? *Please* tell me *they* didn't. It isn't possible is it?'

'Don't ask *me*! When I say love affair, I just mean she loved him, nothing happened, sorry I didn't explain that very well.' Saxon nodded, he looked completely washed out. Toni had had her suspicions since the Glen-Croft visit and also the advantage of being able to read the diaries, her poor boy was hearing it all in one fell swoop. 'I think the sapphire necklace is buried somewhere under my land. Apparently, there's a letter for me with Antonia's will, but Henry Davidson told Dad it's gone missing. I'm thinking of asking Annie, but I don't want to get her in trouble.'

Saxon was trying hard to keep up. All he could picture was Robert Davidson on Toni's fields the other day. Long after Linus had left, he'd stayed, pacing up and down as if looking for something. *Please* don't let his father know anything about the sapphires, he wasn't sure if he could ever forgive that. 'How poorly is Antonia?'

'I'm not sure really, she has a chest infection, why?'

'I'm wondering whether we should give it a week or two. See what happens, get the wedding out the way without these family revelations coming out of the woodwork because you'll need to tell Martin as well.'

'Yeah, can we *please*, wait until after? It's not like they can have any sort of deathbed reconciliation, she sleeps most of the time and when she is awake, she's doolally.'

'Okay, after the wedding then. I'll do some research on the drowning *and* on Flora. She may have been given a different name, was it a legal adoption do you know?'

'No idea,' Toni shrugged. 'You've got this other stuff to do with Alexander tomorrow, the underground chapel. That's got to take priority. I've got two days off, I'll find Sebastian and see what light he can shed.' She heard a low growl and sucked in a breath. If Saxon didn't even like the idea of her seeing him alone, she could never confess to the kiss.

'I'll get away for an hour or two tomorrow, we'll see him together,' Saxon said firmly, wondering what the hell had actually happened between Antonia and Sebastian. He knew Toni was somewhat mesmerised by him, and he'd be damned if he'd sit back and let that attraction grow. 'As for Annie, if she can find out anything, great, but like you said, she mustn't put her job at risk. Bolly will kick our asses if he thinks we're responsible for that.'

Toni grinned. 'You think he likes her then?'

'I'm sure of it, I know that guy like he's my own brother. Now let's get you home.'

'Right, and in the grand scheme of things this may seem pretty insignificant, but I need to phone Pete Alford about the van.'

'He won't even have looked at it yet, love, leave it until Tuesday.' Linus was on the case and poor Pete had been asked to make it a priority. Hopefully, he'd started on Saturday morning, and with any luck, Saxon could deliver it back soon, plus a few other safety improvements, which she'd never know about.

* * *

The Police and Church representatives kept Saxon busy the next morning. He sat with his father and grandfather answering all questions to the best of his ability. Leo, Toni and Annie would also be interviewed later. All in all, it looked like the four of them were about to become local celebrities, at least, until the first flush of excitement had died away. Not one of them craved that kind of attention, but the news crew that arrived at lunchtime were not happy to talk to just Saxon and Leo. If a couple of young pretty girls had been scrabbling about in dark tunnels that made the story even more appealing.

Henry Davidson was very impressed and gave Annie the afternoon off. Even Robert stuck his head out of his office and reminded her to mention the firm's name if she got an opportunity.

There had been no time for Toni to find Sebastian and explain what was going on. It seemed unfair when he was the one with the most right to hear about it. Just before the reporting journalist began to ask questions, against the backdrop of the ruins, she did her best to summon him. It wasn't down to the volume of her shouts, she'd realised that after he'd saved her from the tight tunnel. Somehow, he tuned in if she wanted or needed him.

A few minutes later, Saxon saw Toni and Sebastian together, heads bowed. He gritted his teeth and smiled for the camera thinking it preferable to them having to fit in a visit to the woods later that evening.

Sebastian was able to materialise, no one here would see him, except his two *treasure seekers,* or so he'd thought. Leo glanced over a few times assuming the guy dressed in period gear was someone's attempt at tasteless humour. Not having the slightest idea of fashion through the ages, thought he was posing as Henry VIII. He nudged Annie and pointed. She wasn't sure what she was meant to be looking at so, focussed her attention on giving the cameraman her best angle instead.

By early evening Alexander had got the workmen from the holiday site to erect temporary fencing around the ruins and make the footpath more obvious, especially where it ended. No one had any right to walk past their home to reach Raven Manor, which overnight had become a place of historic interest.

Saxon had persuaded Toni to stay for tea and rustled up some toasted sandwiches. Thinking it a bit crass to whisk her upstairs to his bedroom, but wanting some privacy, they'd adjourned to the snug, a small room adjacent to the lounge, just big enough for a couple of comfy armchairs and a small television. 'I hate all this side of it,' he grumbled. 'Did you see Grandad's face after the fencing was finished?'

'It'll be a five-minute wonder, the few people that are there longer will be the professionals. They won't bother you.' Toni sat on his lap, smoothed his hair and massaged his temples. 'Just relax for the rest of the evening. I need to be at home quite a bit next week. Olly's going to be so highly strung, Mum will need all the support she can get. It's not fair to leave Quando under her feet either, except for when I'm at work.'

Saxon rested his cheek in her palm and felt peace for the first time that day. 'How do you fancy doing something completely different one night this week? Go into town, have a meal and see a film, that sort of thing?'

'Like a proper date night?' Toni grinned. 'Yeah, I'd like that. You don't feel we've sort of been thrown together, do you, Sax, like we had no real say in the inevitability of it all?'

'I do a bit.' He saw her face fall and bent his head so he could kiss her. 'That's not to say I don't think it's the best thing that's ever happened to me.' He snuggled her against his chest remembering he had some good news to share. 'Your van's outside by the way. I forgot to tell you earlier.'

'Oh, that's great, thanks for getting it sorted. Has he left the bill?'

'Yeah, it's not too bad, he was able to reuse older parts for most of it.'

'Most of it? I thought it was just the exhaust?'

'The MOT was due a *month* ago, didn't you realise?'

'Oh *hell*,' she groaned out the words. 'I thought it was the end of July.' She began to trace the pattern on his t-shirt paying close attention to the nipple area.

'That's in two days' time,' he spluttered. 'Even if you'd been right, you wouldn't have got it fixed and road worthy by then and *stop* trying to distract me.' He took her hands firmly in his own. He'd been horrified by how much work the van had needed. Brake discs, three new tyres, the exhaust of course, plus a lot of welding. Pete had also done a full service, replacing all the wipers and a brake light. Everything else on his schedule had been put on hold to get it finished. Linus wasn't shy about calling in a favour when he needed one. The bill would show the barest essentials, the MOT test, the wipers, one tyre and a second-hand exhaust. The rest would be a back-hander which Saxon would pay in cash. Linus and Alexander had sorted Pete out, so she'd never know. Yet again his father had surprised him. Twice in three days, things were looking up.

'I expected it to need some welding, I'm surprised it passed. I love that old van, but I have to change it this year, somehow. It scared the shit out of me the other day when I thought I was going to break down in the middle of nowhere.'

That was like spun honey to his ears, please, *please* let her accept the offer of a job. If a car was thrown into the equation, surely, she wouldn't turn it down. He tried to think of every possible way he could ask her again.

Toni freed a hand and gave him a tap on the head. 'You're miles away.'

'Was I?' Now wasn't the time to mention the job, it would be overshadowed with everything else that was going on. 'We're getting an invite from the Bishop at some point in the week. For *God's* sake don't go swearing in front of him.' They both laughed when he realised what he'd said.

'We *must* fit Sebastian in tomorrow. I managed to explain really quickly what was going on, but I don't think he understood what everyone was doing there. He kept saying things in my ear about strange gents and doodlebugs, it was *really* hard to concentrate on the questions.'

'You did okay, don't worry, it should be on TV tomorrow night. Did you know Bolly saw him?'

'Saw who?'

'*Sebastian*, he thought it was some token Tudor dress up guy. I guess all Ravels and Thorpes can see him. Just play it down if he does mention anything, say you didn't notice.'

'No probs. By the way, I'm meant to be inviting you to supper one night this week, it won't be as grand as the Bishop, I'm afraid.'

A hell of a lot more daunting though. 'Great, any night you like, we're really cracking the parent thing, aren't we?'

'So far so good. Bolly will be there, so you'll have plenty of support and I know Mum likes you.' She started to wriggle off his lap. 'I'm dying to drive the van, if it's been MOT'd it'll be all like new again.'

Unable to disguise his laughter, Saxon found the keys and they went out onto the drive.

Vanessa saw them briefly and painted on a smile. 'You must let me cook you both supper one night soon,' she enthused. 'I do a wonderful cheese and mushroom omelette.'

Saxon smiled, pleased with what he believed, was his stepmother making an effort. 'It's true, she does make a mean omelette.'

'In that case, I'd love to. It may not be until after the wedding though.'

'Whenever you like, just let me know the night before, I like to pick the mushrooms fresh in the morning,' Vanessa trilled. Saxon had just given her a lovely smile, perhaps all hope was not lost after all. First get the trollop out of the picture, secure the land, and then... Linus would have to go. Gorgeously, handsome Saxon would be in need of some serious comforting after all that.

'Vanessa in designer heels picking funguses doesn't exactly go together.' Toni said as soon as they were alone.

'It's *fungi*,' Saxon rolled his eyes. 'Surprisingly it really is something she does well.'

'I'll take your word for it.' All thoughts of mushrooms were forgotten as she opened the door of the van. 'Thanks again for this, I appreciate it.' She gave him a kiss before switching on the engine. 'Listen to that, perfect or what?'

It still sounded like what it was, a heap of junk as far as Saxon was concerned, but at least it was a *safer* heap of junk for a while longer.

* * *

Quando ran in tight circles, constantly stopping to try and squat. 'Just have a poop if you're going to!' Toni said, looking a bit embarrassed.

'Do it here, on Ravel land, not in the woods, otherwise, we'll have to pick it up.' Saxon added.

They were taking a walk across Toni's fields before seeing Sebastian and their eyes were drawn to every slight bump or mound. 'Twenty-eight acres is a big area to search and don't forget at least two-thirds of that is being used at the moment.'

Do you make any money from what the land produces? Saxon asked.

Not exactly, Dad sort of rents it back from me, but that really covers what I'd give them for living at home, so it all evens out. I hope my letter can be found and there's something more specific.'

'Or Sebastian gives us a clue, I have a feeling he's the one who buried it, but he's not exactly forthcoming, about the sapphires.' Saxon barely managed to stop himself from tripping over Quando.

Toni watched with dismay as her dog decided the best place to sort himself out was right in their path. 'He wanted us to find his church stuff, we've done that. Does one orb constitute Holy relics, saved from the Tudor tyrant?'

'I think they're planning on lifting the altar tomorrow, so fingers crossed.' Saxon suddenly screwed his face up, 'What the bloody hell are you feeding that dog?'

'Chicken and rice mostly, but he found a packet of Dad's Torpedoes last night and scoffed the lot.'

'That's *liquorice*, no wonder. The poor little thing's going to have a very sore ass after this.' Quando eventually finished and looked extremely sorry for himself.

'I feel bad, I can't leave him so much, you're going to have to start coming to my house more.'

Saxon nodded, hopefully, this invitation to tea would break the ice. They'd decided Saturday for the date night in town. The weekend after was the wedding. His grandad had already offered to have Quando, and Toni had gratefully accepted, as the family were all staying overnight in a large country hotel, six miles away. She had a room to herself and he'd been invited to share. It would be their first night together, a really big deal as far as he was concerned. Knowing Toni, she'd have far too much to drink, and he'd be too much of a gentleman to take advantage, but he couldn't help a small frisson of pleasure at the thought of what might be.

Sebastian waited impatiently by the Hunters' Stones. He knew they were coming and he was desperate to hear more news.

Yesterday had been very confusing, men holding long sticks with furry heads. Toni had explained that they were to speak into and called them, *microphones*. 'Phone, like a magic telephone?' he'd asked. She'd laughed and said 'Something like that' and then she'd told him to 'stand back, he was putting her off.' After growling a reply and watching the talking sticks for a while, he'd taken himself down to the underground chapel to see what was occurring.

'You're muttering to yourself, that's a sign of madness, Sebastian.' Toni would have run to hug him, but she was mindful of being with Saxon.

He wanted to swing her up into his arms. *Ah no, the boy is hither also, which is just as it shouldst be... hast to be. Find the necklace and break the curse.* 'I speak oft to mine self, I warrant I can trust everything I say and receive a sensible answer also.'

'You're still pissed off about yesterday, aren't you? I was just worried someone would see you, my brother did, you know.'

'Aye, he wouldst, being blood kin. Those other gents wouldst never know, not unless I desired it.'

'Is it easy to show yourself to others?' Saxon asked, coming closer and pointedly grabbing Toni's hand.

'Nay, I wouldst be wiped out for many a day. I can liken it only to swiving a great many wenches, all in succession, dost ye comprehend?'

Luckily Saxon was saved from answering, as Quando, now quite recovered from his 'Torpedo ordeal', bounded up to Sebastian and started to pull at the large folds of leather on his boots.

'Saints in heaven, a new hound dog, and a rascally little cur.' He looked at Toni. 'This one belongs to ye, methinks? *'Down'* he bellowed and watched with satisfaction as Quando quickly did as he was told. 'Saxon, hark well, dogs and wenches shouldst be treated the same. A firm hand and obedience shalt be thine to savour. They must always know who is master.'

Toni now knew a softer side to Sebastian. This was all bluster. It was still a tad annoying though. 'Stop spouting off rubbish and tell us what you thought of the chapel? And by the way, I thought you couldn't go underground?'

'Once daylight wast allowed in, I couldst also enter. I warrant those gents must move the altar. I hast some vague recollection of knowing this.'

'That's *exactly* what's happening tomorrow.' Saxon informed him. 'We've been invited to meet the Bishop by the way.' If he'd wanted to impress Sebastian he'd certainly done it with that statement.

'The Lord *Bishop*,' he said reverently. 'Thou art *most* honoured.'

'Sebastian, I may not get to see you much over the next few days, my sister's wedding is Saturday week and I'll be needed at home. After that, we want to try and find the necklace, will you help us now? There's a missing letter and I don't know if we'll have enough information. You must tell us *exactly* what you told Antonia.'

'I shalt miss ye, little wench.' He heard a sharp intake of breath from Saxon. 'Thou also, young Thorpe,' he grinned. 'I shalt not take what is thine, dost not be afeard.'

Toni did bite that time. 'I'm not bloody chattel. No one *owns* me.'

'Aye wench, as we well know. Behave if ye can, when meeting God's valorous envoy and wend soon to tell me about it.'

'We'll make time for that. What if they find something below the altar?'

'I shalt be keeping mine own eyes on those gents.'

'There is one other thing,' Saxon thought now was as good a time as any to mention it. 'We'd like to hear your full story, you did say weeks ago you'd tell us.'

'Thou hast mine word, when we art close to recovering the Sapphire-Heart.' He leaned over and gave Toni a quick peck on the cheek, partly to kill the subject and partly because he couldn't help himself. Saxon's cheeks began to colour. 'You want one too, Knave?' He laughed and took a step forward. 'I shalt shake ye by the hand instead.' While pumping Saxon's hand, he shouted, 'Up hound.' Quando wagged his tail and looked adoringly at Sebastian. 'Remember, speak to thy wench with such a tongue, verily she shalt gaze upon ye in the same way.'

He left them, to make of that what they would. The studded dog collar came fleetingly to Saxon's mind... and just as quickly faded, when he saw the look on Toni's face.

Chapter Seventeen

'Did you really expect to turn up at the Bishop's Palace in that heap of junk?'

'We 4got to mention the drowning to Sebastian xx.'
'Morning gorgeous, I'm on it XX'
'Ok laters XX'

'They want someone part-time behind the bar.' Annie pointed to a sign on the wall.

'When Karen first reduced my hours, I'd have jumped at it, but now with...'

'Sax.' Annie interrupted grinning.

'I was going to say *Quando*, but yes, Sax as well.' Toni admitted. 'I don't really want to work evenings, but I'm desperate for some more money. I had to borrow £130 from Dad to pay for the van.'

'That's pretty cheap considering all the work he did.' Annie only knew what Toni had told her.

'Yeah Pete's a good guy, and it'll keep me roadworthy at least. I need a new job, Annie, something that's going to pay at least double what I'm earning now. I suppose I'll have to start looking further out of the village.'

'What about the one that Sax offered you?'

'I don't know if he was serious.' She took a bite of her chicken and salad sandwich and considered the possibilities of being part of the new development. Was it only six weeks ago she'd been so against it? Even now, she wished it wasn't happening, and the countryside could be left alone, but trusting Saxon had made a huge difference to her way of thinking. It would be good for the community, as long as *Linus* wasn't ever allowed a free hand to expand. That immediately brought her thoughts back to her own land and the letter. 'I found some old diaries of my great-aunts the other week when I was cleaning the cottage for Olly.'

'Gosh, how exciting. Any steamy boyfriend secrets?'

'Not really, a few local names, kids she used to play with, that sort of thing. The fact that she didn't get on with her sister and, um towards the end, the reason she left me the land and Olly got her cottage.' She felt uncomfortable not revealing everything, she'd never kept secrets from Annie, before Sebastian came into her life.

'Well?' Annie prompted when Toni stopped to eat a bit more of her lunch.

'She believes there's something buried there, some old treasure. To be honest, I didn't think much about it when I read it at first, but now...'

'Now that we've already discovered another sort of treasure.' Annie interrupted again. 'Perhaps we need to start looking, those fields go down to the coast, right? There may be another tunnel.'

Toni shook her head, pleased with the reaction, it might help with what she had to ask in a minute. 'There's certainly no caves or anything there, the coastline is flat, which is why the very bottom of the fields flood sometimes during a high tide or very bad storm. Actually, I'm surprised Linus isn't after them to build a lido. Anyway, don't get me started on *him* and don't say anything to Leo about the diaries yet. I haven't admitted to Olly I was snooping about in the attic. Aunt Antonia left a trunk full of clothes and another full of handbags and crap. I'll have to let her know before new tenants move in, she should have a proper sort through. The thing is Annie, my *bestest* friend in the *whole* world...'

'What are you after?'

'Well, apparently there's a letter addressed to me with her will, or there should be. Henry told Dad about it the other day when they were checking the deeds. It's missing though, misfiled probably. Do you know if he found it, and if so, um, what's in it?' She couldn't look Annie in the eye, instead studied her packet of crisps and read every single ingredient.

'Of *course*, I wouldn't know what's in it. How could you ask me that?' She should really let Toni sweat for a few minutes. 'Do you want me to find out?' She grinned.

'*No*... maybe... well yeah. But not if you get into trouble. Sorry, Annie, I'm desperate to know if there are any clues.'

'I'm meant to be going through the filing cabinet to search for that very thing, believe it or not, I just haven't had time. I'll make it a priority and if I can open it I will. Don't get your hopes up though. These old letters are stuck down pretty firmly.'

'It's not *that* old, I think it was all done the same time as she deeded the land and made her will, so less than ten years ago.'

It was on the tip of Annie's tongue to say Linus Thorpe and Robert Davidson were in some sort of cahoots over those fields, but conscious of her confidentiality agreement and knowing Toni would never sell them, she wasn't too worried. Now with the mention of treasure *and* a missing letter, she was starting to feel differently. Robert had been searching for something in his father's filing cabinet and she'd felt at the time it was odd. Especially as he'd come out of the office without any files. He'd also made no requests for her, or Henry's personal assistant, Mrs Dale, back on a part-time basis from convalescence, to look for anything. 'I'll see what I can find out, talking of which, I'm going to have to run up that blasted hill now, or I'll be late back.'

'Every time.' Toni grinned and gave her friend a hug. 'You know Sax is coming to the wedding now, and as you're still my official plus one, we'll all be sitting together. I've made sure Olly knows to put you next to Leo, he's not bringing anyone.' Annie's whole face lit up.

Deciding against the crisps and throwing the packet into her bag, Toni returned to work early. Karen had just taken delivery of a box of sturdy looking sports shoes, which she was going to put on display in the window with an A5 print-out calling them, *tunnel trainers*. Toni picked one up and grinned. 'God knows what's going to happen beneath our green fields and woods from now on. We saw a lot of other turnings when we were exploring, people are going to get lost if they're not careful.'

Karen nodded. 'Hopefully, in our footwear.'

Toni looked shocked until she realised her boss was joking. It had sowed a seed, however, maybe one of those other turnings did reach as far as her land, and if so... *Bloody hell*, she couldn't let anyone else find it first.

'Sebastian,' Toni called, quietly moving away from where a crowd of teenagers had taken over Smugglers' Knoll.

'Dearest girl, ye art hither alone, and only a few weeks after saying ye wouldst not see me for a while. Is something amiss?'

'A few *weeks*, one *day*, Sebastian.' Toni had to laugh. 'I wanted to know if the tunnels that lead from the coast to the ruins also run west? I'm worried people may start to explore.'

'Nay, sweetheart, shouldst any callow youth wend thither, those gents shalt meet with a dead end. I know every inch below these woods, they originally stopped a long way afore the Manor.'

'Yes, we noticed a stretch was man-made, did the smugglers do that?'

Sebastian shook his head. 'Nay, the priests. They couldst wend through and make good their escape, that wast well afore mine time of course.' He saw her relax and snaked an arm around her shoulders. 'Give me a quick kiss ere ye go.'

'What? *No.*' She unhooked his arm and looked at him in exasperation. 'Sebastian, you're outrageous,' *and bloody gorgeous.* 'Why do you and Sax seem so alike, when you couldn't be more different?'

'Art thou so sure we art different, mine love?' His eyes twinkled.

'I shouldn't see you alone, it's too dangerous.' Sebastian's laugh was so loud Toni couldn't understand how the group of teens failed to hear it.

'I am dangerous, but tis not the danger ye meant. Methinks ye like it if the truth be known.'

Toni felt herself being lifted and was soon at his eye level. *'Don't.'* It was meant to be a stern reproach but came out as a squeak. 'I must think of you as a very dear cousin or uncle from now on.'

'That shalt not stop me. One day, I shalt tell ye of mine great-uncle Harold who swived every one of his three nieces. That gent wast shameless, 'twas his undoing though, he came to a bad end.'

I'm in so much trouble, Toni gazed at his dazzling smile and deep green eyes. *Think about Saxon, think about the night coming up in the hotel.* That did the trick. 'Laters.' She said as casually as possible, and struggling out of his grasp, dropped back onto her feet and practically ran out of Raven Wood feeling sure she could still hear his laughter as she put the key in the front door of the farmhouse.

Later that evening, Toni, feeling a bit guilty over her encounter with Sebastian and determined to put him to the back of her mind, phoned Saxon.

'Hello, love, this is a nice surprise, much better than a message. Do you want to FaceTime?'

'Err no thanks, I've got a deep cleansing, mud mask on my face. It looked grey on the packet but Leo's just told me I look like a smurf and threatened to take a photo. I'm barricading my bedroom door as we speak.'

'You really should get a lock.' He laughed, trying to imagine Toni sitting in front of her door with a blue face. 'Any news?'

'I was going to ask you that but I did see Sebastian quickly, after work.' She heard his breath hitch and tried to keep her voice neutral. 'It was just something Annie said about the tunnels possibly running as far as my land... I needed to know.'

'Yeah, I totally get that.' Saxon forced himself to think rationally. He was a ghost, a sodding ghost, what could he do? It wasn't really about that though, it was more about Toni's feelings. 'I've got some news and I take it the tunnels aren't a problem?'

'Ooh good, I hoped you might. No, they're not, apparently, all the other turnings come to dead ends eventually. I have a hunch that whatever is buried in the fields we're going to have to find with shovels. What have you found out?'

'Something about the drowning, there was very little online, I took a look at the church records, and you'll never guess what?'

'You're right I'll never guess, get on with it.'

'You're very bossy for someone that looks like a smurf!' He teased. 'The couple involved are both buried in the graveyard. I'm sending you pics of the headstones now but I'll tell you the inscriptions and you can study them later. Okay,' he rustled a paper and began to read her the names while she looked at the photos on her iPad. 'Emma Louise Thorpe, born 1881, died 1903. Beloved daughter of Victor and Linda Thorpe. Only sister of James. Tragically left us, now in God's hands.

There's more, are you still listening, you've gone quiet? This gets quite complicated.'

'I'm keeping up.' Her eyes had already strayed to the second of the three photos he'd sent. The wording on that stone was harder to read.

'The next two are your family, father and son and they both died in the same year as Emma.' He heard her gasp of surprise and continued to read from his notes. 'John Ravel, born 1836 died 1903. And the last one was his son George, I couldn't make out the wife or son's name, but the year of death was 1903 again.'

'Curiouser and curiouser... actually, thinking about it, his son must have been Francis, Antonia's father, the one that threw her out. Did anyone in our family have a normal life? Or one that wasn't connected to each other's families?'

'Who knows? Looks like we're following in the tradition.'

Toni felt a glow of pleasure as his words sank in. 'You reckon we're going to be connected then?'

'Aren't we already?' he held his breath and a spilt-second before the silence became uncomfortable he heard her say *yes* and let himself breath again. 'That was difficult, I was worried for a minute.'

'I didn't want to sound too keen,' she giggled. 'But yes, Sax we're definitely connected. I think we always were even during the years I thought you were a total jerk.'

'Charming! Shall I tell you the rest of this story, it's pretty dark and twisted?'

'I've got to go and de-smurf myself, can you message it all across for me, or shall I phone you again after?'

'I'll message it, what should I bring tomorrow?'

'Oh, I don't know, flowers are a safe bet. Anything colourful, Mum doesn't have a favourite.' She blew him a kiss and smiled when he texted some back, a few seconds later. So, he'd implied they were going to be connected forever. No doubt he'd change his mind after an evening in her father's company.

Saxon typed quickly and sent a few links. All joking apart, their families were seriously messed up. If what Sebastian had first told them about the Vikings and the Normans was true, history had carried on repeating itself down through the generations. Well, it would end here, he wanted a future with Toni and it was going to be a good one.

* * *

An evening at home and he still has to talk to that blasted girl. Vanessa stomped away from Saxon's bedroom door. She hadn't bothered to meet Robert today. What would he make of her *no-show*? He hadn't contacted her so far and quite frankly she didn't really care. Since she had a younger man on her mind again, Robert had paled into insignificance, along with Linus.

Perhaps she could persuade Saxon to invite Toni over before the wedding, she couldn't imagine they'd go a whole week without seeing each other however busy the Ravel household was with preparations. Breakfast together, yes, that would be something different, she'd suggest it later.

Field mushrooms grew plentifully in the surrounding area and oddly, picking and cooking them was something Vanessa enjoyed. More importantly, she also knew of some that should never be touched and certainly not added to a cheese omelette. Annoyingly, both she and Saxon would have to display a few minor symptoms, this had to look convincing. How very unfortunate that the bulk would end up on Toni's plate.

* * *

'Hi, Sax come in.' Toni showed him into the front room, eyeing the two bouquets and wondering which one was hers.

'For you, Mrs Ravel.' He handed Beverly the larger bunch of mixed seasonal flowers. 'And for you, Olly. Thanks for the wedding invite.'

'Creep.' Leo smirked, on his way to the dining room.

'Thank you, Saxon,' Beverly smiled. 'I'll go and put these straight into water. Supper will be ready in fifteen minutes, so time for a quick drink first.'

Leo was already on the case and came back with some wine glasses and a bottle of Rioja. 'Thought this would go with Shepherd's pie, it is lamb after all. What do you say, Dad?'

'Good choice, son.' Martin glanced across at Saxon. 'Serve our guest first.'

'Thanks, Mr Ravel. Thanks, Bolly.' Saxon began to feel a bit tense. He threw Toni a few concerned looks and when he caught her scowling at Olivia's flowers, grinned to himself whilst still nodding at something Martin was saying. Just as they filed into the dining room, he pressed a small box into her hand. 'You said Olly was letting you wear your own jewellery next week. I thought this might work.'

Nestling on a small white cushion was a thin silver bracelet with a tiny blue stone. 'Oh, Sax, it's lovely.'

'I'm sorry the sapphire is so tiny but I wanted to get you one, just in case there is actually nothing to find. An emerald may have matched the Kermit dress more, but I didn't think you'd mind.'

'Sapphires all the way, for sure. It's wonderful, thank you.'

'My pleasure, wench.' He answered quietly as they sat down next to each other.

As expected, Olivia took over most of the conversation telling everyone about her future home in Cyprus. By the last mouthful of Shepherd's pie, they were familiar with every detail of the tiled pool and the facilities for the wives and families stationed there. Toni was so happy she didn't make one sarcastic remark but was relieved when her father cut in and asked Saxon how his family were coping with the find at Raven Manor.

'Poor Grandad, every charity and historical organisation is crawling out of the woodwork trying to lay some ownership claim on the ruins.'

'That sucks.' Leo grinned as his mother made a tutting noise.

'He'll need to get Henry Davidson on the case.'

'He already has, Mr Ravel, there're no discrepancies with the deeds, they go back to well before 1837 when they transferred to our family and... oh *gosh*, sorry.' The Manor had formally belonged to the Ravels. Saxon certainly hadn't meant to rub the fact in his face.

'It's history, don't worry about it.' Martin's insides churned for a moment until he saw Beverly raise her eyebrows which signified a warning to behave. He gave her a reassuring smile and asked Saxon to carry on.

'Ownership can't possibly be disputed.' He continued more carefully. 'Preservation orders and such, have never been a problem. We can't stop the public interest, but we're certainly not going to advertise it.'

Martin had fully expected the old man to collect any monies possible but didn't voice his thoughts. The way his daughter kept throwing the lad small adoring glances couldn't be ignored. For her sake, he would make an effort and had to admit Saxon was polite, intelligent and it seemed, considerate of his daughter's needs. Pete Alford had let slip a few things about the Astra van. At first, he'd been hopping mad to think they were in debt to the Thorpes, but once he'd cooled down, he'd realised that wasn't really the case. This was something personal between Toni and her boyfriend.

'It's insurance we have to think about.' Saxon continued. 'The underground chapel isn't open to the general public yet, but people will still try and they do so at their own risk. All the appropriate signs are going up and Henry's sorting whatever paperwork is needed. Um, would you like to come over and have a look, Mr Ravel?' he turned to Beverly and Olivia, 'and you ladies as well, of course.'

'Go on Dad.' Toni leapt from her chair and went to give him a hug. 'It's really exciting.'

'Err, yes… I think I would, thank you.' It would be the first time he'd set foot on Thorpe land since he'd been a young boy and with a couple of his village friends had chased the snooty Linus home one day. He tried not to smile, remembering how a cow pat had hit him right in the back of his stripy, private school blazer. No doubt these days the nanny state would call it bullying. He shifted a bit uncomfortably in his chair, had he been a bully? he hadn't meant to be.

Toni beamed at Saxon from behind her father's shoulder. They'd already discussed this and would make sure it was at a time when Linus and Alexander were out of the way.

'What's happening about tea with the Bishop, Saxon?' Beverly asked.

'Oh yes, glad you reminded me.' He turned to Toni. 'Saturday afternoon at three o'clock.'

'Ideal. Do you want me to drive?'

'No thanks,' Saxon answered a little too quickly. Martin and Leo began to laugh.

'Did you really expect to turn up at the Bishop's palace in that heap of junk?' Olivia asked, ignoring her sister's glare.

'I'm going to borrow Grandad's car, I thought it would make it special.' Saxon said before Toni kicked off. This was beginning to remind him of his childhood visits, the constant snipes and bickering, which in turn had made him laugh, or become apprehensive, never quite sure who or what was serious. Was Flora, alive? *Did* she have children? His cousins in America kept in touch but didn't have a lot of interest in their English family. Thank God for Leo and the Ravels, because of them, he'd never felt alone growing up.

When supper was finished, they played a few games of cards, the conversation was kept deliberately family free and the atmosphere remained comfortable. Leo also made a point of noticing straight away if his father's brows began to furrow, Sax looked awkward, or his sisters or mother were about to put their foot in it and steered them all into safer waters.

By the time Saxon said he should be going, he was on first name terms with Martin and Beverly.

Toni walked him outside and thanked him again for the bracelet. 'What do you make of the fact that John Ravel is buried in what used to be unholy ground.' Toni had read what Saxon had messaged across last night, it was still a mystery, just another thing to check with Sebastian?

'I suppose we have to assume it was a suicide. All I could find out was that George Ravel and Emma Thorpe died in a boating accident and John Ravel died a few weeks later.'

'I checked my facts after we spoke on the phone. The year he died, George's son was only one-year-old and I was right, that little boy was Francis. He still lived here, on the farm until he died in the late seventies.

'What about your grandad, Oliver?'

'I remember him a little. Dad's study used to be his bedroom, I was nearly five when he died. My grandma was long gone, even before Leo was born. Do *all* our family stay with us forever? Poor Leo, do you think he knows he's taking on Mum and Dad as well as the farm.'

Saxon shrugged. 'Looks like I'll have the same thing, doesn't it? In another fifteen years, *if* Grandad is still alive, he'll be in his nineties and Dad will be pushing seventy.'

'And you, my gorgeous man, won't be seeing forty again!' Toni laughed at his horrified expression.

'Oh Hell, I didn't think of that. Let's not talk about it anymore. Saturday will work out even better for date night now, we can stay in the city after seeing the Bishop?'

'I want to treat you to dinner, please don't argue. Book somewhere nice for us.'

He was about to say no, knowing that she couldn't afford it, but thought better of it. Instead, he would find a decent inexpensive restaurant. 'Only if you let *me* pay for the cinema, you can decide what we go to see.' He reluctantly let go of her hand and got in the car.

'Deal.' She leaned in through the window to kiss him goodnight. Quando, who had been well behaved up until that point, started fussing and whining at her feet. She picked up the pup, who was really too large to be carried. 'Tea with the Bishop, Quando, how exciting.'

* * *

Saxon was onsite the next morning when Alexander called to say the altar stone had been lifted, and more relics had been discovered. He watched the foundations of the clubhouse being laid and spent the rest of the day checking over plans and wondering once again how he could persuade Toni to leave Pretty Feet. She was only working on Monday next week, taking the other days as annual leave. He couldn't wait to see her in the bridesmaid dress the following weekend. Olivia had shown him a swatch of the material and it looked nothing like Kermit, much more of a forest green. With her lovely blonde hair, she'd look stunning.

Tomorrow was their big day out. He mustn't forget to invite her over for breakfast either. Vanessa had been going on about it, not taking no for an answer. She was like an annoying wasp, always buzzing around. But, if she was trying to make an effort in welcoming Toni into the family, he should be grateful. Wednesday would be ideal, that way he'd get to see her midweek, before the wedding.

Chapter Eighteen

'Not too heavy on the mushrooms.'

The same dark crimson dress bought in the mall, with a short-sleeved black cardigan and black kitten-heeled shoes would be fitting attire for the Bishop's visit. Toni smiled as her mother nodded approvingly.

Saxon, when he arrived to pick her up, was wearing a dark navy suit, light grey shirt and matching tie. Toni had to agree with her mother's summarization. He looked rather dashing.

'We're a little overdressed for the cinema.' She grinned as he opened the passenger door of Alexander's six-year-old BMW, which to her, looked brand spanking new.

'So, what? you look beautiful, but then you always do.'

Toni sank back in the rich plush seat and decided she was going to enjoy this trip. If her father was spending this sort of money on transport, it would be for something practical. Just occasionally, it was nice to give yourself over to complete unadulterated luxury.

Saxon watched her eyes dart over everything on the dashboard. 'If she was mine I'd let you drive, but I'm under strict instructions, I'm afraid.'

'That's okay if we get offered wine from the holy chalice, I'll have to drink yours as well. I would have been happy going in the Cherokee you know.'

'It needs a good clean inside and to tell you the truth I quite like driving this car.'

'Do you know where the Palace is?'

'You do *know* it's not an actual *Palace*, don't you?' He chuckled.

'Umm, y-yeah, I knew that,' she stuttered feeling stupid.

'You're so cute at times, Ravel.' He laughed.

'Sod off, Sax, don't patronise me. Why *is* it called a palace then, *Einstein*?'

'I don't think it is, not unless it really is one, like Lambeth or Wells. I guess, once upon a time, they did live in castles and palaces. We're going to a large estate owned by the church, they have a care home there with flats and offices. No doubt the Bishop will have the penthouse!'

'It's exciting whatever it is.' She turned her attention back to the car. 'So, Alexander doesn't drive much now?'

'Not at night, his eyesight isn't so good in the dark. He's a good driver otherwise, his reactions are still quick. I'm not keen on him going too far, hence the trip the other day to see the puppies. I've noticed his confidence has taken a bit of a knock since I came back from uni or perhaps it's just that he's quieter in general... Vanessa's influence maybe?'

Toni certainly didn't think Satan was lacking in confidence, but she kept that opinion to herself. 'She does come across as a bit of a ball-breaker. Look at your dad.' She realised she might have gone too far with that remark when he didn't answer. 'I'm sorry, Sax I didn't mean anything by it, Linus was really nice to me when I came over.'

'It's okay,' he gave a tight smile. 'I can hardly blame you for voicing what I've been thinking for ages.' He gave a long sigh, and taking note of where they were, pulled off the motorway. 'Not too far now.' He was well aware his dad had always been a bit on the weak side. Even his mother, who Saxon had loved dearly, had pushed Linus around when she could. The last year or so, since the golf club visits had increased, he had seemed much happier. The threat of a hiding after he'd been through the tunnels, was, of course, a joke. It had also shown a caring side something Saxon always knew was there, but rarely witnessed.

No one had ever raised a hand to anyone in his family, so far as he could recall, unless he counted the suspect slapping noises he heard sometimes walking past Linus' and Vanessa's bedroom. The dubious sounds, which usually ended in whimpering, his *father's* whimpering, forced him to leave the house, and take the dogs for a walk. However late at night, he was unable to remain under the same roof. The thought of what might be going on behind that door was not an image he wanted to go to bed with. Often the dogs would enjoy a midnight run to the ruins and back, though fortunately for him, maybe not for his father, it hadn't been necessary for some time.

* * *

The Bishop lived in a large, light and airy ground floor apartment, in what had once been a stately home, built during the late 1900's. Saxon was correct in thinking part of it was a care home, in this case, exclusively for all levels of the ministerial orders. They had seen a few nurses and nuns walking around to the back of the building as they arrived. Possibly changeover time in their shift pattern.

Toni was fascinated with the décor and amount of shelving, holding what looked like the whole history of England in leather-bound volumes. She also wondered about the Bishop's somewhat casual clothing, was this his *dress-down* robes, or had he just left a layer off? Also, what had come as a surprise was his age. Not the ancient church authoritarian they'd both expected, but instead, a fifty-something, polite and friendly looking fatherly figure, who put them at ease immediately. A priest ushered them through to a comfortable lounge where they were asked to sit. He then pulled a cord near the door and collected a pile of papers on his way back.

'Now that tea is on its way, we can get started.' The Bishop smiled. 'You can tell me all about your adventures discovering the Abbey's secret place of worship, and I'll tell you what was found yesterday, and also a history of the manor, which you may or may not already know.'

The next hour consisted of a resume by Toni and Saxon, from first seeing the small fissure which on closer inspection was actually a cave, to the lifting of the slab above their heads and emerging in what used to be the courtyard of the Manor. All conversation was interspersed with perfectly brewed aromatic afternoon tea, which the priest poured from a large china teapot, accompanied by an assortment of small cakes and sandwiches.

The Bishop showed them photographs of the items that had been discovered the day before. Two chalices and various strings of rosary beads, some wooden, some incorporating semi-precious stones. Also, various gilt frames, the pictures inside mostly rotted away. One or two had survived, because of the dry conditions and the loving way they had been wrapped in heavy waxed cloth. The last and most relevant photo they were shown was of a large crucifix.

'The first discoveries were buried in a lined casket beneath the altar. Then the altar itself was examined. A hidden compartment was spotted and the crucifix was found wedged inside. From the church's point of view, it is one of the most exciting discoveries in years, possibly in my lifetime.'

Saxon studied the photo. 'Is it gold?'

The Bishop nodded. 'It needs to be authenticated, but yes. You can't tell the size by the photo of course, but it's over two feet high and very heavy. If it is solid gold,

I can't even begin to calculate the value. Although the relevance to the church is far greater than any monetary benefit.'

'The detail is amazing. I'd love to see the real thing. Will it stay in this country?' Toni asked.

'I hope so, I will raise a good case to keep it, but of course, it depends where it originated from. If for instance, it was gifted from Rome, then... perhaps that's its rightful place. God will guide us. Now then, talking of home, I have some information that will be of interest to the both of you, I'm sure. It's quite remarkable that I am drinking tea with representatives of both significant families in the Abbey's history.'

He missed the look the two of them gave each other. Toni thought, if the Bishop knew half of what they did about their *significant* families, it would make his Holy toes curl.

'We first have records of Ravel Manor, dating back to 1482, that would have been the reign of Edward IV.'

'That old?' Saxon interrupted.

The Priest's lips thinned, but the Bishop smiled and carried on. 'It is likely the only thing that remains of the original building is the tower and the main supporting walls. Over the years, it was rebuilt several times. However, by its very name, it belonged to your family, at the beginning, Miss Ravel.'

Toni nodded, conscious that she had a large mouthful of cake, just at the moment he'd singled her out.

'We can only assume the family were in support of Henry Tudor when he came to the throne, otherwise, it is unlikely they would have retained ownership. Now then,' he produced more photos and handed them both a copy. 'Can either of you read that?'

'For, great fins and to make...' Toni shrugged and looked at Saxon.

'It's not fins,' he tried hard not to return the Bishop's grin. 'For great *sins*,' he clarified, 'and a-atonement?' he offered and saw a nod. 'I, Louis Richard Ravel gift the Manor for a period of... I can't read the rest, sorry.'

'No matter, we have a typed copy, I'll read it to you. For a period of one hundred years to the church, no rents to be paid. After this time, it shall revert to the Ravel family, for their personal use.' He put the paper down and removed his glasses. 'Those may not be the exact words, but it is a reasonable summarisation. We also know, during the reign of Henry VIII, the Ravels changed their name to Raven and took back the Abbey. To protect the monks and priests, we think. The Ravels originally came from France, they were strong in the true faith and in great danger from the Protestant King. The name Raven may have been to deflect interest. Whatever the reason, they allowed secret worship below the Manor, for many years.'

'Erm... your holiness, do you know what the sin was?' Toni asked, pretty certain she'd addressed him incorrectly.

'Much of the history of that time was recorded by the church, their view on matters would be very... hmm, how can I say, narrow-minded. They lived by strict orders, and that is how they saw the world around them. It seems, this Louis Ravel, raped his own sister and the young daughter of a nearby household.' He looked at Saxon, 'an ancestor of yours, a Thorpe. Both these girls went on to give birth to sons. Now then, they were married off very quickly so we can't be sure Louis was the father in each case, but I assume it's what everyone thought.' The Bishop was quite surprised by the absence of shock on his visitors' faces. They looked almost resigned to hearing these sorts of stories. 'These two boys went on to become the main heirs and heads of each household.'

Saxon cottoned on to their lack of concern and gave Toni a surreptitious nudge. 'Gosh, that's terrible, those *poor* girls.'

'Oh yeah,' Toni piped up, 'what a bast... dastardly thing to do.' She cringed and avoided eye contact with Saxon at all costs.

'What happened to Louis, Your Grace?' Saxon asked quickly.

Your Grace, bloody hell that's what I should have called him.

'He was murdered, soon after the second boy was born, found strangled in his bed.' The bishop handed them both an A4 file. 'There're copies of all the prints I showed you earlier and a brief history of the Manor, including what we've discussed. Raven reverted back to Ravel in 1700. Perhaps by then, the name wasn't synonymous with the Catholic faith, it certainly wouldn't have been so prominent. As far as the Thorpe's ownership went, the house and some thousand acres of land changed hands around 1836. According to rumour, it was won in a gambling debt by Geoffrey Thorpe. Leaving the Ravels with about half of their original land. I assume a lot of that was sold off and the remainder is Ravel Farm, as it stands today? We don't know if that's a true historical fact, of course, but it makes it all sound a lot more interesting, even if gambling is not to be condoned. As you are probably aware, the large house was destroyed by fire soon after. Whether a kitchen accident, or arson, who knows? I have a feeling the former owner, Edward Ravel, would not have parted with his home and land easily and it would not have sat well with him afterwards.' He stopped and looked at his watch. 'I have been much longer than I intended, no wonder Father Bartholomew is looking so tense. Your family history is fascinating.'

Later that evening when they were finishing dessert and had spent the entire meal talking about gold, rape, and murder. Saxon declared the remainder of the evening to be Thorpe, Ravel and Raven free.

They held hands through the film, a romantic comedy that thankfully, didn't require much concentration. During the journey home when a family topic threatened, it was quickly quashed. Toni described the hotel they'd be staying in for Olivia and Josh's reception and asked if Alexander realised what he was letting himself in for, having Lucifer and Quando together for the best part of two days?

* * *

'Dad's very quiet.' Linus said to Vanessa and Saxon, the following evening. 'Anyone know what's wrong?'

'Don't fuss.' Vanessa answered looking bored. 'They all go quiet and withdrawn when they get old.'

Saxon looked at her in annoyance. 'It's because Aunty Sarah isn't there to answer the Skype call for the second week in a row. She doesn't even bother to send a message if she can't make it. Grandad sits waiting for up to half an hour, just in case.' If ever there was a good time to talk to him about Flora this would be it. *I can't, we agreed, not until after the wedding.*

'Don't get uptight, Saxon, it's not good for you.' Vanessa moved behind his chair and began to massage his shoulders. 'I'm sure if I lived in the States I wouldn't skype my parents every week.'

Saxon sent a silent plea across the table and Linus, as if waiting for years to be asked for help, jumped up from his chair. 'Stop fussing the boy for *God's* sake, he doesn't want you touching him all the time, he has a girlfriend for that.'

The silence went from uncomfortable to deadly. Vanessa's hands gripped Saxon's shoulders and he felt the tips of her nails digging through his t-shirt. Whether he was in shock or some deadly paralysing venom was flowing from her fingertips and oozing into his skin he wasn't sure, but the ability to move seemed to have left him.

'Don't be so *ridiculous*,' she finally spat. 'He knows I'm just very empathic to his moods, and anyway, it's nice to feel a bit of muscle for a change.' She sneered at Linus and thankfully for Saxon, released the death grip, so he could slide onto the next chair and from there, get up and take refuge on the far side of the kitchen. 'I'm *very* aware he has a girlfriend, you've embarrassed everyone for no reason and made a complete and utter fool of yourself.' She turned to Saxon and forced a smile, a bit miffed that he'd moved away. 'Did you discuss which day would be best for breakfast?'

'I thought mid-week, perhaps Wednesday? I know on Thursday she's home alone, waiting in for deliveries.'

Vanessa's mind began working, home alone, that meant if it took a few hours for the symptoms to kick in, no one would be around to help. 'Actually, darling, Thursday would be ideal for me and they never deliver to the village first thing. A well-cooked breakfast and an hour with you would set her up nicely.'

He was a little irritated that she'd asked his preference and then ignored the answer. 'Okay if Toni's happy, Thursday it is. Um, Dad, can I have a word with you about something.' He took Linus' arm and guided him out of the room, afraid he was about to speak up for the second time in his six-year marriage. Somehow, he didn't think his father would survive two acts of rebellion in one evening. 'Sorry, just had to get you out of there, let's join Grandad and cheer him up a bit. When the coast is clear I'll come back and grab some beers.'

Linus patted his arm. 'You're a good boy Saxon, plenty of your mother in you, thank goodness.'

* * *

Toni silently screamed every time Olivia went into meltdown during the next few days. Outwardly, she kept her cool and tried hard to be supportive of every imaginary disaster and possible negative outcome her sister could dream up. Each one more horrific than the last. Thank goodness her sister had left this afternoon to stay with Sophie, for two nights. They would all benefit from some well-deserved peace and quiet.

Yet again, she was aware that they hadn't spoken to Sebastian. There was all the Bishop's history about the Manor that she wanted to share and most of all, the recent finds, especially the gold crucifix.

Annie popped around for a quick visit on Wednesday evening to say there was no sign of the letter in the filing cabinet or any of the files and she'd been through every single one. What she didn't say, was at the first opportunity next week, she intended to search Robert Davidson's office.

They spent an hour playing with Quando, and Toni showed her the wallpaper she planned to decorate Olivia's room with. Hopefully enlisting the help of her father and Saxon, by playing the *male bonding* card.

Leo, discovering Annie was in the house, kept finding reasons to interrupt them. In the end, Toni asked him to join them, but first, grabbed a bottle of something nice so they could toast Olivia's absence, for want of a better excuse. On Friday morning, she'd return home to spend a quiet day with her family and that night would be her last in the farmhouse, as Olivia Ravel.

* * *

Early on Thursday morning, Toni took Quando for a walk down to the strawberry fields and back. The pickers, mostly students, were camping close by and rising with the sun, were already out working, keen to earn as much as possible in a short time. Toni stopped briefly to chat to a few that didn't seem to object too much when Quando bounded through the plants to greet them. As they were all kneeling or sitting, they were pretty much at his mercy.

Following a shower and deciding on a light, floral summer dress, she left the house again, this time alone. More walking, perhaps she'd lose a few pounds, especially if she didn't like the look of the omelette. Mushrooms were okay in very small doses, it was only because Vanessa had offered, and Saxon had seemed so pleased, that she hadn't had the heart to refuse, now she was wishing she had.

After breakfast, they were planning to drive to the site so she could see what progress had been made. From there, she'd walk home having to spend the rest of the day cooped up indoors, waiting in for various deliveries for her sister. It would at least be an opportunity to forget everything and relax in the shade with a good book, as long as she could hear the doorbell. Olivia would never forgive her if she missed the last-minute essentials needed for her life in Cyprus. Her flight leaving first thing on Monday morning.

* * *

Vanessa, was still furious with Linus' words the other night, but had noticed how Saxon had come to her rescue and bundled his father away before he could spout off any more rubbish. She turned her attention to the morning's foraging. The first blow was not being able to find any Destroying Angels, which would have been perfect, being pure white and virtually undetectable when mixed with the common and safe field mushroom. Perhaps it was just as well, they were *so* poisonous, it would be difficult to use a small enough quantity in hers and Saxon's omelette to produce just a few minor symptoms. Also, she'd have been tempted to keep one back for Linus, and that really *would* be too much of a coincidence.

Instead, she spotted a familiar friend, another pale fungus she'd used on occasions to get time off school, just a little to make her throw up in front of her mother, any more and she would have been in serious trouble. The effects would be quicker than she'd have liked, but hopefully, Toni would still make it home before she felt them.

'Three different bowls Vanessa?' Saxon commented as he sat Toni at the kitchen table and poured them all an orange juice.

'Oh, um, yes, yours has extra, because of the physical work you're doing at the moment.' She wished she could slide her hand across her stepson's pecs. 'And um also, there's a choice of cheddar or stilton?'

'Cheddar please, and not too heavy on the mushrooms.' Toni said politely, wondering if whatever was glistening on Vanessa's mouth was lip gloss, or drool. It hadn't gone unnoticed how her gaze had lingered over Saxon. Feeling a bit possessive she reached for his hand under the table.

'Stilton for me please and plenty of mushrooms,' Saxon requested. 'I'll have Toni's share.'

'Okay,' she said brightly, turning her back to the table and hiding what she was doing. Apart from one or two, Saxon would certainly not be getting any of the mushrooms destined for Toni's plate.

The three omelettes were served quickly one after the other, Toni getting hers first. She was a bit dismayed by the number of mushrooms and would have asked Saxon to swap, he seemed to have less, but she didn't like stilton, so that wasn't an option.

By the time the other two had finished, she'd managed to eat half. The looks Vanessa kept sending her, and the constant 'Don't you like it?' and 'I picked them especially', made her feel well and truly guilt tripped.

'I'll finish it.' Saxon offered, taking her leftovers.

'*No.*' Vanessa shrieked, lunging for the plate and hurrying to scrape it off in the waste disposal. 'Sorry,' she giggled nervously, looking at their bemused faces. 'Yours was cooked first, Toni, it'll be cold by now. Shall I make you a fresh one, darling?'

Saxon looked uncomfortable, he didn't like her calling him that at the best of times, certainly not while his girlfriend was sat next to him. 'No thanks, that was very nice, but we should be going now.' He threw Toni a look which implied, *right now.*

'Thank you *so* much, Vanessa, that was yummy. Sorry I couldn't finish it.' She followed Saxon out into the fresh air, the lingering taste of mushroom already making her feel a little queasy. She didn't let on, within an hour she'd be home and by then, no doubt, perfectly alright again.

'I can't believe how much work has been done here.' Toni studied what was marked out by the deep trenches. 'It's exciting.'

'You're standing right in the main reception.' Saxon had planned to hold off a bit longer before talking jobs, but he couldn't help himself. 'Please think about that job offer, I'd really love it if you worked here, and like I said, you can choose which area you fancy.'

Toni took a deep breath, was she ready for that level of commitment, especially if things didn't work out between them? This wasn't the time for what-ifs and not making a decision, if she wasn't careful all the jobs would be taken and she'd be stuck working twenty-two hours a week, in a shoe shop, on minimum pay for the rest of her life. 'I could quite see myself sat here.' She walked to where she thought a desk might be fixed and looked at him, a little shyly.

'*Really*, do you mean it?' Saxon beamed and picking her up swung her around.

'Woah, don't do that after those mushrooms, they really didn't agree with me.'

He put her down quickly. 'You do look a bit pale, you should have said, I've seen you eat fried mushrooms before.'

'Yeah, I don't *hate* them, the odd ones you get with a fry up are okay. I never go for mushroom soup or risotto in a restaurant though, they tend to be stronger tasting. I'll be fine, the walk home will do me good.'

'Are you're sure, I can drive you?'

'No, really. I'm going to cut through the woods, and just so you know, I'm not looking for Sebastian, but if I do see him I'll fill him in on what we've learned.'

Saxon was so happy she was going to accept a job and Saturday night was getting close, there was no way he would risk a row. He would have to let this mention of Sebastian pass without comment. 'Text me when you get home and let me know how you're feeling. Oh yeah and drink plenty of water.'

'Will do, Doctor Thorpe. What're your plans for tomorrow?'

'Here for the morning and then making myself beautiful for the wedding, and for you of course.' He laughed.

'Sax, you're already the most beautiful man I've ever seen, I can't wait for Saturday night.'

He was listening for a punch line and when none came, kissed her goodbye. He saw her wave as she reached the bottom of the hill and then she was swallowed up by the trees. Only then did he realise she had felt a bit clammy in his arms.

'Heigh-ho, Antonia, verily, I hast been awaiting ye for such a long time.'

'I saw you a few days ago. But I do have lots to tell you.'

Sebastian's eyes grew round with the stories of his ancestors. He'd already known most of it but enjoyed hearing the story from Toni's lips. The main find, the one that had impressed the bishop so much, was quite a revelation. He'd stayed in the underground chapel and watched them move the altar but had left before the crucifix was discovered. 'Methinks these things hath been returned to whither they belong. Now just the Sapphire-Heart and mayhap I hast done enough to be forgiven and received into heaven.' He said almost wistfully.

'Is this what it's all about Sebastian, forgiveness? What did you do that's so terrible? You weren't anything to do with the drowning, were you?'

'Drowning? I hast never stood guilty of that sin I warrant. To what dost ye refer, darling girl?'

Toni took a step back and looked at him sternly, he laughed loudly and closed the distance. 'Emma Thorpe,' she said quickly.

'Aye, Emma, that tricky ladybird. A more accomplished flirt ye never didst see.' *Except for Alice Greymoor, a story for another day*. 'Mistress Emma Thorpe took both Father and Son to her sleep chamber.'

'What, both at the same *time*? Together?'

'*Antonia*, thou shouldst not bethink or jest of such things, of course *not* at the same time. The son hadst a wife and child, but Emma wast like a drug. When he discovered his ladylove between the sheets with his own father, he planned to kill himself and that lady also. The father, a fusty old gent, wast full of remorse but 'twas too late. Mayhap he wast mad with love or he hadst hoped to get her with child and produce a second son? Thou shalt find many elderly fathers in our bloodline, always trying to produce a second son. Samuel Ravel, mine own grandson, sired seven daughters afore his poor wife gave birth to a boy and promptly died as the babe made his long-awaited appearance.' He stopped when he noticed Toni was swaying slightly. 'Art ye quite well, dear heart?'

'Yes, carry on, this is fascinating, as are all your stories. I think I ate something that didn't agree with me. I'll be fine.'

'Thou must tell me to cease, Antonia, shouldst these ailments worsen. I have digressed from the story. The fusty gent hanged himself, not far hence. His family cut him down and tried to disguise such wrongdoings. The Vicar wast having none of it, suicide wast an unholy sin and couldst not be ignored.'

'Saxon was right, that's why he's buried in the corner of the church, outside what used to be the original wall. Oh *ow*.' Toni gripped her stomach as a shooting pain tore across her abdomen feeling as if it was slicing her in two.

'What ails ye wench, ye look most whey-faced.'

'I'm going to be...' she barely managed to turn away before vomiting.

'Sebastian watched helplessly as she fell to the ground and began to rock.

'I'm in terrible p-pain, get Saxon, he's up on the top field,' she pointed in the direction of the coast.

'I dost not wish to leave ye, sweetheart.'

'Sebastian, *please.*'

Saxon heard the call emanating from the edge of the woods, he looked around, none of the workers indicated they'd noticed anything. When he heard it a second time and recognised Sebastian's voice he had a terrible feeling something was very wrong. He raced down the hill and burst into the wood landing in Sebastian's strong arms.

'Come apace, our girl is not looking in goodly health and she asks for ye.'

It took less than a minute to reach her. Saxon fell to the ground and pulled her gently towards him.

'Tis her woman's time, perchance, her *menses?*' Sebastian whispered as if the word shouldn't be spoken at all.

'No, it's not.' Toni moaned. 'Sax, my stomach, it's *so* bad.'

'Send for the apothic. She hast the sweats and hath taken on the colour of ashes.'

Saxon debated calling for an ambulance. It would be too difficult to try and direct them to the site. The hospital was a half an hour's drive away. In the end, aware he was wasting precious minutes he decided it would be quicker if he drove. 'Out of the way Sebastian.' Saxon swept Toni into his arms and proceeded to climb the hill and get her into his car. 'Hang in there, love.'

'It must have been Vanessa's cooking,' she joked, feebly, before everything went dark.

A cold feeling of dread went through Saxon, they'd eaten the same thing, mushroom omelette, would he be next? 'I have to hurry, it could be food poisoning. I have to get her to A&E before I become ill myself.'

Sebastian watched them leave, ignoring the other men on the building site, they couldn't see him anyway. 'Mine dearest girl, be safe. Whoever Aaneee is, let that gent be worthy.' His eyes narrowed. Vanessa, the wench from the ruins, he knew she was a danger. *I shalt kill ye, mine lady, ere ye harm the ones I love.*

Chapter Nineteen

'We'll have to take a rain check on that coffee.'

By the time Toni was put in a hospital gown, had a dextrose-saline drip attached and blood taken, Saxon had vomited twice. Luckily both times, in the disposable cardboard bowls the nurse had thrust at him.

'Has she woken up?' He asked for the third time, after the medical team had also taken his blood to rush off to the lab.

'I'm not sure, but right now, *you're* my patient and from what you've told us, it definitely sounds like you both ate some toxic fungus. It would help if we knew exactly what it was. You say your stepmother is on the way?'

Saxon nodded and tried to get off the trolley, but the staff nurse wasn't being overly helpful. She kept telling him to sit back so she could monitor his heart rate. The first thing he'd done when they'd arrived, was phone Toni's family and then his own. Linus answered and said Vanessa wasn't at all well and had been violently sick. Hearing what had happened, he'd told Saxon they'd come straight there.

'I *really* need to see my girlfriend.' He tried again.

'Let me go and find out how she is. Apparently, it's a good sign the symptoms showed up so quickly. With some types of mushrooms, they lie dormant for quite a few hours, which can cause irreversible damage.'

Saxon hadn't needed to hear that and lay fretting, waiting for news. When, a few minutes later, he heard his father's and even Vanessa's, voice, from the other side of the curtains he felt a huge burden lift. He didn't feel quite so relaxed when Martin Ravel could also be heard, demanding to see his daughter.

As soon as the lab results were back, the doctor explained that Saxon's and Vanessa's kidney and liver functions were within normal limits, they obviously hadn't ingested very much of the poison. They would be monitored for a while longer than allowed to go home if all was well.

Toni burst into tears when some hours later, Saxon was finally allowed into her cubicle. She clutched his hand and told him she had to stay overnight. 'I have to be out by Saturday, I'm going to be a bridesmaid,' she sobbed.

The doctor looked sympathetic but wasn't going to be swayed. 'It was extremely lucky you didn't eat the whole omelette. I highly doubt that we're dealing with a particularly *dangerous* variety of fungi, considering how much you *did* eat. But you have suffered some nasty effects, your blood pressure is high and you said yourself, you could feel your pulse racing. I want you to have IV fluids for at least the next twenty-four hours. We'll take bloods again later today and tomorrow morning, and then, depending on how you are, make a decision.'

Martin looked a bit disgruntled, wanting someone to blame, and Saxon, being the only possibility, was getting the evil eye. 'She doesn't even like bloody mushrooms.' He snarled.

Toni tried to persuade Saxon to leave with his family, she was worried about him driving, at least this way, Linus could follow behind and make sure he got home safely. She was also desperate to use the commode, which definitely wasn't going to happen while he was around. The staff nurse recognising the familiar predicament, was quite firm when she told him that her patient would settle much better if she was left alone to sleep.

Vanessa seethed all the way home. That detestable girl was going to recover after probably only one night's stay in the hospital. Those mushrooms couldn't have been the same ones she'd used when she was younger. Had they been, she was pretty certain Toni wouldn't still be alive now. She felt like shit and to top it all, at the bottom of her basket she'd found one Destroying Angel. It had quickly been disposed of and all evidence hidden, just in case there was going to be some sort of enquiry. What a shame the tiny killer would turn to compost beneath Linus' precious climbing roses. No doubt they'd suck up the extra energy and grow to twice the size, just to spite her.

The earlier dream of sitting in the back seat and comforting Saxon had turned into the horrid reality of sitting next to Linus and listening to reasons why she should rest during the afternoon, and he'd go and play a round of golf, to get out of her way.

Saxon received a call from Toni later that evening. She sounded very weak but in better spirits. The blood tests were showing signs of improvement, she'd been upgraded from nil by mouth to sips of water, with a promise of a cup of tea soon if she didn't throw up again. He wanted to drive back and see her, but she made him promise not to. In the end, they both had to content themselves with *miss you*. Neither would quite commit to using the *L* word, but both silently thought it.

Debating what to do next, an early night or watch a film, Saxon was surprised when his father knocked on the bedroom door.

'Um, is this a good time for a chat?'

'I guess, come in and sit down.' Saxon invited.

'Are you feeling better? Vanessa says she's still pretty rough, but she looks okay, to be honest.'

268

'I'm fine, Dad, don't worry and I've just spoken to Toni, she's a bit better as well.'

'Ah, splendid, um about Vanessa... do you think she's been acting a little oddly, lately?'

Saxon hadn't been expecting that and thought at first his dad was joking, but as the silence fell he realised he was deadly serious. 'Honestly? *Well*, I've always thought she was odd, like in a highly-strung way.'

Linus' smile didn't reach his eyes. He actually felt a bit sad, and today's events had brought a few things home. 'I wonder if it's my fault, perhaps I don't say enough...' he sighed. 'She's very jealous of Toni, I think it's just new younger blood, but watch your back.'

'Are you saying she'd physically do her harm? Do you think she *knew* about the mushrooms?'

'Good heavens *no*,' Linus quickly dismissed the remark. 'She was sick as a dog all the way to the hospital. I'm not very good with that sort of thing, smells and stuff.' He shuddered. 'No, I meant Vanessa preys on people's weaknesses and Toni appears a little... *innocent* at times. Which brings me to another topic.' Linus stood up and began hopping from one foot to the other, unable to stand still. 'Well, it's about the land she owns. I don't think she's aware just how profitable those fields could be. Robert Davidson is pretty sure building permission of some sort will be allowed there within the next few years. He's so convinced he wants to buy in. I wouldn't do anything underhand, she'd get a very good price from us.'

'I can't have this conversation with you while I'm lying here like an invalid.' Saxon got up from the bed and led Linus unceremoniously down the stairs and into the snug, where he thought they would have some privacy. 'Sit down, Dad and for God's sake listen, once and for all.'

Vanessa, hearing the ruckus, followed at a safe distance making sure she remained out of sight as her stepson began to lay down the law.

'Toni will *never* sell that land. She has big plans and they don't involve housing, well apart from *animal* housing.' He stopped to calm himself. Linus, about to speak again must have seen the warning note in his son's eyes and wisely, kept quiet.

'I love Toni and I want a future with her. Actually, I don't see a future of any kind, if she's not in it. Those fields *are* going to become a nature reserve. I'm going to help her and *you*, are going to help as well.'

Linus, realising everything Saxon was saying, came from his heart, decided it was the time to finally surrender. He also felt a large lump in his throat over the invite to become involved in their plans. 'Okay you win, if that's what she wants, then that's what she'll get. I'll tell Davidson, all deals are off. And yes, of course, I'll help. I love you, son, never think otherwise. It's hard sometimes, with Dad taking such an active role in your life. He did it so early on, I guess, we, your mother and I, just accepted things. I even though that you, err, loved him more than you loved me. Christ almighty, how pathetic do I sound?'

'You never had to feel that way, of course, I love Grandad, *and* I admire him, but you're my father, maybe we all forgot that along the way.' He pulled Linus into an embrace.

'So,' Linus began, a bit flustered. 'You've found the one, eh Saxon, your soul mate? Will you pop the question?'

'I hope so, but it's far too soon. Seeing her in the hospital, kind of gave me a nudge though. Let's see how things are at Christmas.'

And a happy Christmas to you, Martin Ravel. Linus chuckled, wondering how his old adversary would cope with that news. 'A New Year's Eve engagement party, perhaps? Did I ever tell you, your mother and I did that very thing?'

Vanessa silently fumed and tiptoed along the hallway to the kitchen. She didn't bother to acknowledge the men when they came in a few minutes later, to 'rustle up a tin of soup', Linus was saying. If Saxon thought he could lead her on and drop her at a whim, he was sorely mistaken. Somebody was going to pay and this time there would be no mistakes.

* * *

Toni called Saxon twice on Friday, the first was to say she was now allowed to eat and as long as she kept everything down without the help of medication, she was pretty certain the doctor would discharge her later. The second time, she was crying and told him they wanted to take one last blood sample and now she wouldn't know anything more until much later.

He did his best to console her, promising to speak quickly with Sebastian who would no doubt be worrying. He'd also collect Quando, it was one less job to worry about if she got home late. '*If?*' She'd sobbed down the phone. 'If *not,* she'd be signing her self-discharge papers.'

Before he'd taken his second step inside the woods, Sebastian was at his side.

'How fares our girl? Is all well and the duplicitous witch hanged?'

Saxon removed the strong hands that had his arms in a vice-like grip. 'She's recovering, hopefully out of hospital by this evening. Um, which *witch* are you referring to?'

'Your stepmother, that *evil* doodlebug cannot be allowed to live, she attempted murder most foul!'

'It was an accident. I confess to not liking her much but she's not really a bad person, not to *that* extent.' He didn't say he'd voiced his own suspicions to his father, only the night before.

Sebastian made some kind of growling noise and spat on the ground. 'Beware young Thorpe, I warrant that lady is no good. Ye shouldst throw a spanner at her.'

Saxon thought he couldn't possibly have heard that last bit correctly It would be safer not to comment, and anyway, Sebastian had disappeared. He'd never seen him so angry.

Quando at least was pleased to see him, and while he was chatting with Leo and Olivia, there was another call from Toni. Everything her end seemed to have speeded up and she was coming home, just waiting on the pharmacy porter to deliver her medication to the ward.

'Thank Christ for that.' Leo grinned.

Olivia breathed a sigh of relief and tried to hide the few tears that began to trickle down her cheeks. The family had kept quiet about the seriousness of what had occurred until she'd come home today. She wasn't sure how she felt about that. Yes, she'd had a wonderful time with Sophie, but wasn't happy not to have been at her sister's bedside when she'd been so ill.

'She didn't want you to know, Olly,' Saxon, guessing her thoughts gave her a hug. 'I won't stay, as much as I want to see her, this is family time.'

Olivia sniffled. 'This morning when I saw my bedroom I went mad. Where does she think I'm going to get ready tomorrow morning? Then I heard the news and it just wasn't important anymore. At least she's left me a bed to sleep in, even if it *is* surrounded by rolls of wallpaper and paint match-pots.' She gave a small laugh. 'When I found out how poorly she'd been, I even said a proper actual prayer, I haven't done that for years. Thanks, Sax,

I haven't told you how happy I am that the two of you are together.' She gave him a kiss on the cheek. 'See you tomorrow.'

'You're going to be a beautiful bride,' he said, feeling moved. 'Josh is a *very* lucky man.'

* * *

Toni didn't so much as glide down the aisle in front of her sister, as walk extremely cautiously. Concentrating on putting one foot in front of the other, she crossed her fingers beneath her bouquet in the hope that she didn't faint in a heap before the Vicar. The beads of sweat on her forehead seemed to disappear when she saw Joshua's face as Olivia finally stood in the doorway of the small village church, on Martin's arm.

She'd spied Saxon sitting five rows back with Annie and hoped the competent make-up girl had done enough so she'd appear rosy-cheeked and blooming with health. It couldn't be further from the truth. Her lab results had been bordering on normal and although reluctant, the consultant had reviewed everything and declared her ready for discharge, with a follow-up programme, mostly involving her own GP. The main problem was eating, she just didn't fancy anything and because of that, was feeling weak and quite light-headed. However, no one need know as long as she remained upright and managed to spoon a few mouthfuls of the wedding breakfast past her lips. She'd get through the day and still have her special night. The last thing she wanted was to let Saxon down.

He wasn't fooled, but went along with the charade, making sure between the lengthy photo shoots he was constantly in the wings, ready to prop her up, with the excuse of a cuddle, or make sure there was always a convenient chair nearby.

The meal was fantastic, they had both opted for the fish choice, and thankfully, Toni was able to eat at least half of it. After the speeches and the final toast to Mr and Mrs Luscombe, they sat outside in the fresh air with family, waiting for the evening celebrations to start.

At half past seven, on the dot, as per the order of the day, it was time for the cutting of the cake. An iced masterpiece topped with a sugared, fighter jet and the Cypriot flag. A very strange adornment, most of the older guests felt. Toni thought it was pretty awful, but of course, she didn't say, just sniggered quietly into Saxon's ear when the small plane toppled to the floor as soon as the knife made contact with the bottom tier. Josh grinned good-naturedly and announced, he was an Aircraft Technician and not a pilot, so this definitely wasn't a bad omen. Polite laughter echoed through the room with a bit of heckling thrown in from his RAF colleagues. It was soon swallowed up as the distinctive intro of the first dance began to play and Josh took Olivia's hand to lead her onto the dance floor.

'Are you up for this?' Saxon asked, discreetly, as other couples began to join in. Toni didn't hesitate but through the evening when they danced to other slow songs together, Saxon braced himself to take her body weight when she started to flag.

By midnight, they were finally alone in the bedroom; the four-poster which earlier in the day had looked rather magnificent, now began to appear a bit foreboding. Toni went into the bathroom to quickly prepare.

Saxon disappeared next and when he came back he slipped under the covers, took her in his arms and kissed her. 'Go to sleep now, love, you need it.'

'Sax, *no*, this wasn't the plan. It was meant to be special.'

'The thought of having you in my arms all night while we sleep together *is* very special.'

'B-but I wanted more, for both of us. You've been so attentive all day, it's not fair.'

'This is enough... for now,' he murmured, affectionately, before kissing her again. 'There'll be other nights, lots I hope. Plenty of chances to make up for this one. Now sleep and get well, that's what I really want.'

She didn't have the strength to argue anymore and snuggled her back against his chest, his arm came around and brushed against her breast gently. When she awoke eight hours later, they were still in the same position and she knew for certain what she'd suspected for a while, she was in love with Saxon Thorpe.

* * *

Annie's own happy memories of the wedding and Leo, were very fresh in her mind as she arrived at work on Monday morning. This was her best chance to search Robert Davidson's desk. According to his diary, which she'd checked last thing on Friday afternoon, he wouldn't be in until after lunch. There was no excuse for her being in here, he didn't like using any of the office juniors and certainly not a lowly apprentice.

He had his own secretary, Mona, and all the staff were aware that the two of them were *carrying on*. There were more than a few jokes going around the office, about whether or not the smarmy solicitor could make Mona moan. She was at the dentist this morning, very convenient, Annie thought, as she made a start on the two drawers that were unlocked.

It was unlikely Mr Davidson Snr would call her, he was ensconced in a meeting with Alexander Thorpe looking into indemnity clauses should some hapless tourist fall into the underground chapel or trip over a small gorse bush. Also, Mrs Dale was in this morning. All being well she had at least an hour to make use of the spare keys, *borrowed* from Mona's pigeonhole, which unlocked all the drawers and wall cupboards. Taking a sip of tea, she was careful to put the cup down on the blotter and emptying the contents of the first drawer onto the floor started looking for an envelope, addressed to Antonia Ravel.

Robert Davidson hadn't liked the sound of the voicemail from Linus, earlier that morning, saying, 'There were things to discuss, re the deal and he'd meet him in the office at ten o'clock, if he was free?' He had a bad feeling that the milquetoast that was Linus Thorpe, was getting cold feet. No doubt Vanessa had told him not to waste their money. Perhaps he should have included her in the contents of the letter, but he hadn't wanted to. The affair was losing its attraction and not only that, he'd seen a certain look on her face recently which left him uneasy. No, he hadn't been sorry that she'd missed their last two 'trysts'.

Expecting a free morning, he'd called Mona last night, forgetting she was undergoing root-canal treatment, poor cow. She wouldn't be feeling up to their usual evening get together either. It looked like this would be a family night in, listening to his children argue, and watching his wife stuff cheese and onion crisps while she watched Coronation Street.

So, he was not in the best of moods when he entered his place of work at five minutes to ten.

Linus entered the building almost immediately after. He was a little nervous, knowing how keen Robert was about the land. However, it had never been a foregone conclusion that Toni would've sold. Maybe he could get away with saying he'd done his best but no joy, unfortunately, that was the end of the matter.

The reception area was deserted and Henry's door was closed. Linus, remembering his father was there, gave a tentative knock. 'Sorry to disturb you, chaps, I'm just next door if you fancy going for a coffee after, Dad?'

Alexander smiled, it was a rare treat to catch Linus alone and as long as he didn't want to discuss any business propositions or his latest game of golf, he was good company. 'We're just about done here, if you're not going to be too long I'll chat to Henry for a while.' Just at that moment, they heard a crash and a lot of shouting followed by a cry, from the other room.

'I say, that sounds like young Amy,' Henry said, getting up from his chair.

Linus hurried across to Robert's office and threw open the door. There were papers strewn across the desk, a cup of tea had been knocked to the floor and broken china lay amongst the brown liquid that was seeping into the parquet flooring. Alexander and Henry came to a halt and all three men were in time to see Robert, his hands around Annie's upper arm, shaking her and oblivious to his audience, shouting something about sapphires. Mrs Dale, had also left what she was doing in the storeroom and stood behind the men wondering what all the noise was about.

Linus walked over the mess and tried to grab Annie's other arm, with a view to freeing her. 'What on *earth* has got into you, Rob?'

'Into me?' he sneered at Linus, finally letting go. 'Are you pulling out of our deal, yes or no?'

'Err... um, well.' He glanced at his father and at Annie, who was in tears. 'Good girl,' he soothed, 'go over and stand with Henry.' Seeing Rita's daughter so distraught gave him a modicum of strength. 'Yes, to answer your question, the deal's off.'

'You're utterly *pathetic*.' Robert spluttered, his already red face beginning to take on a purple tinge. 'You always were, in school, in business, in your marriage, Christ, no wonder you can't keep Vanessa in your own bed.' The warning sign was not the hurt look in Linus' eyes, but the sounds of indrawn breath from Henry and Alexander. Robert chose to ignore it. 'Well I don't need you, I'll put my own offer to the Ravel girl, one she won't be able to refuse.'

'He's after the treas...' Annie started.

Robert swung around and glared. 'As for you, you little twit, you're fired. Get your stuff and be out of this building within the next two minutes, or I'll press charges.'

'W-what do you m-mean?' she stuttered.

'Theft, of course, you had no business in here, I caught you red-handed, going through my private, *locked* cupboards.'

'I told you I w-was looking for a specific letter when you first came in.'

'Look, old chap, you can't treat the young lady this way.' Linus said hesitantly.

Alexander started to push his way into the room, he had no idea what was going on, but he knew a bully when he saw one.

'Leave this to me, Alex.' Henry put a hand on his friend's shoulder to stop him. 'Um, Amy, is this about the *thing* I wanted you to find? The err envelope I asked you to search for thoroughly, in *every* room?' He gave her a quick wink.

'Yes, Mr Davidson.' She didn't bother to correct her name, it was hardly important at that moment.

'You took it, didn't you, Robert?'

'I don't know what you're talking about, Father, took what?'

'The letter from my filing cabinet?'

Robert made a dismissive snort. 'I haven't been anywhere near your filing cabinet.'

'That's not true.' Annie piped up, feeling a bit more courageous. 'I saw you there a few weeks ago, you took a file out.'

'How *dare* you.' Robert seethed, taking a step in her direction.

Annie slunk back and Alexander and Mrs Dale moved in front to shield her. Linus also entered the fray, his hand curled into a fist and struck in the direction he hoped would do some damage.

Much to Alexander's surprise, because he hadn't thought that punch would dent a marshmallow, Robert yelled and dabbed at a trickle of blood running from his nose.

'That's it, you all witnessed it, assault. I'm phoning the police.'

'We witnessed *you* assaulting a young girl.' Henry said calmly. 'A member of staff who was following *my* instructions. I have no idea what was in that letter, I respect my clients too much to pry. I can't *prove* you took it, but I believe you did, and I can only imagine it states some reason why the land that Antonia Ravel left to her great-niece is more valuable than we thought.' He glanced at Annie. 'I think maybe your friend already knows the truth.' He saw Annie nod. 'Take yourself out of here Robert and don't come back. We'll sort out something, but you certainly won't be working in this practice again.'

'Now wait a minute, I've just been hit in the face by *Linus*.'

'Says who?' Alexander asked coolly. 'I saw you walk into the door in your hurry to get away from what you did to young Annie here.'

'That's preposterous and you know it.' Robert said, not looking quite so confident anymore.

'Yep, sorry Rob, that's how I saw it as well.' Linus added smiling with satisfaction. He'd known Vanessa was at it, but having her affair thrown in his face, in front of his father, didn't make him feel great. Any vindication he could feel, however small, was going to help.

'And I saw it too, you *swine*.' Mrs Dale added, getting a bit carried away by the excitement.

'Leave now, my boy, before charges really are made against *you*. I sincerely wish you all the best, for the sake of the family.' They all stood and watched as Robert packed a few things into his briefcase, dropped the keys into his father's hand and stormed off without saying another word.

'Take the rest of the day off Am..., my dear. Business, as usual, tomorrow.' Henry walked slowly to his office, he seemed to have aged ten years in the last ten minutes.

'Go on Annie.' Alexander nodded. 'I'll stay with him. Linus, we'll have to take a rain check on that coffee. Whatever you were planning with Davidson... well, I'm glad you came to your senses.'

'Yeah, I've had a lucky escape.' He gave a rueful smile. 'Do you have your mother's car, Annie, or would you like me to drop you home?'

'My mother's car?' she looked at him quizzically. 'Fancy you knowing I share with Mum. Err, actually if it's not too much trouble, yes, please. I feel a little shaken after all that.'

Linus kicked himself for nearly putting his foot in it. Alexander watched them leave, then braced himself and opened Henry's door, ready to supply a shoulder, should his old friend need one.

* * *

Answer your damn phone. 'Thank *goodness*, Sax, I've just had a really frazzled call from Annie. We have to speak to Sebastian right away and start looking for the necklace. People know. Can you get away now?'

Sebastian lifted Toni gently and sat her on his lap, much to Saxon's dismay. He liked the ghost, he really did, but just how long would he remain in their lives? He would never tolerate this sort of behaviour from any *mortal* man. After this latest treasure escapade, he and Toni needed a serious talk and hopefully, she wouldn't accuse him of overreacting. If she thought he was laying down the law, it could be the deal breaker in their relationship.

'What ails ye young Thorpe, thou hast a face as long as a witch's tit?'

Toni began to giggle but stopped abruptly when she saw Saxon wasn't amused. She climbed off Sebastian's knee, which she'd just begun to feel she was sinking slightly into anyway and moved next to him. 'Tell him,' she hissed. 'Tell him we want to hear his story, no more excuses.'

Saxon tried to forget what had just happened, this was important. 'We think some other people may know about the Sapphire-Heart, so we need to start looking for it today. But first, Sebastian, you have a promise to keep.'

Sebastian nodded. 'Thou art right, the time hath come. I fear ye shalt bethink less of me when I reveal what I must.' He took a deep breath, closed his eyes and pictured himself as a young boy running around the grounds of Raven Manor. 'I shalt tell ye the story of the

Sapphire-Heart but first, I must start at the beginning, at the hour I was born. The year of our Lord, 1660…'

Chapter Twenty

'Thou hast blood on thy face, Sebastian.'

Jane Heston clung to her mother's arm and screamed with pain. The rag she'd been biting on had fallen to the floor long ago, and no one had bothered to replace it. Moving her legs further apart she squatted even lower and with an almighty push, delivered a healthy baby boy.

'A bastard fer a bastard,' her mother said, with a voice as remote as it was cold. 'Chestnut, like ye and his grandfather, well then, a goodly wish on ye girl, yer going to need it. What shalt ye name the brat?'

'Sebastian, fer his father,' Jane said weakly, putting the babe to her breast where it began to suckle noisily.

'His *father*! Ye shouldst hath lain with an honest working man if ye couldst not keep yer legs together, at least ye wouldst be wed anon. Reginald Sebastian Raven shalt not beholdeth ye any more than Thomas Thorpe didst gaze mine way, once mine belly wast swollen.'

* * *

By ten years old, Sebastian could read, write a little and knew the history of the Ravens and Ravels. His father had insisted on it, preparing the way for the possibility of naming his bastard and only son, as his heir. Having been wed for nearly twenty years and having two living daughters but burying another, alongside his two sons, he was getting desperate. The only thing holding him back was the similarity in looks between Sebastian and Thomas Thorpe, Jane's father. How he hated that family. It was the reason he'd initially sought out the pretty kitchen maid. It didn't matter that her father rarely acknowledged her, his blood would still boil when he found out it was a Raven that had taken her innocence.

Reginald glanced at his left hand, and an intense rage came over him when he recalled how casually William Thorpe, one of Jane's half-brothers, had sliced three fingers off. Afterwards, he'd thrown down his sword and laughed, saying he wouldn't fight a cripple, everyone in the hall had laughed with him. They'd all chosen to forget the reason the fight had started. William had broken off his betrothal with Anne Raven, Reginald's fifteen-year-old sister, leaving her bereft and broken-hearted, while he went on to marry a lady of the court, all for social advancement.

Eventually, after another two years had passed and it looked unlikely he would father any more legitimate children, he named the young Sebastian, heir of Raven Manor, moving him into the large family home, and paying Jane enough coin to make her forget she had ever birthed him.

By the age of seventeen, Sebastian could add fencing and fluent French to his list of accomplishments. He even accompanied his father on a visit to Court. King James hadn't been in attendance that day but it hadn't taken the shine off the visit and Sebastian's good looks won the hearts of many noble ladies. The fact that he remained a bit rough around the edges only enhanced his charm. The only thing that marred the visit was his father's clear instruction to deny his true faith, should he be asked. Thankfully the topic didn't arise.

That same year, both his stepmother and birth-mother died from influenza. A deadly disease which swept mercilessly through the small village, killing indiscriminately, rich and poor alike. He mourned them both, one for a boyhood memory and the other, for a generous, welcoming lady that had gladly accepted him into her home. He never knew that the reason for her kindness was due to the fact that her ravaged body was no longer expected to undergo anymore fumbling beneath the bedsheets in an endeavour to produce a male child.

Life was as perfect as it could be for Sebastian. He had two half-sisters, both older, who adored him, his pick of village girls, eager to satisfy his lusty nature and even, an uneasy alliance with the Thorpes, because of his mother's connection. They would not have been so civil, had they known he was regularly bedding his half-cousin, Marjorie Thorpe. Niece to Thomas Thorpe, Sebastian's own grandfather

Everything changed soon after his twentieth birthday celebrations. Talk of his arranged betrothal, which had, for the last year, been foremost in his father's mind, began to dwindle, as did any other interest shown to him. The reason being his father's new wife.

'Sebastian!'

He heard his father's call and rushed down the stairs to greet him. A month away on business was a long time to be left alone with only servants for company.

'Come, son and maketh thy bow to thy new stepmother. The Greymoors art a most influential family, am I not the luckiest of men that Alice didst accept mine offer of marriage? We wast wed a sennight ago, in London. *Well*? What say ye?'

Sebastian gave a deep bow and welcomed his father's lady. As he straightened he saw the look of disinterest change as she openly appraised him.

'A *fine* son ye hast husband. I warrant we can findeth a goodly position for him, once thy true heir is born.'

Sebastian remained silent but tried to meet his father's eyes, the older man kept looking away, obviously uncomfortable but also, not prepared to correct her statement. A feeling of betrayal, hurt and then self-preservation began to flood his core and looking more carefully at Alice, he gave his most beguiling smile. She flushed slightly and his dark green eyes twinkled. He'd yet to meet any girl or woman, that was immune to his charms.

His half-brother, Nicholas, was born seven and a half months later. A testament as to why the comely, blonde-haired Alice had accepted an older man who was lacking in hair as well as fingers. Reginald was deaf to any suggestion or servants' gossip that the babe looked rather too healthy to be premature. He was declared the rightful heir with some small compensation for Sebastian, promised.

Nicholas, was definitely not, as Reginald wanted to believe, his own flesh and blood, but the result of endless nights of passion between Alice and her own brother, George Greymoor.

An extended trip to the country by the siblings, two years prior to Nicholas' birth, had already resulted in the appearance of George's official ward. A blonde, blue-eyed baby girl, who was quickly given the Greymoor name.

Having a second set of friends die in an accident and leave an orphaned infant was too much of a coincidence. So, when Alice found herself with child for the second time and the hapless Reginald was thrown in her path, marriage it seemed, was the only choice left. Learning that her suitor owned a large country estate, sweetened the blow a little, even if she did not relish the thought of country life.

She easily persuaded her admirer, that he owed himself a second chance to fill the house with an army of strong sons. 'Who could rely on one heir?' she'd argued. 'Anything might happen.'

Over the next few years, Sebastian became a fine distraction, and although taking his own wife, an obvious act of defiance in his father's eyes, also gave Alice two healthy children. If Reginald chose to believe the boy and girl, both sporting the most alluring mix of dark green eyes and chestnut-brown hair were his own, so much the better.

Her life was not bad, but Alice pined for George and eventually persuaded Reginald, that her brother should join them at Raven Manor.

By the time Nicholas, had reached his ninth year, George had moved in permanently. His ward, Marie, accompanied him, and Sebastian often found himself looking at the pretty eleven-year-old and imagining Alice at that age. There was something else he thought he witnessed in the young girl, a hint of madness.

The brother and sister, fully aware of the family resemblance, started to plot Reginald's demise. Sebastian's removal would have to follow soon after, he was becoming far too suspicious.

Charges of theft would do nicely, George decided, after learning of the Sapphire-Heart. The necklace, he told Alice, was making its way, by ship to London and thought to be a gift for Queen Mary. He couldn't expect the captain, an acquaintance of his, to hand over such a treasure, but this stretch of coast was renowned for smuggling, many a sturdy ship and master had met a watery end at the hands of wreckers.

The siblings planned that George, would eventually be ensconced in Raven Manor as official guardian to his niece and nephews. Alice being so distraught, would declare never to marry again. George, if he had to for proprietary's sake, would wed some mealy-mouthed simple girl, who would live in ignorance, or should she prove difficult, would be packed off to a madhouse.

Their plans started to come to fruition when George managed to acquire the necklace just as he'd hoped. He had no money to pay for it, but as dead men tell no tales, neither can they recover their debts. George made quite sure that *that* particular loose end was taken care of. The next day he offered to accompany his brother-in-law during his rounds, visiting the tenant farmers.

George arrived home in a terrible state the same afternoon, the body of Reginald draped over the second horse. 'The ground wast so wet,' he gave by way of explanation to Alice and Sebastian. 'I gazed as the horse's legs didst shoot out in all four directions, thy beloved husband,' he looked slyly at his sister, 'hadst not a chance, tis a terrible tragedy. Verily, I am most sorry for ye also, Sebastian, what a blow, the loss of thy father and thy home.'

'Mine home?' Sebastian said, looking surprised. 'I may nay be heir, but methinks ye shalt find writ within the clauses of mine father's will, that I hast a home for life here, at Raven Manor. Also, mine goodwife Ann, and any future issue I beget.' He didn't miss the looks that passed between them and it sowed the first seeds of doubt. He reasoned that yes, his father was getting on and wasn't as strong as he'd once been, but, he was still one of the best riders in the county. An accident of the nature George described, was most unlikely.

The moment that Alice clasped eyes on the Sapphire-Heart, she nestled the large stone in her palm and declared she would never let it go. They would have to find another way to deal with Sebastian.

George paced the floor of her bedchamber and began to shout. 'A ship hath gone down and its crew perished for this very purpose. I am *grossly* out of pocket after paying the smugglers *and* I hast done murder fer ye, sister. Not once, but twice already. I dost not bethink Sebastian's head shalt cave as easily as the old gent's and I am not of a mind to try. What dost thou suggest, Alice, if it not be theft?'

Alice thought quickly, an unpleasant smile played about her lips. 'Let it be rape, that shouldst suffice well. 'Twill not be difficult to entice him to mine sleep chamber.' She daren't admit to George that it would hardly be the first time. 'Thee, mine dearest brother shalt save me from the murdering clutches of the rogue, so traumatised with his father's loss and the fact he is not the heir, he must taketh revenge on the one he holds such bitterness towards.' She smiled again, 'Dost not forget tis *thy* son who is the eldest and shalt inherit everything.'

George looked doubtful, 'Sebastian is wed to Ann and I want not his filthy hands on thy body.'

'His wife is of nay consequence; her bags shalt be packed in less time that mine late husband's cock wast able to stay erect. Sooth, most times he wast not even able to swive me, it hadst gone soft apace.'

George laughed out loud and undressed quickly. 'I, on the other hand, own a lot more staying power, as ye well know, sister of mine heart.'

Sebastian had heard every word. They'd thought he was away for the evening but he'd come home early and hearing raised voices, had stopped to listen. In a murderous rage, he tried to calm down long enough to think where the children were. His own two green-eyed beauties were tucked up safely in bed. He'd looked in on them only moments ago. He guessed at this late hour, Marie and Nicholas, the boy who he'd only just discovered was not related to him in any way, and certainly, no true heir, were also in their rooms. He picked up his sword and stood outside of the master bedroom composing himself, then anticipating the scene of depravity, threw open the door.

Sebastian liked to take his women imaginatively and a little roughly, if they were game, but to see the degrading act that the brother and sister were in the throes of, and, knowing what they had done and planned to do, completely turned his stomach.

'Standeth straight, Greymoor, I shalt not run ye through from behind whilst thy whore of a sister hides her face in the pillow. Madam, hadst I known thy preferences leaned to the more... *adventurous*, I may not always hast behaved such the gentleman in thy bed.'

'Shut thy mouth, Sebastian.' She looked fearfully in George's direction, he had quickly disentangled himself and picked up his own sword.

Sebastian smiled coldly. 'Ah, thy dear brother George didst not know. Tell me, Greymoor, didst thy *truly* believe mine father sired your niece and younger nephew? It seems our mistress of the bedchamber hast fooled us both.'

George, growling out a string of curses was too angry to think straight or control his movements and his swordplay was at the best, haphazard.

Nicholas, reading by the light of a dying candle, heard the uproar from his room directly above and rushed down to see what was happening. Thinking it rather humorous that his Uncle George had no clothes on and was playing sword fights with his elder brother, he ran between them to join in the game. Sebastian immediately stepped to one side to try and deflect George's aim. He was nowhere near quick enough. The nine-year-old was struck by a blow from his father that sliced through his small chest. He looked at the bed, managed to gurgle out the word *mama*, and was dead before he hit the floor. Alice let out a heart rendering scream.

Sebastian dropped his sword and knelt down to lift the small body. George was momentarily in shock but seeing his enemy in such a vulnerable position, raised his sword for what he expected to be the death blow.

Sebastian had kept one eye on his opponent and this time he acted at lightning speed. Grabbing his sword in his left hand, he thrust it upwards just as George stepped into its range. The point pierced his heart easily, not having the protection of any clothing whatsoever to push through.

Alice looked from the body of her son to the one of her brother and began to grab fistfuls of hair, trying to pull it out by the roots. As Sebastian placed Nicholas carefully onto the bed, her eyes began to roll.

'Alice, hast a care and looketh to thy kin, there is much to be done.'

The sound of his voice had some effect and her mind began to focus. 'Sebastian, ye shalt *not* get away with this. I shalt see ye hanged.'

'Dost not be motley-minded, 'twas self-defence. God and his saints, thy brother wouldst hath slain me ere I didst hold the body of your dead boy.'

'I warrant tis not how I witnessed it. Thou murdered Nicholas and when his uncle came to his aid ye didst strike him down in bitter cold blood.'

'Ye art *raving* wench, ye dost not know what thou art declaring.'

'I shalt swear ye instructed the smugglers to procure the Sapphire-Heart. That shalt cook thy goose well and truly, Sebastian Raven.'

'Sapphire-Heart?' He followed where she was looking and saw the large stone shining in the candlelight. 'Is that from the wreck? Alice, what *art* ye bethinking, that stone canst never be seen?'

'Thou didst it all for revenge,' she snarled, 'Tis what I shalt tell the Judge. He shalt put on his black cap when ye come before him, *filthy* whore's bastard.'

Sebastian was too shocked by the night's events and now, these false allegations to think rationally. As he made a grab for the necklace, Alice reached for her jewelled dagger and he felt a white-hot pain in his shoulder.

'I'll *kill* ye afore thou take that necklace from me.'

'Mistress, thy son and thy brother art lying dead, is that all ye can bethink of?' He pulled the dagger out and the wound began to bleed profusely just as she launched at him with a pair of scissors. He felt the second cut to his body, this one not nearly so deep but still painful. That was the point he knew only one of them would leave the bedchamber alive and forced her arms behind her back.

Alice, almost past the point of insanity, began to scream filthy obscenities and vile curses.

'I'll ram these blessed stones down thy *throat* if ye dost not cease.' Sebastian threatened.

'Ye wouldst not *dare*,' she goaded, 'Hark well, for upon mine soul I shalt curse ye. Thy son, wilt grow strong because he is also of Greymoor blood. But, he shalt also know ye for the murdering swine thou art, and so shalt his son and the ones that follow.'

Alice felt the grip on her loosen and she looked at Sebastian in triumph. Her threat of cursing him was having the desired effect. Soon he would beg her forgiveness. 'Each one of thy bloodline shalt struggle to beget the next male heir and wilt never knoweth the comfort of a second. *One* only, to carry thy shame down the long line of Ravens. Imagine, Sebastian, ye shalt never be taken into heaven. Thou canst walk in the forest and gaze at what befalls thy miserable kinfolk. If...' The grip had tightened again and too late she realised, he had been pushed to his limit. 'Ye art cursed forever.'

Sebastian had heard enough, he rose up and did what he had threatened, grabbing her chin and prising her jaw open, the chain and smaller stones were shoved forcibly inside her mouth. Alice struggled for breath, as she felt his fingers at the back of her throat. It was the large, rough cut Sapphire-Heart that finally cut off her oxygen supply. When he could stand no more of her gagging noises, he reached for the jewelled dagger and slit her throat, curious to see one of the smaller sapphires appear from where the blood came seeping. 'And that mine fine lady is the true end of ye.'

Not sure what to do next, Sebastian was horrified to see his seven-year-old son stood in the doorway, clutching a small comforter and sucking his thumb. 'Sooth, little brother, allow me to guide ye back to thy bedchamber, thou art having a bad dream.'

The boy let himself be led away and tucked beneath the blankets. 'Thou hast blood on thy face, Sebastian.' He said before falling into a deep sleep.

* * *

Sebastian gave a long, loud sigh and looked at his spellbound audience. 'So now ye know the sort of man I am, and ye will revile me.'

Toni had tears pouring down her cheeks. She'd run out of tissues and resorted to using her sleeve. 'The *horrible* bitch deserved everything she got, but that poor little boy, what happened to the bodies, and more to the point what happened to you?'

'And this curse stuff?' Saxon asked. 'Why would it affect the Thorpes, it's just your son's descendants, isn't it?'

'Another day…' Sebastian began.

'No,' Toni demanded. 'No more *other* days. Answer the questions *now*!'

Both men looked slightly shocked with the vehemence in her tone.

'Methinks thou art overcome Antonia, but I shalt finish the story. Verily the bodies went into the underground chapel, I wast in no state of mind to bethink what else couldst be done, nor take notice of what else lay hidden. I wast certain I wast the only one mine father had told of that place. Some weeks anon I returned to move them. Those were the only two times I ever descended into that chamber. The secret of the holy place shouldst hast been passed on to mine own son, when he wast older, but I never hadst the chance to tell him. An acquaintance took the bodies of Nicholas and George out to sea and made sure they were well weighted. That gent wouldst not touch a dead wench though. So, I brought her to the woods and buried her mineself.'

'The woods? Did you, err remove the sapphires and bury them separately.' Toni asked.

Sebastian shook his head. 'Nay, that land wast still part of the forest then. As for thy question, Saxon, about the curse, ye recall I mentioned Marjorie, mine half-cousin?' They both nodded. 'Well I didst not pay heed at the time but I hadst got her with child. As she increased, Robert Thorpe, mine half-uncle, hadst his eye on her also. He wast a fair few years older, but he took her for his wife. She told me a few years anon he believed the child to be his. That little minx wast hedging her bets with the two of us methinks. His younger brother, William, the one mine father had fought, had no issue, so Marjorie's and mine own child became the Thorpe heir.' He gave a snigger.

'And you took her word for it?' Toni asked, not able to hide a smile.

'I knew mine own child, believe me, Antonia. Also, if the rumours be true, Robert Thorpe wast impotent. Now, what else didst ye ask?'

'What happened to you, of course?'

'Ah well, mine poor little son told everyone that his *brother* hadst blood on his face that night. I'm sure he told them a goodly amount more. I wast a wanted man. I took refuge with an uncle, mine mother's brother, Arthur Heston, the famous smuggler.' There was a note of pride in his voice.

'Never heard of him.' Saxon muttered.

Sebastian glowered slightly but carried on. 'I worked with those folk for eight months, which is how I know of the tunnels, 'twas inevitable I wouldst be found eventually. When there is a large enough bounty on a gent's head, smugglers' codes of conduct count for naught.'

'Smugglers' codes of *conduct*.' Saxon sneered and felt a painful jab in his ribs from Toni's elbow.

'How were you caught and what happened to your wife, you haven't mentioned her much?' Toni reached for Sebastian's hand feeling a bit cross with Saxon for being so sarcastic.

'Ann wast a sweet wench, I shouldst not hadst wed her, 'twas as I said, an act of defiance when mine father hurt me so badly. I sought out the comeliest and most buxom maiden in the village. We hadst no issue. She wed again after I wast... gone. I wast glad for her, she deserved a valorous man. Mine son, with Alice, when he wast of age, reverted to the name of Ravel, mayhap to distance himself from the shame.'

'And the two girls?'

'*Two*? Ah, ye include, George's ward. Alice and George's elder brother and wife, took her in. Mine own little darling, I am pleased to tell ye, wed a local, widowed gent and lived a long and joyous life. She hadst no surviving issue of her own, but wast a most goodly mother to his three young children. I gazed from a distance but I didst not show mineself to anyone for many years.'

'Sebastian, if all this is as you say, then I'm descended from *Alice*.' Toni said looking a bit shocked.

'Dost not be afeart on that score, mine blood is the stronger. That lady's incestuous issue, with her own brother, is the one to heed. Who knows what madness flowed through the young Marie Greymoor. I heard a rumour some years hence that she had born three sons, all from different fathers. She never wed, so they hadst the name Greymoor, also.

'You weren't *hanged*, were you?' Toni felt Saxon squeeze her hand and instantly forgot he'd just pissed her off.

'Mine death wast not met dancing on the end of a rope. I wast on the run, *sooth* through these woods, verily running for mine life from men and hounds. I hadst a sword and battle-axe, but I hadst not the stomach to kill more men. I ran up the hills and to the cliff edge,' He saw Toni's eyes open wide and he nodded. 'I plunged forward to the rocks and sea below. I knew a moment of blessed peace and then, alas, I hadst returned to these damn Hunters' Stones and men were running past as if I wast not there. Tis as she said, I shalt wander the woods forever, or until the curse is broken.'

'Until two sons are born to one father. It all makes sense now.' Saxon said.

'I hast gazed and waited for over three hundred years, even the passionate lovers hast not succeeded. I am doomed.' He said mournfully.

'We'll start with the Sapphire-Heart tonight,' Saxon said decisively. 'Can you meet us on Toni's land, at around eleven o'clock?'

'Time means naught. I know night and day tis all. Call me, and I shalt come.'

'One last thing.' Toni asked gently. 'What were the names of your children?'

'Ah, wench, I bethought thou wouldst wish to know. My son wast named Richard and mine little daughter, Flora.'

Chapter Twenty-One

'Not all mine kin can inherit mine fine upstanding physique.'

Sebastian, whose father was a Raven, and grandfather a Thorpe, really *was* responsible for all the Thorpes and Ravels living in this village. The Thorpes, courtesy of Marjorie the minx and the Ravels... well, because of Alice the slag.

On top of all that, Toni pondered, whilst getting ready to go out for the third time that day, was that the first Viking and Norman families led all the way to Leo and Saxon, fascinating stuff. Thank God over three hundred years had passed and she and Sax were far enough removed to have a relationship of their own, at the most they would be something like ninth half-cousins. She couldn't stop thinking about the similarities in Sebastian's story and Saxon's home life. The weak father figure, the younger stepmother who lusted over her stepson, okay, Sebastian kind of let himself be lusted over and took full advantage of the situation, by the sound of it, but still, it was quite uncanny.

Dressing in dark gear and creeping around her fields with Saxon, waiting for Sebastian to appear, was almost laughable. It was only the note of slight hysteria in Annie's voice that had prompted such swift action. If Robert Davidson really did believe a priceless necklace was buried here somewhere, he wouldn't walk away.

'I feel a bit guilty leaving the other two out, especially after what Annie did. I had a long chat with her on the phone, she told me everything, but I expect you've heard it all at home.'

'Yeah, Dad threw a punch,' Saxon said proudly. 'I'd like them here as well, but we need Sebastian, speaking of which, where is that blasted ghost? Didn't he say we only had to call and he'd be here?'

'I didst, and I hast come!' Sebastian said loudly, ignoring the fact that both Saxon and Toni nearly jumped out of their skins. 'Now then, I must receive mine bearings.' He stood very still, trying to avoid the beams of torchlight. 'Knave, remove that cursed light, it shines in mine *eyes*. We must seek one and a half oaks.'

'I don't think there are any *half* oak trees left. There are plenty of whole ones bordering the next field, shall we walk over and see if you recognise one?' Toni suggested.

Sebastian grabbed her hand and began to march away. Saxon, was left to carry the shovels and follow behind. When they'd nearly reached the border of fields two and three, Sebastian smiled. 'Methinks that may be the very one. Dost ye see how the mature tree splits in four ways towards the top of the trunk? Tis familiar.' When they reached the base of the large imposing oak, he circled it and kicked the ground. 'Saxon, verily tis whither ye must dig.'

Toni heard a muttered '*verily*' and '*whither*' interjected with some quite coarse language about where he'd like to shove them, coming from her normally placid and polite boyfriend. Sebastian really did bring out the worst in him and she stopped for a moment to consider the future. If Sebastian remained in Raven Wood after all this was over, she couldn't just abandon him. Would Saxon understand that, how could they condemn Sebastian to such a lonely life now that they knew him? She took a shovel from Saxon and began to help.

Sebastian made it abundantly clear with pointed looks and mumblings about the fairer sex, that this was not work fit for wenches, but much to his annoyance his opinion was completely disregarded.

After three hours of solid digging, and both complaining of the most enormous and painful blisters, Saxon shone his torch on what turned out to be small bones, most probably a hand. Sebastian gasped and tried to squash himself into the pit, but there was barely room for the two of them.

'Christ, how exactly did you bury this body, it's certainly not lying flat?' Saxon scrabbled around using his fingers, which were now bleeding. 'Oh God, I think this is the skull.'

'I didst bundled her in, she wast laid as a babe might.'

'In the foetal position.' Toni whispered, unable to drag her eyes away. 'Sebastian, you and I need to get out and give Sax some more room.' As she said the words Saxon began to use his t-shirt to scrub furiously at something. 'The *Sapphire-Heart*?' Toni asked.

'Still wedged in behind the jaw-bone.' Saxon said quietly, trying to remove the biggest stone without doing any further damage. He handed it up and hoisted himself to sit on the edge of the pit. Toni sat down beside him, spellbound by the ethereal necklace that held so much poignant history for both of their families.

'We need to think very carefully about how we play this.' Saxon said thoughtfully. 'The chapel business below Raven Manor and now *this* discovery less than two miles away?'

'You're right,' Toni agreed. 'We'll never be left alone, people would come here for all the wrong reasons.'

'I've looked up everything on the web I can possibly think of, there is no record of a *named* ship being wrecked during that particular time period, certainly not off this coast. And the Sapphire-Heart isn't mentioned either. To be honest, love, and I can't believe I'm saying this, I think you should keep it.'

'But it's not right, surely there are laws, the treasure trove act or whatever it's called?'

'There are… but the necklace could be broken up and used for something good *if* that's what you wanted to do? I think it's the actual size and clarity of the sapphire that makes this so valuable, more so than the age.' Saxon only knew this because he'd been specifically researching sapphires. This stone was bigger than the examples he'd seen online, it was impossible to gauge anything else at the moment it was so filthy and even an expert wouldn't be able to tell in this light. 'It *is* a family heirloom of sorts, it just happened to be stored outdoors on your family land, rather than in someone's jewellery box inside the house.'

'What do *you* think Sebastian?' She asked, unsure of what to do. 'It was destined for Queen Mary, which makes our present Queen the rightful owner, doesn't it?'

'I know only what I overheard George Greymoor speak, mayhap 'twas a pack of lies. Wouldst he hath risked such a prize lost in the watery depths? That gent most likely arranged it stolen from a Nobleman's residence. Sooth, a ship didst go down around that time, but the wreckers I came across during the months anon hadst no knowledge of such a prize. Methinks it wast a story to impress Alice. In any case, Kings and Queens hast riches in abundance, thou shouldst wear it, mine darling wench.'

Toni gave a short laugh. 'I could never wear it knowing where it's just been.' She did take the time to really study it though. The name *heart* was a very generous description of a large triangular shaped sapphire. It was the tiny stones around the edge that actually gave it the shape. There were a few smaller sapphires set along the length of the gold chain and they were interspersed with pearls. It was certainly beautiful. Even the clasp was made from two more of the precious stones. It made her giddy to think of the actual value. 'What exactly did you mean Sax, something good?'

'Your nature reserve, or even something more ambitious, a proper sanctuary of some kind, to do with this part of the coast, seabirds, seals...'

Sebastian looked as if he was about to explode. 'Thou wouldst use these fine gems for *filthy* animals. Wherefore?'

Toni's eyes were shining with excitement and she was totally oblivious to his misgivings. 'Yes, of course, we could look into registering it as a proper charity. I don't think Dad would be much help with that side of things, perhaps... Alexander would point me in the right direction?' When had she started to think so differently about Satan? It could have been when she'd first seen the plans for the lodges, or when he'd helped Karen, or she'd seen Quando curled up happily on the old man's lap. Even today, he'd been prepared to perjure himself in a bid to get justice for Annie.

'I'm sure he'd love to get involved.' Saxon said. 'He needs more things he can do from home now. Your Dad and Leo would help in more practical ways. Toni, this could be a wonderful opportunity to get the two families working together. That can only be good, especially for us.'

'I wish *not* to be ignored and I hast one request if it be true ye art going to do this thing with squawking birds and sea vermin.'

Saxon gave Toni a wink, she grinned back and put a hand on Sebastian's arm. 'No one is ignoring you, what did you want?'

'Look closely at the clasp of the necklace, two small square cut sapphires. I err, recall they were the last thing to disappear inside…'

'*Don't* say it…' Toni interrupted.

'Her mouth.' Sebastian finished, giving a nod of satisfaction. 'I crave ye to promise me thou shalt keep them. They wouldst make a fine set of earbobs.'

'He's right,' Saxon smiled, 'You should have something for yourself and they *would* look very beautiful.'

'Very well, you notice I didn't need too much persuading,' she laughed. 'And I've already thought of a name, *The Sapphire Sea Sanctuary*, what do you think?'

Sebastian was slightly out of his depth, but Saxon nodded enthusiastically 'Why not, it should have a catchy name, and just think about the polo-shirts and sweat-tops you could provide for the staff or sell online.'

'You certainly have inherited your family's business brain. In a good way,' she added quickly and went across to kiss him forgetting Sebastian was still there and that they still had a six-foot-deep hole with a human skeleton to consider. 'I can't keep this from my family, I shall have to come clean about the diaries. And of course, Annie knows some of it already.'

'I'd like to tell Grandad everything, if you're okay with that?' He saw her nod and felt instantly relieved. His grandad always knew the right way to do things. For now, he'd keep the news from his father, it made him a bit sad but he couldn't help remembering seeing him here with Robert Davidson, not that long ago. According to Annie, Davidson had had some knowledge of the sapphires, he just had to hope his father didn't and that his interest had been purely in the land. After hearing about the punch to the solicitor's face, Saxon's hopes for Linus were growing by the day.

'Sebastian, how exactly did Antonia know about the necklace?'

'I told her, and she asked her father for the land, mayhap that gent gave it as a peace offering, I know not. She never begged to search, as ye hast done, tis strange, but then she never heard mine story, ye art the only ones to learn such knowledge of past kinsmen.'

'Well, it was her *brother*, not her father that gave it to her. So, I'm guessing Francis didn't show any remorse or forgiveness. Once she'd moved away the idea of searching probably became difficult, or the romantic notion was better than the reality. I'm really honoured that she wanted me to have it.'

'Before we discuss anything else we need to decide about *this*.' Saxon pointed to the pit next to where they stood. 'Do we really want Alice Greymoor/Raven's bones discovered?'

'That lady must not be disturbed, tis not right.' Sebastian said immediately.

'Actually, I agree, I think we should fill it in again as quickly as possible,' Toni said. 'Like right now.'

'I desire to climb the golden stairway and meet mine maker. Whether that gent shalt allow me to stay I know not. Methinks I may still not hast done enough. *Sooth*, Knave, begin thy toil.'

Saxon folded his arms and frowned as something suddenly occurred to him. 'You knew the *whole* time where the Sapphire-Heart was buried. You led us straight to it, we could have done this the *first* week we met you.'

'Quite right.' Toni added. 'We've been talking about this necklace for *weeks* and found it in a few hours.'

'Aye, ye art correct, but there hadst to be an order to things. The Holy relics first and then mine story.' He looked at Toni. *There is also the curse to break and I desired ye to fall in love first.* 'There is still much to do here. Saxon, hast ye not picked up the shovel yet?'

Toni didn't dare look at either of them for fear she'd burst out laughing.

* * *

Toni spent a full day explaining everything to do with the Sapphire-Heart, to her family. Difficult, without being able to mention Sebastian. The following day it was Saxon's turn to speak to Alexander. She arrived to give him some moral support.

'How was it?' He asked, showing her inside.

'Pretty much as I said on the phone, they're going from complete amazement over the whole thing, to outrage at Robert Davidson and absolute determination that I keep the necklace. I had to say it was just a hunch to start looking around the oldest trees.' She smiled. 'Leo's gone all protective over Annie, after what happened to her at work. I mean it's cute I guess, but bloody hell, she was only grabbed and shaken a bit roughly, if it was any worse he'd be committing murder right about now.'

'There's already too much of that in our family history.' He gave a small laugh. 'What did you say about Antonia's affair?'

'Dad knew something pretty serious had happened and he also knew there had been rumours connecting her to Alexander, but I'm not sure he'd put two and two together or maybe he didn't want to accept it? He knows now, of course, but I haven't mentioned Flora, yet. Alexander will have to understand that Dad will want to read these after he's finished with them.' She indicated the diaries under her arm. 'Antonia was his aunt after all, and if Flora's still around, they're related as well.'

'I know, I appreciate you're giving him a chance to find out first.'

'Grandad, we'd like to talk to you about a couple of things.'

Alexander looked at Saxon, and then at the old notebooks under Toni's arm and wondered what revelations they had in store for him this time.

Vanessa also wondered and walked outside onto the patio. Taking her place by the open window, she felt somewhat frustrated that she had to resort to eavesdropping again.

Sometime later when they all emerged from the study, Alexander was in a state of shock, but it was fast giving way to a steely resolve to put right his own wrong in the long list of what seemed like never-ending and inevitable occurrences between the two old families. There was also a bubble of excitement, which he wouldn't quite give in to, just yet.

'Are you sure you don't want to tell your father about the err, other thing, Saxon?' He asked.

'The Sapphire-Heart, I will do soon. We chose to talk to you tonight, knowing he was at the golf club and because it was sort of linked with the Antonia stuff.'

'Thank you both for this. I have a lot to think about.'

'Keep the diaries for a few days, to read properly,' Toni offered generously.' She'd been through them again with Saxon and regretfully, scratched out the words ghost or anything similar. Sebastian would come across, at best, as an odd character, in Antonia's written records. If Alexander wondered who it was, he would be unlikely to ask Toni, why would she know the answer to that question?

'It's up to you Grandad, what you tell Dad and Aunty Sarah about Flora. Martin will know eventually, so it can't be kept a secret.'

Alexander nodded. He'd spoken to his daughter a few days ago, when she had actually skyped first and was very apologetic about missing him the previous two times, but she'd been in hospital having her gallbladder removed. He'd sympathised, kept his thoughts to himself that her husband should have let them know and transferred some money across, to help with the medical costs. 'I'll see what I can find out first, but I think I'll tell Linus, he'd appreciate knowing.'

Once again, Vanessa had overheard family secrets and these were the ones that finally pushed her over the edge. *No* Saxon, *no* sapphire necklace and if Linus' hints were anything to go by, he was on to her affair.

She felt the walls close in around her and as they did, planned the next move, starting in the cellar. 'There you are my beauties locked up nice and tight.' The keys would be in the desk drawer, in Alexander's study. She'd have one prepped and ready to take at a moment's notice, the cupboard could remain unlocked afterwards, as long as the keys were replaced, no one would be any the wiser. Now she just had to carry on listening to conversations until she heard what was needed. A meeting between the two sweethearts where they'd be quite alone, perhaps walking the dogs, as they often did.

She didn't need to wait long, two days later the perfect opportunity arose.

'Going to see if Sebastian's around or if he's made it to heaven yet haha xx'

'Ur up early, Ravel, u off to the woods or shingles? I'll meet u xx'

'Ok leaving now, shingles. xx'

'I'm meant to be on site, but want to see u first xx'

'Grandad, you're going to the site this morning, aren't you?'

Alexander nodded. 'Problems?' He poured another coffee.

Vanessa quietly put her cereal bowl in the dishwasher and kept her back to them both.

307

'I'm meeting Toni down on Shingles for a while. Can you let the crew know I'll be a bit late?' Saxon picked up his car keys and hurried off. He did want to see her, it was true, but he also didn't like her being alone with Sebastian. Hopefully for all their sakes, Sebastian Raven would get his wish about entering heaven, sooner rather than later!

Alexander chuckled. 'It must be true love if they're meeting in this awful weather.' He said to Vanessa, and when he got no reply, found he was alone in the kitchen.

A few minutes later Linus appeared. 'Dad, look what I just found on Vanessa's dressing table, I think this is what Robert Davidson took from Antonia Ravel's file. God knows how it fell into Vanessa's hands. Even if they *were* carrying on, he would never have given it to her and by the way, where's my wife going in such a hurry with one of the hunting rifles? It's still closed season, not that she's ever shown any interest.'

Alexander clutched his chest and concentrated on his breathing for a moment. 'Quick son, bring your car around to the front as quickly as possible. I think Saxon and Toni could be in danger. I'll phone Ravel farm and tell whoever's there to meet us at Shingle beach.'

* * *

Toni slowed the van when she saw Annie approaching the farm. 'I'm just going to meet Sax at the beach for half an hour before he goes to work, do you want to meet up later?'

'The *beach* in *this* weather, you must be mad? Drive carefully, it's very misty. Leo and I are doing breakfast, sure you won't join us instead?'

'Another day.' Toni waved and drove off reaching the empty car park. Annie had been correct with her warning, she could hardly make out the top of the cliff path. She toyed with the idea of waiting for Saxon but really was keen to see if Sebastian was still around.

There was no answer at first and, although knowing deep down it would be better all-around if he had climbed his *golden stairway*, she would miss him dreadfully.

'Mine darling Antonia, I am still here, tis not as I desired... ah well, I am pleased thou art hither. Methinks the curse must also be broken afore I may leave this place.' He didn't give Toni any time to protest, just wrapped her in his strong arms and kissed her full on the lips.

'Stop it,' she laughed. 'Behave.'

'I'm glad I heard you say that, at least.' Saxon walked into the cave and squared up to Sebastian. 'This *has* to be the end, you must realize it.' He turned to Toni, and for a moment faltered, what if she said no, could he bear not to have her in his life? 'I don't want to give you an ultimatum, but I have no choice. Either you leave here with me now and we don't see Sebastian again, or you carry on. All the job offers etc will stand and I'll always be a friend to you, but that's all. I can't do this anymore. I thought because he was a ghost and it was just messing around, it didn't matter. But I'm afraid where you're concerned, love, it matters very much. I guess I'm jealous.'

Toni burst into tears. 'He'll be so alone though.' She said between her sobs.

'I'm so sorry to do this, but I have to.' Saxon closed his eyes and tried to come to terms with the fact she was going to stay in the cave. He began to walk away feeling numb, it was a few seconds before Toni's voice penetrated his dashed hopes.

'Sax, of *course*, I choose you, wait, I'm coming.'

He looked at Sebastian, expecting to see anger or upset, but the ghost's eyes were wide open and he was staring at the front of the cave. Saxon looked to see what was there, he made out a figure, it was... *Vanessa*. For a moment, things didn't quite compute, but as Toni drew level, he saw the rifle and blocked her path, using himself as a shield.

The shot when it came, felt like fire ripping through his upper body. He couldn't catch his breath and the more he tried, the more everything around began to shut down. As he crumpled to the floor he heard a scream, Toni's?

Vanessa, panicking, dropped the rifle and began to run.

Even in the poor light, Toni could see his skin was taking on a grey pallor. 'I love you, I love you so much, don't die, Sax I've always loved you, even when I didn't know I did.'

Sebastian watched and felt as if his heart would be ripped in two. He knew what he had to do, but first, he had someone to kill.

A small crowd was quickly gathering at the top of the cliff, mostly the workers from the holiday site, alerted by the gunshot. Two cars pulled into the carpark. Leo jumped out of the first, and followed by Martin and Annie, rushed across to see what was happening. Linus and Alexander emerged from the second, also hurrying to see what everyone was looking at.

Their eyes were drawn to what was going on at the top of the cliff path. Vanessa Thorpe seemed to be moving in some kind of frenzy toward the edge. Linus ran towards her, his eyes not completely on his wife but also the strangely dressed man at her side, who had a look of... Saxon about him.

'Thou cannot save the wench.' Sebastian eyed Linus critically, 'Not all mine kin can inherit mine fine upstanding physique, thy body is puny as mine father's wast, but methinks ye art a goodly man. Dost not worry about thy feeble frame. Find a wholesome mistress to desire, one who shalt love ye back, and wed her with haste. This doodlebug viper is evil and shalt now pay the price. Thy son lies in the cave below, dying by her hand. Go apace to his side, thy work hither is done.'

To the spectators, it seemed that Vanessa was standing still, head bent, perhaps listening to whatever Linus was saying. In actual fact, she was being held in a vice-like grip, one strong hand across her mouth and her head tucked firmly against Sebastian's chest.

As Linus reached out, Sebastian shook his head and smiled. He was finding this amount of physical contact difficult but summoning a last burst of strength, made sure she could also see him. 'Come for a stroll with me, witch. I know ye and tis time to meet thine end. 'Twill not hurt... much.'

Linus tried one last time to grab Vanessa, but they had already taken a step over the edge. In the time it took for her body to crash onto the rocks below, Sebastian had returned to the cave.

'You're back.' Toni sobbed. 'I don't think he's going to make it, what'll I do?'

'There is naught thou can do, mine dear, sweet, lovely girl.' He crouched on the ground next to her and dropped a kiss on the top of her head. 'There is something *I* can do, however, but I am afeard I shalt lose myself.'

Toni stopped crying just long enough to try and work out what Sebastian had said. 'What do you mean, *lose* yourself?'

'Thy sweetheart is dying, methinks his last breath will come anon ere *Aaanee* can help him. I must give him my very... soul.'

In the time she'd known him, Toni had never seen Sebastian look nervous, everything but. 'You're going to merge somehow, aren't you?' She watched him nod. 'But you wanted to go to heaven, that's what all this was for.'

'Mayhap, God in his mercy shalt forgive me, but I doubt it.' He didn't admit to just adding Vanessa to his list of victims.

For the briefest moment, Toni let go of Saxon and touched his face. 'I love you, Sebastian, not in the same way I love Sax, but I *do* love you.'

'I know dear heart, tis why I must do this, for ye… and for him.' *Mayhap if young Thorpe dies with no heir the curse shalt be broken?* Sebastian only dwelt on that thought for a few fleeting seconds. He couldn't do it, not only was he fond of Saxon, but his feelings for Toni had grown very strong.

'It will still be *Saxon*… won't it?' Toni asked tearfully. She wanted more than anything for him to live, but at what cost?

'Methinks I may be thither,' he held his thumb and finger closely together, 'a tiny bit. But hast no fear, it shalt be thine own true love from now to the day he dies, hopefully, a valorous long time. Kiss me goodbye, Antonia.'

As she did, Saxon's chest stopped rising and they heard distant sirens and running footsteps coming across the shingle.

'We must hasten.' Sebastian pressed his lips to Toni's one last time and at the crucial moment when the kiss would have deepened, he left her. The surrounding air froze and then, returned to normal. As Leo, Linus, Martin and a few of the others burst into the cave Saxon took a large gasp of air.

* * *

In the days following, eyewitnesses reported seeing what they assumed was a young woman, committing suicide. It hadn't been easy to make out properly through the mist, but she'd been alone, and although walking strangely towards the edge, even reluctantly, some said, she very definitely threw herself over. It was no accident. Her poor husband had done his best to stop her.

Four men saw something entirely different but, doubting the proof of their own eyes Martin and Leo failed to admit to seeing a large red-haired man, in strange costume, pulling Vanessa to her death, in fact, sweeping her in his arms as he stepped off the very edge of the cliff right in front of them.

Alexander had seen this man before, in the woods talking to his grandson. He'd also been told tales by Antonia, sixty years ago, not that he'd believed a word of it of course. Ghosts! utter nonsense, or so he'd thought. 'When you feel ready,' he said to Linus, 'you can tell me everything. I saw him as well.'

* * *

The day of Vanessa's funeral was also the day Saxon came home from hospital. The ambulance team, seeing the amount of blood loss, had feared the worst. But the consensus of opinion was, he had been extraordinarily lucky, and the fact he'd survived such a well-aimed gunshot at close range was a testament to his general fitness and good health.

Alexander and Linus were only gone from the house briefly and although Saxon had offered to accompany them to the crematorium, Linus insisted he stay behind and rest.

'Dad, you missed a phone call from Henry. Apparently, everything's straightforward, but he's putting it all in the hands of his new partner and he'll talk to you later.'

'That's fine,' Linus nodded. 'Henry's winding down, he'll be fully retired by Christmas.'

'Won't he miss it?' Saxon asked.

Alexander came into the conservatory carrying a tea tray. He'd been concerned about his friend after the incident leading to Robert's departure. 'His heart's not in it anymore, but he said he's planning a long visit to his daughter in Canada, in the spring, one of the grandchildren is getting married. In the meantime, his daughter-in-law has taken him very much under her wing. Mona, the PA, was so disgusted hearing about Robert's affair with Vanessa that she went and told his wife everything. He may be a good divorce lawyer but I don't think he's going to come out of his own, very well.'

Saxon took a sip of coffee and remembered the second phone call. 'The bank phoned as well, they wanted to know when you plan to go in and sort Vanessa's safety deposit box. You only need the death certificate, they said. No security questions or anything like that.'

Linus nodded. 'I went through all this with her other account. I knew all the answers even though I didn't get asked. Street she grew up in, Wayland road. Maiden name, Jenkins and Mother's maiden name, Greymoor.'

Saxon had the strangest feeling, almost as if satisfaction, justification and retribution were all vying for supremacy inside of him. Later when he was trying to explain it to Toni he was unable to put it into words.

* * *

A month later, Saxon got ready to accompany Toni on the last visit to Glen-Croft. This time Aunt Antonia really was dying and the family was visiting in shifts, so someone would always be with her.

Alexander rushed out waving a letter as they were about to get into the car. 'I won't ask to come with you, some things are best left. I have good news though, I think I've traced Flora, I think I've found my daughter.'

The room was light, and the window open. 'She made us promise to leave it this way, until the end.' Lizzie, the carer, sniffled. 'Call me if there's any change,' she gave Toni's hand a squeeze, 'she was one of my favourites, you know.'

Toni sat and stroked Antonia's hand for half an hour telling her the news she'd have asked to hear, had she been able. 'I'm working for the Thorpes now, Aunty, can you *believe* that? And guess what,' she took a quick look behind, making sure no one was hovering in the doorway, 'we found the Sapphire-Heart.' Antonia's lips gave a small twitch but her breathing remained slow and shallow.

'I'm just nipping to the loo; hold her hand until I get back?'

They swapped places and Toni left the room. As soon as Saxon touched her, Antonia's eyes opened and seemed to focus. Saxon's silver eyes turned to dark emerald green and he smiled. 'Go in peace, mine little wench.'

She gave a small sigh of pure happiness.

Saxon rang the bell totally unaware of what had just happened, by the time Toni returned, it was all over.

Epilogue

The wedding had taken place three years ago, and when Saxon put the ring on Toni's finger, it was the first time she saw his eyes change colour, ever so briefly. The second time it happened, was a year later, the night she gave birth. She knew then a tiny piece of Sebastian was still with them.

Today was a birthday celebration. The men had congregated around the barbeque, as men do. Alexander, Martin, Linus and Leo were in their element, discussing projects and the success of their joint venture, the Sapphire Sea Sanctuary. Josh listened politely but preferred to cast glances across at his very pregnant wife.

Toni sat in the warm sunshine between Beverly and Olivia and looked out over the large, not quite so pristine lawn, now that Quando had found another ideal place to bury his latest bone. Lucifer, Oxeye and Damocles watched from the sideline with bored expressions. She passed a jug of orange juice to Rita and asked how the house was taking shape.

Rita couldn't have been happier when Linus had proposed, she'd accepted immediately, but declined the offer of moving into the Thorpes' home. Instead, Alexander had bought the house next door to her cottage, which conveniently, was on the market, and given it to them as a wedding gift. Linus had big plans and she was quite content to let him proceed with knocking down walls and turning the two semis into one substantial detached home.

Under Annie's watchful eye, he was also having some input with the extension to the café and gift shop at Sapphires. It really had become a family concern.

Annie had moved to Ravel Farm and lived happily there with Leo. Deciding a career in law wasn't for her, after all, she'd taken very little persuading to accompany him to Australia, for six months. Since their return, he really had settled and knew the farm was the only place he wanted to be. Annie had developed a taste for working outdoors and could hardly believe her good fortune when she'd been asked to manage the sanctuary. 'I just don't have the time to do it properly,' Toni had said. 'I'll be looking in often though and I'm more than happy to be a bit more hands-on with the animals. And we can always make time to sit and have a coffee under my favourite oak tree. I love that it's part of the picnic area. Have you noticed how it divides into four at the top of the main trunk? I absolutely didn't want that one dug up.'

In the early days, when the site was first being developed, Robert Davidson had become a real pest. Often caught mooching around the area after dark with a small torch, he'd inevitably had an accident and fallen into, what would become the seals' pool, breaking his ankle and his wrist. It was then, they'd had to put a stop to it once and for all. Threats of trespass and breaking and entering would not look good on a divorce lawyer's record. The name of the building taunted him and yet he didn't make the connection, so sure the treasure was still buried and waiting to be discovered. He would spend the remainder of his life not quite coming to terms with the situation.

The doorbell rang, Alexander hurried to greet his daughter, Flora, his granddaughter, Susan and her husband, and his two great-grandchildren.

'I *still* find this completely overwhelming.' Flora smiled waving at Martin and Leo. 'So much family.'

The boy and girl sidled up to Linus, 'Great-Uncle, will you take us to the ruins later?' Linus nodded indulgently, while he found Susan a seat.

'If your mother says it's okay.'

Susan nodded and turned to Rita. 'Did you and Linus enjoy the trip to Boston?'

'It was wonderful, Sarah and the family were *so* welcoming and what a fabulous place to celebrate our wedding anniversary.'

The conversation petered out as everyone watched Saxon deposit his two small sons on a blanket, far enough from the glowing charcoal, but near enough so they could be watched by both groups of adults. His eyes immediately sought Toni's and shone with love.

Cards and presents discarded, the two-year-old twins were more interested in their new puppy, a birthday present from Alexander. The sable-haired little boy, the spitting image of his father, grinned at his brother, his silver-grey eyes flashing with pleasure. The second twin, his red, chestnut fringe, falling forward, grinned back and pointed at the small black Doberman, 'Down Raven,' he squeaked, the pup dropped to the floor like a stone. His green eyes twinkled with merriment, the spitting image of... *his* father.

Toni walked across to Saxon and took his hand, her other touched the small square cut sapphire earrings. If there ever *had* been a curse, which the jury was still out about, as far as she was concerned, they had well and truly, in the most unprecedented and unique manner possible, broken it.

Author's Note

I confess to not knowing if farming auctions actually take place or if muck-spreading really is the main topic of conversation amongst farming families, in their local pubs. I hope my concept of rural village life is received as I meant it to be, entertaining.

I make no apologies for Sebastian or anything else pertaining to the 17th century. After many hours of research, I was totally confused and resorted to what I hope is acceptable within the confines of this particular story. My aim was to make him a romantic, provocative figure, both endearing and slightly bizarre.

Authenticity, has its place, but if we cannot escape and totally immerse ourselves in a story without worrying if thee and thou have been used correctly, tis a great shame, methinks.

Happy Reading
Alison McKenzie

Alison McKenzie

FROM THE
FUTURE,
WITH L♥VE

*The clock is ticking for these
time-crossed lovers*

Also by this author

FROM THE FUTURE, WITH LOVE

An invite from her best friend to spend the summer in Scotland, and celebrate her twentieth birthday, is just the thing Robyn needs to put some positivity back in her life.

On the long drive from Devon, she is strangely drawn to a man she finds collapsed and bleeding in the middle of a wheat field. There is something about this dark-haired, dark-eyed stranger that's more than mysterious.

The last thing Robyn expects is to become entangled in a romance before even crossing the border, but she feels an inexplicable connection, and perhaps Shay, feeling it too, or due to his bang on the head, starts dropping hints about life in another time.

From the Future, With Love is a love story with a time-travelling twist, and a reminder that today's actions have future consequences.

The Sapphire Heart is Alison's second
novel to be published

Imaginary worlds and situations that are realistic
enough to create that ounce of belief that they could be
real, is a common factor that can be found
in all her stories.

Follow Alison on Facebook
https://www.facebook.com/plymouthauthor

Or visit her website
www.mckenziesisters.com

If you have enjoyed this book, please leave Alison a
review on Amazon.
She would love to know your thoughts.